Something shifted between them,
as if a veil were yanked away...

"I don't understand it," Lia whispered. "I think I've been robbed."

"What happened?"

"I was just putting away the drugs that were delivered today. See this?" She reached up and tapped empty spots, and then she turned to face him. "Morphine and everything containing codeine."

Cal's eyebrows shot up.

"I had a full supply."

"You're sure—Of course you're sure." He studied the shelves up behind her shoulder, his peppermint gum-scented breath filling the tiny space between them. "Maybe they were accidentally moved out of place. Let's search through all the drugs."

"I already did that!"

"Well, we'll do it again. And then probably again. Hey, don't worry." He lightly touched her forehead and pressed away the frown.

It was when he brushed strands of hair back from her face that something shifted between them, as if a veil were yanked away, abruptly bringing into focus a nameless emotion. He stopped smoothing her hair. Surprise registered in his eyes, and she sensed hers reflected the same. Slowly he tilted his head downward until only a hair's breadth separated them...

Sally John is a former teacher and the author of several books, including *A Journey by Chance*. Much like the citizens of Valley Oaks, Sally and her husband, Tim, live in the country surrounded by woods and cornfields. The Johns have two grown children.

After All These Years

SALLY JOHN

HARVEST HOUSE™ PUBLISHERS

EUGENE, OREGON

Scripture verses are taken from The New English Bible, ©The Delegates of the Oxford University Press and the Syndics of the Cambridge University Press 1961, 1970. Reprinted with permission.

Cover by Garborg Design Works, Minneapolis, Minnesota

Published in association with the literary agency of Alive Communications, Inc., 7680 Goddard Street, Suite 200, Colorado Springs, CO 80920.

"Just Come In," words and music by Margaret Becker, © 1989 His Eye Music (SESAC). International Copyright Secured. All Rights Reserved. Used by permission.

AFTER ALL THESE YEARS
Copyright © 2002 by Sally John
Published by Harvest House Publishers
Eugene, Oregon 97402

Library of Congress Cataloging-in-Publication Data
John, Sally D., 1951-
    After all these years / Sally John.
      p. cm.
    ISBN 0-7369-0881-1 (pbk.)
  1. Female friendship—Fiction. 2. Vandalism—Fiction. I. Title.
    PS3560.0323 A68 2002
    813'.54—dc21   2002003319

Printed in the United States of America

04 05 06 07 08 09 10 / BC-MS / 10 9 8 7 6 5 4

To

Kaiya Grace John,
at the beginning of your journey

Acknowledgments

My fictional characters always draw breath from the real world. I'd like to thank those people in my world who so graciously give of themselves. This story would not have been written without them.

⌒

Thank you:

Leila McGrath, for inspiring the essence of *Lia*; and Lynn and Janet Fyfe of the Orion Pharmacy, Orion, Illinois, for creating *Lia's* store and expertise.

Martha Nieto, for giving *Isabel* an incomparable heritage; and Myrna Strasser of WDLM radio station, for animating *Isabel's* career.

Sue Laue, for your passion for journalism I caught years ago and passed on to *Tony*; and Juanita Arellanos and Pastor John Jairo Cano of Colombia, for rescuing *Tony*.

Michael Skelton, for the *Valley Oaks* map, without which I would have become lost; and Tracy Charlesworth, for your excellent critiquing and the hours of brainstorming.

Chip MacGregor, agent, and Kim Moore, editor, for your unfailing enthusiasm and direction.

And, as ever, Elizabeth, Christopher, and Tim, for being there.

⌒

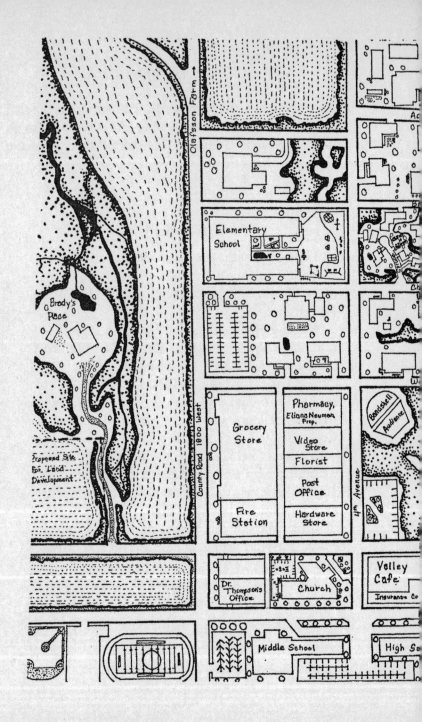

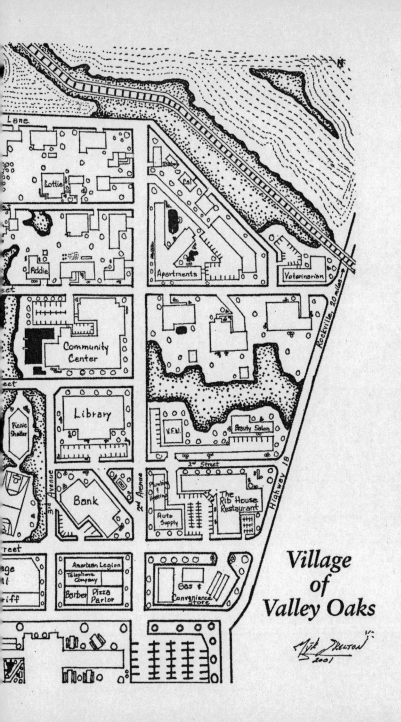

Village
of
Valley Oaks

Prologue

Man plans his journey by his own wit,
But it is the LORD *who guides his steps.*
—Proverbs 16:9

Leon, Mexico

The bus rolled along a cobblestone road toward the outskirts of the city, its motion stirring the summer dust and heat through the open windows. Distant dry hills shimmered under intense sunshine.

Two women sat side by side. Though not of the same generation, they mirrored one another. Their eyes were wide set and the color of deep caramel that foretold of brilliant flecks on a different day. But not today. Today an identical vertical crease separated the brows of each.

Both women were small, though the older one was rounder. She wore her silver-streaked black hair in a single thick braid down her back. Her blouse and skirt were bright floral prints, a rainbow of colors. The lines in her face spoke of hard work, her hunched shoulders of strength. The relaxed pose of her mouth exuded a contrary peace. A large mesh shopping bag engulfed her lap.

The younger woman was also of Mexican heritage, but there was an air of otherworldliness about her. Perhaps it was in the angle of the jeans-covered leg and the sandaled foot that stretched across the aisle, blocking it. Or in the jaunty hang of the backpack slung over a slouched shoulder. Or in the cut of her layered shoulder-length hair with its copper highlights.

Her face, however, was different. The Americanism was fading from her face.

"*Abuela*," the younger woman said, addressing the mature one as grandmother and continuing in Spanish, "I'm not going back. May I live with you?"

The older woman silently studied her granddaughter for several moments. The only indication that she heard the question was a slight tilting of her head. "Of course. But what about your studies?"

The young woman didn't reply.

"How long will you stay?"

"Until…" She pulled in her foot and shrugged the backpack onto her lap. "Until I want to breathe again."

Evanston, Illinois

"What about college?" The tall man slouched over the table in the updated suburban kitchen. A weariness was etched in his eyes.

At the counter a young woman spooned tea into a silver infuser, set it in a pot, and then poured steaming water over the leaves. Each motion was efficiently executed, wasting no energy. "I've changed majors."

"Past tense?"

Her black ponytail swished at her waist as she carried the teapot over to the table and set it beside two porcelain cups. "Past tense. It's done." She kissed the top of the man's head and sat down across from him, tucking her long skirt beneath her. "Dad, don't worry."

He opened his mouth as if to offer a customary retort and then closed it. Retorts were for another day. But not today. Today his navy blue cardigan hung haphazardly, his blond hair hung unbrushed down the nape of his neck, a book lay beside him unopened. Everything about him represented all that was not customary on this day.

His daughter reached over and squeezed his hand. Like him, she had a determined chin, a small nose, and high cheekbones. Also like him, she was taller than average, though not lanky. Unlike him, her eyes were black and slightly almond in shape with long black lashes, a reflection of her mother's heritage. "Dad, the path is clear, and it's full of good works already prepared for me to do."

"You're too young to know any better. How will you live? How will you make ends meet? For goodness' sake, how will you survive the *emotional* work of two?"

She chuckled and pushed up the sleeves of her sweater. The distinctively unconstrained response diminished the hints of Asian femininity. "You of all people know that I'm not in this alone."

"But how—*how* can you give up your dreams?"

She squinted momentarily, as if a bandage were being ripped from a wound. Then her features fell again into their tranquil lines, though now there was a hint of resolve in the set of her jaw. "I didn't. They were just replaced, changed by Someone who knows better. It will work, Dad. It will work."

One

Valley Oaks, Illinois

"She's a gift." Gina Philips nuzzled the two-month-old bundle of tawny fur. "From me and Brady."

Isabel Mendoza laughed as the kitten batted a paw at Gina's white lab coat. "She's adorable! But why would you give me a gift?"

"Because," the vet's voice softened and her deep green eyes glistened, "you have a new emptiness in your heart right now. She'll help soften the pain. Here, take her. Snuggle a bit."

Isabel accepted the little animal, who promptly curled against her neck, just above her heart. She blinked away her own unshed tears and waited for the tightening of her throat to ease. "Aww. But I can't afford—"

"I said gift. Entire kit and caboodle sort of gift." She knelt behind the receptionist's counter, straightened, and set down a yellow plastic pan overflowing with bags of litter and kitten food. "This is for you. We'll make an appointment later for spaying and shots."

"Gina, thank you, but I can't let you pay for—"

"Sure you can. Do you know how many books Brady sold this year? And the corn and bean market forecast is excellent."

Isabel smiled at her new friend. The California native had lived in Illinois for less than three months and already knew all about crops and Brady Olafsson's personal business. Isabel

14

teased, "Not to mention, Dr. Philips, that you're a millionaire." Gina had recently won a lawsuit against a wildlife preserve. The preserve's negligence in animal care contributed to Gina being attacked by an elephant, a situation which caused permanent injury to one of her legs. Though the lawsuit was not something Gina had wanted to pursue, her legal actions guaranteed that the elephants would receive better care.

Gina laughed. "I think all of Valley Oaks is waiting with bated breath. When and if a settlement check arrives, I'm going to post a message on that big board outside the Community Center so everyone will know immediately."

"Don't you think news can spread faster by word of mouth?"

"A few months ago I would have said no way. Now I know better! Seriously, Isabel, this kitty won't cost much. I'll do the work myself, and Dr. Swanson doesn't mind if I use his facilities here."

Isabel stroked the cat's silky fur with her thumb. A mild purring sputtered like the kick start of some minuscule motorcycle. She sighed. What was it that people said about being single and owning a cat? Something disparaging. But...this warmth against her skin felt comforting in the air-conditioned vet's office. A distinct sense of coziness enveloped her, planting images of family gatherings, sounds of laughter, scents of frying tortillas and spicy— "Cumin. No, that won't work. Nutmeg! She looks like nutmeg, don't you think?"

Gina smiled. "Her coloring reminded me of your eyes. Nutmeg is a perfect name."

"All right, Nutmeg it is. Thank you, Gina. And thank Brady for me, too."

"You're welcome, from both of us."

Isabel took hold of Gina's left hand and made a show of inspecting her third finger. "Did I miss anything while I was gone?"

Gina yanked her hand back. "You know you would have heard, even in Mexico."

Isabel laughed. "So, what have you been up to besides falling more and more in love?"

Gina rolled her eyes as a rosy blush spread across her face to the roots of her dark brown hair. "Well, I've been digging my heels in here at work and at Aunt Lottie's. I convinced her to have air-conditioning installed. And Brady just got back from a two-week signing tour."

"Ouch. How did the first separation go?"

She grinned. "Big phone bills. Really big. We decided the heart does not grow fonder, it just aches a whole lot. Oh, there's a Chicago reporter coming today to interview him for some special article. Brady says it's no big deal, but I think it's rather exciting."

"That's Brady, downplaying the attention. What's the article about?"

"Something about well-known Christian personalities for one of those Sunday supplement magazines. The guy's meeting me here so I can show him the way out to Brady's place."

"Your more-than-likely fiancé is going to put Valley Oaks on the map yet."

The blush returned. "Isabel! We hardly know each other."

"Uh-huh. Hey, how are your parents doing?" Isabel had met Maggie and Reece Philips two months ago when they were in town for a family wedding.

"Making progress. Mother keeps saying Dad's a new man. Neither of us can believe he's taking an entire month off work, but they're scheduled to leave for Venice next Tuesday. He even promised to leave his cell phone at home. To tell you the truth, I think Mother's still skeptical."

"It's difficult to accept that someone can change so dramatically."

"You're right. But he keeps sending her flowers, and he's home for dinner five nights a week rather than five times a month. They've hit art galleries every weekend. Still, she hasn't begun to pack yet. Brady thinks it will just take time for her trust to build, but anything's possible with Jesus."

"Amen to that. Well, Nutmeg." The kitten lifted its tiny head. "Let's go home."

The bell above the front door jangled, and a man walked inside. He eyed Gina behind the counter. "I'm looking for Gina Philips."

"Hi. I'm…"

Their voices drowned in a rushing noise that suddenly filled Isabel. The room slipped out of focus. It was as if the air itself evaporated, leaving a vacuum where there should have been oxygen to breathe. *Tony?*

The magnetism still radiated from him, the energy palpable even before he spoke a word. Even before he turned those piercing deep-set eyes toward her.

"*Izzy?* Izzy Mendez!"

Mendoza, she corrected silently. "Tony."

He flung his arms around her, giving her and the kitten a friendly hug.

Gina asked, "Izzy? I haven't heard you called that."

He kept an arm around her shoulders. "She only lets *extremely* close friends call her that." He peered down at her and winked. "And *we* were extremely close friends, weren't we?"

He wasn't teasing. Though she could tell she was familiar to him, he didn't remember her. She saw it in the tilt of his head, in the cocky grin that scrunched his left cheek alongside the narrow aristocratic nose. Isabel turned toward Gina. "College nickname. Seven years ago."

He dropped his arm. "Right. English lit."

Try journalism. She changed the subject. "So you're a big-time reporter now?"

He shrugged a shoulder. "*Chicago Tribune.* What are you doing?"

"I'm a small-time radio announcer for a local station."

"That's fitting. You always were quite the talker."

She gave him a tight smile. He had remembered one fact correctly. One out of three was par for Tony. He still looked good, even in crumpled khakis and a pale yellow short-sleeved knit shirt. In shape. His coffee brown hair cut in a professional style.

"How'd you end up here?" he asked.

I'm from Rockville! Just down the road! Remember? This conversation was becoming an inane guessing game on his part. "Hey, I've got to get this kitty home. And Gina's been ready to close up shop here for a while."

"Isabel," Gina said, "why don't you have dinner with us since you two know each other? Brady's cooking."

"Thanks, but I haven't unpacked yet from my trip, and I'm scheduled for the early shift tomorrow."

"All right. Here, put Nutmeg in this box. You don't want her underfoot on the drive home."

"Thanks." She grasped the box under one arm, the pan of litter and food in the other. "Nice seeing you, Tony."

"You too, Izzy. Take care." He held the door open for her. She bumped into the jamb trying to fit through.

"Need some help?" He grinned.

"No. Thanks!" She made her clumsy way outside and across the parking lot. Even after the door finally clicked shut she felt his eyes on her, studying. They were blue, the bright blue of the Mexican sky. Hidden behind them was a razor-sharp mind that too often sidetracked itself with rabbit trails.

But he would remember. Eventually he would remember, and that would be worse than him not remembering.

Tony sat in Brady Olafsson's large country kitchen, digesting the best home-cooked meal he had eaten in years. Maybe in his entire life. His mother was an artist who never had been much of a cook. His dad's place was in his law office. No time for role reversal and domestic chores in that relationship.

The couple here was intriguing. It was Brady who had cooked dinner while Gina changed her clothes after her day with the animals. He watched them now as the author loaded the dishwasher and the girlfriend scooped warm cobbler onto plates. The aroma of cinnamon and apples filled the room.

"Tony." She glanced at him now. "You'll have ice cream, won't you?"

"You bet."

They made an attractive pair, both tall and slender. Brady resembled a lanky, brooding model for western wear. Gina was the quintessence of a California chick. Not the blonde, brainless brand, but the one glowing with health and natural beauty sans makeup, lit up by a 1,000-watt smile. He hadn't quite figured out their relationship yet, but long before he saw Brady greet her with a kiss that almost embarrassed even him, Tony sensed she wasn't available. An air about her had kept him from crossing an invisible line into flirting with intent.

Maybe he'd look up what's-her-name. Man, he had pulled "Izzy" out of some deep subconscious pocket. Now there was a looker. That thick, chin-length layered hair with its subtle copper highlights…that petite figure…heart-shaped face…the wispy suggestion of a Hispanic accent… She assaulted his senses like a Marine beach landing.

Brady slid into the chair across the oak table from him. "You're welcome to spend the night here, Tony. I've got plenty of room."

"Thanks. I appreciate that, but I've already checked into the Rockville Holiday. I want to transcribe the tape, and then I'll probably write half the night away."

"I know that syndrome." He grinned.

Gina served them the cobbler, vanilla ice cream melting around the edges. "Odds are that neither one of you will stay awake after this."

"Mmm, probably not." Tony scooped up a large spoonful. "Mind if we keep talking, though?" They had primarily chatted up until now, covering life's basics.

"Not at all. What's your premise exactly? Maybe I can gear my answers toward that."

Tony fiddled with the tape recorder. If he told them the real reason behind his article, they'd kick him out in two seconds flat. He pressed the play button. "Christian artists are making a significant impact on society today. I'm localizing it, just talking with Midwestern artists."

"What sort of impact? Negative or positive?"

His rehearsed evasion came easily. "Well, for example, you're big business. What would you say is the impact of your books?"

Gina laid a hand on Brady's. "Mind if I jump in, Tony? I know lives are being changed for the better. Readers enter into a world of fiction and come face-to-face with the reality of Jesus Christ."

"You sound like Brady's number one fan."

"No, just speaking from experience. I wasn't a Christian before I read his books."

"Really? Perfect. Mind if I interview you, too?"

"Not at all, but not tonight." She stood. "I'm bushed and I'm going home."

That answered one question. They didn't live together.

"Tony." Brady looked at him. "Are you a Christian?"

"Agnostic."

Gina sat back down. "Have you read Brady's books?"

"Not yet. They're all stacked and waiting on the night-stand even as we speak. This is my 'delve into Brady Olafsson' week."

The author spread his arms. "My life is an open book."

Gina groaned and stood again. "Now I'm going."

"I'll walk you out, sweetheart." Brady slipped his hand around hers.

"Nice meeting you, Tony," she said. "Hey, you could interview Isabel. She's sort of in the Christian entertainment business."

"How so?"

"She works at the Christian radio station. She knows a lot about the music world."

"Could make a good sidebar. Thanks."

Brady said, "You might give her a few days, though. She just returned from Mexico where her grandmother died. They were pretty close. Excuse me, I'll be right back. Gotta kiss my girl goodnight."

"Don't blame you. Nice meeting you too, Gina."

"Goodnight." They left.

Mexico! That was it! Isabel Mend...Izzy...Izzy Mendoza. Grandmother... That last spring break of college... Leon, Mexico.

Images burst from an old memory. Desert. Relentless hot sun. Poverty. Children racing about, laughing. Cool dark bars. Tequila.

He whistled a note of disbelief. Izzy. How could he have forgotten?

Two

Calhoun Huntington slipped into a back pew of the Valley Oaks Community Church alongside those parents who insisted on keeping their squalling babies and overactive toddlers in the sanctuary during the service. He didn't want to add his own disruption to the music now by walking toward the front. He should have come earlier.

He rubbed his tired eyes. What he should have done was leave Tammy's earlier last night. Last night? Try this morning. At least he'd arrived home in time for a quick shower. He scratched his jaw. No shave though. Oh, well. Brady kept telling him Jesus wasn't interested in appearance. He just wanted his heart.

An open hymnal touched his knee. Cal glanced down at the kid sitting next to him and nodded his thanks.

Tammy didn't understand this hunger of his, this craving to sing and be taught by Pastor Eaton. Church wasn't that important to her. But she had been a Christian longer and seemed to know more than he did. She didn't care for any of the churches where she lived in Twin Prairie, the county seat 23 miles west of town. And that distance, she said, made his church too inconvenient. Distance or lack of sleep made no difference to him. He had been coming regularly for almost three years now. Tammy had only been around for a couple of months.

The song ended. Cal yawned and pulled a pen from his shirt pocket, tuning out Tammy's voice and the annoying squiggler beside him. There was something more important going on here. He opened up his Bible along with the pastor.

After the service, Cal found his old friend Brady outside on the sidewalk. "Yo, Brade." He noticed Gina standing at a distance with others. Most of the congregation mingled outdoors in the late-August morning sunshine.

"Cal. You look like you were rode hard and put away wet, bud. Third shift?"

"You might say that."

"Ah, Tammy date night."

Cal tilted his head toward the parking lot. "Who's the city slicker with Miss California?"

"Reporter from Chi-town. It shows, doesn't it?"

"Yeah. It's the way his clothes hang. Silk. Tammy had me in Rockville one day, trying on clothes like that. Didn't have the same effect."

Brady laughed. "With a neck size of 20, I think you're talking custom-tailoring."

"That's what Tammy said. So what's he up to? Visiting you or the famous vet?"

"Me. Gina won't give any interviews. Part of the settlement agreement. If she doesn't talk about the elephant abuse she witnessed, the zoo folks won't blacklist her. Come on over and I'll introduce you."

As they maneuvered through groups of people, Gina caught Cal's eye and smiled. In his opinion, she was one classy lady, a good match for his friend. "Olafsson, when are you going to put a ring on that gal's finger?"

"Soon, but don't tell anyone."

He laughed as they neared Gina. "Like nobody suspects it."

"Hi, Cal!" She gave him a hug. "Suspects what?"

"That you're the prettiest woman in Valley Oaks."

"Better not let Tammy hear you say that, mister."

"No problem. She's the prettiest woman in Twin Prairie." He held his hand out to the stranger. "Cal Huntington."

"Tony Ward, *Chicago Tribune*. Nice to meet you. I take it you're a friend of Brady's?"

He nodded. "Ever since we put on our first helmet and set of shoulder pads. Anything you need to know about him, ask me."

"Thanks." He reached into his back pocket and pulled out a pad and pen. "I'll probably take you up on that. What do you do for a living?"

"Jacob County deputy sheriff." The guy wrote it down. Cal knew he had better things to do on a Sunday afternoon than talk to this note taker. "I live here in town. Name's in the book. Gotta run now, though. Nice meeting you. Bye, Gina." He averted his face and raised his brows at Brady.

His friend wasn't slow on the uptake. "I'll walk you to your truck. Be right back, Tony."

When they were out of hearing distance, Cal murmured, "His eyes aren't right."

"All reporters look like that."

He snorted. "Shifty-eyed?"

"Gina says they're missing something. You can't connect with them."

"Be careful with him, bud."

"I know what's missing, Cal. I'm just praying for the man."

"Yeah. That, too. See you around." He clapped Brady's shoulder and climbed into his pickup.

Cal always felt the urge to run interference, to protect his friend. A few years back, Brady's fiancée, Nicole, ran out on him. She had damaged him in a basic sort of way, leaving him almost...fragile. Cal complained his friend had lost his quarterback nerve. Brady described it as meekness, a realization that Christ was taking care of him, and not to worry. Cal worried. He didn't feel the need to tell Brady that he had thoroughly investigated Gina a few months ago, even before she made the national news.

Now he'd run a check on Tony Ward. Brown hair, blue eyes, 5' 11", 160, early 30s. Silk.

Cal pulled his own notepad from the glove compartment.

Lia Neuman parked her car in the alley parallel to the old brick building and cut the engine. The wipers thumped to a halt. The last notes of a praise song dissipated in the rain's staccato beat. She turned toward the passenger seat. "Welcome home, Chloe."

The little girl stirred, her face scrunched against a pillow propped against the door. A gentle snore escaped her mouth.

Lia closed her own eyes for a moment and breathed a prayer of thanks. They were finally home...home in Valley Oaks where home felt as it should...safe, even here in a dark alley at 11:30 P.M. in the midst of a torrential downpour. She should have left Chicago earlier in the evening, but things got complicated telling her parents goodbye and dealing with Chloe's hesitation to leave the only home she'd ever known. And then the rain began, slowing their journey to a snail's crawl.

But they had made it. Tomorrow she'd begin sorting out those complications, most of which should simply cease to exist because she was here and not there. Chloe was all hers. The pharmacy was all hers. Well, except for the small-business loan and her parents' money, which they insisted was an early inheritance rather than funds to be paid back.

She loved her new situation. Escaping the big-city environs and living in a town like Valley Oaks was a longtime dream come true. She was a pharmacist and now her own boss, the proprietor of a well-established business. The apartment above the shop meant she didn't have to leave home and Chloe in order to work. The small back room served as a private entrance off the alley. It held the stairwell to the apartment and tripled as a cramped laundry room, office, and storage space. The pharmacy itself was a manageable size with plenty of shelves to expand the gift selection.

Everything she needed or wanted was right here within this corner portion of a turn-of-the-century brick building. God was good.

Not bothering with the umbrella now, Lia got out and hurried around the car. She unlocked the store's back door, opened it, and flicked on the ceiling light, thinking that Chloe's hesitancy would change in the morning. When she saw her new bedroom set and the special case to hold her stuffed animal collection, she'd feel better about this move. The child was only nine, but at times projected an uncanny resemblance to a 17-year-old's attitude.

Lia opened the car door, leaned inside out of the rain, and unbuckled Chloe's seat belt. "Can you wake up, sweetpea?"

Chloe's groan answered in the negative.

The girl was really too heavy for Lia to carry, but she didn't exactly have another choice. She smiled wryly to herself. No other choice. That philosophy pretty much summed up her life. Her backside was sopping. "Honey, wrap your arms and legs around me." Chloe obeyed. With an "oomph," Lia straightened and pushed the door shut with her hip.

Suddenly a car swung into the alley, its headlights and a spotlight reflecting through the rain and nearly blinding her.

It lurched to a stop in front of her car and a large man emerged. "Is there a problem?" he called.

Heart pounding in her throat, Lia quickly backed away, throwing herself off balance. She cried out just as the man caught her.

"Whoa, steady there, ma'am." The bass voice materialized from somewhere above her. "Here, let me help."

She struggled against what felt like a brick wall with arms. "No!"

"Ma'am, I'm the deputy sheriff. Sorry if I startled you."

A policeman? Relief flowed through her, turning her arms to rubber. Chloe's legs slipped.

"Here, let me take him. Her?"

The weight evaporated. Lia hurried inside behind him and closed the door. "Her. Thank you!"

In the bright light she recognized him, though they had never met. He was the local deputy she noticed sometimes cruising the small town's streets or sitting in his car beside the highway that ran along the edge of Valley Oaks.

His wide-brimmed hat and long dark brown slicker dripped. He scanned the room. "Where—"

"Upstairs. But wait a sec." She stepped over to the laundry corner and pulled towels from a stack on the dryer.

Chloe's arms were around his neck, her legs dangling. She briskly rubbed down the girl's back.

He took off his hat. "Mind taking that?" He spoke softly as if not to waken the little girl in his arms.

"I'll hang it on the hook here."

"Thanks. It's a frog strangler out there tonight. You're the new pharmacist, right? Eliana Neuman?"

She laughed and draped a towel about her shoulders. "I hope so or else you'd better arrest me for trespassing. Do you mind carrying her upstairs, Deputy?"

"No problem. And the name's Cal. Cal Huntington."

"Nice to meet you. I go by Lia. And that's Chloe you're carrying." She led him up the enclosed stairway. Behind her he jangled, no doubt with the police paraphernalia beneath the raincoat. At the landing's turn, she saw that he filled the tight space, but his step was light. He reminded her of an incredibly large brown teddy bear.

Heart still madly pumping adrenaline, Lia babbled. "What good timing that you came when you did! I didn't know how I was going to manage."

"Just doing my rounds when I noticed some activity in the alley. Do you live here?" His tone expressed disbelief until she opened the door at the top of the stairs and flipped the light switch. "Whew," he approved, "I guess you do! Man, the last time I saw this place, it was a pit. Unlivable and chock-full of junk. Fifty years' worth of trash collection."

"That trash collection turned into a gold mine for the Bentleys in the form of a yard sale. I'm sure you know the former owners." Lia surveyed the cozy apartment she had spent the last two months renovating. The old wooden floors shone beneath scattered braid rugs. The kitchen and living room ran together with two side windows facing Walnut Street. Soft yellow paint, white lace curtains, and used furniture from home had worked wonders.

"Chloe's room is right through here." She led him down the short hall past the bathroom to one of two bedrooms at the front of the building. It didn't matter that the rooms were tiny. Each had a window facing the lovely town square across Fourth Avenue.

Lia turned on a low-watt bulb and smiled to herself as she pulled back the comforter. She had splurged on this room, buying a white canopy bed Chloe had admired once and accent pieces in the girl's favorite shade of cardinal red.

Cal carefully set Chloe down, and Lia pulled off her sandals. They left her snuggling into the pillow.

"Deputy, would you like a cup of tea?"

His smile was nice. It crinkled his eyes. "Cal. And, uh, no thanks."

"Oh, you probably don't even drink tea! How about some coffee?"

The smile widened into a grin, transforming the intimidating shoulders and square jaw into an approachable neighborhood cop. "Now coffee I'd consider, but I need to get going. I'll take a rain check, though."

"You got it." She followed him down the stairs. "Stop by again sometime so Chloe can meet you. She won't remember a thing."

"Will do. Goodnight, now."

"Thanks again. Goodnight."

Lia shut the door behind him, flipped off the light, raced back up to the bathroom, and turned the shower's hot water handle on full force. Her wet clothes had chilled her to the bone. She clipped her long hair atop her head and jumped into the spray.

"Thank you, Jesus, for bringing Cal at just the right moment. Bless him. Keep him safe in his work tonight." She broke into a praise chorus.

"Mrs. Neuman!" There was a pounding on the open bathroom door.

Lia screamed.

"It's me! Cal."

"Oh!" She gulped a breath. Her heart was certainly getting a workout tonight. She peeked around the edge of the opaque shower curtain, grateful not to see his face and yet still embarrassed at his apparent proximity. She turned off the water and called out, "Yes?"

"You left your keys in the door."

"Just a sec! I'll be right out!" She held the curtain before her as she stepped out of the tub and pushed the door shut.

Eyeing her heap of wet clothes, she quickly toweled off. What was the proper thing to do here? Mom had never discussed this scenario. When a police officer enters your apartment and— Her long terry cloth robe hung on the back of the door. It would suffice.

He stood in the kitchen beside the sink, which was a good distance around the corner from the bathroom. His face was apple red as he shifted his weight from one foot to the other. "I, uh, knocked," he said, averting his eyes. "You need a doorbell and a new alarm system."

Lia bit her lip to keep from bursting into laughter at his discomfort.

"I noticed your purse in the unlocked car, so I brought that up, too. Do you need anything else?" He made eye contact somewhere above her head.

"No, but thanks."

"Okay. I'll lock the door and your car. I thought I heard you were from Chicago."

"I am."

"Then you know you should keep doors and cars locked."

"But this is Valley Oaks! I feel so safe here."

"People are still people, Mrs. Neuman. They take advantage of the unsuspecting. You need a deadbolt, too."

"By the way, it's *Miss* Neuman. And my friends call me Lia. I think I'd consider you and me friends, given the fact that you were in my apartment after midnight while I was in the shower. Hmm?"

A small smile played at his lips as he turned and strode to the stairwell. "Yes, ma'am."

The giggle she had been holding in bubbled out. "Goodnight, Cal."

"Goodnight. Lia."

Cal chewed himself out as he punched the doorknob's lock and pulled the door securely shut behind him. He vocalized his lunacy while opening the driver's door of Lia's old model Volvo and jabbing the automatic lock button, rain still spattering off his hat and slicker.

"Huntington, this is exactly what happened to Patterson. Get yourself into a dubious situation and allegations start flying." He strode to the squad car and kicked a tire before yanking open the door. "You could've thrown the keys in on the floor and simply locked up. No, you've got to play Mr. Considerate and hike all the way back upstairs. You hear her singing in the shower and you still don't duck out."

He climbed in and drove out of the alley.

At least she didn't *seem* like the complaint-filing type.

Yeah, that's what Patterson thought.

Cal shook his head. She was nice. He had recognized her shower song from church. And most of what he had heard about her indicated that she was an asset to the community. She had even lowered some prices on pharmaceuticals. Townsfolk appreciated that in a big way. Her business should grow.

Tammy's mother worked for her and wasn't too keen on the woman. He couldn't put much stock in her opinion, though. Dot Cassidy wasn't too keen on anybody.

He cruised down Main Street and headed for the all-night Gas Mart. Maybe he should make his whereabouts known... just in case.

So it was "miss," huh? Interesting. The daughter appeared to be nine or ten. Lia must have been a teenager, probably too young to marry. Said something about her, sticking things out like that, becoming a pharmacist and now buying her own shop. Probably family money. She was cute with her long swinging ponytail, little nose and a mouth that kind of curved up at the corners like a bow tie. There was a vague hint of Asian heritage in the shape of her dark eyes and matching dark hair, but not much of one. The only accent was Chicago style, big city and borderline aggressive. Confident might be a better word. Her black hair hung to her waist. Except when it was pinned up for a shower.

He laughed at himself and pulled into the gas station. Tomorrow he'd pick up a deadbolt and install it for her. Make amends.

Of course if Dot found out then Tammy would find out, and then he'd have amends to make with her... *Women!*

Three

Isabel rapped her knuckles on the glass window on the upper half of the pharmacy's front door. A moment later she saw Lia hurrying down the aisle, shrugging into her white lab coat.

Lia unlocked the door and opened it, the small attached bell tinging. "Isabel! You didn't have to come this early. Goodness, you didn't even have to come in today. You just got home."

"Yes, I did have to come."

Her friend drew her inside.

Isabel set down the cardboard box, Nutmeg's undignified traveling case, and accepted Lia's hug.

"Isabel, I am so, so sorry about your grandmother."

"Thank you." She wiped away a tear. This was why she had come early. She wanted to get this over with, this seeing everyone for the first time after her *abuela*'s death…this pain hitting afresh, like a paper cut that couldn't heal because she kept touching it.

They clasped hands in silence. In a subtle way, the moment intensified Christ's comfort more than words could. They sniffed and then smiled through tears. Isabel sensed this was another reason she came today. After her grandmother, Lia was the most joyful woman she had ever met. Such women knew the depths of sorrow firsthand.

Isabel hadn't heard the entire story. Lia had arrived in Valley Oaks only that summer. When she came to church and met Britte Olafsson and Isabel, an instant rapport sprang up between the three of them. Since that time, she and Britte had pitched in at the shop and the upstairs apartment, helping their new friend get her feet on the ground.

"Isabel, your box is *moving*."

"Look." She lifted out the kitten. "Her name is Nutmeg. Gina gave her to me. I thought Chloe would enjoy playing with her today."

"Oh, how sweet! She'll want one."

"Well," Isabel cleared her throat, "Gina happens to have this mama cat out at Brady's, and Brady is not exactly a kitten kind of guy. I thought it'd be a great 'welcome to Valley Oaks' gift, so I called Gina. There's a kitty earmarked for Chloe if you give the okay."

Lia's eyes were wet again. "Thank you, Isabel. You've all been so thoughtful."

"Hey, we're just grateful to have you here. You kept the pharmacy in town. I can't wait to get you singing in the choir and to a book club meeting. Now, when do I get to meet Chloe?"

"We snuggled a bit this morning, and then I told her to go back to sleep. We didn't get home until midnight. It was such an unbelievable day! Speaking of the choir, you'll have to ask Cal Huntington what he thinks about my singing."

"Cal?"

Lia relayed the story, ending with her rendition of a hulking teddy bear avoiding eye contact.

When their giggles finally subsided, Isabel said, "He's my neighbor. And he goes with Dot's daughter, Tammy."

Lia shook her head. "I will never get the hang of all the interrelationships in this town."

"Oh, just give yourself six months. It took me a year, but you're smarter than I am. All right, put me to work."

Like most Monday mornings, this one kicked into high gear promptly at nine o'clock, two minutes after Dot Cassidy waltzed in to take her place at the cash register beside Lia in the back of the store.

Isabel enjoyed her role of chatting with customers and covering the front register. The simple changes Lia had already incorporated exuded a pleasant small-town environment. Her pharmacy area was located at the back, with the drugs and counter in one corner and a waiting area in the other with four new wicker arm chairs and a coffee table holding magazines. Besides the regular array of drugstore items, the pharmacy now carried distinctly more tasteful cards, organic herbal teas, Brady's books, delightful gifts for any occasion, and an assortment of candles, their delectable scents permeating the shop.

Cal walked in before ten o'clock, carrying a paper bag with the hardware store's logo and a drill. "Morning, neighbor."

"Good morning, Cal." Isabel winked at him. "I've heard you were upstairs already! Don't you think Lia's done wonders with the place? Especially the *shower?*"

"Like I saw *that*, Miss Nosy Mendozy," he bantered, although his tan deepened three shades and his jaw worked furiously on a piece of gum. "Why don't you announce it on your show?"

"Maybe I will." She trailed after him down the aisle and held her breath as he ambled by the collectible figurines. For his mammoth size, his movements were surprisingly graceful. She breathed again. "What's with the drill?"

Over his shoulder he threw her what she called his cop glower, a look that said, "I'm asking the questions here, lady, not answering them."

She scrunched her nose back at him.

"Izzy!"

She whirled around. Tony stood there, holding the door open while dear old Mrs. Anderson lumbered through it, thanking him on her way out.

Here was another reason she had needed to come early this morning...needed to fill her day with busyness... "Hello, Tony."

The lopsided grin spread slowly as he leaned against the counter and crossed his arms. "Ah, my day is a success. I've tracked you down."

"How did you—"

"Uh-uh," he wagged a forefinger, "can't reveal my sources, but I know you work here on Monday mornings, your day off from the station."

He knew more than that. She saw it in his eyes, a glint of familiarity. He had remembered. A dread reality settled like wet cement on her bones. She heard footsteps behind her and turned to see Lia.

"Isabel, do you mind helping out back here? Cal's going to put a deadbolt on the door and— Oh, hello."

Tony extended his hand. "Hi. Tony Ward, old friend of Izzy's. In town to interview The Author." He nodded toward a display of Brady's books.

"Lia Neuman, pharmacist. Nice to meet you." She looked at Isabel. "I hate to interrupt—"

"No interruption. I'll be right there."

"Thanks." She strode back down the aisle and glanced over her shoulder. "Izzy?"

Isabel shrugged in reply. She hadn't allowed Tony's special name for her to surface since college. "Tony, we're swamped. I need to get to work."

"Right. You don't want the blue hairs to get restless. How about dinner tonight?"

"Tonight is—"

"Open. No work. No church service. No book club. No teen group." He tilted his head, brows raised. "Rib House in town here?"

Avoiding him would be impossible. With resignation, she gave in to his persistence. "Are you staying in Rockville? I have errands—"

"Name the place."

"How about the Italian Village, just off Route 18 on Fifty-second."

"Got it." He sauntered to the door. "Six o'clock work for you?"

She took an unsteady breath. "Fine."

Like that paper cut, Tony Ward wasn't going to go away.

"Cal, you didn't have to do this." Lia followed him into the back room.

"No problem. Comes under the job description of keeping Valley Oaks citizens safe."

She studied the back of his head as he knelt on a knee, emptying tools from the paper bag onto the floor. His hair was a light brown, the type that would age into silver. Its bristly texture hinted at shorn curls similar to that on a teddy bear. "How about that coffee now?" she asked.

He looked up, and she noticed his eyes were a vivid green. "You've got a store full of—"

"Oh, I always have a pot going right here." She went to the laundry corner that contained a sink and a counter just large enough for the coffeemaker. "I keep a carafe out in the shop for the customers." She handed him a large mug. "Which you would know if you'd ever been a customer here."

He gave her a guilty smile. "Guess I'm just on the healthy side."

"What, you never need toothpaste?"

With a sideways glance, he sipped his coffee. "Mmm, great coffee. Hey, don't let me keep you from your *customers*."

"Right. Oh, if Chloe comes downstairs, just tell her you're the teddy bear who carried her in last night." She walked back into the store, smiling to herself at the look on his face. The gauntlet had been tossed the night before when he terrified her by walking unannounced into her apartment. Teasing him about not patronizing the shop was her payback. The teddy bear remark put her ahead. It had rendered him speechless.

She stepped behind the counter where Dot handed her a bottle of capsules.

"This needs your okay. And this one here."

"Thanks, Dot."

Her only full-time employee was a bit of a puzzle. In her mid-50s, the platinum blonde was well-preserved, petite, always fashionably dressed, and pretty. But one minute she resembled an airhead embellishing the latest rumor, and the next she was efficiently advising a customer about his prescription. Like a fixture at the pharmacy, she had worked there almost for as long as the Bentleys had owned the place. Lia happily kept her on because she knew the business. Legally she could do everything regarding a prescription except give it to a customer without Lia's approval first. Rightly, the customers trusted Dot's knowledge.

At the moment Lia sensed an icy draft floating in her direction despite Dot's normal tone of voice and smile. What in the world could have happened between the time Lia left to chat a moment with Cal and now?

Cal. Yes. What was it Isabel said? He was dating Dot's daughter, Tammy. *Oh, Lord, these small-town relationships...*

When there was a lull in the activity, Lia said, "Dot, your Tammy certainly has herself a catch. Cal is so thoughtful and professional."

Dot was never at a loss for words, but her tongue seemed to be in a stranglehold. "Uh, what's he doing here?"

"Installing a deadbolt. I met him last night. He was patrolling the alley and saw me unloading Chloe in the rain. He stopped to help and noticed the flimsy lock on the back door. Now here he comes today offering to take care of it."

"That's our Cal." She glanced over her shoulder and lowered her voice. "Between you and me, I think they'll be engaged soon."

"Congratulations," Lia whispered.

Dot gave her a conspiratorial smile as three customers walked up.

Lia sighed inaudibly. If Dot knew her better, she'd understand there was nothing to worry about. Lia had no intentions of stealing Cal away from his intended. Chloe's father had cured her of even the thought of sharing her life with a man.

~

Lia bounded up the stairs behind Chloe, both of them giggling. It was evening, after dinner, and they had just raided the store's candy shelf. Homemade fudge and a generous array of licorice, candy bars, and chewy drops filled a basket.

They raced to the couch and plopped down cross-legged. A cartoon video awaited in the VCR and a fluffy newcomer named Soot lay curled up on the rug, purring.

"Chloe, it wasn't too bad of a first day, was it?"

The girl concentrated on unwrapping a candy bar, her chubby cheeks hidden behind her chin-length black hair falling forward. She resembled Lia only slightly. The Asian hint about her eyes was less pronounced, evidence of another generation removed from her grandmother's ancestry. Chloe's royal blue eye color was a beautiful blending of her mother's almost black and her father's light blue.

"The vet was nice, wasn't she?" Lia prompted. Gina had delivered the kitten that afternoon.

Chloe nodded. "I like Soot. And Isabel was funny."

"She's my new best friend here. What did you think about the school?" They had registered Chloe that afternoon while the store was closed for a 45-minute noon break. She would begin fifth grade next week when school opened.

The girl shrugged. "It's old. Not like home."

"I know. Little towns have a lot of old things, like this building. But at least we have a video store right next door."

"Maybe they'll give us a key!"

Lia laughed at the image of the slovenly owner being overtly kind. "And we can get videos any time! Let's check out the Community Center tomorrow. That's fairly new and just down the block. You can sign up for gymnastics again if you want."

Chloe scooted over and laid her head against Lia's arm.

"Oh, sweetpea, I know it's hard and that it will take time to get used to everything. Just remember Jesus is taking care of us. I think we'll like it here. But Chloe?" She put a finger under the girl's chin. "You tell me when you don't like something, okay? Promise me you will."

"Okay, I promise."

"Thanks." She kissed her forehead. "All in all, I think it was a pretty good day, not easy, but pretty good."

Chloe nodded, a somber pose on her lips.

"I just wish you could have met the teddy bear."

"The *peppermint* teddy bear."

"Peppermint?"

"I remember he smelled like peppermint."

Chloe's grin was the reward Lia needed. The answer to prayer. *Thank You, Lord. Please, please make it work out here.*

Four

Isabel fussed at herself for choosing the Italian Village. She had forgotten about the candlelight and cozy booths. On the spur of the moment, at the pharmacy when Tony invited her to dinner, it had simply been the first decent restaurant that came to mind.

Across the table in one of those cozy booths, Tony scanned the room. She remembered that about him, his incessant curiosity about everything.

The waitress, a disinterested young woman, asked for their drink orders.

"Diet cola, please."

Tony raised a brow at her and asked for a beer. When the waitress left, he said, "Ah, Izzy, no tequila? You disappoint me. Don't you remember?"

"I remember."

"I envisioned us tying one on—with tequila, of course. For old times' sake. You know, trip the light fandango down memory lane. Have a few laughs over our youthful indiscretions. Thank God that we made it, eh?" He was animated, from cocked brow to tilted head to half smile to shifting shoulders, arms, and hands.

Her own body felt strangely still. Normally she would be matching him gesture for gesture. She had always been expressive. In college, other students were either annoyed or entertained by the twin-like mannerisms she and Tony shared. Their personalities enmeshed, creating a one-two punch effect whether they were interviewing or hanging out at the local pub.

But that was a long time ago. She gave him a tight smile. "I thank God every day that I made it."

"Uh-oh, I see a pattern here. No tequila. Friend of The Author's girl. Thanking God." He leaned across the table. "You, Izzy Mendoza, are a Christian." It was an accusation.

"Flimsy evidence, Ward, but your investigative skills are intact. I am."

The waitress served the drinks and asked for their food order. Though the pizza was a favorite, Isabel balked at sharing one with Tony. It seemed too intimate somehow. *Now that's ridiculous...* She chose the spinach ravioli, he the lasagna.

Isabel sensed the cogs whirring away in his mind.

He set down his glass. "Your grandmother. She would have influenced— Oh, jeez-louise. Foot-in-mouth disease, as usual. I heard she passed away recently. I'm sorry."

Isabel looked away. "Two weeks ago. And yes, she was a major influence on my decision."

"She didn't like me much, did she?"

"She guessed at only half of what you represented in my life. She didn't like you *at all*."

For a split moment, his features froze.

Isabel laughed. "It was our lifestyle she hated, not you. My *abuela* prayed for you." She didn't mention that she too had prayed for him through the years.

"That makes total sense." He glanced toward the ceiling. "So what half didn't she guess?"

Isabel felt a blush erupt over her entire face and neck. Conversing with Tony was the equivalent of tap dancing on a minefield. She couldn't come up with a nonexplosive answer, one that wouldn't ignite emotions.

"You're prettier than I remember." His voice was low. "There's a depth of life about you, like a rose in full bloom."

"Say, how about those Cubs this season?"

He laughed. "Izzy, I'm serious."

"If you say so. Now what do you want to know?"

"Ah, we seem to have a trust issue here."

The past rushed at her, nothing specific, just negative emotions en masse.

"Iz, the comment about your being pretty wasn't empty flattery. I may have dished that out in college, but it's not my professional style now. I *have* grown up. Well, to a certain extent, at any rate. However, I would like to ask you a few questions for the article. Do you mind?"

"N-no."

The waitress placed salads and garlic bread before them.

Tony picked up his fork. "All right. If I say Brady Olafsson, what's the first thing that comes to mind?"

"Off the record?"

He stretched out his arms, tanned beneath the short sleeves of his white cotton shirt. "No wire. No pad and pencil."

"He's for real."

Dissatisfaction flickered in his eyes. "Do tell."

"I mean it. Genuine good guy. I doubt there's anything I can tell you that you don't already know."

"I take it you're friends?"

"Yes. We became acquainted through church. His sister Britte and I are close."

"Since?"

"About four years ago. I moved out to Valley Oaks when I took the job at the radio station."

"And?"

"And what?"

"Did he put the moves on you?"

She clenched her jaw and glared at him.

"I mean, why wouldn't he?" He waggled his brows.

The obvious. Brady was engaged at the time. She had no intention of revealing that bit of information.

Tony's face brightened and he held up a finger. "Unless one of you was involved."

She kept her stony silence.

"Izzy, Izzy, why is there no trust? Okay, moving right along. What do you know about the zoning of the property adjacent to his?"

"Digging for dirt?"

"Just trying to see the big picture. Thought you might want to add your two cents worth to balance school board members' opinions. All seven of them who wanted a housing development out there. On the record."

"He sold his property to Gina. As a zoning board member he voted against the development and for the preservation of history and a wildlife refuge. The town is divided on the issue, but then they often are. Nothing dark and sinister under that bush."

"Is it Christian versus non-Christian?"

"Hardly."

The waitress delivered their entrees. "Finished, ma'am?"

Isabel eyed her half-eaten salad. The thought of meeting with Tony had squelched her appetite all day. "Yes, thanks." She watched him interact with the waitress in that totally captivating way of his. The young woman was emerging from her shell. Isabel had always liked that about him, his ability to draw people out. At the moment she didn't want to be drawn out, but it probably wasn't the correct response. *Lord, I need some courage.*

After the waitress left, Tony commented, "This is pretty decent food here."

She smiled at his surprised tone. "More so than you'd expect outside of Chicago?" she teased.

"That's nice."

She focused on her plate of fragrant garlicky tomato sauce and pasta.

"You actually looked at me. And even smiled."

It was true. Avoiding eye contact was her self-defense. She gave herself a mental shake and raised her eyes to meet his again.

Tony had bright, laughing eyes, full of anticipation at what the next moment might bring. Their blue pulsated with all the vibrancy of the sky. Deep-set and dark-lashed, they had first drawn her in over seven years ago. Tiny crow's feet had etched themselves around the corners.

A deep recognition flashed between them. She turned away.

"Izzy, you're so familiar to me, but it's as if you've changed so much you're unrecognizable. Does that make sense?" His tone was sincere.

"There's a Bible verse that talks about being a new creature in Christ. Does that make sense to you?"

"No."

"Jesus invaded my life several years ago. I can't see or hear Him, but He walks and talks with me. It's a supernatural reality, the purpose of which is to make me resemble Him more than I resemble myself."

"Now you've totally lost me."

She smiled. "He is pure goodness and light, Tony, and He is my best friend. College was a dark time for me. The memory is that of an alcohol-induced haze."

"But we had such a blast."

"It was nothing compared to the blast I'm having now."

He smacked the tabletop. "The apartment on Linden."

She set down her fork, all pretense of eating gone.

"Izzy, how long did we live together?"

"Three months, give or take a few days."

"Hmm. You'd think I'd have remembered something like that."

Yes, you would think so, she silently agreed.

He shrugged, as if in dismissal. "There's no accounting for those wild and crazy days."

Isabel drove home. The miles stretched endlessly as she vainly tried to shut the mental floodgates Tony had pried open. The past was not to be contained. Scenes from their college days flowed, carrying a rash of emotions.

She parked in front of her small rented house, which didn't have a driveway or garage. She got out and stood in the quiet. Willows grew across the street above train tracks that were set in a shallow gully. When trains rattled by, she saw only their tops.

The evening's first stars winked against a navy blue sky. She gazed at them while the evening's conversation with Tony reeled unbidden in her mind, mingling with a darkness from the past. It all nibbled at the fringes of her equilibrium.

"Isabel."

She turned to see her neighbor walking across his yard. "Hi, Cal."

"You're standing in the middle of the street."

She walked around her car and stepped up on the curb. "So give me a ticket for jaywalking."

Methodically, he pulled a piece of gum from his uniform's shirt pocket, unwrapped it, scrunched it into his mouth, and began chewing. "You all right?"

"Yeah. Why?"

He shrugged his big shoulders and slouched against her car. "Your voice sounds funny."

"I just had dinner with the reporter who's interviewing Brady."

"Tony Ward?"

"You've met him?"

"Yep. Why'd you have dinner with him?"

Isabel crossed her arms. Under the cover of the deepening twilight she frowned. "I knew him in college."

"Small world. If you don't mind my saying, you should have told me you were seeing him. I don't trust the guy."

"Huntington, don't you ever get tired of playing the *cop*?"

Ever since Isabel had moved next door to Cal two years ago, an easy, teasing rapport defined their relationship. Suddenly, it disintegrated on the spot. Isabel felt the heaviness in Cal's silence.

"Cal, I appreciate your concern, but he's an old acquaintance who wanted to talk about Brady for his article, add some local flavor."

"Do you know him well?"

She bit her lip. "It was a long time ago. About seven years. We were both pursuing majors in journalism. He was a senior, I was a sophomore. We—we dated for a short time right before he graduated."

Cal pulled himself up to his full height, unsnapped another shirt pocket and slipped out a tiny spiral pad and pencil. "Look, Isabel, I don't mean to offend you by *playing the cop,* but this Ward guy rubs me the wrong way, and he's about to tell the nation the nitty-gritty details of my best friend's life. Exactly how is he going to interpret those details?"

"I don't have a clue."

"You do. You just don't know it. Where did he grow up?"

She tightened her crossed arms, pressing them against the nausea beginning in her stomach. "Highland Park. I met him at Illinois State University."

"What do you know about his childhood?"

Snippets of long-ago conversations came to her. "No financial worries. His dad is a lawyer, his mother some sort of artist who doesn't cook."

"Any siblings?"

"I think a younger sister."

"Tell me what you know about his high school career. Sports? Gangs?"

"No, neither. His mind is sharp, but school bored him. He almost didn't graduate. He drifted around for a year, then his dad gave him an ultimatum. He joined the Navy. Four years later he went to college. He said he's been with the *Tribune* for about six years. His father probably knew somebody who knew somebody, but still, he must be very good at what he does."

"Which is exactly what?"

She spread her arms in a helpless gesture. "Cal, I don't know. We haven't been in touch. He's a reporter. He writes about what's going on in the world." Was it a lie to omit the fact that she had seen Tony's byline once and never again read the Chicago paper?

"Is he married?"

"No. He said work is his life."

"Why did you stop dating?"

"It wasn't serious between us. He graduated two years before I did and he moved on. And this is getting way too personal, *Deputy*."

"It's for Brady's sake."

"Brady's a big boy. He can take care of himself. And you know, the article is about other Christian artists, too. Brady might rate two paragraphs, hardly major exposure. Now, you'll have to excuse me. I'm very tired." She strode up the front sidewalk, ignoring her friend's thanks.

Five

Promptly at six o'clock Friday night Lia bid Dot good-night and locked the shop door behind her employee, grateful no customer remained. She turned to Anne Sutton, a part-time employee. "Whew!"

Anne grinned. "Told you those discounted carnival ride tickets and Autumn Faire T-shirts would bring in the business."

"But can I cancel tomorrow morning and not open?"

"A Saturday? No way! At least you're only open until one. Okay, I've got this register closed out."

Lia appreciated her friend's down-to-earth personality. Mother of three and assistant girls' basketball coach, she wore her dark hair in a no-nonsense ponytail and, more often than not, a smile. "Anne, thanks for staying late tonight."

"No problem. It's Autumn Faire weekend. The whole town lives at Franklin Park, including Alec and the kids. My kitchen is closed for the duration and car pools cease to exist."

"Chloe couldn't wait to go tonight. I'm so glad your girls invited her."

"It was Mandy's idea, and for once Amy agreed because she happens to like her little sister's new friend. Even Drew says he doesn't mind her, and he's 16 and usually can't stand little kids! Lia, you've done a good job. Chloe's an adorable child. And Mandy says she's smart as a whip in school."

Lia laughed. "After only two days?"

"Well, if it's an exaggeration, it's a positive one anyway. I told them to check in with us at the pavilion at seven. They'll probably be too full of ice cream and funnel cakes to eat dinner with us."

"What's a funnel cake?"

Anne moaned, "Mmm, a piece of heavenly food—but deep fried. Can I do something else to help you close up shop?"

"No, no." Lia ushered her to the door. "Anne, I can't thank you enough for helping me out."

"Goodness, you're paying me."

Lia blinked at tears that were welling up. "It's more than the hours you put in as an employee. You and Isabel and the others have kept me going."

Anne gave her a hug. "Oh, Lia, it's our big God who's taking care of all of us."

"I know. The details He's orchestrated this week alone amaze me! Chloe has friends already because she's in your Mandy's class. Isabel arranged for Gina to give her a kitten. Dot and I are swamped but you, Addie, Isabel, and Britte all jump in with two hours here, four hours there—and I don't think one customer has gone away unhappy."

"Eliana, you are the one who has made such a difference. This shop is Crabtree and Evelyn, a Galena boutique, *and* a country general all rolled into one. It's such a pleasure just to walk in here. I love being a small part of it."

Lia waved her hands, clearing away the praise as she would smoke clogging the air. "Enough of the mutual admiration society. I just needed to emote at the end of a very satisfying week. Now, go, so I can finish up. I don't want to miss my first pork chop dinner and country western dance!"

Anne smiled and stepped out the front door. "All right. See you at seven. Maybe we can talk about a raise!"

Lia laughed as her friend began weaving her way through the throngs of people meandering on the street. Along the front of the shop, two blocks of Fourth Avenue were barricaded to traffic for the festival. Just the other side of it, the town square called Franklin Park was lit up like a Christmas display with white lights strung through the picnic pavilion and trees. The band shell glowed like an enormous jewel in one corner. Another corner resembled a miniature carnival midway. In the center of the square, surrounding the fountain, a myriad of booths and tents housed arts and crafts. The air was heavy with enticing scents and sounds.

The phone rang at the back of the store as she shut the door. She dismissed the fleeting thought of letting the machine pick it up. Her business was to serve Valley Oaks. Sometimes that meant taking a doctor's prescription after hours. Once this summer she had even delivered medication to a distraught mother with an ailing baby and a traveling husband.

"Valley Oaks Pharmacy. This is Lia Neuman."

There was no reply.

"Hello?"

She heard it then... Someone's faint breathing.

"Who is this?"

Click.

"No!" she cried. She punched the asterisk button, the six, then stopped. Why waste the money? The call would be from a cell phone, untraceable.

Her hands shook and the receiver missed its mark, crashing to the floor. She grabbed it and slammed it on the hook.

Anger somersaulted over fear, and then fear over anger until she felt only a mass of roiling emotions. Fear won out.

"Chloe!"

Lia ripped off her lab coat, smacked her hand over the light switches, ran upstairs, grabbed her keys, raced back down, missed the last two steps, and tumbled to the floor. Tears sprang to her eyes. "Oh, dear God! Don't let this happen!"

Anger got the upper hand again, and she sprang to her feet, straightened her denim skirt, and tightened her ponytail. "Nelson will not control me. He *will not*. Lord, cast him from the face of the earth!"

Fear nipped at Lia's heels as she scurried across the street. Chatter, shouting, laughter, carnival music, and squeals from the ferris wheel filled the evening air. How would she ever find Chloe in all the ruckus?

More than likely the youngsters would gravitate to the carnival area. She hurried to the far corner, her heart beating erratically. The rows between game booths and rides were chock-full of kids of all ages, walking, standing, running, shouting, laughing. She studied the faces passing by. "Lord, please help me find her."

A hand touched her shoulder.

She whirled around into a brown uniform.

"Lia. I guess you couldn't hear me calling you."

"Cal! Have you seen Chloe?"

"No."

Lia swiveled her head, eyes sweeping the area. "I must find her. She's here with Anne Sutton's daughters."

"They'll turn up eventually."

"I can't wait until *eventually*!"

He gently grasped her hands and lowered his face, forcing her to stand still and meet his eyes. "Lia, what's wrong?"

A wave of fear constricted her throat. "I can't find her!" she choked.

"Is she missing?"

Lia struggled, fighting for control.

"Was she supposed to meet you?"

"At seven."

"It's not six-thirty yet."

"But I need to see her *now*!"

"She's fine. The Sutton girls are dependable. She'd stay in the square with them, wouldn't she? She's new here. I'm sure she'll stick close."

Lia's knees wobbled. She gripped his hands that still held hers and drew strength from his calm solidity. "But kids will be kids."

"And this is where the action is, where they'll hang, in the middle of this crowd."

A blonde appeared at his side. "There you are, Calhoun!"

He straightened, dropping Lia's hands. "Tammy. Hi."

"Hi yourself, big guy." The young woman stretched on tiptoes and planted a kiss on his cheek.

Lia willed herself to stand still and act normal. Cal was right. The children would stay put.

The stranger tossed her white-blonde shoulder-length hair and pouted glossy mauve lips. "I wanted my little nephew to meet you, but he's over there on the merry-go-round."

"I'll be working here all night. Catch me later. Have you met Lia Neuman yet?"

"No," she turned toward her, "but my mother has told me all about you." Her tone had gone flat.

Cal said, "Lia, this is Tammy Cassidy."

It took her a moment to respond. "Oh! You're Dot's daughter! Nice to meet you finally." Her voice was tight. She felt the polite façade slipping.

Tammy shook her outstretched hand. "Likewise, I'm sure."

"I have to go."

As she turned away, Cal called, "I'll keep an eye out. Where are you meeting?"

"At the pavilion."

Again Lia scrutinized each passing youngster. The garish lights and music compounded the frantic beating of her heart.

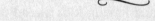

"Tammy, I can't hold hands while I'm on duty." Cal untwined his fingers from hers.

"Well, you were holding hands with *her*."

"Who? Lia? I was trying to calm her down. She was spinning around like a chicken with its head cut off."

Tammy squeezed his forearm. "My hero with the beautiful green eyes. Saving a damsel in distress. What was her problem?"

"She can't find her daughter."

"Oh, yeah. Mom told me she had a *daughter*. And no *husband*."

"Kind of like half the world. Tammy, I need to move on. I hope you're not staying late and driving home in the middle of the night."

"Twin Prairie is only 23 miles down the road." She fiddled with a button on his shirt. "Of course, you could invite me to stay in town."

"I'm sure your mother would put you up."

She slapped his chest. "Oh, you! Whenever you're wearing that uniform, you just tune me out."

He heard the hurt beneath her exasperation. "Tam, it's a discipline thing. If you're not a damsel in distress, I gotta move on."

She stomped her foot on the ground. "I *am* in distress! I miss you!"

Cal laughed and walked away. "See you."

"Goodbye!"

He strolled through the crowd, studying the faces. Some of the kids were familiar to him, the older ones because they'd been in trouble, the younger ones because they were children of his classmates. That fact always brought him up short. He couldn't imagine having kids already. Come to think of it, he couldn't imagine having a *wife*, let alone kids. He and Tammy were on the same wavelength with that concern. It was one of the things he liked about her. Right after her looks.

She was a lot younger. They hadn't known each other growing up in Valley Oaks, but he knew she had won different beauty pageants, county fair queen kind of stuff. She could have been a model, but instead settled in Twin Prairie where she taught preschool. She was good-looking.

Speaking of looks, what did Lia's little girl look like? Would he even recognize her? She had been asleep that night. He knew her hair was shorter than her mom's, but just as black. When he had laid her down on the bed, he noticed her creamy skin, like her mom's. What was it called? Porcelain. That was it, like dolls. Two china dolls plunked down in the middle of Valley Oaks.

Cal made his way to the picnic area. Long lines of people stretched from the food tent, eager to get the town's famous grilled pork chop sandwiches. He greeted folks, rounded the end of the lines, and spotted Lia in the nearby playground, kneeling before a dark-haired little girl and hugging her tightly.

Well, that situation was resolved. Apparently the new pharmacist was a little high strung when it came to her daughter.

That niggling corner of his mind stirred. What was it? Yeah…that was it…the outdated alarm system. And the back door's flimsy lock. Apparently Lia wasn't overly concerned when it came to home security. But wasn't that and the kid's security one and the same?

Hmm. Something didn't jibe here.

Six

Tony popped the last of his pork chop sandwich into his mouth. They certainly did know how to cook around these parts, he had that to say for them.

He chided himself for the uppity attitude. Not everyone south of Chicago was a closed-minded bigot who thought a whining voice set to twanging guitars was music. Take Izzy, for instance. Though unsophisticated, she had gone to college and was bilingual and bicultural. No, he had to admit that the majority of Valley Oaks residents he had met so far weren't the stereotype he imagined. Homemade and maybe a bit hokey, but decent and open. Only those three men in the café the other morning displayed true redneck colors. They drove big ugly trucks, spoke loudly, chewed loudly, and teased the waitress mercilessly. From their undisguised scrutiny of his person, he figured their notion of him was highly suspect. He did what he could to display his own rendition of machismo, winking and smiling at the waitress before making a mental note to leave his Gucci loafers at the motel from now on.

He looked across the picnic table where Dot Cassidy sat, dabbing daintily at the cole slaw dressing at the corner of her mouth. She was older, attractive, and no doubt a knockout in her younger years when the platinum didn't come from a bottle. The tone of her eager friendliness, though, led him to believe that she was the town's leading gossip who bent stories as easily as she batted her mascara-laden eyelashes. Her husband probably drove one of those big ugly trucks.

Tony gave himself a mental shake. He was a journalist. Professionally, he needed an unbiased posture when researching a story. Even if he threw out three-fourths of what Dot told him, there would be useful nuggets. He focused on her again, shutting out the noise and bright lights of the Valley Oaks annual ritual called the Autumn Faire. "Excuse me?"

"I was wondering if you would use my name." She pulled a compact from her purse and proceeded to apply another layer of bright pink lipstick.

"Yes, Mrs. Cassidy. Unless you want to remain anonymous."

"Tony, please! I told you to call me Dot. And my goodness, no, I don't want to be anonymous in something the whole nation's going to read!" Although no one was sitting near them, she leaned across the table and lowered her voice. "Now, I don't like to say anything derogatory about Brady, but the guy is not perfect. Nobody is. Did you know his dad was married to Gina Philips' mother? We were all in the same high school class."

"Wait a minute. Brady's *related* to Gina?"

"Well, not exactly. It happened way before Neil married Barb and they had Brady. The Olafssons are rich farmers, so he was a spoiled kid. Had the money and the looks to get away with anything. He sure could play basketball." Admiration slipped into her voice. "Made the state all-star team his junior *and* senior year. No one's done that before or since."

If I hear that fact one more time—

"What I'm saying is, life came easy for him. He got everything he ever wanted." Dot's smile bordered a smirk. "Except Nicole Frazell. She hightailed it out of here, leaving him high and dry and out a $10,000 ring."

"He was engaged? When was this?" Tony jotted down the name in his small notebook.

Dot tapped the page with a long, pointed pink fingernail. "That's one *z*, two *l*s. Let's see. That would have been about four years ago."

"What happened?"

She shrugged her hot pink padded shoulders. "Most people thought Nicole was nuts to let Brady slip through her fingers. I, on the other hand, imagine he just didn't have what it took to keep her happy."

A movement caught Tony's eye beyond Dot. Uh-oh. Izzy was making her way through the picnic shelter. She stopped for a moment to talk to someone, but she kept glancing in his direction. The shelter's yellow lights cast a muted glow on the subtle deep red tones of her thick hair. The chin in her heart-shaped face appeared more pointed and determined than usual.

He surreptitiously closed the notebook and slid it into the inside pocket of his lightweight sport coat. "Until this article comes out, Dot, I'd appreciate it if you'd keep the specifics of our talk here confidential."

"My lips are sealed."

Yeah, right. He swallowed the laughter that threatened to burst and hid his face by searching his pockets. He pulled out a business card and handed it to her. "If you come up with any other," he dropped his voice, "*inside* information, would you mind calling me? The motel number where I'm staying is written on the back."

"Don't you have any more questions for me now?"

Izzy was only one table away and approaching rapidly. He stood and offered his hand to Dot. "Afraid not. You've been a great help. Thank you."

She shook his hand. "I'll be glad to give you a call. We could talk half the night away. It sure doesn't seem like I told you much."

Tony disagreed. Her tidbit was priceless. Nicole Frazell left the Valley Oaks Golden Boy floundering in the dust for *some* reason.

Isabel was fuming. Dot Cassidy knew her pharmaceuticals like nobody's business, but she also knew how to twist words into nonsense. Tony Ward had no right to accept that woman's version of today's *date* let alone anything she had to say about Brady!

Having wound her way through the perpendicular rows of picnic tables, Isabel reached where they were seated just as Tony stood. She caught Dot's voice, demurring something about not telling him much. *Ha!* That'd be the day. If it were true, it'd be an answer to the prayer that only formed in her mind three minutes ago.

"Hello, Izzy." Tony smiled.

She cringed. Now Dot knew the nickname she abhorred. Shiny new merchandise for the gossip peddler. "Hi, Tony. Dot."

"Tony," Dot's tone accused, "you didn't tell me you two knew each other. And where does the name 'Izzy' come from?"

He said, "In college—"

"We were," Isabel cut in, taking no chances, "acquainted. Eons ago. Am I interrupting an interview?"

Tony replied, "Not at all. Have you eaten?"

"Yes. I was wondering if we could talk."

He turned to the woman whose photographic memory was recording every nuance between them. Isabel hoped her jaw wasn't obviously clenched. "Dot," Tony said, "it has been delightful. Will you excuse me, please?"

"Only if you promise me lunch next time!" she giggled. "Just kidding. Thank you for dinner."

"You're welcome. Goodbye."

Isabel added her goodbye and headed to the edge of the shelter. She veered off into the grass toward the street, nearly pitch black compared to the brightly lit park.

Tony caught up with her.

She snapped, "I wonder if the *Tribune* knows how it lucked out on this assignment?" Cattiness underscored her tone. "Your expense account won't take much of a hit at the Valley Oaks Autumn Faire."

"That's what you think. We had the whole dinner with creamy slaw *and* cherry pie à la mode. Where are we going, by the way?"

"A quiet place." She led him across the street to the front steps of the library. The lights, music, and laughter were muted here. Anger still churned in her stomach. No doubt Tony sensed it by now. There was no reason to mask it. She propped her hands on her hips and faced him. "Tony, what are you up to?" In spite of the attempted bravado, her voice quivered.

He walked the few remaining feet to the stoop and sat on a step, lounged back, and clasped his hands behind his head. "Am I missing something here?"

"Don't answer my question with a question! You always did that."

"And aggravated you to no end."

That knocked the wind from her sails. She let the silence stretch between them while she struggled against remembering.

"Aggravating you, Izzy, was one of my favorite pastimes. If I kept you going long enough, your *r*s would start rolling like crazy and oh!" He clapped a hand to his chest and closed his eyes. "The way vowels would dance around in your mouth, like they were something physical! And then you'd start spewing forth in Spanish. You were *the* most intriguing young girl I had ever met."

He used to say her speech was music to his writer's ears. Whenever she was upset, she'd inadvertently slip into the rhythm of her parents' accent. He would catch her unawares, egging her on to exasperation. "Tony, you were *the* most annoying guy on campus."

"Which intrigued you."

Which intrigued me, she silently assented, *as well as your charm, your handsome face, and your intelligence. Probably in that order, in the beginning anyway.*

He sobered. "It was an intense three months, wasn't it?"

Again, she didn't reply.

"Go ahead, yell at me, preferably in Spanish. Mine's a little rusty."

"Do you deserve a scolding?"

"What do you think?"

"Tony!"

He leaned forward and braced his elbows on his knees. "Izzy, I'm not meaning to aggravate you. I'm simply trying to get at what you're really asking me. You know what I'm up to. I'm writing an in-depth article about the Christian artist's influence on today's society."

"All right, I'm really asking what are you doing talking to Valley Oaks' clearinghouse of gossip?"

"I recognized her as such."

"Then why are you giving her the time of day?"

"I'm interviewing lots of folks in an attempt to get a more rounded view of your author."

"Did she tell you about her daughter Tammy and Brady?"

"Is this gossip?"

"No. She told me her side of the story, he told me his, and I saw some of it. Brady and Tammy worked together on a committee for the Faire last year. Tammy went after him, flirting, asking him out. He wasn't interested. Her ego was bruised. Her mother has held Brady in contempt ever since, blaming him for the entire situation."

"Which leads you to believe her opinion is a little biased." He chuckled. "Come on, Iz, give me more credit than you would a baboon writing this piece, huh?"

"You'll not just take her word for something?"

"I won't take anything she says as fact unless two others substantiate it. Fair enough?"

Isabel crossed her arms. His track record didn't promote trust, but that was personal, something between the two of them. And it was a long time ago. She took a deep breath, again pushing aside the memories. "Promise?"

"Promise."

Her temper fizzled. With a start she recognized a bad habit she thought was long gone. Angered at the drop of a hat, she would fuss and fume for a while, and then feel better. The sight of Tony sitting with Dot had ignited it. Tony seemed to be igniting too many emotions.

She shook her head. "Sorry. Dot is just a needy person."

"She seems pretty self-sufficient to me. Hey, I think I hear a band warming up." He was changing the subject.

Isabel glanced toward the square. The giant black grills used for cooking the pork chops were shut. The crowd of food-tent workers and patrons had dwindled. People were gathering nearer the band shell where park benches had been removed from the concrete slab, opening it up for dancing.

She felt deflated. How she loved the Autumn Faire! This was her fourth one, and she had been anticipating for weeks the great fun and camaraderie it offered. And now here she was stewing over Tony's presence. He was an outsider...he was going to tarnish this year's memory...but then again...he didn't have to, did he? After all, her reaction was her choice.

He was as needy as Dot, but he didn't recognize it in himself. Maybe he had never seen Jesus in action. Maybe she could at least give him a glimpse of that. That, after all, was what he needed to experience for his article. *Lord, love him through me?* "Come on, Tony. You've got to catch the full flavor of this weekend. Let's dance."

"It's country." His tone balked.

"Ward, you always did have a snooty side. Now, wouldn't it serve your best interests if you joined in rather than stood at a distance and observed like a condescending city slicker? Potential interviewees might see you as approachable if you do a little," she lifted her arms and stepped sideways, "line dancing."

He stood. "Good grief. You've gone Christian *and* country on me!"

Seven

Cal stood eye to eye with Brady and asked, "In public?"

His friend grinned. "Breaking new ground here. Watch my backside?"

"Always." He returned the grin and punched Brady's shoulder, and then he walked on.

Cal continued patrolling the more or less circular edge of the Autumn Faire crowd gathered near the band shell. Things were winding down elsewhere in the park. He thought about Brady, who had just let him in on the latest developments with Gina.

Five years ago the guy was a basket case, working long hours at three jobs. He was teaching high school English, farming with his dad, and writing instead of sleeping, desperate to publish his stories. Writing was the love of his life, though Brady had tried to convince himself it was Nicole.

Cal had never warmed to her. She and Brady met at college. She always had a prissy look on her face and looked down her nose at Valley Oaks. The worst part, though, was her influence over Brady. She discouraged him from joining in the usual affairs with his old friends. Over time he became less sure of himself. After she left him and he pulled that crazy stunt chasing after her in California, things really went haywire. Brady stopped trying to convince Cal to trust in Jesus.

At first Cal was relieved, until he realized the impact of what that meant. It didn't mean Brady went carousing with him. The guy never did that, hadn't even in high school. No, it meant that if what Brady believed all these years was not true, then life really was hopeless. Looking back, Cal knew it was the impetus he needed. Even when he didn't swallow everything the guy preached, he had always depended on Brady's steadfastness. When that was gone, Cal finally started reading the Bible and the other books Brady had given him.

After a time he confronted his friend. "Is it all a lie?" Cal asked. He would never forget how Brady's face crumpled.

Since then their friendship had deepened. Cal watched over him, and in time Brady's faith worked like a grappling hook to pull him from despair. The process spoke louder than all the words Brady had spoken. Cal began to trust Jesus. Scars remained in his friend, leaving Brady vulnerable. Cal ran interference for him, much as he had during football when Brady played quarterback.

And now there was Gina. It seemed Brady had found true love this time because he wasn't a basket case with this woman. He was just...contented and happy, happier than he'd ever seen him since sophomore year when they blew Clifton High out of sectionals.

Cal stopped now and scanned the crowd in the dim light, the bright band shell a backdrop behind it. He saw Isabel with that reporter, Tony Ward. They were laughing like old friends. Well, maybe they were. But he was still an unknown in Brady's life. Tomorrow Cal would grab some computer time and see what he could learn about the guy's background. It was apparent Isabel didn't want to pursue the subject. She was still snubbing him.

"Cal!" It looked like Lia coming through the shadows toward him. A little girl followed.

"Hi."

She smiled. "Hi. Chloe, this is the Peppermint Teddy Bear, Deputy Huntington."

Chloe held her small hand out. "How do you do, Deputy Huntington? Thank you for taking care of me last week."

Whoa! Where had this kid come from? "You're welcome, Chloe. It's nice to meet you with your eyes open."

She giggled and turned to her mother. "Now may I?"

"Yes, sweetpea. I'll be right over." The girl hurried off. "She can't wait to learn how to line dance."

"It's tonight's big event."

"So I hear. Cal, I need to ask you a favor. Another favor. I promise, I'm truly not a nuisance."

He believed her. Somehow he couldn't imagine her as a nuisance. She was calmer now than earlier but still not as sturdy as she had been that rainy night, even after he had surprised her in the shower. "What can I do for you?"

"Will you walk us home in about an hour?"

He couldn't help but glance to the left of the band shell, over the heads of those in the crowd. He could see the pharmacy just across the street, not even a football field's length away. "No problem."

"Oh, good. Thank you so much. We'll find you!" She began to walk away before turning and calling over her shoulder, "I can't wait to learn line dancing either!"

Now why in the world would a woman who left the key in her door be afraid to cross the street with half the town standing nearby?

Tony thought the scene surrealistic, more Dali than Rockwell. But then maybe that was simply his jaundiced eye seeing ulterior motives and underlying issues hiding behind this Mayberry façade.

The band shell glowed, a half moon of floodlights penetrating the dark night directly in front of it while carving shadows just beyond the circle of light. Band members clunked around the stage in their cowboy hats and boots, preparing to play their non-music. He was certain Rockwell had never depicted such a moment.

Then there was Dot, queen of the know-it-alls who, according to Izzy, relayed only bits and pieces of all she knew. At the moment she held court, surrounded by yakking women, undoubtedly of similar ilk. Where were the men? That was an easy one. At the beer tent down the block, around the corner. Where he should be. A cold one might take the edge off this mushrooming cynicism.

But...the story was here. The Author was making his way toward the stage.

Off to one side stood Cal Huntington, his bear-width shoulders and unblinking gaze erasing any benevolent Sheriff Andy Taylor aura. He had been friendly enough when they met, but Tony suspected the guy was borderline redneck. The law and order department did not exactly roll out the welcome mat for outsiders here.

Valley Oaks was a cultural desert. The pharmacist stood out as different, though her features only faintly suggested Asian heritage. She was obviously Chicago born and bred. Then there was Izzy, his hot Latino ex-girlfriend who was still hot, not only in her jeans and boots, but under the collar as well. She hid it fairly well, but she was angry at him. About what, he hadn't a clue.

She turned to him now, tilted her chin to meet his eyes and leaned closer to be heard above the noisy crowd. "You're laughing at us."

He blinked. The woman's talents were being wasted at a Christian radio station. "Why would I do that?"

"We're unsophisticated. The thing is, Tony, most of us know it and don't give a hoot. Write *that* down in your little notebook." She tapped his lapel and raised a brow.

Yes, a beer would definitely help, he thought again, giving her a self-deprecating smile. Sophistication wasn't the point. He was out to prove whether or not Brady Olafsson was authentic, but he couldn't exactly tell Izzy that.

"Ladies and gentlemen." Brady was on the stage now, speaking into a microphone. "May I have your attention, please? As a member of the Entertainment Committee, I'd like to introduce tonight's band, but first, on a personal note..." He paused.

The crowd stilled. The guy did have a presence about himself, Tony had to admit.

Keyboard music began playing softly. It sounded like an old tune. He noticed a blonde sitting at the instrument. She didn't look like a country musician. Hadn't he met her? That was it. Band teacher married to a relative of Brady's. Lauren something or other.

Brady continued, "I'd like to welcome our new vet to her first Valley Oaks Autumn Faire. Oh, excuse me just a moment." He pressed a finger behind his ear as if to hear better. "Ah, she's correcting me. All right, *assistant* vet."

Tony looked to where he was directing his smile. He could see even in this light that Gina's California tan had turned a deep crimson.

"When Gina arrived this summer, one of the first things she noticed was how fast news travels around Valley Oaks. As we all know, sometimes it's true, sometimes not. Well...the news I hear these days is that she and I are engaged, so I thought I'd better set the record straight."

There was laughter and a few whistles. Tony recognized the background music now, something about where the journey leads.

"The fact is, we're *not*. But...Angelina Philips, I love you. And I'm wondering what you're doing the rest of your life?" He chuckled. "I'd sing this if I could carry a tune."

Laughter drowned him out for a moment.

"Where does your journey lead from here? Down roads unseen, midst stars flung wide? I have but one request of you, dear." He took a deep breath. "And so...the question is: Will you marry me?"

There were more whistles and catcalls and cheers while poor Gina covered her red face with her hands.

"Folks, I don't know if we have a yes or a no here, but that's the latest news from Valley Oaks. I'll let Lauren introduce—Oh, it looks as if we may have an answer on the way. Or else she's going to strangle me." He grinned as the crowd parted for Gina. When she reached the stage, he leaned over far enough for her to grab his vest and give it a good yank. He tossed the microphone toward Lauren and jumped down. The crowd erupted into applause when Gina's arms went around his neck.

Lauren spoke loudly into the mike. "I'd strangle him myself."

Tony rolled his eyes and nudged Izzy beside him. "Bit of an exhibitionist, isn't he?"

Tears streamed down her face. "Are you kidding?" she sniffled. "That's the most romantic thing I've ever witnessed. He just publicly declared how much he loves her!"

"Yeah, well, what if the feeling isn't mutual?"

"Oh, the whole town knows it's mutual." She wiped at her cheeks. "This was just a formality. I wonder if he has a ring?"

A woman standing nearby turned, pressing a tissue to her eyes. "He just pulled it out of his vest pocket."

Izzy joined the woman in an exaggerated "Aww" and brushed away another tear.

Tony shook his head in disbelief and touched Izzy's arm, urging her a short distance from the others. "Is this guy truly for real?"

"I told you he was!"

"You're saying this wasn't all an act? That he's not just yanking heartstrings to promote his image?"

Izzy narrowed her eyes, studying him. "Tony, if you don't get it yet, you'd better spend some more time with him."

Lia jabbered about the evening to Cal. The loud country music faded as they crossed the dimly lit street behind the band shell. She felt at ease with him, but she didn't kid herself. It was his obvious physical strength and the gun in his holster that calmed her anxiety. Chloe skipped ahead of them, slowing now and then to slip into a line-dance step.

Cal chuckled. "I think your daughter had a good time at her first Autumn Faire."

A tiny fist of dread pressed against her chest, and for a fraction of a second her lungs could get no air. Would it never go away? "Yeah, she had a grand time. Cal, she's not my daughter. Her mother…was my sister."

He stopped.

She waited for him to process the information.

"Was," he said. "Then—I'm sorry. When?"

"Almost six years ago. Kathy died in a car accident. I've been Chloe's legal guardian since then."

"What about her father?"

"He's never been a part of the picture." *Not as a father or husband, except to his other, legal family.* "My new friends know. Isabel, Gina, and Anne, the pastor and his wife, they all know. I just don't bring it up in casual conversation because then I have to talk about my sister dying." She exhaled. "People always learn about the situation eventually."

"Especially in Valley Oaks. So it's not a secret? Chloe knows?"

"Oh, yes, she's always known. She remembers her mother. You're welcome to spread the news. Not that I can imagine you spreading gossip, even if it is true."

He gave her a soft smile.

They continued their stroll across the deserted street, and she realized that he fit as naturally as Isabel and the others in her small group of new friends.

"Lia, aren't you concerned about what people think?"

"I haven't had time to be concerned about that. I probably should be, considering my livelihood depends on people thinking well of me. Maybe I should put a sign in the window: The pharmacist is not an immoral slut."

He laughed loudly. "You don't mince words."

They reached the door where Chloe waited, dancing on the sidewalk. Lia fumbled with the keys. "Cal?"

"Sure, I'll walk you inside."

She threw him a smile.

"But there's an if. *If* you tell me what happened between the time you left the keys in the back door last week and tonight."

She pushed open the door, jerked out the keys, and shoved them back into her skirt pocket. A night-light softly lit the shop's interior. Her niece raced down an aisle. "Chloe! Wait!"

"I have to go to the bathroom!" she yelled over her shoulder.

Cal touched her elbow as he shut the door. "Lia, what's going on?"

Once again anger shoved aside the fear. How ridiculous! To fuss at Chloe for simply hurrying to the bathroom! She refused to live this way. "Oh, nothing, Cal. I'm being silly."

"Do you want me to go upstairs?"

"No."

He dropped her arm.

"Thank you, though, for offering."

"Lia, you're not the silly type. I hope you'll clue me in."

She didn't respond.

"Did you order a new security system?"

She nodded. "It's being installed next Tuesday."

"All right." He opened the door. "You've got my number."

"I do?"

He gave her a thumbs-up. "Nine-one-one. See you."

She bolted the door behind him and hurried after Chloe. *Dear Lord, don't let me need that!*

Eight

Dead air!

Isabel raced along the studio hallway, coffee sloshing over the sides of her mug and scalding her hand. Swerving into the control room, she bumped into the door frame. The remainder of the coffee splattered across the front of her yellow cotton shirt.

She rounded the corner of the L-shaped desk, shoved the chair aside, flipped a switch on the large computerized board, jerked down the microphone, and slapped on the headphones.

"Whoops! I apologize for that, folks." She gulped for air as indiscreetly as possible and set down the empty cup. "This is Isabel Mendoza at WLMD. We just heard from…" She read from the monitor the list of artists and their songs. "Today's forecast calls for another 24 hours of clear sky with a high of 73 and a low tonight of 50. It's currently 64 degrees. Perfect Labor Day weekend weather and great for the Autumn Faire out in Valley Oaks. We'll have national and local news at the top of the hour. The national news update is next. It's 8:30, and you're listening to WLMD-FM, Rockville, Illinois."

She pressed the appropriate buttons and switches, grateful that contemporary broadcasting was not a complicated process.

What was complicated was Tony Ward.

She hooked the chair leg with her foot, slid it over, and sank onto it. With a loud groan she laid her head on the desktop and closed her eyes.

Last night at the Autumn Faire had been fun... Well, after she had chewed Tony out for talking to Dot, anyway. She had deliberately set aside old hurts, wanting Jesus to be more evident in her attitude toward him. Eventually she had coaxed him into joining the large group of square dancers. Other women loved him, of course. After a time even the guys warmed to him. He really was more charming than ever. They had all laughed at his two-left-feet version. At midnight he walked her home.

Now, as the news droned on, she read from the monitor. A long set of songs and a program about house renovation was queued. With computerized pre-programming these days, her physical presence wasn't necessary much of the time. But she loved the challenge of live radio and had talked the manager into letting her do the Saturday morning slot. She often scheduled an interview and church bulletin information after the children's stories.

There was plenty of time to grab another cup of coffee. She headed back down the hall, empty mug in hand. She needed coffee desperately. Fifteen minutes ago she had gone for some. Her mind wandered light years away, and she forgot to watch the large clocks that were never out of view around the studio. She wasn't even aware of the broadcast until everything went quiet.

Isabel entered the kitchenette located in a nook across the hall from the lobby. She had drained the pot the last time and now prepared fresh coffee. As it dripped into the carafe, she tuned her ears to the worship music. When it gave way to the house renovator's voice, the pot was full and still she sat, not having heard one word of one song. Wearily, she stood and poured herself a mugful of coffee.

Tony's presence stirred so many memories and emotions. They had kept her awake most of the night. What was she supposed to do with them? They had been buried for years. No problem. Forgotten, right? That's what God did with them. Forgave them and forgot them. She would rebury them. Same thing as forgotten.

A banging on the front door disrupted her thoughts. She was the only one scheduled at the station today. Generally the secretary, engineer, and manager didn't come in on Saturdays. Isabel kept the station locked. She left the tiny kitchen area and entered the lobby. There was a glass door, a small entry, and then another door. She saw Tony outside, waving his arms and grinning.

Wham! All those half-buried emotions flung themselves at her with tornado force. Her second cup of coffee slid to the carpeted floor. She stared at him. He stopped waving and shrugged, questioning.

Isabel went to the doors and opened them.

"Sorry, Izzy. Didn't mean to scare you."

She pulled the exterior door shut behind him on the pretense of making sure the lock clicked, but in reality hiding her unguarded expression. "You just startled me." So to speak.

"That's amazing out there! I've never seen so much corn! And it's growing to music!" His gesture encompassed the surrounding fields that always echoed with the broadcast. Except for a sliver of highway at the end of the long drive and the two radio towers, eight-foot-high corn stalks blocked views in every direction. "It's gotta be the tallest corn in three counties."

In spite of her discomfort she had to smile at his exaggeration. "Tony, what are you doing here?" She retrieved the mug from the floor, making a mental note to scrub out the stains before she went home.

"Nice outfit. Designer?"

She glanced down at the brown-splattered yellow shirt and the khakis damp from waist to ankle along her right leg. "*Again* you don't answer my question. I thought you were leaving today."

"I am. On my way out of town right now."

"This isn't the route between Rockville and Chicago."

"Yeah, yeah, I know. Listen, I was thinking. I need to spend more time with The Author. And you." He spread his arms, palms up. "You were right, Iz. I don't get it. None of you add up. For one thing, you were all *dancing* last night. I know for a fact that Christians don't dance, they don't chew, and they don't go with girls that do."

"Last night's square and line dancing was more like a PE class." She gave her head a slight shake. What exactly was he getting at? "Tony, Christianity isn't about rules."

"News to me. Anyway, my editor can't spare me to work more on this right now. It's a freelance kind of thing, no deadline. I'll be back in a week or so. I plan to stick like glue to Brady, except when he's at his laptop. Then I'll hang with you. Find out what makes *you* tick." He finished with his lopsided grin and a cocked eyebrow.

She stared at him, silence hovering between them.

Silence. Except for fuzzy static.

"Oh, no!" she cried and raced down the hallway. "Not again!" It was a repeat performance at the controls.

"This is Isabel Mendoza, uh," she ruffled a stack of papers searching for the news she had read at 8:00. "It's..." she glanced up at the clock, "um, 8:57," *45 seconds late, an eternity in air time,* "and here's our local news."

She read 90 seconds' worth and then tuned in to the national news already in progress. At 15 seconds shy of nine o'clock she repeated the weather forecast, identified the station, then released control to the children's story hour that had bounced off some orbiting satellite during the night, imbedding itself into the station's system.

She blew out a breath.

Tony chuckled from the doorway. "Nice job."

She rolled her eyes.

"Again. I caught your 8:30 segment on the drive out."

"That was no segment. That was at best a snafu."

"Oh, well. I hear that Christians aren't perfect, just..." he paused, "forgiven." His tone was unmistakable.

"Tony, your charm flies right out the window when you start mocking."

"I know. One of my many bad habits." He came around the desk and took her arm, urging her from the chair. "Walk me out."

With dragging feet she made yet one more trip down the hall.

At the door he said, "I guess it's why I'm coming back. I want to know what that means."

"Know what what means?"

"Forgiven. What does it look like in the nitty-gritty details of everyday living?" He leaned over and gave her a friendly kiss on the cheek. "I'll call you."

Isabel watched him walk outside to his car. *Forgiven.* How in the world was she going to answer that question? She used to know what forgiven meant in the nitty-gritty details. But that was before Tony Ward had reentered her life, delivering a whole bunch of ugly baggage with "Izzy Mendoza" written on the ID tags.

Tony pulled out onto the two-lane county highway, leaving behind the one-horse operation of a broadcast studio. It was...quaint, just a small building with a pleasant, homey feel about the rooms that were bright with windows overlooking cornfields and blue sky. The requisite towers and satellite dishes were in a small clearing across the blacktop drive that widened enough for a handful of cars to park.

It had been a kick to hear Izzy's voice sing out across the rustling corn. She had a beautiful voice, whether whispering or fussing at him in Spanish or singing.

Singing?

Hmm. Did she sing? He felt a distinct notion that she did. Not that he remembered specific incidents...Beyond visiting her grandmother in central Mexico, his past with her remained a memory of impressions. Intense, but just impressions.

Like holding her hand.

Or passionate discussions about...politics...journalism...religion. Religion? They went to church with her *abuela*.

Laughing with her.

Convincing her to move in with him. The apartment on Linden. That last semester he had ended up in a one-bedroom, his roommates dropping out or graduating.

Why couldn't he remember clearly? Brushing her cheek just now with a kiss had been an automatic farewell. As if he had done it all the time. It was a kiss between friends, as if their living together had gone a step beyond physical intimacy, as if they truly cared for each other.

Whoa. That was a scary thought. Was *that* what had separated them in the end? He couldn't remember why or how they split, but at 26 he would have been a blur on the horizon at the first sign of a truly caring relationship. He had a shot at writing for the *Trib,* and he was not about to let anything like a college girl distract him from his goal to be the best reporter that ever walked Michigan Avenue.

That could explain her anger, although seven years seemed like an awfully long time to hold a grudge. Especially since she was into forgiveness.

Well, it would be a trip to delve into her psyche. She and Brady professed a faith that was a sham. Why had they fallen for it?

"Speaking of trips," he spoke aloud and reached for his cell phone. Hopefully his travel agent could book him a seat on the red-eye to Los Angeles that night. He'd track down Nicole Frazell tomorrow, get her version of the Brady Olafsson broken engagement, catch the red-eye back, and be in the office on Monday. Piece of cake.

Cal strode across his and Isabel's adjacent backyards and entered her screened-in porch. He knocked on the kitchen door. When he heard nothing, he pounded a couple of times.

"Hold your horses, Cal!" Her voice carried through the open windows from somewhere inside the house. Two minutes later she opened the door, her hair wrapped turban style in a bright purple towel. She wore a scruffy "3-on-3" blue T-shirt and jeans. "What?"

"How many times have I told you to keep your porch locked?"

She folded her arms and tapped a bare foot.

He blew out a frustrated breath. That wasn't the fight he meant to pick. "Can we talk a minute?"

She took a moment before answering, her thoughts evidently elsewhere. "Sure. Come on in."

He stepped up into her kitchen and went to the table, taking notice of the full coffeepot and glass jar of cookies. "Truce?"

"I didn't know we were at war."

"Come on, Mendoza. You've never answered the door and snapped 'What?' at me like that before."

She bit her lip. "You just want some good coffee."

He grinned. "And a cookie."

She poured him a mugful and set it on the table with the cookie jar. "Excuse me a minute."

Cal always liked stopping in at Isabel's. Her comfortable rented house always smelled good, usually with the scent of fresh coffee and fresh-baked cookies. She wasn't all sugar-and-spice femininity, though. The thing about Isabel was you could talk to her almost the same as to a guy. It probably had something to do with her having four brothers.

She came back, her hair combed and hanging damp. She poured herself a cup and sat down across from him. "I'm sorry I snapped."

"No problem. Great coffee." He was tiptoeing. He hated tiptoeing. "Look, I don't want to disturb you again by talking about Tony Ward—"

"It doesn't disturb me to talk about him!"

Now that is a convincing tone.

"I was just tired the other night. And besides, I told you everything I know."

Well, she had been avoiding him, but he wasn't going to go into that at this point. "I spent the morning on the Internet. Do you know anything about his sister?"

She sipped her coffee and gazed toward the window above the sink. "I never met his family. He mentioned a younger sister."

"She died. About two years ago."

Isabel's eyes swiveled back to him. "Died? What happened?"

"She was a missionary in Colombia. The way I read it, some guerillas didn't like Christian visitors."

"She was *martyred*?"

He nodded, watching the implications sink into her awareness before he said, "He's out to crucify Brady."

"Cal, you don't know that. Maybe he's searching for the real truth."

"You're thinking like a girl, Mendoza."

She scrunched her nose at him.

"Did you know he was nominated for a Pulitzer this year?"

"A Pulitzer? You're kidding!"

"Investigative reporting. He exposed some scam an insurance group was running that involved laundered drug money."

Isabel walked to the sink and stared out the window. "But Brady's just Brady, Cal. He's authentic. He has no skeletons in the closet. Tony can't hurt him."

"The likes of Tony Ward can hurt anybody. Why do you suppose he didn't interview me? He interviewed half the town, but not his subject's best friend."

Isabel turned. She looked pale. "Why?"

"Because there'd be no reason to ask me the kind of stuff he's digging for. I wouldn't bother to answer those questions. When is his article coming out?"

"I don't know. He's coming back in a couple of weeks. He said he doesn't understand us Christians yet. I really think he's curious about our faith. We know Brady's praying for his salvation because he always thinks of that first. Maybe Tony's coming back is part of the answer to his prayer."

"I'm still blown away when that happens. You know, when God answers Brady's prayer in a way I can see with my own two eyes."

"Don't your prayers get concrete answers?"

"Well, I haven't gotten shot." He headed toward the door.

"Is that all you need, Cal? To not get shot?"

"Pretty much." He opened the porch door and turned toward her. "I could pray for you though."

"For me?"

"Yeah, you don't look so hot right now. Are you sick?"

Her forehead crinkled.

Oh, swell. Now she's on the verge of tears. Mendoza is never on the verge of tears.

"No," she whispered, "but will you...will you pray for Tony's soul, too?"

"Sure." *Right after I pray that I won't have to nail the weasel for slander.*

Nine

Lia parked her car behind three others at the curb in front of Isabel's house. Across the street, trees lined a gully where the railroad tracks ran. Four modest houses and a brick apartment building bordered the right side of this block of Acorn Park Lane. At the far end was the vet's office. Two blocks back at the other end was the north edge of town where Anne and Alec Sutton lived in their renovated farmhouse. Chloe was there now, visiting Mandy and being baby-sat by Amy, although of course that wasn't a term Lia used any longer in front of her niece.

Lia's fingers ached. She loosened her grip on the steering wheel.

Lord, please keep her safe... Oh, that's all I seem able to pray these days! I'm sorry!

It was Thursday, almost a week since the first phone call. A new alarm system had been installed at the shop. If it went off, a siren sounded, which in her opinion wouldn't help a whole lot considering they lived in the business district where the sidewalks rolled up at 5:30 P.M. But also a signal would be sent to the security office. They were to call her and then, if she didn't answer, they would notify the police.

Still...she had received two more phone calls and now today a letter. Intangibles that wouldn't trip an alarm system.

She blinked away tears of frustration. Valley Oaks exuded comfort and safety. *Just look at Isabel's house.* Architecturally it was nondescript, but the sight of its cheery yellow siding and clean white shutters was like seeing a friend eagerly waiting to give you a hug. Two large maple trees filled the front yard. A rainbow of perennials bordered the sidewalk that led from the street to the stoop, then along the front of a flower-filled planter and around the left corner of the house.

She took a deep, calming breath.

Isabel had told her that Cal lived next door. Lia briefly studied his home, which was larger than Isabel's. It resembled him in a way, square and solid. A wonderful porch with brick pillars supporting its overhang covered the entire front of the white house. Above it a second-story window jutted out. There were trees and junipers around, but no flowers. A guy's kind of place. He emerged now from the front door. She climbed out of her car and met him at the curb.

"Hi, Cal."

"Hi, Lia." He smiled, the sides of his face folding accordion-style and his green eyes crinkling in a pleasant way. His teddy bear-trimmed hair was damp. He wore a short-sleeved plaid shirt and jeans.

"Do you have a minute?"

"Sure."

"I'm headed into Isabel's, but—" She pressed together her lips, which insisted on trembling.

His eyebrows shot up. "*Now* will you tell me what happened?"

"Friday night, right before I left for the Faire, I got a phone call. There was another one on Monday and yesterday. And...and this today." She pulled the envelope from her shoulder bag and handed it to him.

"Tell me about the calls."

"They came on the shop line, right after closing hours. I just heard breathing on the other end the first two times. Yesterday there was a scratchy whisper that said, 'You can't hide.'"

Cal carefully removed a piece of lined notebook paper from the envelope and shook out its fold, holding it by a corner. He read aloud, "'Your history.' Hmm. I suppose that means 'You *are* history.' They can't spell, can they? It's written in crayon on school paper. Lia, I think it's kids with nothing better to do than to pull a prank on the new person in town."

"There's more. Chloe's father— Oh, where do I begin?" She covered her mouth with her hands, but the gasp still escaped.

"How about his name?"

Lia closed her eyes for a moment and steadied herself. She lowered her hands. "Nelson Greene. He lives in Evanston. He doesn't have visitation rights. He kidnapped Chloe twice when she was a toddler. About six months ago, after strange phone calls, he showed up at the playground where she was playing with friends. They talked and he gave her a doll. Now Chloe wants to get to know him."

"Did you get a restraining order?"

"My sister did after the first time he kidnapped her, even though he didn't hurt Chloe or run. He just took her home. The cops found them that night. The second time...He came back a few months later. Chloe was three. He took her from day care and then went to Kathy's workplace. We pieced the story together after the accident. She never would have gotten into that car if Chloe weren't in it. Since then, Nelson has stayed away...until this year. I was in the middle of trying to buy the pharmacy and figure out the move. I just wanted to get us away as soon as possible. He has his own family."

"He's *married?*"

"Yes, with four older children. He was Kathy's boss. He was in the habit of wanting Kathy back whenever his wife kicked him out. I don't know why he's interested in Chloe now. Some latent altruistic sentiment..." She was going to lose it.

Cal squeezed her shoulder. "Listen, Lia, he's never written a note like this before, right? I mean, this is kids' stuff." He studied the envelope. "The postmark is faint. It looks like Rockville, though. More than likely it's not him, but I'll let the department know. Somebody will patrol around your place tonight. I'll swing by later. Where is Chloe now?"

"At the Suttons'. Alec is there with all the kids."

"Do they know?"

She shook her head.

"Lia, you've got to tell others. Your friends, the school. All right?"

She tucked a strand of hair behind her ear. "I thought we'd be safe in Valley Oaks."

"Maybe you should work on a restraining order."

"Maybe. I don't want him in her life! Oh, Cal, I'm sorry. That was a major unloading on you."

"Hey, I get paid for this kind of stuff."

"You look like you're going out. With Tammy?"

"Yeah."

"She seems like a special young woman. Besides being beautiful."

He nodded slightly. "I'm glad you told me about the situation. All right if I hang on to this letter?"

"Sure. Thanks, Cal."

"See you."

She watched him climb into his truck parked at the curb, then squared her shoulders and looked at Isabel's house. *I hope it's what it looks like—a friend with her arms wide open because I really, really need a hug right about now.*

Isabel opened her front door and saw a forlorn Lia Neuman standing there, her long black ponytail askew and her dark eyes unfocused. Isabel pulled her inside and gave her a bear hug. "Welcome!"

Lia fiercely hugged her back. "Oh, thank you! Sorry I'm late."

"No problem. I told you this so-called book club is extremely casual. It is so casual we don't always discuss books. You know everyone, don't you?"

"Hi, Lia!" a chorus of voices sang out behind her.

Isabel watched as her new friend joined the group of women oohing and aahing over a particularly large diamond on Gina Philips' left hand. Newcomers Lia and Gina would fit in as naturally as Isabel had herself four years ago. Observing the hugs and gentle camaraderie, she smiled. Christ's love was palpable whenever they gathered. It was the only thing they all shared in common. Well, that and a passion for reading.

Tonight was their first meeting of the season, the first Thursday in September. If anyone were regarded as leader, it would be Celeste Eaton. Her situation automatically placed her there: She was the pastor's wife, the oldest at 39, and the creator of the group. Years ago she rounded up mothers who, like herself, needed a regular evening away from their little ones. They called themselves Club NEDD, an acronym for what they did together: nurture, eat, and dabble in discussions about books which they may or may not have had time to read that month.

Still, Celeste shied away from overtly leading. With her pixie face, splash of freckles, naturally wavy brown hair of medium length, quick smile, and soft, lilting voice, she led by serving. They all adored her.

That original group of mothers with toddlers now all had teenagers. Anne Sutton added her calm, solid presence.

Addie Chandler sparkled with pizzazz, seeing everything through her artist's eye. Athletic Val Massey never let up on encouraging them to do aerobics at home whenever they finished reading a chapter.

Younger women completed the group. Britte Olafsson, who could pass for Brady's twin with her height and blonde good looks, taught high school math and coached the girls' basketball team. Band teacher Lauren Thompson and music teacher Abbey Swanson always left enthusiasm in their wake. And now there was Gina, the California transplant newly engaged to catch-of-the-century Brady. She was a veterinarian with hopes to bring elephants and other wild animals to the area.

And lastly, Lia Neuman... As a pharmacist, she was a wonderful addition to Valley Oaks' business community. Isabel recognized how deeply Lia was grounded in her faith. She admired her generous spirit, energy, and fun-loving attitude.

Tonight, though, all that was quite obviously missing.

The women would have celebrated anyway with food and singing, but Gina's engagement gave them a proper excuse. After agreeing on a novel to read before next month, most of the group left. Isabel watched from the door as they walked down her front steps. Light splashed through windows onto the dark lawn.

Anne leaned over Isabel's shoulder and called out, "Spoilsports!"

Britte turned from the sidewalk, laughing. "You're just a stay-at-home mom, Anne," it was an ongoing joke between them, "with nothing better to do than hang out here half the night! *We* all have to go to work tomorrow."

"You call what you do *work*? Showing teenagers how to add and subtract and shoot baskets?"

"How many times do I have to tell you? Calc is *not* adding and subtracting."

"Not to mention flirting with the new principal."

Britte only shook her finger in reply and kept walking toward the street.

Isabel nudged Anne with her elbow. "Say goodnight, Anne."

"Goodnight, Anne!" she mimicked.

Britte waved from her car parked at the curb. "Goodnight!"

Isabel shut the door. The late night air was cool. She sat back down in her favorite chair, a padded rocker. The earthy Anne pinched up the front of her capri pants, crossed her ankles and gracefully folded herself down onto the floor.

"Annie, your boss might fire you if you keep harassing her like that."

"The school board loves me." She grinned. Her husband was a member this year. "*They* pay my assistant coach's salary, not Coach Olafsson."

Isabel laughed. She glanced at the couch where Nutmeg had nestled herself between Celeste and Lia. The women were deep in conversation, legs tucked under their long skirts. Their similarities went beyond their clothing. Something about their spirits reminded her of her grandmother. That was it... All three women possessed an awareness that could only possibly develop after years of seeing with two sets of eyes. One pair saw the visible while the other saw the invisible. Isabel had ignored her *abuela's* teaching until later in life. As a result, her eyesight wasn't as keen as it could have been. Time had not only been wasted, it had been misused. Her vision would never reach the sharpness of theirs.

And she blamed Tony for that.

Celeste patted Lia's hand and turned to Isabel and Anne. "Lia has just told me that Chloe may be in danger from her father."

"What?!"

Lia nodded. "As I've mentioned, Nelson doesn't have visitation rights. He wasn't named on the birth certificate, and after his drunk driving killed my sister, I haven't wanted him near Chloe." She took a shaky breath. "Cal said I should tell you... Within the past week I've received three phone calls. With the first two, no one said anything, but the last one was a whispered 'You can't hide.' And a letter came in the mail saying 'You're history.'"

Before continuing, she closed her eyes briefly. "What I haven't told you was that Nelson often threatened to take Chloe. He did twice, and the second time ended in the car accident. He showed up at the playground six months ago and talked with her—without our permission. He didn't take her, but... It happened after hang-up phone calls."

Anne shook her head. "Oh, hon, you must be a basket case! Do you want to live with us?"

"Or me?" Isabel added.

"Or us?" Celeste finished.

"You all sincerely mean that, don't you?" The tightness around Lia's mouth relaxed in a smile that lit up her eyes. "I feel like God just gave me six more shoulders to carry this nightmare. Make that eight with Cal's. I think we'll be fine in the apartment. The problem is not going to go away. We're not in physical danger from him. And he has a wife and kids, so it's not like he wants to disappear with Chloe. It'll sort itself out."

Celeste said, "Cal will take care of the police side of things. I hear he's even investigating that reporter, what's-his-name, who's writing about Brady."

"Tony Ward," Isabel filled in the blank. "The whole town is excited about a big-time Brady article, and Cal's gone off the deep end looking for ulterior motives."

"You and Tony are friends, right?" Lia asked. "He called you Izzy in the shop."

Celeste and Anne turned wide eyes in her direction. "Izzy?"

"Yeah, yeah." Isabel paused. She needn't go into everything. "I knew him in college."

"Knew him?" Anne prompted.

"We were both in journalism." No reason to go into their living arrangements of so many years ago. "We dated for a short time right before he graduated, when I was only a sophomore. I never heard from him again."

Anne and Celeste exchanged glances.

Isabel's heart thudded. She had been off all evening. Now she heard the bitter undertones in her criticism of Cal and superficial description of Tony. None of that would be lost on her friends. She reached for a fair middle ground. "But then, I never tried to contact him again either."

Gentle Celeste smiled. "He's awfully charming. And nice-looking."

On the floor, Anne swung her legs out behind herself and began doing pushups. "Surface stuff, Celeste. I'm sure our *Izzy* wasn't *taken* with him."

Isabel rocked the chair with a vengeance. She simply did not want to get into her past, but these were her friends and their assumptions were on target. "All right. I was nuts about him. There, I said it."

They all burst into laughter.

Anne crumpled on the floor. "He is *way* cute, Dizzy Izzy."

"He really is," Lia agreed, "Busy Izzy."

Celeste giggled. "How about Fizzy Izzy?"

Isabel walked to the front door and opened it. "I think it's time you all went home."

Amid peals of laughter and hugs, they filed past her, calling out more renditions of her name as they strolled down the sidewalk.

"Mizzy Izzy!"

"Tizzy Izzy!"

"Wizzy Izzy!"

She leaned against the door frame and watched them drive away. The fact that she had deceived the women who loved her best made her feel sick.

Ten

Cal shifted in his chair at the kitchen table in the apartment above the pharmacy. Chloe's blue saucer eyes hadn't left his face for the past ten minutes. The little Sutton girl, Mandy, giggled behind her hand.

"Girls!" Lia reprimanded. "You're being rude to Deputy Huntington."

Grinning, Chloe turned to her aunt, nodded, and pointed her thumb in his direction.

Lia's dark eyes widened. "Chloe Neuman! If you two are finished, please excuse yourselves!"

"Excuse me! Excuse me!" The girls popped off their chairs and raced across the small kitchen into the hallway, laughter trailing behind them.

"Cal, I apologize."

"What was that all about?"

Lia grimaced. "Chloe is on the lookout for a dad."

"A dad? Oh... I see. I guess. I mean..."

She laughed. "Yes, you've got it. She thinks you'd fit the role perfectly, Peppermint Teddy Bear. But don't look so panic stricken. I'm not in the market!"

"Kids are..." He shrugged his shoulders, at a loss for an inoffensive adjective.

"They seem to make you uncomfortable."

"That's putting it mildly. They unnerve me. Give me an escaped convict any day."

"Weren't you a kid at one time? Or were you born wearing a sheriff's uniform?"

95

"I was born wearing a football uniform. Just grew up into the other one."

"I see. How about some coffee now?" She carried their plates to the sink and switched on the coffeemaker.

"That doesn't sound like a traditional Chinese beverage." He had just finished wolfing down the best egg rolls and kung pao chicken he had ever tasted.

"Neither does apple pie. It's my father's medley of European genes taking over. When my sister and I were little, he'd make coffee after a meal like this to go with his pie, which *he* had baked. Mom would just smile—my parents are still absolutely devoted to each other—but Grandmother, watch out!" Lia shook her hands, then pressed them to the sides of her head as she shuffled around in a circle, squealing out a string of Chinese phrases.

He laughed. "I think I'd skip the coffee. Do you speak Chinese?"

"Only when I'm very upset. Angry upset. Frustrated upset, I sing."

"You were frustrated upset in the shower?" he teased.

"No, Deputy, just glad to be home. Mind if I shut this window? It's getting cool in here." She struggled with the old wood-framed window behind the table.

He touched her shoulders and gently pushed her aside. "Let me."

"I really am independent when you're not around. Impressively independent."

"I'm sure you are. Oomph." The window rattled and banged shut. "I'm surprised these old things still open and close at all. I could probably replace the sashes, that might help."

"Cal, you've already done so much! First the deadbolt and new lock, then the doorbell this week. Not to mention lugging Chloe upstairs and ordering me to install the alarm. And now this Nelson business."

"Maybe I'm just looking for another home-cooked meal."

"Open invitation on that. I love to cook. You don't even have to work for it. Of course, you could buy your toothpaste downstairs here. Aspirin. Maybe a card for Tammy."

"Okay, okay. Want me to shut this window while I'm at it?" He went into the other end of the combined kitchen/ living area separated only by the beginning of a braid rug.

"Please. Then have a seat. I'll be right in with dessert."

He manhandled the other window behind the couch, then sat in the chair, anticipating the apples and cinnamon he smelled warming in the oven. Lia's apartment was small, but clean and neat. The recliner was a soft leather, worn and comfortable, located across from a plaid couch. A television and a couple of lamps and tables filled the room. An afghan, a painting of snow-capped mountains, silk-looking flowers, and small family photographs made it feel comfy and lived in.

He watched Lia as she prepared a tray. She was probably 5' 8", shorter than his Tammy by a few inches, but still taller than average. Tammy was on the scrawny side compared to Lia, whose angles were more rounded, making her softer-looking. She usually wore skirts and collared shirts beneath her white lab coat. Tonight she wore a light blue, soft-looking short-sleeved dress belted at the waist. He hadn't seen her in spandex. She was attractive and would probably look pretty good in spandex. Although it wouldn't fit her personality. She was outgoing and yet...quiet. No, that wasn't the word. She was...serene. Her long black hair swayed with her hips. Whenever she laughed, which was frequently, her black eyes lit up, sparkling through incredibly long lashes.

He wondered why she was single. Then he remembered Chloe. Major disadvantage there.

Lia set a tray on the coffee table; then she handed him a huge piece of apple pie with crumbly topping and ice cream melting beside it.

"Whoa. I'm going to sleep through the third shift tonight."

"You don't have to eat it. I'll send the pie home with you."

"Can't I eat this *and* take the pie home?" He grinned.

"Is that kind of like eating your cake and having it too? Here, coffee will help keep you awake. Black?"

"Thanks. So why are you still single?" The question slipped out. "Sorry, hazard of the trade, pumping you like that."

"No problem." Lia curled up on the couch, coffee mug in hand. "I told you. I'm impressively independent." She grinned before growing serious. "Oh, there are lots of reasons. I've been preoccupied with school and Chloe, of course. Buying the store and moving to Valley Oaks. And a long time ago I decided that I want no part of marriage unless I meet someone who treats me like Dad treats Mom, and he treats her like a queen. And then the guy would have to adopt Chloe as his daughter. Bit of a tall order, huh?" The clipped, emotionless words rolled from her tongue. She'd evidently rehearsed them a time or two. "How about you?"

He shrugged and swallowed his first bite. "Just not particularly interested, I guess. Mmm. This is the best apple pie I've ever tasted. Well, since we're on the same wavelength here, I vote we can be friends without all the other rigmarole. I mean, I'll fix whatever you need around the place, and you can feed me."

"It's a deal. Tammy's welcome, too. I'm sorry she couldn't come tonight."

"Mm-hmm." He felt unguarded with Lia already. She was easy to talk to, comfortable to hang with. But he wasn't about to honestly relay Tammy's reaction to Lia's invitation. His girlfriend was...prejudiced. No two ways about it. And it didn't take a rocket scientist to figure out how she got that way.

While he was installing the doorbell earlier in the week, Tammy's mother had overheard Lia invite him—and Tammy—to dinner. Later Dot had raised her brows, made fun of Chinese food, and declared she still believed that Chloe was Lia's daughter. Tammy had flat out refused to come, but he had already accepted and said he would go without her.

And now, he wasn't sorry that he had.

A short time later they stood in the kitchen as she drained the coffeepot into a traveling mug for him. She glanced at him out of the corner of her eye. "Dare you to go tell the girls goodbye."

"Uh—"

"Double dare."

"How about I clean up the kitchen instead?"

"They're just short people, Cal."

He turned on his heel, marched down the hallway, and rapped his knuckles on Chloe's open door. The kids looked up from where they sat on the floor, playing with the little black kitten. "Goodbye, girls."

Mandy, a tiny version of her mom, Anne, waved. "See ya, Cal." Like mother, like daughter. Casual and familiar.

"Wait!" The little china doll climbed onto the bed and stood up, motioning to him.

He stepped beside her. "What?"

She wrapped her arms around his neck and squeezed. "Thanks for coming over."

Feeling awkward, he patted her shoulder. "Uh, you're welcome. Bye now."

He rejoined Lia in the kitchen, accepted his coffee mug and a foil-covered pie dish. "Strange girl you've got there, Lia. Normal kids don't hug cops."

"Ha! She hugged you?"

"Yeah. You really should teach her not to go around hugging strangers."

"Oh, Cal, you're not a stranger. Besides, don't you want children to feel safe with you rather than afraid?"

"Safe, okay, but hugging? Give me a break."

Lia slipped an arm under his and around his waist. He held up the dish and mug as she leaned her head against his shoulder and gave him a quick hug. "Of course hugging. That's what teddy bears are for!"

"I'm supposed to be a tough cop, not a stinking teddy bear." Cal shook his head, but couldn't help grinning as he climbed into his truck. Both the china dolls were strange...a nice kind of strange.

He drove from the alley behind the pharmacy and around the block to the front of it. Although he was on his way home to get ready for work, he decided to play the tough cop first and visit the video store housed in the same old brick building as the pharmacy. Much of the block had been built in the early 1900s. A florist was on the other side of the video store, also part of the same building. The post office butted up against that. Next, a narrow walkway leading to the alley separated the post office from the hardware store on the corner.

He parked between the lines painted directly in front of the darkened pharmacy and got out. Light shone in a second-story window, probably from Chloe's room. The other window was dark. He guessed that would be Lia's bedroom. From the looks of the kitchen, she'd be in there a long time.

A faint garlic aroma lingered in the air. He smiled. Maybe it was his breath. He unwrapped a piece of gum and thought again about how much he had enjoyed dinner. Tammy could take some lessons from Lia. On second thought, that wasn't such a good idea.

He strolled into the video store. To the left of the display shelves near the front, he spotted the owner, Mitch Conway, at the checkout counter. They'd gone to school together, but Mitch's hair was already thinning, and he had a good start on a beer belly. They hadn't gotten along since Cal won the MVP football award in seventh grade. Of course, it didn't help their relationship any that Cal won it every year after that. Coaches were always on them about teamwork on and off the field.

Cal raised his voice above the pulsating music. "Hey, Mitch."

"Good evening, Cal. Help you find a movie?"

"No, thanks. Just stopped in to ask you to turn the noise down."

He cocked his head and crossed his arms across his barrel chest. "Noise?"

"You gone deaf on me, Mitch? It's a little loud in here. It's a little loud outside."

"Come on, Cal. It's Saturday night. My kid and his buddies like to hang out in the back room and play video games and ping pong. They brought in a jam box. Gotta turn it up full blast to hear it. No harm. I don't mind. It's not like we got any businesses open in downtown Valley Oaks at ten o'clock."

"You've got neighbors. Lia Neuman lives above the pharmacy with her niece."

"No kidding. Did she complain?"

"She didn't have to. Your kids are making a racket in the alley." He didn't mention how it vibrated in Chloe's room.

"Hey, at least they're off the street."

Like 13-year-olds have any business being on *the street.* He had picked up Mitch's son once for curfew violation.

"I close at midnight. What's the harm if what's-her-face didn't complain?"

"I'm complaining, Mitch. Cool it, or I'll give you a ticket for disturbing the peace."

"Ain't nobody's peace being disturbed except maybe yours. You sick? You were in that pharmacy an awful long time. Figured it must be a real special prescription the doctor ordered." His grin was more of a leer.

Cal's eyes narrowed. He caught himself gripping the counter. Not a good sign. "Consider this your first warning, Mitch. And by the way, I only give one."

He walked away before he gave Mitch a citation for being obnoxious.

Eleven

Who's ringing the doorbell at seven o'clock on a Saturday night? Isabel stuck one more pin into her French twist and smoothed her flowered sundress. The weather was still warm. The open weave cardigan should suffice. Slipping on gold hoop earrings, she padded in her stocking feet to the front room, crossed it, and flung open the door.

"Tony! What are you doing here?"

"Picking you up for the party. You're late, by the way." He wore his charming lopsided smile, a white T-shirt, black slacks, and a grey sport coat. "But that's okay. You're definitely worth waiting for."

"*You* were invited?"

He made a tsk-ing noise. "Still underestimating me, Izzy. Of course I'm invited. And it's all because of you."

"Me?"

"Two weeks ago you challenged me to come back and put Brady under a microscope—"

"Those weren't exactly my words—"

"And he thought it was a great idea and suggested I start with his and Gina's engagement party tonight, which is at his parents' farm, for which I need directions. Are you going to make me stand out here all night?"

Isabel felt her entire body sagging. "Why didn't you call? How do you know I don't have other plans for tonight?"

Those deep-set blue eyes grew serious. "You would have let me know before now if there was a special someone in your life." From behind his back he produced a potted mum plant bursting with burnt orange blossoms. "The grocery store didn't have any fresh flowers tonight."

"Tony!" It was an exasperated groan. "I was planning on going by myself. I'm tired. I probably won't stay long."

"I don't mind leaving early. I can drive us."

"Oh, come in. Leave the plant outside on the step. Thank you; it's pretty. Have a seat." She hurried toward the hallway. "I'll be right out."

She shut her bedroom door, sank onto the carpet beside the bed, and buried her face in the comforter. "Jesus, I can't do this. I can*not* do this. Why, why, *why* did You bring him back?" Straining her ears, hoping for an audible voice, she forced herself to take three deep breaths. "Okay, okay. Use me. Be real to him through me. Open his heart to Your saving grace. And give me patience. Oh! I didn't mean *that*, Lord!"

"Tony, you're not watching the road." Isabel felt his eyes on her again. "We have to make a left-hand turn after this curve."

He shifted his gaze toward the highway. "I caught your show. Nice interview with the teacher."

"I'd been at the studio since five. Somebody has to manually turn on the AM then, so I was running on empty. Not very spontaneous."

"Let's try again. That was a nice interview. You did a good job."

She met his glance.

"Izzy, you have a great radio voice and personality. You're fun to listen to."

"Thank you."

"That wasn't too hard, was it?"

She didn't respond.

"It's a Christian thing, isn't it? Not accepting praise. It's worm theology. We're all worthless creatures."

"No, we're not. God created us. He loves us just the way we are. He gave me this voice and personality."

"Then don't get so down on yourself. You do that a lot."

"Well, I'm not perfect."

"Do you have to be?"

"No, but—"

"So can't you accept yourself like God does? Recognize my compliment for what it is: my opinion—which I think is a pretty fair assessment—of your ability. Say thank you and forget it."

"I don't want my ego getting in the way."

He chuckled. "Not much danger of that. I truly don't believe you have an ego. You seem totally unaware of yourself."

"Turn left up there." Strange. Tony was teaching her a lesson on God's acceptance. She should be the one teaching him. "Why are you familiar with these Christian concepts?"

He signaled and made the turn before answering. "My sister...got into it hot and heavy." His jaw tightened.

"And?"

He shrugged.

"Is that why you're so set against faith in Christ?"

"Say, how about those Cubs this week?"

The subject was off limits for him. And she couldn't tell him that she knew from Cal about his missionary sister being killed. Yet... "I'm sorry her conversion evidently turned you against—"

"Drop it, Izzy." He turned toward her, eyes narrowed and mouth distorted. His voice was almost a growl. "You have no clue."

"I don't, but God does."

They rode in silence for a few minutes. The county highway was like a dusky tunnel through cornfields, the tall stalks partially brown as the time for harvest drew near.

Tony slowed as they approached dozens of cars parked on the narrow shoulders. To the left the Olafsson farm came into view, more cars crammed onto its long blacktop drive. Tony whistled. "This must be the place. Picture postcard, corn belt farm. Circa turn of the last century, gracefully restored into this one. Ni-ice place."

It was beautiful. A long white fence bordered the drive. At the end of it stood white barns to the right; to the left, a large white square house with black shutters. The last rays of the setting sun glimmered gold in the third-story windows. "Brady's grandparents built the original place in the early 1900s. We probably should park out here if you don't mind leaving your car along the side of a county road."

"Nah, not this serviceable, nondescript car. Good thing I left the Porsche at home, though." He caught her raised brows and smiled. "I don't have a Porsche. I'm a reporter, remember? I can drop you off at the door. Save you a trip in those shoes, which are fetching, mind you—"

"I can walk."

Tony parked and then hurried around the car to offer an elbow. She grasped it to steady herself as her high heels wobbled on the gravel scattered at the highway's edge.

"Izzy, when we leave, I'll pick you up at the end of the drive."

"Tony, I can catch a ride with somebody else. My house is out of your way. There's a quicker route from here to Rockville."

"Oh, didn't I mention I'm not staying in Rockville this time?"

There was no motel in Valley Oaks. "Where *are* you staying?"

"Brady actually invited me to stay with him, but I thought that would be just a bit too much togetherness for the both of us. So I rented a furnished apartment for a month. More reasonable than hotel rates, plus I'll save all that driving time and gas money. I'm just down the street from you." He grinned. "Don't look so happy."

Her thoughts scrambled, leaving her wordless. She let go of his arm and stopped. He couldn't do this!

"Hey, Iz, I promise not to bug you too much, even though you are the closest resemblance to a friend in a hundred-mile radius."

"Tony!"

"What?"

Emotions bombarded her. Ferris wheel stomach...her very bones melting in warmth that enveloped her like the desert sun...those Mexican sky blue eyes promising the world...

No!

It had all been a lie, all those emotions, all those words of endearment. "You left without saying goodbye," she whispered, the long-buried ache pressing the uninvited accusation through her lips. "We were living together, and your hometown *girlfriend*—whose existence had never even been mentioned before—came for graduation with your *parents*."

He stared at her. "I— Hometown girlfriend? Oh, you mean what's-her-name. My folks and her folks thought— Ancient history. I saw her maybe once after that weekend."

"I had to pack my bags and make your apartment look as if I'd never existed. You practically shoved me out the door ten minutes before they arrived. I had given you *everything*, and suddenly I wasn't worth an introduction." *Everything*. She had given him herself...that which should have been given to her groom...and she had paid in spades for her foolishness.

"Izzy, I was a jerk in college. I admit it!"

"You can't live down the street from me!" As always, her arms gestured, embodying feelings she couldn't form into words. "You can't!"

"Izzy!" He grasped her flailing hands and held them to his chest. "What does me living down the street for a few weeks have to do with our college relationship?"

She bit her lip to keep from crying aloud. *Jesus, help me!*

"I'm sorry, Izzy, I'm sorry. I hurt you, didn't I?"

"It doesn't matter."

"Of course it matters!"

He wouldn't understand. She wasn't about to waste her breath trying to explain. "It was a long time ago. I'm just...I'm just tired, and I don't want to live under your microscope!" She tried to pull her hands away, but he held them fast.

"Brady is willing to."

"Brady's Mr. Macho Mature. I'm just—just—"

"You're just *real*."

She hung her head and willed the tears not to fall.

"Izzy," he said softly, "it's my job."

Dear Lord. She tried to pray, but the thoughts wouldn't form. She had good reason to be angry and hurt. Why should she let it go? Tony had walked out on her and never looked back. He didn't know the devastating consequences their behavior played on her psyche and her plans for school. If he was going to pry into her life after all these years, he deserved to be chastened and made to feel guilty. He owed her. He didn't deserve her forgiveness. He didn't deserve—

An understanding pierced her like a flash of lightning. Of course he didn't deserve forgiveness, but then neither did she, and yet Christ offered it. She lived in that grace every single day of her life.

No! Use somebody else, Lord!

Isabel resisted the impression that she knew came from God. She knew it came from Him because it involved letting go of her so-called rights and caring for someone else who had so obviously been plunked down in the middle of her path. She also knew that resisting would leave her even more miserable.

All right! I give up! Jesus, let me see him through Your eyes, not mine.

At last she raised her face and met the blue eyes boring into hers. Tony was just a man. Lost in his crusty world of exposé journalism, he was a field waiting to be harvested.

"All right, Tony," her voice shook, "live down the street from me. But your microscope works both ways. And my job...my job is to make sure you know Jesus loves you."

Twelve

The Olafssons certainly know how to throw an engagement party, Lia thought as she wound her way carefully through the crowded dining room, protecting a plate piled high with scrumptious-looking food.

It was a warm evening. Nodding to acquaintances, she drifted through open French doors onto the patio. Strands of tiny white lights crisscrossed the area like a thousand stars. Designer perfume floated on the permeating fragrance of dry cornfields. People chatted to a background of humming insects.

Earlier she had visited with the newly engaged couple. She wondered why Gina's parents weren't there.

"Brady didn't want my dad talking me out of it."

Brady laughed. "Not true!"

Gina grinned. "Well, you proposed while they were halfway around the world!" She turned back to Lia. "He actually tracked them down in a hotel in Venice—I think it was the middle of the night here—and asked my dad for my hand in marriage."

"How sweet!"

"But strange. They knew before I did what he was planning to do at the Faire."

"What are your parents doing in Venice?"

"Reports indicate they're falling in love all over again. It's a sort of second honeymoon after hitting a bumpy spot in the road. It seems to be working. Mother has called three times just to giggle."

Lia spotted the engaged couple now. Gina and Brady stood hand in hand, talking with Isabel and Tony. They were a striking couple. Actually, they were both striking couples. Tony was quite a few inches shorter than Brady, as was petite Isabel compared to Gina. The engaged couple resembled solid Olympic athletes, even though Gina walked with a slight limp.

Isabel and Tony were less defined. There was a casual and yet intense air about them, as if they belonged, like two peas in a pod. They both gestured now, almost flamboyantly, both talking at the same time. Lia wondered how either got a word in edgewise. She couldn't imagine these high-energy personalities sitting still together. Maybe they were more jumping beans than peas in a pod.

Tony reminded her of guys she had known growing up in the Chicago area. His heritage was written in his boyish good looks, in the sport jacket that hung just so, in his confident and polite manner. He would have lived nearer than she to Lake Michigan's shoreline.

It struck Lia that Isabel's background was quite different from Tony's. Her friend had been born in Mexico, the fourth of seven children. The large family had moved to East Rockville when she was four. Her growing up years were full of noisy love and little money. Isabel looked especially pretty tonight. Her autumn-colored floral print dress reflected her personality and set off the copper highlights in her hair.

The crowd parted and Lia noticed Tammy in a corner of the patio, seated alone beside a glass-topped table. She hurried over.

"Hello, Tammy. I don't know if you remember me. I'm Lia. Mind if I join—"

"Cal's sitting there."

"Oh." She halted, the plate inches above the table, her knees bent at a half-sitting angle. She grinned and straightened up. "Didn't see him."

The blonde batted her eyelashes. She had amazingly long eyelashes that appeared to be the ones she'd been born with.

"Tammy, I'm sorry you couldn't make it to dinner last week. I've been hoping to get to know you."

"Well, I'm pretty busy. I don't live in *Valley Oaks*." There was a hint of condescension in her voice.

"But you grew up here, right? Your mother told me you're a preschool teacher."

Tammy made a noise with her mouth shut. It was probably a sound she made when annoyed with a three-year-old toddler.

Lia plowed ahead anyway. "I'm so grateful she didn't want to leave when the Bentleys sold the pharmacy. I don't know what I'd do without her."

"Lia!" It was Cal's voice booming above the crowd's.

She turned and saw him approach, carrying two plates. "Hi, Cal."

"Have a seat."

Tammy protested, "There's no chair."

"There's one right there." He pointed an elbow at the one Tammy had saved for him. "I don't mind standing. Here, Tam." He set down a plate of lettuce and fruit. "Sure you don't want any roast beef?"

She made that noise of exasperation again.

"Sit, Lia. Please."

"Well, thank you." She unwrapped silver from a linen napkin and speared a forkful of pasta salad. Lunch was a distant memory.

Cal stood over them and bowed his head for a moment while Tammy daintily tore apart a piece of lettuce.

Lia studied them. Cal the teddy bear, Tammy the Barbie doll. What was the connection that made them a couple?

Cal wolfed down a bite and dug into his back pocket. "Here, Lia, before I forget again." He handed her a piece of paper. "Cell, pager, and home numbers. In case you need me when I'm not on duty."

"Thanks. I didn't have any phone calls or letters this week. Maybe it's as you said, just kids."

Tammy swung her crossed leg. "What's going on?"

Cal caught Lia's eye over his raised fork. He was leaving it up to her. She wondered how much to reveal. After all, Tammy was Dot's daughter. Whatever she said tonight, Dot would hear tomorrow. But then again, Chloe's safety might depend on the whole town knowing. She cleared her throat. "I'm getting hang-up phone calls, and I've been concerned that it's Chloe's father. He doesn't have visitation rights, but he may try to take her."

Tammy contorted her face in dismay. "She can't see her own dad?"

"It's a long, complicated story. He has a wife and kids. Chloe's never been part of his world."

"Hmm." She chewed her lettuce.

Cal said, "I made some calls this week. Nelson Greene is still employed, still a vice president at the software company whose name you gave me. Nothing unusual going on as far as fellow employees, no vacations planned. Evanston cops don't have any recent record of him, none since the accident."

Lia smiled in relief. "Thanks, Cal. That makes me feel so much better."

Again Tammy emitted a quiet sound of vexation and then wiggled out of her chair. "Cal's my super sheriff, aren't you?" She caressed his forearm.

"Yeah, right. Oops, careful." His plate wobbled.

"Are you *still* eating? I want to go talk to Jimmy."

"Go right ahead. I'm going to sit down and finish. This is great stuff. Mrs. Olafsson has been one of my favorite cooks since I was 12." He slid into her chair, shoved aside her plate, and smiled up at her. "I'll catch up."

Tammy pouted her lips, which were shaded a nice coral that matched her slinky dress. "Oh, you." She leaned over and kissed his forehead. "Goodbye, Lee."

Lia smiled. "Goodbye, Tammy."

"Tam, her name's Lia."

Lia thought she heard her breathe "*Whatever*" as she walked away.

Well, "walked" wasn't quite the right word. The tall slender blonde waltzed. Amazing how some women moved as if their bones were composed of fluid. Tammy was an extremely attractive woman and Cal was a good-looking, hunky sort of guy, but the phrase "striking couple" did not come to mind.

"Lia, I've got your coffee mug and pie plate in my truck."

"No hurry." She grinned. "You can return them when you come in to buy toothpaste some time."

He laughed.

They finished their buffet dinner, conversing as easily as they had the week before in her apartment. Lia half expected Cal to apologize for his girlfriend's thinly concealed cold shoulder, but he didn't mention her at all. She respected him for that. Tammy was obviously insecure and naturally felt left out when Cal gave his attention elsewhere. Well, she'd just have to invite them both over for dinner again and wear down her defenses with hospitality. She could include Dot. Maybe that would get Tammy there. Then she'd have to invite Dot's husband, too. That was it! A staff party with spouses!

Lia laughed at herself. Her parents would say she was a bit desperate to win friends and influence people, albeit her livelihood did depend somewhat on those people.

"Life just got in the way, Izzy."

"What?" Walking toward her house, she looked over her shoulder. He stood as if rooted to the sidewalk, a few strides behind her. She stopped. "What are you talking about?"

Tony studied her in the dim light cast from distant stars and street lamps. Whether it was her tears earlier or their twosome-like proximity at the party, he didn't know, but she had grown familiar tonight. Just now, as she had breezed ahead of him, that familiarity had mesmerized him. "Us. Life just got in the way of us. I'm sorry I never said goodbye. I'm sorry I ignored you when my parents and that girl came for graduation."

She turned and went to the door.

He followed. "I did call. Once. I remember calling your home. A kid answered, probably a brother? He said you were in Mexico."

She shrugged, rummaging in her purse. "I went to my grandmother's that summer."

"Did I promise you anything? Did I mention marriage?"

"Tony, you know you didn't. Neither of us were ready for anything that resembled a permanent relationship."

"Even though we lived together?"

A painful expression crossed her face before she turned and thrust a key into the door. "Thank you for the ride."

"Izzy." He clasped her wrist. "I asked: Even though we lived together? Please. I need an answer."

"Everybody lived together. I was just your flavor of the month."

"Three months. And I never *lived* with anyone else, before or since."

"Tony." Her tone chastised, her brown eyes narrowed. What had he called that brown with its tinge of lightness?

"Honest, I didn't. Did you? Not that it's any of my business—"

"No."

"What does that say for us?"

She pulled open the screened door, pushed the inside door wide and flicked a switch, illuminating the front room. "I forgot to leave the light on."

He persisted. "What it says, Izzy, is that we had something special going."

"So? Life got in the way."

"Life got in the way. You went back to the dorm because my parents came for graduation, I went home, they took me to Australia as a surprise gift, you went to Mexico, the *Trib* called."

"Goodnight." She went inside the house.

"Wait." He grabbed the screen door and held it open.

"Tony." She faced him. "What do you want me to say?"

"Nothing. It's what I want to say." His eyes stung. "I stood beside you tonight, talking to others. Your eyes sparkled, their raw sienna—that's what I called them—that incandescent brown dancing under those little lights. I saw how that wildly colored dress defined your heart, so bright and creative and generous. We finished each other's sentences. We laughed." He paused. "And now I remember. I remember that before I knew you, I never saw colors. I never laughed before or since as much as I did in our months together. More than any professor, you made me believe I could write. Oh, Izzy, you were so easy to love."

She stared at him.

He wanted to take her in his arms, but he held back. Her distrust of him ran deep, and he couldn't blame her. He gave her a tiny smile.

Isabel blinked, nodded, and shut the door. But just before it completely latched, she reopened it and leaned outside. She planted a soft kiss on his cheek; then she quickly backed away and closed the door.

Thirteen

The pharmacy was bright with sunshine, and balloons and streamers were floating everywhere, just the way they did during her grand opening celebration in August. But where were the customers? The doorbell rang. People were coming! Lia raced frantically up and down the aisles. Where was the front door? The doorbell rang incessantly. Doorbell! Oh! They were using the alley door, pushing the new doorbell!

Lia raced through the back room, yet she couldn't reach the door. The bell buzzed and buzzed. Why hadn't she told Cal she wanted chimes or at least a singsongy ding-dong? Maybe just a simple ding?

She smacked a hand to her ear and woke up. What a crazy dream! It must have been Barb Olafsson's heavenly three-layer chocolate cake.

The annoying buzz sounded again. And again.

This wasn't a dream. Someone *was* at the door!

She rolled out of bed, grabbed her robe from the chair, and glanced at the clock radio's red digital numbers. It was 1:24 A.M. Did someone need medication? She hurried to the kitchen. Street lamps bathed the room like a giant night-light. She propped her hands on the counter, boosted herself to lean over the sink, and peered through the lace curtains. The angle was wrong. She couldn't see the door. The buzzing continued. What was going on?

She flipped on the stairwell light and went down. The buzzing stopped. At the bottom of the steps was a small, high window beside the door. She twisted the rod, opening the

117

tiny horizontal blinds. The alley was empty. Across it, a spot-light shone brightly above the empty loading dock of the grocery store.

Lia shook her head. Had she only imagined the doorbell ringing? Her icy bare feet on the linoleum floor told her she wasn't still dreaming. She padded back up, turned off the light, and shut the door at the top of the staircase. Halfway across the kitchen, she went back. There was a flimsy old-fashioned latch on the door that she never bothered to hook. She hooked it.

Her heartbeat tickled in her throat. *Jesus, protect us.*

"It's a prank," she said aloud. "Some silly kids' prank. I can...I can live with that. It's not Nelson Greene. He's foolish, but this is childish, vexing behavior, not threatening."

She tiptoed into Chloe's room. Enough light shone through the front window blinds that allowed her to see her niece sleeping soundly, sprawled crossways, only partially covered with the comforter. Such peace and trust in the soft, even breathing. Soot was snuggled up against an arm. *Dear Lord, thank You for this precious child. Protect her from Nelson. And please give me wisdom.* She pulled the comforter over Chloe.

Back in her own room, Lia took the extra quilt from the back of the chair and spread it on the bed. The apartment was chilly tonight. She hugged herself against the cold sheets. Time to get out the flannels. Maybe even time to turn on the furnace.

Sleep came quickly. And then the doorbell buzzed again. Eyelids heavy, she peered at the clock. Only 2:16. Did she have to get up? Obviously no one wanted her to answer the door. Chloe slept through anything. The buzzer went again. And again.

Cal would ask her for details. She certainly wasn't going to sleep anyway. With a groan she threw back the covers, grabbing her robe and, from a drawer, socks. She paused in the kitchen to slip into them. At the stairwell her hand hovered above the light switch. Maybe it'd be better not to warn them. No doubt the light had shone before through the alley window at the bottom of the steps and chased them away.

With one hand on the rail and the other trailing along the wall, she made her way down in the dark, turned the corner landing, and continued. The buzzing let up only long enough for someone to repress the button.

Without touching the blinds she had left open, she peeked through. It was dark. Too dark. She could barely see the outline of the grocery store. Its floodlight was out! There were shadows by the door, but she couldn't make out faces or even how many figures stood there silently jabbing her doorbell. Lia flipped the switch to turn on the outdoor light. Nothing went on.

They'd tampered with her light bulb! This went beyond a prank.

She yanked up the blinds and shouted through the closed window, "What do you want?"

There was a muffled yell and two figures raced away.

"Oh!" She swished shut the blinds and stomped up the stairs. "You'd think kids would have something better to do in the middle of the night! Like sleep!"

In the kitchen she slid onto a chair at the table. Should she call the police? She'd say, "Some kids rang my doorbell." They'd reply, "Oh? And?" What could they do? She could call Cal. He mentioned at the party earlier tonight that he wasn't on duty, but why disturb him? He couldn't do anything either.

Her father had warned her that she would encounter prejudice in a small town. Being a single mom/aunt and half

Chinese were two strikes against her. In Chicago she blended in. Here she stuck out like a neon sign blinking, "I'm different! Hate me for it!"

Her stomach hurt. What should she do?

She shuffled over to the couch and lay down, pulling the afghan over her. Curled up like the kitten, she waited. *Lord, please don't let them come back.*

Twenty minutes later she heard a violent shattering of glass.

Lia cried out, jumped up and ran to grab the cordless phone. She punched 911, circling the apartment and turning on all the lights in the living room, kitchen, and bath.

The answer took too long. Her explanation took too long. The woman's calm voice didn't calm Lia. She heard no siren in a town barely ten blocks wide!

What was going on downstairs? She couldn't hear anything.

"Ma'am, please stay on the line."

"I'm calling Cal." She hit the off button. Where was Cal's number? In her dress pocket? No, she had put it in the kitchen drawer.

Pager? Cell? House?

Middle of the night. Try house. Her hands shook. It took two tries.

The other end rang and rang. At last an answering machine picked up. Answering machine!

She held the off button and listened. As if nothing had splintered her sleeping hours, hushed night sounds echoed in her ears.

Her whole body shook now. She punched in his cell number.

"Yo."

"Cal! Someone's trying to break in!"

"Lia?"

"I called 911, but nobody has come!"

"Slow down. Tell me what happened."

"A window broke. I heard a loud noise like glass breaking."

"The big front one?"

"I—I—" She didn't know!

"It's probably the little back one. The alarm would have gone off if it were the front. I'm just three minutes away. Are you upstairs?"

Tears flowed now, choking her throat.

"Lia, talk to me."

"I'm upstairs. They kept ringing the doorbell!"

"Who? When?"

"Before."

"Is Chloe there?"

"She's asleep."

Cal's voice soothed during the long three minutes. "All right, I'm on Main. Turning in the alley now. Man, why is it so dark back here?"

She heard tires squealing outside.

"Lia, it's the back window." A door slammed shut. "Looks like a rock or something was thrown through it. The door's locked. Nobody's inside, hon. Come on down and let me in."

She stood in the middle of the kitchen, frozen to the floor, shaking.

"Lia?"

"Y-you're sure?"

"I'm shining my flashlight at the window. The hole's too small for someone to climb through. Go to the stairs and turn on the light. I'm hanging up now to call headquarters and let them know I'm here. Okay?"

"Okay." She slowly crossed the kitchen, unlocked the door at the top of the stairs, and went down one step at a time. At the bottom she saw the window blinds bent and askew. "Oh!" she moaned.

"Lia!" Cal called through the window. "Open the door."

It felt as if she floated beside another person going through the motions...until Cal held her in his arms. The fears of the night poured out, her face buried against his chest. Her entire body shaking, she cried wildly.

"Shh, Lia, it's all right."

After a time, the tears slowed. "Oh, Cal, I am such a pathetic phony!"

"Pathetic phony?" He smoothed her hair back from her face and smiled down at her.

She sniffled and dug a tissue from her robe pocket. "Impressively independent, my eye. I can do it all by myself! Yeah, right, except cope with a little harassment!"

"Here, sit down and let me look things over before the cops get here." He guided her across the room to the desk chair.

"By the way, 911 works great around here." Sarcasm helped mask the fear.

"There was a major accident out on 18. They needed everybody. It happens."

She watched him crouch below the window. The overhead light was on. He must have switched it on when he came in. Bits and pieces of glass had sprayed across the floor. A brick lay against the opposite wall, near the closed door that led into the store.

"Lia, there's blood— Let me take a look..." He knelt in front of her and raised her left foot. Red splotches dotted the bottom of her white sock He checked the other foot before stepping over to the sink. "You must have walked through the glass and cut yourself on one foot. Mind if I wet this towel here?"

"No." She pulled off her sock. "Ouch! How weird! I couldn't feel anything a minute ago, but now my foot stings like crazy."

"That's good. It tells me you're not in shock." He slipped the warm damp cloth under her heel and lifted it. "I can't see any glass. Do you have antiseptic and bandages?"

When his eyes met hers, a tearful giggle caught in her throat.

He grinned. "Yeah, I suppose in a pharmacy you might have one or two."

She stood. "I'll get some."

"No you don't." He scooped her up as if she were a bride.

She cried out and flung her arms around his neck. "Cal!"

"There's shattered glass everywhere." He stepped to the door, glass scrunching beneath his shoes.

"It's locked. The key is in the top left-hand drawer of the desk."

Balancing her in his arms, he leaned sideways and easily fished out the key. He unlocked the door, pulled it open, and carried her through. "Bandages. Tell me where."

"If you ever shopped here, you'd know where. Put me down in that chair. I can prop my foot up on the table. First aid stuff is in the far right aisle."

He strode down the aisle, chatting the whole time. "Handy-dandy place you've got here, Miss China Doll. Bet you never run out of toothpaste." He reappeared, opening a package of latex gloves. "I took a pair of these, too. You can send a bill to the county sheriff's department." Putting on the gloves, he knelt again and gently he took her foot into his hands. He examined it more closely. "I see two nasty slices, but nothing major sticking out. Maybe you should have the doctor look at it tomorrow, though. In the meantime, I'll wrap it."

She studied the top of his head. "China doll?"

He glanced up. "I don't mean it in a derogatory sense."

"I know." She bit her lip and grimaced.

"Sorry. One more." He misted antiseptic over the cuts.

"They hate me."

"Who hates you?"

"Whoever did this. I'm half Chinese and that makes me an oddball in Valley Oaks and that frightens them."

"Well, I know one thing for sure."

"What?"

"You sure don't have china doll feet."

His impertinent comment cut through the frustrations and made her laugh. "So what? My dad is 6' 2" and wears a size 12 shoe. You know, that's not a very nice cop thing to say to a victim."

He patted the top of her foot and smiled. "But if she's my friend and it makes her laugh, I think it's the *right* thing to say, don't you?"

By 4:00 A.M. Cal had bandaged Lia's foot, swept the back room clean of glass shards, nailed cardboard over what remained of the window, and written down the sequence of her eventful night.

He stood in her kitchen, prepared to go home until he looked over at Lia. She sat in the corner of the couch, huddled under an afghan, nibbling on a fingernail. Her eyes were wide, her fair skin paler than normal. Like a china doll, she looked fragile, as if the slightest disturbance might make her crack.

"Lia, how about if I stick around until morning?"

"You don't have to. I'm not going to sleep anyway." Her voice was lower than normal, but had lost all trace of assertiveness.

"I'd feel better if I stayed."

She nodded. "All right. Do you want the couch?"

"No, I'll just sit here in the chair." He sat down and raised the footrest. "Why don't you go to bed?"

She shook her head.

As his eyelids grew heavy, he watched her staring at nothing in particular, obviously shaken to the core.

"I'm here, Miss Impressively Independent. No need to worry." He drifted off to sleep.

Fourteen

Tony sat at Izzy's kitchen table, drinking coffee and reading the Sunday *Trib,* a surprising find at the Valley Oaks gas station. A loud banging on the back door startled him. Through the yellow eyelet curtain that covered the door's window he could see a hulking outline. Uh-oh. Maybe Izzy did have a boyfriend. Worse yet, maybe this was one of her brothers.

Tony opened the door and the deputy sheriff quickly strode inside. Sidestepping quickly before getting stepped on, Tony said, "Good morning! It's Cal, right?"

The big guy didn't pause in his wordless lope across the kitchen.

"Cal, how about some coffee?"

"No." Cal halted at the threshold leading into the living room and hall. "Mendoza!" he yelled.

"What?" Isabel's distant voice drifted through the small house.

"Can you take Lia's kid to church?"

The cop looked as though he needed coffee. He resembled Smokey the Bear without the hat and smile. His eyes were puffy. His plaid shirt and khakis were slightly more rumpled than they had been last night at the Olafsson farm and damp from the fine mist falling this morning. A bristly shadow covered the square jaw. Tony poured a cup and stuck it in his massive hand.

"Thanks."

126

Isabel came into the kitchen, wearing a silky cream-colored blouse beneath a deep brown skirt and cardigan, carrying a pair of heels. "Cal? What's wrong?"

"Somebody broke the alley window at Lia's and harassed her half the night ringing the doorbell. She's skipping church this morning—"

"Is she all right?"

"She's shook up. Cut her foot on the broken glass. Nothing serious. Mostly just exhausted. She asked me to take Chloe to church, and I thought— Well, do you mind?"

"Chicken." Isabel brushed past him and took Tony's mug from his hand. "Kids give him the willies."

Totally understandable, Tony thought as he retrieved a bag of coffee beans from the freezer.

Cal asked, "So can you do it?"

She sat at the table and drank from Tony's cup. "Of course. I'll call—"

"She's in my truck."

Isabel jumped up and pushed his shoulder. "Cal! Go get her! How could you leave that little girl out there?"

"She slept through the whole thing last night. She's fine."

She practically shoved him out the door. "Men! First *you* show up," she shot a glare at Tony, "because you can't go to church by yourself—"

"I didn't know what time—"

"Yeah, right. And Cal can't even take care of a child for half an hour." She sat back down and strapped on her shoes. "Oh, poor Lia."

"Do you have much vandalism in town?" Nice change of subject.

"No. Everybody knows everybody. Some kid will brag about this and sooner or later a mom will get wind of it and tell Cal. Kind of takes the fun out of it. You're making more coffee?"

"Pot's empty."

"I don't want more than this cup—"

"Yeah, well, that cup was mine." He paused, his hand holding the carafe midair. Something passed between them, a recognition that they'd been here before...

The back door opened. "Chloe!" Isabel hurried toward the little girl entering the kitchen. She embraced her and then helped her out of a red raincoat. "Want some breakfast?"

Chloe big blue eyes were wide. "Do you have any more of those chocolate chip cookies?"

Isabel laughed. "How about a scrambled egg with them?"

"Okay." She slid into a chair.

"Cal, come in and sit down. You look awful. Have some breakfast."

Tony opened the fridge and pulled out a carton of eggs. "Boy, am I glad you two came along. No one offered *me* any breakfast. Hey, Iz, I'll make my famous frittata. Remember?" He saw the look on her face. It was an almost imperceptible widening of the pupils of her eyes, a momentary dread washing through her. Overt references to the past disturbed her. He stuck his head back into the refrigerator. "Got any peppers and onions?"

"Little girls don't like peppers and onions."

"I do," Chloe piped in. "Aunt Lia always cooks with peppers and onions."

Cal said, "I do, too, but I've got to go home. Thanks anyway."

Isabel reached around Tony and took out a jug of orange juice. "Huntington, were you up all night?"

"Well, yeah. Lia got me on the cell coming home from Tam—uh, Twin Prairie. I helped her clean up the place and nailed some cardboard over the window. I'll get some boards and seal it up better this afternoon."

"Think it's kids?"

"Yeah."

"You," Chloe's chin quivered, "you told Aunt Lia *you'd* take me to church."

"Well, Isabel said she'll take you. I don't know where the Sunday school is. And besides, I gotta go get ready."

Isabel patted Chloe's head and set a glass of juice before her, scowling at Cal. "We'll see Cal at church, hon. I think he'd better go comb his hair. Not that he's got much to comb. What do you think? Hey, maybe you can spend the afternoon at Mandy's."

Cal caught Tony's eye while Isabel chattered away at Chloe.

He raised a spatula in parting and smiled.

The big guy looked miserable as he shut the door.

Isabel said, "Tony, you don't have to cook. I'll do it."

"I like to cook. Remember?" He winked.

Her shoulders slumped, giving her an abject demeanor that surpassed Cal's. So much for joyful Christians.

Isabel pushed Lia's doorbell as she eyed the boarded up window. It resembled how she had felt with Tony in tow all day: broken and hurting inside, but not showing it, keeping stiff boards nailed up all around her true feelings.

Her true feelings had been nagging at her since last night. Why was it she could still feel anger toward Tony as well as that old tickle of affection? Why was it that little things like inadvertently taking his coffee mug unnerved her?

What a perfectly dreary day! Nonstop rain, Tony at her elbow, Lia's close encounter with small-town prejudice. She shivered.

Tony pulled her close beneath the umbrella he held above them. "Cold?"

"It's freezing."

"Feels more like November than late September and only the second day of fall, huh?" He peered over his shoulder. "Is that the cop's truck?"

She looked over his shoulder at the small lot behind the grocery store. "Looks like it."

"Something going on between him and the pharmacist?"

"No. You heard him mention Twin Prairie this morning. Tammy Cassidy lives there. Dot's daughter."

"Ahh."

She felt as if she'd said too much. "Tony, you don't have to stay."

"We already talked about this. Hanging with you is my assignment. Brady gets a turn tomorrow."

"This is kind of personal. A girl thing."

"Unless Huntington is here."

The door opened and Lia stood there, long hair loose about her shoulders, a grateful smile lighting her face. "Come in!"

Isabel hugged her. "Lia, I am so sorry."

"Thank you, but I'm fine now. A little sleep works wonders. Hi, Tony. Let me take your coats. I'll hang them here." Coat hooks lined the wall beside the door, near the washer and dryer. "Come on upstairs."

"Lia, you're wearing blue jeans! I don't think I've seen you in anything but skirts."

"Shh, don't tell my mother. She'd have a cow."

Isabel smiled. Somehow, even in jeans and a baggy red cable-knit sweater, her friend was still the essence of femininity.

They entered the cozy apartment. Cal sat in the recliner in the living room area, facing a small television.

Tony strode across the kitchen and plopped onto the couch. "Bears playing?"

Cal grunted in the affirmative.

Lia's raised brows mirrored her own. They smiled. "Tea?" Lia asked.

"Thanks." Isabel sat at the table. "Tell me what happened last night. Cal didn't give out any details."

"Oh, it wasn't anything. Just kids. They rang the doorbell, I turned on the light, and they took off. Then they did it again, and I shouted through the window. Does Tony drink tea?"

"Yes." *Doesn't he?*

She set before her a porcelain cup and saucer painted with tiny flowers. "Then, about three o'clock I heard the window break. I called 911, but they didn't show up right away, so I got Cal on his cell. He arrived first. That's about it."

"Do you think it's related to the phone calls?"

"Probably." She emptied the coffee carafe into one mug, filled another with tea, carried them to the men, and then joined Isabel at the table.

"Lia, did Cal tell you about my experience?"

She shook her head. Dark circles were like smudges under her eyes.

"Nothing like this. Just a general attitude of 'you don't belong.' Snide looks in the grocery store. One note that told me to go back to Mexico. When I was living in an apartment, a bag of cow patties was left outside my door."

"Eww. Gross."

"Tell me about it. Since I moved next door to Cal, though, no problems. Something about having a cop for a neighbor, I guess. Of course, I don't interact too much with people outside the church. Not like you with a business."

"I thought things were going all right. Customers responded well when I lowered prices and added the gift section. But..." Tears swam in her eyes.

Isabel squeezed her hand. "But what, Lia?"

"I'm sorry. I guess the rough night is catching up with me."

"We shouldn't have come."

"No, no. I need your company right now. Last week I heard from the big prescription drug group that covers Agstar employees."

"Like half the town?"

"Exactly. The group is removing independents like myself from their approved list."

"Oh, Lia."

"I can't make it without them. And who's going to shop here and pay $30 for a prescription when they can drive into Rockville and pay five?"

The implications were staggering. Isabel didn't know what to say. "Besides threatening your business, think about the incredible inconvenience for all those families."

"Well, $25 is $25. That covers a lot of inconvenience. Between you and me, I suspect the Bentleys knew this was coming." The tears spilled over now.

"Oh, Lia," she said again and scooted her chair closer. She wrapped her arms around her.

Cal's voice boomed across the room, "Everything okay?"

They nodded. Isabel winked and whispered, "That's his cop voice."

Lia said, "I think he's getting hungry. We thought we'd order pizza. Will you stay?"

"Sure. Sounds great. Where's Chloe?"

"Anne invited her to spend the night." She shrugged. "Even though it's a school night, you gotta break some rules now and then. So?"

"So? What?"

She shifted her eyes toward the guys.

"Huh?"

Lia whispered, "Tony."

"Praying for him." She knew the words were flippant because they left a hollowness in their wake.

Lia tilted her head, studying Isabel's face for a long, silent moment. "And is anyone praying for you?"

Fifteen

Lia thought it was an awkward gathering of dinner guests around her kitchen table. Isabel shot thinly concealed scowls in Cal's direction and avoided eye contact with Tony. Cal's face had settled into a rough frown when it became evident the Bears were losing. The look suited his sheriff's uniform, not the soft fleecy gray sweatshirt he wore. Tony was quiet, a totally opposite demeanor from the other times she had seen him.

Cal had arrived early that afternoon, boards, nails, and hammer in hand, intent on sealing the window ahead of the predicted rainstorm. He learned Chloe wasn't home, probably sensed Lia's tentative manner, and promptly invited himself to watch the game on her television, saying, "How about if I keep an eye on things here during the game?" Isabel and Tony had popped in unannounced. Lia didn't feel like playing hostess, but she was grateful for the company.

It was the anchovies that finally broke the ice.

Cal helped himself to a piece of pizza that was unofficially designated as Isabel and Tony's pizza. Lia and Cal were sharing one with different toppings.

Isabel reached over and scooped the slice right off of his plate. "You said you wanted meat and no anchovies. Eat your own pizza."

Everyone stared at her.

Cal deliberately transferred the piece back to his own plate. "Changed my mind."

"You can't. There won't be enough."

134

"You and Tony are going to eat an entire large pizza?"

"Yes. What of it?"

Tony rearranged the pizzas, sliding the anchovy-laden one toward Cal. "Izzy, he's bigger than I am, and he carries a gun. He can eat whatever he wants."

"Oh, Tony, he's about as tough as Nutmeg and Soot."

"Mendoza," Cal growled, "you've never taken pizza from me before."

She grabbed the piece back. "And you've never taken it from me either."

Tony rearranged the pizzas again. "Cal, she's got a point. I tried it once. Wet hen comes to mind."

Cal smiled. "I can see that."

"Yelling in Spanish."

Cal chuckled. "Yeah, I heard her do that once, all the way from inside my house. She was mad at a *recipe*."

Tony was grinning now. "Let's hope she doesn't get mad on the air!"

Isabel swallowed a bite. "Oh, like you guys are perfect. I saw Cal throw a lawn mower once, halfway across his yard. And you, Tony. I seem to remember you swearing at newspapers and magazines. I certainly hope you don't do *that* anymore."

"Hey," he protested, "I don't have to be perfect. You three are the Christians."

Lia exchanged glances with Cal and Isabel and then smiled. "Tony, do you really believe that?"

"Christians are always passing judgment on others, as if they don't lie and cheat, etcetera, etcetera. They're perfect. Supposedly."

"Have you personally spent much time with Christians?"

He shrugged. "Izzy and Brady."

"And is that what they do?"

He appeared unfocused, as if he were lost in thought for a moment. "Brady seems to go out of his way not to be condescending." His eyes flickered toward Cal. "I wonder if it's a show for my benefit."

Cal shifted in his chair. "It's not."

"But then, you're his best friend." Tony's smile softened the words. "I'm just trying to be honest. I'm here because Izzy challenged me to watch Christianity up close."

Isabel touched his arm. "And what about me? Is my attitude judgmental?"

"No, but you're always surrounded by people who agree with your point of view. What would you be like in a different environment? Say Chicago, for example, where most of the world is blatantly anti-Christian. Valley Oaks obviously isn't without its problems, but it is basically a nonthreat to you."

Isabel nodded and helped herself to more pizza, the one without anchovies. "You're right. I..." She shrugged, a blush creeping across her face. "I've thought about it. I don't know."

"Tony," Cal asked, "what was your sister like?"

Tony's jaw tightened briefly. "Good work, Detective." He took a deep breath. "Ladies, my sister was a missionary, martyred in Colombia two years ago."

Lia's heart went out to him. "Oh, Tony, how awful!'

Isabel squeezed his arm and whispered, "I'm so sorry."

Cal added his sympathies.

They sat quietly for a moment. Tony said, "What, no formula explanations? Most Christians have to tell me why."

Isabel shook her head. "There is no pat reason. It's a terrible tragedy, and we grieve for you and your family."

Tony bit his lip. "Thank you. Cal, to answer your question, Joanna was messed up with drugs, became a Christian, and headed overseas to save the world." He gave them a small smile. "She always was impetuous. Okay. Back to the subject at hand. You're saying you're not perfect."

Lia explained, "No, we're not. We should be recognizable by our love, not our judgmental attitudes. Do you see love in us? A giving, caring attitude?"

"Yeah. Izzy just proved it. She's eating a piece of the *other* pizza."

They laughed.

Lia ached for Tony. She knew the unbearable hurt of losing a sister. Unlike him, though, she also knew the comfort of friends who loved her in ways that carried her through the worst of it. She prayed that Tony's heart would be opened to that kind of love.

"I really, *really* hate Scrabble," Cal announced as he and Tony dodged raindrops and jogged to his truck parked across the alley. They climbed in it and he started the engine, flipping the heat on high. "Especially with people who probably aced every English class they ever took."

Tony laughed. "Izzy and Lia play for blood."

"And you don't?" Cal grinned. "Have you played with Brady yet? He's the worst."

"Not yet. Maybe we'll do that this week."

He pulled out of the alley onto Walnut. "So how come you haven't interviewed me?"

"You're too close, Cal. I needed a broader view of him. But you know his reputation. Generally speaking, the town adores him. I doubt I'm hearing anything you wouldn't tell me."

Cal hoped it wasn't a stretch on the truth. Tony was growing on him. He had a sense of humor. He hovered attentively over Isabel without overwhelming her. He seemed like a regular guy in spite of the sweater. What would Tammy call it? Cashmere, that was it.

"I was wondering, though... Was Brady always so well liked?"

"I'd have to say he earned it. Shoot, you've seen the farm he grew up on. Not many like that around. Things came pretty easy for him, and, yeah, he was kind of a snob as a kid. But in high school, when the sports counted, he was phenomenal and turned into a team player. Town pride is wrapped up a lot in school spirit, and we won plenty of trophies in those days. Now he's got his books. Valley Oaks is proud of him. Have you read his stuff?"

"Not yet. How about you?"

"Sure. You gonna read them?"

"I can't write an article about an author without reading his books. Do you think the girls will be all right tonight?"

Cal didn't answer right away. They had left Isabel at Lia's to spend the night. He offered to stay, but they didn't want to put him on the spot with Tammy, not to mention Dot, which meant half the town. Now, he second-guessed his decision. He didn't like abandoning Lia, even with Isabel for company. She still seemed pretty strung out, practically jumping out of her skin when the doorbell rang. The first time they looked through the kitchen window and saw Isabel's car. The second time it rang they expected the pizza delivery, but it still startled Lia. He had dismantled the ringer before leaving. "I don't anticipate a repeat performance. They'll be fine."

"Did you and Izzy ever date?"

Cal laughed. "Nah, my type is tall and blonde. Isabel's like one of the guys. You know, if I need a hand at the house, she's right there, little as she is. Comes from her having a bunch of brothers, I guess. You dated her, right?"

"Right. We…" He paused. "We were tight for a short time, until I graduated."

"What happened?"

"Neither of us were ready to settle down. I moved on. We lost touch with each other. She's grown into quite the woman."

Cal glanced at Tony's face in the light of a passing street lamp. "Are you dating now?"

Tony barked a laugh. "No way. She can't wait until I'm out of here. I represent the youth she wants to forget. Besides, my type is also tall and blonde."

"Remind me not to introduce you to Tammy."

"Like I said, you're bigger than I am *and* you carry a gun."

Cal smiled. "Just keep that in mind, Ward, and we'll get along fine."

"Don't worry, Cal," Lia spoke into the phone, smiling at Isabel across the bedroom. "Thanks for feeding Nutmeg… Yes, now go to sleep. Goodbye." She hung up the phone. "Cal is such a teddy bear."

Isabel nodded, impressed with Cal's thoughtfulness toward Lia. "He reminds me of my oldest brother."

"I don't know about that. He's too good-looking to be thought of as a brother."

"Cal? A heartthrob?"

"I didn't say heartthrob!"

"It was in your tone."

"You want to talk about tone, *Izzy?*"

She groaned. Tony's nickname was catching on.

Lia laughed. "Anyway, thank you for staying."

"You're welcome. I know *I* wouldn't have wanted to stay alone." She had invited Lia to spend the night at her house, but Lia insisted she needed to face her fears. She was jittery, though, prompting Cal to offer to stay. "We certainly couldn't let Cal spend the night, despite his big brother/teddy bear status."

Lia dug through a dresser drawer. "No way. Here, these should work." She pulled out a pair of silky pajamas, a lime green with tiny multicolored flowers. "They're kind of small on me."

"They're so pretty! Lia, I sleep in sweats or shorts."

"Me too. It's not like we have to impress anybody. Sometimes, though, I like to feel pretty, just for myself. A little pampering is okay. If those fit, keep them. They're only polyester."

Isabel, in the armchair, hugged the pajamas, speechless for a moment. "Thank you." She watched her friend crawl onto the bed and sit cross-legged. "Lia, do you mind if I ask you something personal?"

She shook her head.

"Do you want to impress anybody in that way?"

"What you mean is, am I lonely? Do I want a husband?"

Isabel smiled. "I guess that's probably the issue."

"I think it would be best for Chloe to have a mom *and* a dad, which is asking for the moon. And I know the moon is possible with God, but the guys I dated disappeared in about 30 seconds flat after they understood my situation." She lifted a shoulder. "I've put the thought aside for so long. I wanted to be a pediatrician and marry one. I wanted us to live in a small town and take care of people. Then Chloe turned three, Kathy died, my parents had their careers. Mom's a librarian and Dad's an econ professor, both at Northwestern University. Kathy and I were always close. Chloe was like a daughter to me from the day she was born.

I really wanted to raise her. So I went into pharmacology. With the science and math I'd already had, it didn't take me too long to catch up. We lived with my parents until this summer. They encouraged me to go ahead and find my small town. The Valley Oaks Pharmacy fit the bill. Part of my dream came true."

"And so your answer would be?"

"Do I want a husband?" She grinned. "Oh, why complicate matters? No. How about you?"

"Why complicate matters?" Isabel repeated, laughing. "Seriously, I've been happy as a lark, living in Valley Oaks, working at the station, singing in the choir, leading the high school girls' Bible study. Then Grandmother died and—" She paused. "In Mexico I felt this ache, like I belonged there. I'm not so content anymore. I've been looking into short missions trips. And now Tony has been pointing out what a sheltered life I lead." She inhaled deeply. "*Short* missions may not be the answer."

They stared at one another for a moment. Isabel stood. "It's too late for this heavy conversation. Your eyelids are half closed."

Lia followed her down the hall. "I think I'm finally ready to sleep. I'll turn off the lights. Cal said the deputy on duty tonight would drive through the alley often."

"Well, you can count on Cal being out there, too. Please wake me if you can't sleep. Are you sure Chloe won't mind if I use her room? I can sleep on the couch."

"Chloe won't mind. Soot might though."

"I hope not. I've got to show off my new jammies to somebody!"

Cal sat on a wet park bench in the town square, across the street from the pharmacy. As the upstairs lights went off, he slid from the seat and headed down Fourth Avenue. He'd walk past the other shops and the post office, circle round into the alley, and pray that God would fill the block with extra guardian angels tonight. His two favorite women slept here.

Whoops. Make that two of his *three* favorites.

Sixteen

Lia locked the pharmacy's front door and twisted shut the blinds over its window. It was closing time, Friday night. "Chloe, you did a fantastic job!"

The little girl smiled as she wiped a dust cloth over the wooden countertop. "It's fun working in the store. I like the cash register the best. Can I have a raise?"

She laughed. "You've only been at it for three days!"

The front door knob rattled, and then someone knocked. Lia felt the immediate tightening in her stomach. At least she wasn't literally jumping anymore. She peeked through the blinds. It was Cal. Though she hadn't seen him since Sunday night, he had called every evening to check on her. There had been no more harassment.

She opened the door. "Well, I suppose I can let our neighborhood cop in after hours."

"Sorry." He stepped inside, Isabel's kitten climbing across his brown uniform-covered shoulders. "I tried to get here before six. Isabel asked me to deliver her cat. She said you didn't mind keeping it for two nights."

Chloe squealed and hurried over. "Don't let her fall!"

He grasped the kitten and handed her down to Chloe as if she were a dirty diaper.

"Be careful!" she ordered.

"Cats are pretty good at taking care of themselves."

Chloe frowned as she turned and headed down the aisle. "I'll take her upstairs to play with Soot."

"Sweetpea, will you bring down the pie for Cal?"

Her niece continued toward the back room, whispering to the kitten.

"Chloe!"

"Yeah!" she yelled.

Lia stuck her hands in her lab coat. What had happened to her chipper little employee?

"Pie?"

She looked up at Cal. "Mm-hmm. Banana cream okay?"

His eyes widened. "More than okay. But, about dinner tomorrow night..."

An awkward moment passed between them. "Cal, I know. Dot told me today that you all won't be coming, that Tammy doesn't like Chinese food." *Not that I was going to make Chinese.* "But I already had the pie made." She attempted a smile. *Just be gracious. It's not his fault.* "I like to bake."

"Tammy and I have this, uh, understanding. Um..."

Lia balled her hands into fists. He was a big boy. Let him explain it. It had been silly coming from Dot, embarrassing even.

"Um, we sort of have a standing dinner date on Saturday nights."

"Of course. I shouldn't have imposed."

His face reddened.

Well, it's not my fault your girlfriend and her mother are superficial racists. "It looks like you're dressed for work tonight."

"Yeah, I usually put in a few extra hours at the home football games before my shift. Hey, you and Chloe could come. It doesn't matter if you don't like football. It's kind of a town social gathering."

"I like football fine, but..." Without warning, tears sprang to her eyes. She turned to the counter and began straightening things that didn't need straightening. If the social gathering was made up of a bunch of Dots and Tammys, she wasn't about to go anywhere near it. She blinked rapidly. "I have some work to do."

"Any phone calls or notes this week?"

She shook her head. "I'd better go hurry that pie along. Chloe probably got sidetracked playing with the cats."

"I gotta go. I'm late already. Maybe I'll stop by tomorrow."

"Okay." She followed him to the door. "Thanks for bringing Nutmeg over. Bye." Lia shut the door on his goodbye.

He pushed it back open. "I'm on duty tomorrow night, too. I'll drive by every half hour or so."

"That'll be good. Thanks." Again she shut the door, this time locking it.

She strode down the aisle, yanked off her lab coat, smacked the store's light switch, turned on the alarm system in the back room, and ran up the stairs. "Father," she muttered, "I am sorry for calling Tammy and Dot names. Forgive me. And I'm feeling like such a victim, which is totally *asinine*!"

She found Chloe giggling on her bed with Soot and Nutmeg, all three rolling together.

"Chloe."

Her niece sat up and smiled, her short black hair mussed.

"You were rude to Cal. What's wrong?"

The smile faded.

"Come on, sweetpea. I thought you liked him."

"Banana cream's my favorite."

"Oh!" She plunked herself down on the bed and threw an arm around Chloe. "I know that, which is why I made two pies. That's not it. 'Fess up now."

"I don't know. He made me mad when he wouldn't take me to church."

Lia thought that over. "Okay. That was rude after he said he would take you. At least Isabel gave you breakfast."

"Tony was a good cook."

"Cal's a cop. He would have given you a box of donuts."

"I like Izzy's cookies better."

Lia glanced at the ceiling. "Anyway, you still shouldn't have been rude back to him."

"Well, why couldn't *he* take care of Nutmeg while Izzy's gone?"

What did that have to do with anything? "You want Nutmeg here, don't you?"

"Yeah, but can't Cal do *anything*?"

Lia sensed that Chloe's trust in Cal as a daddy figure had disintegrated. "Chlo, we have here a lesson in womanhood. I don't know if you're old enough, but it's never too early to hear it. Besides, I'll be repeating it through the years. Now listen closely. A man is not the answer to anything. You need a daddy and you've got one. His name is Jesus. I know you can't see or hear Him, but He's right here and He loves you. Cal's just a man. He's kind, and he's helped us a lot, but he's not perfect. Okay?"

Chloe was somber, a thoughtful look on her face. She stroked Soot. "Maybe I should see my real dad."

Lia hugged her. *Oh, Lord, help! I'm just a woman here, imperfect and lonely!*

"Tony, you spent too much." Isabel watched him set an armload of shopping bags onto the bed in her hotel room.

He headed back toward the door she held open. "Izzy, if you say that one more time, I'm going to buy those diamond earrings you just admired in the Cartier window down-stairs."

"Diamonds! I thought you were just a reporter."

"Inheritance came in early," he muttered.

Isabel bit her lip. Come to think of it, he probably would get all of his parents' money now that his sister... Impul-sively, she wrapped her arms around his neck.

"Hey, keep that up and I'll shut your door and hang out the Do Not Disturb sign." He briefly returned her hug before removing her arms from his neck.

"You won't close it. You promised."

He grinned, his face inches from hers, those deep-set blue eyes fixed on her.

She sobered. "Tony, why are you doing this?"

"Doing what?"

"Number one, you've brought me to Chicago—"

"Uh-uh. I challenged you to visit the real world."

She wrinkled her nose. "And I said yes, of course, but a Saturday night awards dinner requires an overnight stay, not to mention a fancy, *fancy* dress, neither of which I can afford, especially this month considering I spent most of last month in Mexico, which, by the way, is the real world."

"You're getting off track. To continue the scenario. Number two, I get a hotel room for you because I know you won't stay at my apartment. No big deal; I get it at a smidgen of the cost because I know people. Number three, I take you to Marshall Fields' sale of the century."

She giggled. "Year."

"And I buy a dress you look absolutely gorgeous in—ever mindful that it is 70 percent off the marked down price—for one reason only: pride."

She gave him a quizzical look.

"My date has got to be the most beautiful and best-dressed woman in the room. That makes *me* look good."

Isabel wagged a finger at him. "It's more than that, Tony Ward."

He held out his hands, palms up, in a gesture of surrender.

"Number four," she continued, "is I make you promise to be the quintessential gentleman and you *agree*? I don't buy that. What's in it for you?"

"You still don't think I have an altruistic bone in my body."

"No," she shot back, only half teasing now, "I don't. You're a reporter."

He angled his head to one side, and she sensed his demeanor soften. "I'm making up for past sins."

"You can't do that."

"I know. Jesus already did. All I have to do is accept His gift."

"Tony, you know the rhetoric—"

"Naturally. I just spent a week with Brady Olafsson. Not to mention my sister's preaching."

"Why do you reject it so glibly?"

He shrugged and leaned against the doorjamb. "Joanna died and Brady lives in Valley Oaks."

"So they don't count, and the rest of us are a bunch of judgmental hypocrites?"

"Who don't get out enough. Izzy," his voice grew husky and he scanned the room, "I just wanted to treat you."

A smile tugged at her mouth. He was serious. "Really? Why?"

"Now who's asking all the questions?"

"Why?" she repeated, unable to halt the grin spreading across her face.

"Because you're a delightful young woman who deserves to be treated like a princess now and then." He leaned toward her and placed a finger on her lips before she could say anything. "No protests. No explanations. Just leave it. I'll pick you up at seven."

She nodded and waved as he backed out the door, pulling it shut as he went.

Oh, Tony! How could she explain that she *was* a princess? That God gave her indescribable treasures in sunrises, a baby nephew's laughter, a friend's hug, a song? Tony would say those were abstract and fleeting. True, and yet real treasures, she'd argue. But—but—

She twirled around the lush hotel room, past the ceiling-high picture window that overlooked the Chicago River and Marina Towers, and laughed aloud. "But— Oh, Lord! I can't remember when I've had such a down-to-earth, outrageously fun day!"

Seventeen

Isabel closed her eyes against the morning sun beating on her face. She and Tony sat on a park bench, sipping lattes from carry-out mugs with plastic lids. The thick Sunday *Tribune* lay between them, its sections still neatly folded in half. Tired from a late night, they had met a short time ago in her hotel lobby and then found a coffee shop on Michigan Avenue. Conversation didn't progress much beyond greetings and coffee decisions as they walked through the quiet streets to Grant Park.

"Tony, did I pass inspection?" She felt him turn toward her.

"How's that?"

"As a Christian hanging out in the real world of bigwig newspaper types at the most elegant dinner I've ever attended?"

"I think you know the answer to that, else you wouldn't have asked it. You passed with flying colors."

She opened her eyes. "And how's that?"

"You seem to be getting the hang of this asking questions." He scrunched down on the bench, leaned back and closed his eyes. "You made me look real good."

She poked his arm.

He opened one eye briefly. "Okay, okay. I was impressed. You were yourself, Isabel Mendoza, confident, intelligent, blatantly full of integrity without being judgmental when conversations deteriorated into sewer subjects."

"Ha! Showed you, Mr. Ward." She closed her eyes again.

"You're gloating."

"No, I'm not. I didn't do anything. Jesus Christ lives in me, and He likes people and parties."

"He does?"

"See, you still don't know much. It's high time you read Brady's books if you're not going to crack open a Bible."

After a few silent moments, Tony said, "You were the most beautiful woman cheering for me."

She smiled.

"May I kiss you?"

She tapped her cheek.

"No, may I *kiss* you?"

It was as if everything shifted into low gear. Shocked by the sudden change, her heart felt erratic, her limbs like water. She sensed movement, Tony sitting up straight, turning toward her. She didn't budge.

"Nah, forget I said that, Iz. According to quintessential gentleman behavior, I promised not to." He settled back down. "But you sure are beautiful."

Thank You, Father, she breathed. If Tony hadn't answered his own question, she would have said yes.

They headed north on Michigan. At Congress, Tony grabbed Isabel's hand and pulled her from the path of a swiftly turning cab.

He didn't let go until a few blocks later when they entered a restaurant. She wished it were at least another 12 blocks away.

Fortified with more coffee and their first bites of cheese omelets, they finally slipped into their flowing conversational style.

"Izzy, we're definitely out of practice. We act as if we've been up all night."

"Two A.M. is all night for me."

He laughed. "Yeah, that goes for me, too. College was a long time ago."

"Extremely long time ago."

"Has the statute of limitations been reached yet?"

He'd lost her. Maybe she wasn't quite awake yet. "For what?"

"For holding a grudge."

"Do you want all those pancakes?"

He scooped one over to her plate. "I still get these vibes that the sooner I leave Valley Oaks, the better you'll feel. I did apologize for hurting you eons ago, didn't I?"

"But you didn't even know what you were apologizing for." Her fork clattered as it hit the plate.

"So tell me exactly."

"It doesn't matter. It's just that," she glanced up at him, then focused again on her plate, "it was such an ugly time in my life. When I see you in my safe little town, I'm reminded of it over and over and over again."

"Is that why you're more comfortable with me here in Chicago than in Valley Oaks?"

She watched the cheese ooze from her omelet.

"Iz?"

She forced herself to meet his gaze. "Maybe."

"Ah. Progress. Okay, now tell me, what's a Christian to do with her ugly past?"

What do I see you dragging up here...is that for your atoning? "There's this song." She paused and let the words flow through her, felt the music resonate inside. Lowering her eyelids, she shut out Tony's face and began to sing softly.

What do I see you dragging up here?
        Is that for your atoning?
I know you're sorry;
        I've seen your tears,
        you don't have to show Me.
What makes you think
        you must make that go away?
I forgot when I forgave.
        I wish you would...

Just come in,
        just leave that right there.
        Love does not care.
Just come in,
        lay your heart right here.
        You should never fear.

You think you've crossed some sacred line
        and now I will ignore you.
If you look up, you will find
        My heart is still toward you.
Look at the sky,
        the east to the west.
That's where I threw this
        when you first confessed.
        Let it go now.

Just come in...

I will forgive you
        no matter what you've done,
No matter how many times
        you turn and run.
        I love you...

Isabel looked up in time to see Tony brush a finger at the corner of his eye. He twitched his nose. She said, "That's what God says about it, compliments of a Margaret Becker paraphrase."

"So why don't you let it go?"

Her breath caught. "Seven years later...I don't know. Still trying to earn my own way, I guess."

For a moment he stared quietly toward the window beside them, before turning again to her. "My sister jumped on the bandwagon. Literally. Did you ever hear of Sky Hi?"

She tilted her head from one shoulder to another as if the motion could jar loose a memory. "Rock group. They took alternative Christian rock to the nth degree. I'm not well acquainted with their music though."

"Joanna knew their music. She believed it and through it became a Christian."

"People hear the message in unimaginable ways."

"They definitely spoke her language, that of the ex-drug addict. She became a groupie. She went to Colombia because that's where they went."

"*What?*"

"They wanted to minister to the coca growers." Undisguised bitterness laced his tone. "The band left. JoJo stayed, with others, determined to love the unlovable to Jesus. Six of them were killed. Four came back."

"Oh, Tony." She reached for his hand across the table and squeezed it. He tightly held on to hers.

"Someday I'm going to put my investigative skills toward getting the whole story. I've lost track of those four, but I'm just too close to the situation right now. I can't observe it objectively."

"After hearing your praises sung last night at the awards dinner, I'd say that someday you will do it and do a credible job. Probably win the Pulitzer."

He gave her a small smile. "Thanks, Iz."

She smiled back. "Do you want both of those pancakes?"

Tony passed one to her. "That's what I remember about you."

"That I love pancakes?"

"No. That you know how to make me believe in my writing."

"Hmm. That'll cost you one more pancake."

Hours later, after they'd driven back to Valley Oaks and parted ways, Isabel replayed the conversation in her mind. What stood out was Tony's deep distrust of Christian musicians...which came under the umbrella of Christian artists...as did Christian writers...like Brady Olafsson.

Isabel cuddled Nutmeg against her chest, glad to be back home. After Tony dropped her off at her house, she had hurried over to Lia's to pick up the kitty. "I missed this silly cat. Are you sure she was no trouble?"

Chloe smiled. "No. Except she slept with Aunt Lia. Soot kind of pushed her out of my bed."

"Lia, I hope you wore a decent pair of jammies. That's what she's used to, you know. Silk."

Lia laughed. "Can you stay for a cup of tea and tell me all about your trip?"

"Sure, if I'm not interrupting."

"Not at all."

Chloe said, "I'll play with Nutmeg until you leave. I have to do homework."

Isabel handed her over. "Thanks."

The little girl sang as she headed down the hallway.

Lia set a cup before her at the kitchen table. "Chloe and I did some shopping and ate dinner out. Want some banana cream pie?"

Isabel groaned. "Tony and I ate for 24 hours straight. Last night's dinner was unbelievable. There were something like seven courses. Pâté, a scrumptious salmon stuffed in filo with a spinach and Gorgonzola sauce, and then raspberry cheesecake. Mmm."

Lia laughed as she prepared tea. "I do miss Chicago food."

"I can understand that. Hey, is Cal coming over by any chance?"

"I don't think so." There was an odd note to her voice. She sat down. "Sounds like you had a good time."

"Fantastic. I haven't had so much fun in ages. I'm just a bit concerned about some things Tony said." She relayed the story about his sister and the music group. "Cal might be right about Tony having it in for Brady."

"Cal said that?"

"Yeah. I feel bad. I accused him of playing cop like it was a sin he should confess."

"I came close to accusing him of having a racist for a girlfriend." Lia's hand flew to her mouth and her black eyes grew large.

"What?" Isabel couldn't help but smile. "I'm sorry, but you're pretty close to the truth. I just don't think I would come right out and tell him."

"I didn't. It started out with a dinner invitation. I had invited him and Tammy and Dot and her husband over last night. Cal accepted, then Dot told me none of them would be coming because Chinese food makes Tammy ill. And then Cal stumbled around, tripping over his tongue, explaining how he and Tammy have this standing Saturday night dinner date."

"Oh, Lia, I'm sorry. I know that hurts."

"It does. I think I was snippy to him."

Isabel laughed. "No way. If you were, I'm sure he didn't notice."

"I thought we were good friends, but now things are all uncomfortable, as if I'm trying to get between him and Tammy."

Isabel shook her head. "There's nothing to get between. They're not engaged. Cal doesn't even seem all that serious about her."

"But they have this standing Saturday dinner date."

"Which he seemed to have completely forgotten not just once, but twice." Isabel gathered steam, her tone turning sharp. "Maybe his Sundays are still free. You two can be friends on Sundays. Have a standing Sunday dinner date."

"Isabel! I am *not* interested in Cal that way!"

"Well, why not? You think he's attractive. Besides, I don't trust Tammy. Cal needs a good woman. When we ate pizza here Sunday night, I saw his rapport with you, how he paid attention to you."

"The same could be said for you and Tony."

Isabel made a noise of disgust. "Way too much baggage between the two of us."

"Well, I've got so much baggage it'd send Cal running for the hills. Izzy, I think you and I are back to that other conversation."

"About not complicating our lives with men?" Isabel smiled.

Lia grinned back at her. "That would be the one." She raised her teacup. "Here's to the single life."

After tucking Chloe into bed, Lia climbed into her own bed with a calculator and the pharmacy bookkeeping ledger with some notes from her accountant. Tired as she was, this had to be taken care of tonight.

"Dear Father, I need wisdom with these figures."

An hour later she set down her pencil. Tomorrow was the first of October. September had been a good month, with a slight increase over August profits. Based on past business, she calculated what Agstar's prescription plan brought in during an average month. The plan covered 49 percent of her regular customers, 25 percent of them retired and on monthly refillable drugs.

Subtracting that amount from her income put her in the hole.

Thinking that she could cut out company for dinner and not drive anywhere, she subtracted groceries and gas. No more baking *two* banana cream pies.

This put her slightly less in the hole.

Grandpa and Grandma would help pay for Chloe's clothing. Of course, her parents had always done that.

The business loan would carry the pharmacy for a short time…Thanksgiving maybe.

A single tear rolled down her cheek.

She shut the ledger and pushed it away. "Lord, I don't know what You're doing. It looks like we're going under." She drew up her knees and buried her face against them. "Oh, Father, I don't want to go under! Didn't You bring us here? Why would You bring us here just to fail and turn around, pack up, and leave? Pull Chloe out of school? *Why?!*" She poured out her complaints until she could think of no more. "Will You fix it? Please?"

Lia sat quietly, listening for the stillness but hearing only her whiny tone. She clapped her hands over her ears. *Let it* go. *Let it go.* "You gave it to me," she whispered. "It's Yours. I know You love me. I know You love me."

A distant ringing crept into her consciousness. It was the pharmacy line downstairs. She blinked, then looked around her bedroom, waiting for the business machine to click on and stop the ringing. This was a repeat of the past two nights. The message had been only heavy breathing.

Suddenly her private line rang, the jangling of the bedside phone tearing through her nerves like an electric shock. It rang again and then a third time before she managed to grab it. "Hello?"

"Lia."

She recognized the deep voice.

"This is Cal. Are you all right?"

"No. Yes. Why?"

"I'm across the street, your lights are still on, and it's after midnight. What's wrong?"

"I'm just...I'm just working on accounting." She could handle this alone. The loss of the business. The pointless phone calls. She didn't need Cal's help. She had God to lean on. Him and her impressive independence—

"What's wrong?" he repeated.

"Nothing. I'm fine."

"You don't sound fine."

"I'm just tired."

"All right. I won't keep you. Uh, about the pie."

Lia closed her eyes in disbelief. It was the middle of the night, and he was talking about the pie. She thought of how she had dumped it in the garbage.

"I'm sorry I didn't get over to pick it up."

"Banana cream doesn't keep long."

"Yeah, my mom used to tell me that. The thing is..." He paused. "Lia, I feel like an idiot, but I better just say it straight out. Tammy thinks there's something going on between you and me. So I probably shouldn't pick up any more pies. I don't want to hurt her feelings."

She searched for gracious words, reminding herself that he wasn't required to receive a gift from her. It wasn't as if he'd asked for it. "Well, tell her that she doesn't have a thing to worry about, Cal. But I can see her point. I mean, if I were involved with you I wouldn't want you going around having dinner with other women."

He didn't respond.

"Cal, tell her it's just my way of paying you for the doorbell and everything. No big deal. It won't happen again." She leaned toward the window and peeked through the curtain's edge. The outline of his truck sat across the street. His *truck*, not his cruiser. "Aren't you on duty right now?"

"No. Just driving by. The wrought iron bars over the back window were a good idea."

"Cal." She'd used up her supply of good manners. Exasperation inched her voice up a notch. "If I can't make you a pie, then don't check up on me when it's your night off."

"It's my nature. I'm a cop. I'm concerned. It doesn't mean you have to repay me. Jesus does all sorts of things for us, and He doesn't ask for anything in return."

"That's true, but I love Him in return and would do anything—" She heard the words flying unchecked and pressed her lips together to stop them.

"But I'm not asking for any—"

"You know, your analogy doesn't work! Just stop cruising by when you're not on duty."

"Hey, I don't need another woman telling me what to do!" His tone instantly crushed the teddy bear image into a plain old bear.

"Cal, this conversation is going nowhere."

"You got that right! I'll see you around."

She heard the click of him disconnecting.

Eighteen

Tony hauled a chair from the back of the pharmacy, set it near the front counter, and plopped onto it, grinning the whole while.

Isabel shut the cash register drawer and frowned at him. "Why are you sticking like glue to me? I'm simply working at the store, ringing up purchases and dusting. It's nothing to write home about."

"Ha, ha." He shrugged. "I have a few hours to kill. The Author has gone off to the airport to pick up his in-laws-to-be. Now that's nothing to write home about."

Hands on hips, she glanced at the ceiling and shook her head. Hadn't she passed inspection yet?

"Besides, you're exceedingly more intriguing to watch."

"And you're too charming for your own good."

He hooked his hands behind his head and crossed his legs, right ankle resting on the left knee. He wore his usual jeans and loafers, today with a royal blue crew neck sweater that intensified the color of his eyes. The usual lopsided grin spread across his face.

Isabel felt a tickle, as if the floor had just dropped beneath her about a foot. Stunned, she knelt behind the counter and retrieved the feather duster. "Ward, why don't you go buy us some lattes?"

"Because I'd have to drive into Rockville to get them."

She fluffed the duster against his nose as she passed him. "Exactly."

161

A movement at the back of the store caught Isabel's eye. Lia marched down from the slightly elevated pharmacy counter and toward the back room. Phone pressed to her ear, its long cord uncoiling behind her, she spoke sharply, "No!"

Isabel hurried down the aisle. The three people sitting in the chairs exchanged uncomfortable glances. Two women stood in line to have prescriptions filled, conversation halted. Dot frowned.

"No!" Lia's voice resounded across the store. "I will not allow it!"

Isabel slipped into the back room behind her and shut the door against the telephone cord. It was extended to its limit, allowing Lia only a short distance into the small area.

"I don't care!" Her face was red, her mouth a grim line. "No, you can't!" she shouted and punched the disconnect button.

"Lia?"

Her friend's eyes were large and she shook, speechless. She handed the phone to Isabel, pleading silently, and strode out through the alley door.

Isabel carried the phone into the store and laid it on the counter. "Dot, will you hang this up, please?" Not waiting for a reply, she followed Lia outside.

She was bracing herself, palms against the brick wall, head down.

"Lia?" Isabel said again.

Her shoulders heaved. She didn't speak for a few moments. "That was Chloe's dad. Nelson Greene." She muttered something under her breath and then gulped a breath. "Oh, why can't I *handle* this?"

Isabel touched her back. "Handle what?"

"He wants to see her. He has no right to see her!"

Matter-of-fact sentiments came to mind. *He is her biological father. Chloe may have a need to see him. You could work something out.* Isabel rejected them. Now was not the time for reasonableness. She pulled Lia away from the wall and hugged her. "Take some deep breaths, hon. Dear Jesus," she prayed, "comfort Lia. Take away the fears."

They held each other silently.

"Amen. Lia, you've got customers in there. Only you can fill their prescriptions."

She nodded and wiped tears from her face. "Okay. Okay. I'm fine."

"I'll keep praying today. We can talk later if you want."

Lia nodded again and gave her a thumbs-up sign. "Thank you." Her face had gone from beet red to drained of all color.

Isabel followed her back inside, pasting on a smile to hide her astonishment. Hatred wasn't too strong of a word to describe what she had just seen on Lia's face.

Cal rang the doorbell of Brady's log cabin house, thinking about the conversation he had just finished with Isabel. They still were still being careful with each other when it came to Tony. At least she hadn't accused him this time of playing cop.

What was it with women? Ever since he'd begun trying to take Jesus seriously, his relationships with them had gone haywire. He used to have female friends, some of whom he was attracted to in a romantic way and dated, though never one at a time. Now Tammy insisted on one at a time or forget her. And she pouted over his friendships with other women like Isabel and Lia, which made him feel guilty and off center when he talked with them.

The door opened. Brady grinned. "Hey, bud, what are you doing ringing the bell? Come on in."

"You've got company." He pointed a thumb over his shoulder toward cars he recognized as belonging to Tony Ward and Gina. "I need to talk to you privately. Only take two minutes."

"Brady," Gina's voice grew louder, "who is it?" She came into view. "Cal! Come meet my parents." She pulled on his arm.

Brady smiled. "Only take two minutes."

It was a sunny, early fall day. Everyone sat on the screened porch that overlooked a pond and rolling acres of huge oak and walnut trees. He and Tony greeted each other, and then Brady introduced him to Maggie and Reece Philips.

"My best man," he said.

Cal felt a rush of gratitude, maybe even pride. Who needed women?

Maggie and Reece were a striking couple in their mid-50s, California-tanned, and undoubtedly Gina's parents. She resembled her dad with her athletic good looks, olive skin tone, and dark hair. Her smile and bright green eyes, though, were her mother's.

Cal declined iced tea and settled in for two minutes of small talk. "I heard you just got back from Italy."

Maggie laughed. "Don't get me started. I've just met Tony, and even he must be weary of our stories. It was an incredible experience. Almost indescribable, but I keep trying. And this man, here," she nodded toward her husband, "proposed to me while we were riding on a gondola."

They laughed as she held out her left hand for all to see a flashy diamond ring.

Tony said, "It sounds as if there's a Mr. Romance contest going between Reece and Brady."

Reece shook his head. "No way. He wins, hands down. He's years ahead of me in that department."

"But, Dad," Gina winked at Brady, "four weeks in Italy sounds like the ultimate honeymoon."

"Too bad Brady can't afford it. He spends more on flowers for you in a week than I've spent in 30 years." Reece turned to Tony. "So, you were telling us about Brady's books, which you haven't read yet."

Cal suppressed a grin and made his exit. Brady was in good hands. His friend followed him outside to his truck. They leaned against the hood, arms crossed.

"Brade, we might have a problem. Ward was in Los Angeles at the end of August. I found a record of his ticket bought the day he left Valley Oaks."

He didn't immediately respond. "Los Angeles is a big place."

"Isabel just told me about a conversation she had with Tony this weekend, about his sister."

"You already told me about her. Tragic story."

"But I didn't know the circumstances. She went down there with some Christian rock group. Isabel said Ward got really bent out of shape talking about the musicians' influence on his sister. Now even she's concerned he has ulterior motives, and she *likes* the guy."

"Cal, you know firsthand I'm not perfect. I never pretended to be."

"The thing is, Brade, you look perfect. Man, you've always been the role model. Your one lapse into stupidity will get blown all out of proportion."

"Comes with the territory of being a public figure, bud. Territory I didn't choose, by the way. If it makes me look more human to the entire world, then that's for the best."

"I wasn't thinking of the entire world." They exchanged a knowing glance. "Did you tell her yet?"

Brady pulled on his chin.

Cal punched his arm. "She deserves to hear it from you. She shouldn't have to read about it in some newspaper."

Much to his surprise, Tony was enjoying his visit with Gina's parents. Not only were they from California, land of the fruits and nuts, they were Christians. Reece, evidently a Johnny-come-lately to the fold, had been challenging Tony's beliefs nonstop, more so than Brady had. All this, and still he found them delightful. The source of Gina's character was evident.

He steered the conversation to his main reason for being there and finally got around to asking, "What about Nicole Frazell?"

"Ancient history," Brady replied.

Gina's brows went up.

"I'm sorry. I assumed you knew." Tony thought his tone sounded sincere considering he had assumed no such thing.

Brady's eyes narrowed.

Gina said, "Oh, I know about her. My soon-to-be husband was engaged to her. I was just wondering what she has to do with this story."

Tony lifted a shoulder and studied the pad on his knee. "Anything to do with The Author piques my curiosity. She lives in California, right?"

Brady answered, "Last I heard, which was years ago."

"Hmm. Years ago." *Do it, Ward! Go for the jugular! It's your job! Do it, for pete's sake!* He opened his mouth, but nothing came out. An image of Isabel flashed through his mind, turning away from him. "So, uh, you and Gina must be open about your pasts?"

Brady hesitated. "I don't think we've dissected them day by day for each other, but yes, we're fairly open."

"Uh, 'fairly' open. Meaning?"

"Meaning what you're hinting at." His voice deepened. "I was engaged, Gina nearly was. We know what wasn't right about those relationships. If she asks me anything concerning it, I tell her, and vice versa. *Not* that it's any of your business."

And does Gina know enough to ask you about stalking and assault and battery charges? Tony let a silent, awkward moment pass.

Reece made a joke, Maggie talked of dinner plans, Gina excused herself.

Tony allowed the subject to change. He had heard the hint of fear in Brady's angry tone, seen the look of doubt in Gina's lowered eyelids. He had...succeeded.

He declined their dinner invitation. Revulsion toward himself squelched his appetite.

Nineteen

Lia slumped in her car outside the Community Center in the parking lot, waiting for Chloe to come out from her Monday evening gymnastics class. Set in the middle of a neighborhood of hundred-year-old homes, the Center was a modern structure housing gyms, an indoor pool, and various courts.

Dusk had already fallen, though it wasn't yet even seven o'clock. The days were shrinking...as was her budget, which she was wantonly ignoring tonight. She had squandered gas driving the car less than two blocks. As soon as Chloe appeared, they were driving four more blocks and buying a large pizza with the works. Lia felt exhausted in body and soul.

A large figure approached along the sidewalk. It was Cal. He set his gym bag on the hood of her car and angled himself to peer through the windshield, his face a question mark.

Lia sighed and motioned for him to get inside.

He opened the passenger door and slid onto the seat, his teddy bear shoulders filling the interior of her car. He wore a short-sleeved sweatshirt and gym shorts, both damp with perspiration, as was his face and hair. "Hey, China Doll," he puffed, slightly out of breath. "How you doing?"

His soft tone snapped the fragile string of control she'd been holding onto most of the day. Not trusting her voice, she lifted a hand and rocked it back and forth, indicating so-so.

"You look beat."

"Short night, long day," she said, her voice barely above a whisper.

Silence followed. It wasn't exactly awkward. Despite last night's fractious telephone conversation, she considered Cal a friend. After all, he had carried her over a threshold and bandaged her cut foot...he swept shattered glass and waited out the night, dozing in the recliner while she huddled in a corner of the couch...he had sat stocking-footed and watched the football game in her apartment.

"Lia, I was out of line. Last night, I mean. On the telephone. I'm sorry."

She swallowed. "And I'm sorry for telling you not to cruise by on your night off. I really do appreciate your concern."

"Friends?"

She gazed through the windshield. Youngsters straggled out through the Center's double glass doors. "For Tammy's sake, maybe it's best that we're not. You know, somebody's going to see you sitting here, and she'll hear about it. That's not fair to her."

"My job is talking to people."

"You're not in uniform, we're alone in my car, and it's nearly dark."

"So?"

She straightened and looked at him. "Cal, it's the appearance. What would you think if you heard that she were sitting with some guy like this?"

"Nothing." He locked his eyes with hers.

"Because?"

"No reason to think anything."

"You trust her, then. Or you don't care enough."

He didn't reply for a moment. "Or something. So why is it she doesn't trust me?"

Lia shrugged. "She's insecure. She's not sure you care about her."

"What do I do?"

"Well, for starters, don't have dinner at my apartment. Send her flowers. I don't know, Cal. I've never been in love."

"Really?"

She shrugged again.

"I don't think I have either," he said.

"Then why in the world do you let this woman lead you around as if you've got a ring in your nose?"

"Hey, China Doll. That's getting a little personal."

"That's what friends are for."

"Thought we weren't going to be friends." He drummed his fingers on the dashboard. "I'm attracted to Tammy. She's fun to be with."

"A Saturday night dinner you can count on." It was a dig, but the conversation was turning into an uncomfortable counseling session.

He narrowed his eyes to mere slits. "Don't bake any more pies for me. That makes me feel guilty."

"Hadn't planned on baking you any more, Deputy." She returned his stare.

After a moment, his face relaxed. A small smile tugged at the corner of his mouth. "Truce."

"I'll think about it."

"While you think about it, we need to talk about something else. I heard you had a phone call at the store today."

Lia slumped back down in the seat. How many people had been in the shop? Isabel, Tony, Dot, a handful of customers getting prescriptions. All of Valley Oaks probably knew by now. "It was Nelson."

"Has he been calling?"

"N-no."

"You don't sound certain about that. Either he has or he hasn't."

"There have been some hang-ups, but I don't think they were him. He asked to see Chloe. I don't want him to."

"What does she want?"

"I haven't asked her."

"I've dealt with a lot of child abuse cases. Strangest thing. Kids remain loyal to parents, even jerk dads. You might want to talk to her about it. Who knows? The guy hasn't been in trouble. Maybe he sincerely wants a relationship with his daughter."

"It doesn't seem possible after all these years. My dad has always been there for me. He adores my mother. He's smart and giving and fair. I don't know where or what I'd be without him. What's yours like?"

Cal was quiet for a moment. "He was a state patrolman. He died when I was 15. Heart attack. I worshiped him."

"I'm sorry, Cal. Is your mom around?"

"She lives in Florida. I'm on my own. No brothers or sisters. So tell me about the hang-ups."

Lia was still digesting the information about his family life, imagining how painful his adolescence must have been with losing his dad. "Oh. The hang-ups. There's nothing to tell. For three nights in a row, there have been calls on the store line leaving heavy breathing on the answering machine."

"What time?"

"Friday, maybe 10:00 or 10:30, again at midnight. I went down and turned off the ringer. Same thing Saturday. The ringer was off, but the machine records the times it picks up. Last night there was just one, right before you called."

"Lia!" The way he said her name made it an interjection of pure annoyance. "Tell me this stuff when it happens, okay?"

"I can handle it. It's no big deal. There's nothing you can do."

"I've got my suspicions. From now on, give me details so I can investigate."

"Okay, okay."

Chloe opened the back door and climbed in. "Hi, Aunt Lia. Hi, Cal."

Lia turned around. Her niece looked so cute in her leotard. "Hi, sweetpea. How was gymnastics?"

"Great. I did two back handsprings in a row."

Cal whistled.

Lia reached over the back of the seat and slapped a palm against Chloe's. "Way to go, Chloe! Hey, I'm planning on dinner at the Pizza Parlor. Sound okay to you?"

"Yea! Can Cal come?"

In the deepening shadows, Lia wrinkled her nose at Cal, signaling that this was not a good idea. But then again, this dinner wouldn't be at her apartment. "Can you?"

"Monday night football." The answer came swiftly. "Kind of a ritual with a few guys. And I need a shower. Thanks, though."

The little girl remained silent as Cal got out and said goodbye. Lia's heart sank. He had let Chloe down again. Lia chalked up her own stab of disappointment to empathy over Chloe's. *Men!*

"Aunt Lia?"

"Hmm?" She turned.

Chloe was pinching her nose. "He did need a shower!"

They laughed all the way to the restaurant.

"Hey, Brady," Cal whispered into the phone.

"Cal? The game's on!"

"Quick question." Cal carried the cordless phone into his backyard. No reason the guys in his living room needed to hear this. "How do I order flowers?"

Brady burst out laughing.

"I'm serious! You're the expert."

The laughter got louder.

"Come on."

Brady gulped for air. "Is this an emergency?"

"Why would it be an emergency? They're just for Tammy."

"For...?" He still chuckled.

"For?" Cal raked his fingers through his hair. "I don't know for what. Lia thought I should send some."

"Then it's a 'thinking about you' sort of gift?"

"Yeah, yeah. That's it."

"Well, you could call Bev at home tonight if it were an emergency, like if you messed up in a major way. Did you forget her birthday?"

Cal thought a moment. Her birthday was in March, wasn't it? Or May. They'd only been dating since July. "No."

"Then call Bev's shop in the morning. Tell her you want a bouquet of fresh flowers in a vase sent to Tammy's school. Send them to her at work. You get a lot of mileage doing it that way because all her friends and coworkers notice. Anyway, just tell Bev what you want to spend."

"What's it cost?"

"Whatever you want to pay. Twenty-five won't get you much, but a hundred probably isn't necessary in this case."

"Twenty-five dollars for flowers?"

"You've really never done this before?"

Cal sighed.

"Hold on a sec." Brady's voice was muffled, and then he laughed again. "Gina says don't order the Hawaiian special.

Where were we? Okay, choose an amount, then Bev will ask what sort of card you want."

"Card? This is getting too complicated."

"You can do it, big guy. Choose the 'thinking of you' card and ask her to sign it— How do you want to sign it? Love? I love you?"

"N-no." He paced the width of his backyard. "That's too, uh, strong."

"Okay. Why did Lia suggest you send flowers?"

"Because Tammy's insecure."

"You're talking with Lia about Tammy's insecurity? Curiouser and curiouser. How about 'crazy about you'?"

"I'd never say that."

"Yeah, you're right. Oh, man, touchdown!"

"Who?"

"No way. Find out for yourself. You're the one interrupting the game. How about, 'can't wait to see you'?"

"Too...much."

Brady exhaled loudly. "Have a nice day."

"Come on, Brade. Tell me what to sign."

"That's it. 'Have a nice day.'"

"Oh. Yeah. That'll work. Thanks."

"Hey, bud, when Tammy thanks you for the flowers, don't tell her it was Lia's idea."

"I should take the credit?"

"Mm-hmm. Something like that. See you."

Women!

Twenty

Luscious scents of ginger, lemon, and rosemary and the rich sound of Italian opera music filled Isabel's kitchen. She enjoyed cooking, but Tony's special touch had turned ho-hum into extraordinary.

"Izzy, try this." Tony stood at her stove, holding a spoon above a sizzling pan.

She turned from her salad preparations and accepted his offer. Sautéed mushrooms, zucchini, and shrimp burst into a most delectable sensation. "Mmm. Perfect."

"Need more ginger?"

"I don't think so. Shall I drain the pasta?"

Tony forked a strand of spaghetti from the boiling pot and flung it at the wall. It stuck.

"Tony!"

"Best way to tell. Okay, woman, drain it!"

They bustled around the kitchen, setting the small table with seafood pasta, salad, and garlic bread. He lowered the volume of the music and pulled out a chair for her. "*Señorita.*"

"*Gracias.*" After he sat down, Isabel bowed her head.

"Izzy, you can pray out loud."

In all their meals together, she hadn't done so yet. She peered at him.

"Research." His tone didn't mock. He bowed his head. "Just pray like you always do, as if I'm not listening."

O Lord! "Jesus, thank You for the abundance of food that You've provided. Thank You for Tony's friendship. And like

175

I always pray," she smiled, "let him see and hear You in me. Draw him into Your kingdom. Amen."

"Amen. Smiling is allowed during prayer?"

She winked at him. "Peeking is, too. Thanks for grocery shopping and cooking."

"It's the least I could do, considering how you're putting up with me." His sincerity surprised her. "Nice salad."

"Thanks." She watched him eat for a moment. He was different tonight somehow. Distant. "Tony, what's wrong?"

"Why would you ask that? I'm working on a major story and hanging out with my old girlfriend. Life is good."

"You're a big-city guy stuck in Valley Oaks. You love football, but you've brought a video to watch instead. You probably have a string of gorgeous women who would spend the entire night with you, but you're here with Miss Prude. Great pasta, by the way."

"Thanks. Number one, the story is in Valley Oaks. Number two, I won't be here next Monday night. Football will be wherever I am. Number three..." He paused. "I don't and you're not Miss Prude. You're an adorable young woman with convictions. I don't agree with them, but I respect you for having them."

She smiled. "Definite progress. What's the video?"

"It's called *American Dreamer,* and it's about writing fiction and winning contests and falling in love in Paris. Speaking of dreams, is this what you want?"

"What do you mean by 'this'?"

"Doing what you're doing."

"I love what I do."

"But when you were younger, what did you dream about doing?"

Isabel set down her fork and glanced around her cozy kitchen. She did love this little place. She loved her job and her coworkers. But...her dream? "I forget."

"My guess is it had to do with writing. You were in journalism. You wanted to..." He gestured for her to fill in the blank.

And it came to her. "Be a columnist. I wanted to invade people's lives with my wit and insight and *change* them." She grinned.

"So why aren't you? What happened? Christianity get in the way?"

"No. You—" She pressed her lips together.

"I? I what?"

Oh, I'm going to regret this! "You did."

"*I* did? How's that?"

"What I mean is," she slowed her speech, keeping her tone flippant, "life was never the same after you. You swept me off my feet. I don't know. When I picked myself up again, I wasn't thinking anymore about changing the world through writing a column. So what about you? Are you living your dream?"

"Soon as I win the Pulitzer. Back up, Izzy. What were you thinking when you picked yourself up again?"

No. She *wasn't* going to tell him. It was none of his business. "That life was difficult and maybe I'd just take it one step at a time."

"Did you become a Christian at that time?"

"A little later."

"And is that when you tucked yourself away here, sheltered from the slings and arrows of the real world?"

"Tony, you're attacking now."

"I apologize. Do you still want to write?"

"I...I don't know. More salad?"

Tony let the subject shift. The evening's mood lightened as they cleaned the kitchen together. Isabel tried not to notice how well they worked alongside each other, how quickly the task was finished.

He dried his hands, surveying the room. "All right, my dear. Put away that last pot and then close your eyes."

"*Now* do I get dessert?"

"Only if you close your eyes."

She leaned against the counter and shut her eyes. "It must be smaller than a bread box because you've carried it in your jacket pocket."

"Clever girl. All right, open your eyes."

He held a wrapped chocolate bar in front of her face. Caramel. Milk chocolate. Cadbury. "You remembered!" she blurted.

He grinned in his lopsided way. "Of course. I always remember insignificant details. It's your name I couldn't get right."

She stared at it. His remembering pierced her heart, transfixing her.

"Iz, you can have the whole thing. I've got my own."

She thought of the way he used to tuck chocolate into odd places, like her book bag or a kitchen drawer, little surprises for her to find. Long after they had gone their separate ways, she discovered one in the side pocket of a suitcase.

Tony lowered the candy. "I suppose it's a religious thing and you can't have any."

"What?"

"You've probably given up videos and chocolate." He looked like a little boy who had just lost the ball game on his third strike.

She grabbed the chocolate bar from his hand and slid her arms around his neck. "No, silly. Videos and chocolate are no problem. I told you loving Jesus isn't about keeping rules. It's just that you remembered my favorite, after all these years!" Her smile faded when their eyes met. When he placed his hands round her waist, she didn't budge.

His kiss was a feather touch on her lips. It was the most natural moment...but it shouldn't have been. It was as if she had traveled a great distance and just arrived home...but it shouldn't have felt like that.

Tony reached behind his neck and unhooked her hands. "Sorry," he whispered, "didn't mean to do that. Forgive me?"

"I...I, mmm, I think you warned me once."

"That's right, I did." He held her hands against his chest, the candy bar clutched in her fist. "Izzy, when did you start feeling guilty about our living together? Did Christianity do that?"

Why was he talking about this? "The Bible says it's wrong."

"So your answer is yes. But there's forgiveness, right? For the past, present, and future?"

She nodded.

"And when you tell God you're sorry, then you're forgiven and the guilt goes away?"

Again she nodded.

"Then why is it you still feel guilty about it?"

"I don't still—" Tears welled in her eyes and a sob choked off her words. In that instant, she knew what he said was true. She had confessed over and over, not just the living together, but all of it. Still the guilt hung like a necklace of millstones. She knew it, she just chose to ignore it. Most of the time she disguised it well from herself and others.

Then Tony had come, the investigative journalist searching and searching, digging for the real God, pressing her for answers, for authenticity. He had glimpsed behind her mask and now relentlessly peeled away its layers.

Tony held her until the sobs lessened.

Evidently he had hit a nerve. Again.

Dinner churned in his stomach. He hoped the antacids were still in his jacket.

"Izzy? I'm sorry."

Pushing herself back from his chest, she shook her head. "Truth hurts. Not your fault."

She was so beautiful, with her mussed hair, heart-shaped face damp with tears, and wide mouth. Half of her lower lip slipped inward. He knew she was biting it. He remembered the mannerism... whenever she was upset...

The memories bombarded him tonight. He remembered he had been consumed by her that last semester at school. The wild imaginings of a future together had terrified him then, sent him racing off to Australia and then Chicago with never even a cursory reading of alumni newsletters. She was history. He so meticulously buried her in his subconscious, he hadn't even remembered her name.

A new realization dawned on him. No other female had come near to captivating him in the way she had. And now she was a woman, more alluring than ever, in spite of her religion. Or maybe because of it.

"Izzy, I'm leaving." He touched her cheek and kissed her forehead.

The raw sienna of her eyes glistened knowingly. She understood. If he stayed, he would more than likely regret his actions.

Tony returned to his tiny furnished apartment down the street and hurriedly packed a bag. It was still early. He could be in Chicago by 10:30.

He couldn't shake the pall that had settled over him after leaving Brady's place yesterday...after asking about Nicole. Whether it was a journalist's intuition or a simple need to put a hundred miles between himself and Isabel Mendoza, he didn't know. All he knew was that the story was on hold for the moment. Back, back burner.

He grabbed a novel from the nightstand, then paused, his hand in midair. Beneath the thriller lay Brady's books. He hadn't cracked one open yet. He really balked at the idea of reading historical fiction with Jesus Christ as the superhero.

It wasn't like him to disregard research for a story. Background was what gave his work depth. What was the problem here?

Izzy came to mind, as she too often did. Her lovely face, her musical voice.

"Tony, it's a supernatural thing. You can't explain it in strictly human terms or from a human perspective. No way can you understand it. God is here, right now. And evil is in this world, right now, fighting in unimaginable ways to undermine His love."

To read or not to read. Was this a struggle between good and evil? That sounded ridiculous. He could make his own decisions. The intelligent thing to do was to read the silly books. He would even ask Brady for a peek at the fourth manuscript. He'd show God and the devil exactly who was in charge.

Now he was talking to them?

He picked up the top one. It slid from his grip and fell to the floor. He knelt to retrieve it, bumping the other two. They thudded against the carpet. He gathered them, then hit his head against the nightstand.

Tony tossed the books at his duffel bag, a rare curse flying with them.

Twenty-One

Lia's hands shook uncontrollably. She gripped the steering wheel more tightly and stared at the parsonage, an old, pretty, two-story white frame with forest green shutters. Celeste Eaton was hosting tonight's book club meeting. Club NEDD...nurture, eat, dabble in book discussion. Lia had skipped dinner, but she did not want to eat. She had read the book, but she did not want to discuss it. What she wanted desperately was to be *nurtured*.

Well, she would just stay late again until she found a private moment with Celeste. That would mean paying more for the baby-sitter, another wanton expenditure of money budgeted for more important items.

No, this was a more important item. Chloe needed to stay home and get to bed at a decent hour. Chelsea Chandler, Addie's daughter, was 16 and had driven herself over. She needed the job, and Lia needed the time away.

Oh, Lord, what do I do?

Minutes before Chelsea's arrival, Nelson had called, this time on the apartment's private line.

"Lia, don't hang up." The strong voice with its authoritative tone was easily recognizable.

"How did you get this number?"

"Chloe gave it to me."

Chloe?!

"Lia, she called me yesterday. She's my daughter. I loved your sister."

"And what does your *wife* think?"

182

"She's come to terms with it. We both want to see Chloe. And Chloe wants to see me."

"Kathy wouldn't want it!"

"Kathy's not here."

"No! I won't allow it!"

"Lia, biological fathers have rights. I'll go to court."

The unspoken words rang loud and clear. *And I have the money to fight until I win.* It all came down to money.

"I've changed, Lia."

"You just threatened me!"

"With legal proceedings. I promise you, I've changed. Just give me a weekend with her. I'll come pick her up."

Defeat turned her bones to water. "I will talk to my niece." She hung up and marched into Chloe's room.

"You gave him our number? Why didn't you talk to me first?"

"Aunt Lia, please let me see him! He's going to take me to the zoo."

"Grandpa can take you to the zoo!"

The little girl's lower lip quivered. "I want to see my daddy!"

But he killed your mother! Tears streamed down Lia's face. She sat on the bed beside Chloe and hugged her. "I have to think about it."

Now, Lia opened her car door. What was there to think about? She knew what was best for Chloe, and it did not include a visit with Nelson Greene.

Did it?

———

The moment Celeste released Lia from a bear hug, Isabel gathered her into her arms. They stood in Celeste's entryway, a homey shoe- and coat-infested area at the bottom of an open staircase.

At last Lia wiped her tears and gave them a small smile. "Amazing how planks in the eye can be invisible to the one looking out. Thank you for helping me see the resentment I'm still clinging to."

Celeste patted her cheek. "In all of our eyes, Nelson doesn't deserve forgiveness. It's natural you couldn't see the need to do just that. But the more you give up that thought to Jesus, the less power Nelson has over your emotions. There's a great freedom in that."

"And you both think I should let Chloe see him?"

Celeste smiled. "Forgiveness doesn't happen just inside your head."

Isabel added, "She'll be fine, Lia. It's a good plan for when she has that long weekend off of school. If your parents come and get her and you pick her up on Sunday, she won't be alone with him a long time. And you never know, she might have a completely boring time."

"Maybe." Lia opened the front door. "Maybe I'll pray for rain on their zoo outing." Her dark eyes crinkled. "Just kidding. I think. Goodnight, ladies. Thank you!"

As they called goodnight to Lia, Celeste tugged on Isabel's sleeve. "Stay for a minute?" They went back into the living room and sat on the couch. "It's about your friend Tony."

Isabel opened her mouth to protest and then realized he *was* her friend. Becoming more and more so as the days went by.

Celeste's pixie face contorted as if in pain. "You know we all think he's adorable, and we're praying for his soul, but something has come up."

Isabel shivered. Had she found out they had lived together? "What?"

"Brady talked with Peter today. I can't give you specifics because Peter won't give me specifics." She paused. "The gist is that Tony hinted at something, at some information he possesses that could tarnish Brady's image. Oh, Peter said tarnish is even too strong a word, but in the hands of a reporter…" She held up her palms.

"Did Tony threaten to include this information in his article?"

"Not directly. You know how Brady is. He doesn't care. The problem is Gina didn't know. Until now. Tony stirred things up on Monday, but Brady didn't have a chance to talk with her until Tuesday night."

"Oh," Isabel moaned. "Does this have something to do with why she didn't come tonight?"

"I think so. She's…upset. Isabel," Celeste squeezed her arm, "don't overreact."

"Celeste! This is so unfair! Tony is such a jerk!"

"Shh. He's not, honey."

Isabel clenched her fists and closed her eyes, letting her friend's soft voice wash through her. She would strangle Tony Ward!

"I wanted you to know, just in case you can influence him. Brady may not care what's printed about him, but we're concerned about Tony's discretion."

"I don't ever want to see that snake in the grass again."

"Isabel. Weren't we just talking about forgiveness? Tony needs our prayers."

She sighed. "Now *that* I'll have to think about." *Oh, Tony!* He could be so warm and caring and understanding. "But I will talk to him. I can't promise what impact I'll have on him, but I *will* talk to him."

"And pray for Gina and Brady."

"Of course."

"She's..." again the painful pause, "thinking about returning to California with her parents."

Cal's lights were on. He was a night owl even when he didn't work the third shift. Isabel banged on his front door, too energized to simply push the doorbell.

He opened the door. "Isabel. What's wrong? Come in."

"Cal, you knew! Didn't you? You knew!"

"Mendoza, calm down! I don't know what in the world you're talking about. Sit."

His stern tone cut through her anguished restlessness. She sat in a worn armchair and glanced around to get her bearings. Cal's entire home was worn—usually neatly kept—but worn. It had been his grandparents' home. They had built it over 50 years ago and left it to their only grandchild when they passed away. The furnishings had probably been theirs, too. Doilies certainly would have adorned things at one time. No doubt he had pitched them.

He turned off the big-screen television and sat down.

Cal was a decent guy. Why couldn't she fall for a decent guy?

"Talk to me."

"Tony found some dirt on Brady."

He closed his eyes and ran his hand over his face. "What dirt?"

"You tell me! You knew he would dig, and you knew there was something for him to find! Why didn't you warn Brady?"

"I did."

"Well, it was too late!"

"Isabel, I'm in the same room."

She gasped back her screeching tone. "Gina might leave him. At least go back to California with her parents next week. Peter told Celeste, and she just told me."

"You're pretty close with Gina, aren't you? Talk her out of it."

She had already considered this. "I won't know what I'm talking to her about! And I don't want to know!"

"Brady's not perfect."

"Yes, he is!"

"Come on, Mendoza, don't go squirrelly on me. I love the guy, but he's got his faults."

"Is it horrific?"

"No, of course not. It was just stupid. He chased after Nicole. This was soon after you came to town, I think. You didn't know him well then. He was...nuts about her. I thought he was losing touch with reality. Working too hard at three jobs, teaching, farming, and writing but not getting published. Anyway, she called from California, told him goodbye, said she'd mail the ring. Next thing I know, he's gone and it's spring planting time. Two weeks later he shows up on my doorstep, in obvious need of a shave and a shower."

Cal leaned forward, elbows on his knees, and muttered, "Cured me of ever wanting to get serious with a woman, let me tell you."

"Cal!"

"He told me he found Nicole. She said she didn't love him anymore. He realized he'd been an idiot. Then the new boyfriend appeared. Brady punched his lights out."

Isabel gasped. *Brady Olafsson punched somebody?*

"He got arrested. They charged him with stalking—"

"No!"

"And assault and battery. But when he agreed to leave town, give Nicole the $10,000 ring plus damages, and never contact her again, they dropped the charges."

"So it's not on any records."

Cal shook his head. "Ward went to L.A. right after the Autumn Faire. Somebody must have told him about Nicole, and he found her."

"Dot."

"Dot?"

"They talked at the Faire. And, Cal, you know she would. I'm sorry. She's Tammy's mother, but you know she would."

He appeared to mull that over.

"You've known him longer than any of us. You should talk to Gina. She must be scared out of her wits, wondering what kind of weirdo he is. She hasn't known him very long. Should we all talk to her?"

He grimaced. "I'm batting zero when it comes to women lately."

"Cal! Brady needs you!"

"Why don't you talk to her and I'll talk to Ward?"

"No way." She shook her head. "He's mine, soon as he gets back from Chicago." *And he will pay for this.*

Brady had been known to shout "Go away!" at friends and family. Anyone who disrupted his writing time by finding him out on the screened porch at his laptop was considered an intruder. Cal was no exception, but early Friday morning he braved Brady's wrath.

He bypassed the front door and walked along the leaf-strewn stone walk around the log house to the back porch. He climbed the three deck steps and saw him. He wasn't at his laptop.

Brady stood the other side of the screen door, coffee mug in hand. "Cal." He opened the door and stepped aside. He needed a shave. His baseball cap was pulled low on his forehead. "Coffee?"

"Sure."

Brady gazed at him, as if lost in a thought that had nothing to do with the coffee he just offered.

"I'll get it, Brade." Cal hurried into the kitchen, noted it wasn't in its usual neat shape, grabbed a mug from the cupboard, and helped himself to what remained in the carafe. He'd make some more before he left.

Back on the porch, Brady hadn't moved. "Well, you warned me."

"Too late. I'm sorry. I liked the guy. Underestimated his ability to backstab."

Brady gave him a tiny smile. "I like him too, but I could have done without this little episode. Gina feels like she's been through the wringer. I feel like I've been clothespinned to a line, hung out to dry." His voice faded.

Cal looked for signs. Brady was in a bad way, but not strung out the way he was when Nicole left. "You okay?"

"No, but we'll be okay. I think. I mean, she can't believe it. She has to, though, because it's true. All of it. Tony hinted, she sensed something was left unsaid, I told her Tuesday night. How'd you find out, anyway?"

"Peter told Celeste—no details, bud. Just that Tony had information to hurt you. Celeste told Isabel. Isabel told me."

Brady took off his cap, scratched his forehead, and replaced the hat. "That's the kind of stuff that drives Gina up the wall."

"I, uh, I told Isabel the details. She needed to know in case Gina wants to talk with her. And then there's her relationship with Ward. Seemed best to level the playing field."

Brady nodded. "Isabel should know. How do you think Tony found Nicole?"

"Dot. Well, anybody could have given him Nicole's name and that she was last known to be in the Los Angeles area. But according to Isabel, Dot had the opportunity."

"And the motive." They exchanged a knowing glance. "Cal, I know she's an attractive girl, but Tammy is...immature, with no help on the parent front."

"No problem. I don't intend to get serious." Cal shrugged. "So how goes it?"

Brady gazed through the screen, toward the pond. "Reece is having second thoughts. Maggie is unusually quiet. Gina and I..." he let out a breath, "have some issues to work through. At least, I think they can be worked through."

Twenty-Two

Late Friday night Lia stood alone in the dimly lit pharmacy. In the back corner, where the lights were brighter, she stared at the tall shelves that came out from the wall, shaped like a giant "E." They held her large array of drugs. Tablets and capsules neatly alphabetized...topicals in their section...orals in theirs...children's medications separate...the refrigerated items.

Her thoughts raced in every direction and then halted, too scattered to grasp their conclusion. It was incomprehensible. Dread flooded through her. She braced herself against a shelf.

The phone at her shoulder rang. She jumped.

Not now!

It rang again. Again. And again.

The machine picked up. Her message played, then, "Lia, it's Cal. You there?"

She grabbed the phone. "Cal! Oh, Cal! Are you nearby?"

"On the sidewalk. What's wrong?"

"Something...something's not quite right. I think I need a policeman."

There was a knock on the front door. "At your service." He must be on his cell.

She hung up and rushed down the aisle. As the big brown teddy bear in uniform strode inside, she felt a rush of relief and clutched his arm.

"What's wrong?"

191

Gulping for breath, she turned, motioning him to follow. They stepped through the half door that joined two counters. She went between the shelves and stared.

He touched her shoulder. "Lia?"

"I don't understand it," she whispered. "I think I've been robbed."

"What happened?"

"I was just putting away the drugs that were delivered today. See this?" She reached up and tapped empty spots, and then she turned to face him. "Morphine and everything containing codeine."

Cal's eyebrows shot up.

"I had a full supply."

"You're sure—Of course you're sure." He studied the shelves up behind her shoulder, his peppermint gum-scented breath filling the tiny space between them. "Maybe they were accidentally moved out of place. Let's search through all the drugs."

"I already did that!"

"Well, we'll do it again. And then probably again. Hey, don't worry, China Doll." He lightly touched her forehead and pressed away the frown.

It was when he brushed strands of hair back from her face that something shifted between them, as if a veil were yanked away, abruptly bringing into focus a nameless emotion. He stopped smoothing her hair. Surprise registered in his eyes, and she sensed hers reflected the same. Slowly he tilted his head downward until only a hair's breadth separated them.

"Lia." His lips moved the air against hers. "This is not a good idea."

"Right," she breathed, relief and disappointment weaving a tangled mess in her throat.

Cal straightened. "Let's go, uh—" They bumped into each other, unable to turn simultaneously. "You go first."

Wobbly legs carried her to the grouping of wicker chairs. She sank onto one.

He joined her. "Sorry about that. What *was* that?"

"I don't know, but I completely forgot why you're here."

He laughed, tugging at his collar. "Keep the victims calm, I always say."

"Well, you're effective, Deputy."

"Okay, down to business?"

"Okay."

The veil was back in place.

Cal pulled out his pen and notebook from his shirt pocket, trying to keep just superficial eye contact with Lia. A few moments ago he'd totally lost himself in those jet black pools that matched her unbelievably thick long hair. "You just discovered the drugs missing tonight?"

"Just before you called. What timing, huh?"

He nodded, scratching notes on his pad, avoiding the sight of her mouth. It was a perfectly shaped mouth, reminding him of a perky little bow tie. Small, full, velvety. She was trying to smile bravely, and his heart was thumping like crazy. Still. Thank God he had caught himself in time. *Yes, thank You, God.*

"Mr. Swanson picked up his morphine for his cancer pain on Tuesday. I ordered more, but I wasn't completely out. I'm sure I would have noticed that Wednesday when I stocked. Or Thursday—Maybe not Thursday. There was the book club and...other things going on. Today was too busy to stock yesterday's shipment."

"Can you get your records together? Copies of order forms and so forth?"

She jumped up.

He reached out and pulled her back down. "Not this minute."

"Oh, what are they going to think when I order more and haven't filled any prescriptions? It sometimes takes a week to get morphine delivered. There's the DEA paperwork and—"

"Lia, it's okay. Relax. We'll get to the bottom of this."

"Cal! Nobody's broken in! No alarm in the middle of the night! No mess back there! No broken window!"

"But your door has been open during business hours."

"This counter is *never* left unattended."

"Who has access behind it?"

"Dot. Isabel on Mondays. Britte used to work, but not since school started. Addie was here Wednesday. Anne helps on Fridays. Chelsea, sometimes on Saturdays. Chloe has been helping more, but not with the drugs. She wouldn't know anything."

"Does she come in with friends?"

"They're eight and nine years old! And when we're not here in the store, I keep the door between it and the back room locked. Always."

"With the key in the desk drawer beside it."

"Right."

"Which would be easy for anyone to find. Does Chloe know where you keep it?"

"Yes. Oh, no!" She slumped. "Chelsea baby-sat Thursday night. But she wouldn't, would she?"

"Chelsea's a good kid. Kind of artsy, like her mom. Some of her friends are on the fringe, but... Ask Chloe if Chelsea had any friends over that night. Who else has a key to the place?"

"Just Dot. She's here full time and is the only one who really works with me on the prescriptions. Oh, Cal, I can't blame this on Dot or Chelsea or any of my friends!"

"Don't worry about conclusions yet. What else has been going on? Any unusual prescription requests?"

"No."

"We could check prints, but there would be everybody's around the store, and it's doubtful we could match any without fingerprinting half the town. We'd have to shut you down—"

"Oh, please don't shut me down. I don't know how I'm going to make ends meet as it is!"

"All right. I'm going to take a quick look around the back room, and then I'll file a report. Lia, I don't want to frighten you, but if someone did waltz in here and swipe the drugs without being detected, they may try again."

Her eyes widened.

He stood and squeezed her shoulder. "Just be on the lookout. You know I'm close by."

She leaned her head against his arm. "Cal, why is it I need a cop so often in Valley Oaks?"

Saturday morning Cal stepped inside the Valley Oaks Pharmacy, the tinkling sound of the bell above the front door announcing his arrival. All heads turned toward him.

From the rear counter, Lia gave a little wave. He did a quick mental checkup. Last night when he— Whew! What had come over him? He'd never responded to a victim like that before. The china doll was a friend. She was also a great cook, enjoyable to be around, her demeanor and looks always keeping him just a little bit on edge...or off balance. That feeling that kept you...interested. Intriguing dark eyes, unlike any he'd encountered. Sweet bow tie of a mouth. Long, long hair, but not a color that attracted him in *that* way. She didn't attract him in *that* way...except last night...for a brief moment... And now? He stood still and listened. His heart beat normally. Good. He was back in the saddle.

Beside Lia now, Dot frowned. In the center aisle, Mr. and Mrs. Jennings called out a greeting. To the right, Chelsea Chandler and Chloe looked up from behind the cash register.

Cal shut the door and ducked down the left aisle. Where was the toothpaste? He felt Dot's eyes on him. Nuts, he'd have to send Tammy more flowers just for doing his job.

"Cal," Chelsea sang out across the store, "need some help?"

"Uh, no," he called back. "Thanks."

He hated shopping. He especially hated shopping for personal hygiene products—and Lia's store was all personal hygiene—where the entire town of Valley Oaks would know what brand of toothpaste he used in his bathroom.

He rotated his shoulders, shaking off the discomfort. It was prudent that he visit the scene of the crime, even if it meant revealing the contents of his bathroom.

He thought of Chelsea. He liked the kid...in recent years anyway, once she got into high school and behaved more like a regular person. To Cal, anyone younger than 15 was a foreigner to the human race.

Chelsea resembled her mother, almost a 60s-style hippie. Plain, broad but not unattractive faces, no makeup. They had long, wavy dark blonde hair worn often in braids. He glanced across the tops of the shelving units. Actually, her hair was orange today. Must be the Halloween season.

She was an artist, like her mom, and wore strange, flowing outfits. Some of the art students were troublemakers. He picked them up regularly for underage drinking. Never Chelsea, though. She seemed to prefer church activities. He hoped she wasn't mixed up with the underside, but he'd have to ask around.

Cal found the toothpaste. It didn't seem like much to spend. It didn't add much support for a local business. He clenched his jaw and studied the dental floss selection.

What was it Lia had said last night about making ends meet? That hadn't sounded promising.

He strolled around the corner. There were greeting cards. Shoot, it wouldn't hurt to send his mom a card.

He noted four people hanging around the pharmacy counter, talking with each other and Dot as she made change for Hattie Miers. Lia intently studied the computer screen. The phone rang near her. She flinched, but didn't reach for it. It rang again before she answered it. After a moment, her body visibly relaxed, and she pulled a pen from behind her ear.

The store was small. It wouldn't be possible for someone to open the half door in the center of the pharmacy counter, go up one step and back to the drugs without rubbing shoulders with someone else.

He chose the first flowery card that said "Thinking of You" on its cover. Down the center aisle he spotted stationery. He could use a pen. At the end of that aisle he saw Brady's books. Brady always gave him a copy. But if he bought one, it would support Brady *and* Lia. Instead of sending his copy to his mom, he could buy one for her. Stick the card in it. There were large padded envelopes located with the pens.

Chloe appeared before him, holding out a bright yellow plastic basket.

He blinked.

"For your stuff."

"Oh." He dumped his purchases in it, accepted the handle, then turned down the last aisle, pretending he didn't feel as if he were carrying a purse.

Candy bars. Hmm...

He eventually made his way to the front register. Chloe took care of ringing things up while Chelsea bagged them and chatted. "Did you see the fall wreaths? They're on sale. One of those would look great on your front door."

"Wreath? No thanks."

She nudged Chloe and rolled her eyes. "Bachelor."

"So how's junior year going?" he asked.

"Great. My favorite class is woodworking."

"No kidding. Bet you're the only girl in there."

She laughed. "Yeah, actually that part's kind of fun, too."

"Staying out of trouble?"

"Of course. My mother would kill me otherwise." It was her standard response, spoken in her customary open way. "How about yourself?"

"Just looking for it." He paused, counting his money out for Chloe. "Know of any?"

"The usual, Cal. And you know as much as I do."

"Sometimes." He knew who drank. Which parents didn't stop the parties. He knew who smoked and what they smoked. He had a lead on the current LSD supplier. He knew who was on probation, who was doing community service. But he didn't know— "Morphine, Chelsea."

She stared at him. "Don't doctors use that stuff?"

"A high is a high."

She shook her head. "*My* friends swear grass and beer is all they do. They know I'd kill them otherwise."

"I'm not talking about your friends."

She met his gaze. "I haven't heard."

"Keep your ear to the ground? This one involves theft and innocent people. Okay?"

She handed him his plastic shopping bag, concern erasing her smile. "Okay."

The bell dinged again as he left. He felt ten pairs of eyes boring into his back. It reminded him to stop by the florist two doors down the street.

Cal drove into the vet's parking lot. He parked his truck beside Gina's car.

At the florist's, he had gone a little hog wild. Bev was one intense saleswoman. It was fall, mums were on sale. He'd walked out with a mum for Tammy, of course. One for Lia, who definitely needed cheering up, but he'd probably keep it himself because he didn't want it to look as though he was treating her any differently. Trouble was, he couldn't figure out if he would have given her a mum before last night... One for Isabel, because she really was a great neighbor and her yard was full of flowers. And one for Gina.

Another bell jangled above a door. It was almost noon, closing time, and the waiting room was empty. He sat, feeling downright un-coplike holding the potted plant on his lap.

A few minutes later a collie appeared, followed by Dick Mackenzie and his kids, then Gina. After exchanging greetings, the family and dog left.

Gina turned to him. "Cal. Hi."

He held out the plant. "You have to stick it in the ground. And then you have to stick around to see it come up next year."

She blinked rapidly and bit her lip.

"Sorry."

She took the plant. "It's not your fault."

"Well, I thought I'd put in my two cents."

She pulled a tissue from her white lab coat. "All right."

"He made a stupid mistake, but it's the worst he's done in 33 years. And it was out of character. The second dumbest thing he's ever done was not telling you. He would never hurt you."

"I know."

"So you'll stay?"

"If I don't, will he stalk me?"

"No!"

"He did it once, Cal! In a sense, at any rate."

He felt his face flush, but the confusion in her eyes froze the shout of protest on his tongue.

"He deeded his property to me! He gave up his most cherished possession. If I hadn't moved to Valley Oaks, he would have followed me, leaving all his friends and family and moving halfway across the country just to be near me."

Their eyes locked. The aftermath of her words melted something in Cal, and he sensed his cop glare soften. "Gina." He paused, grasping for words to define his emotions. "Brady is like Jesus to me. Not that he's perfect, but most of the time I can count on him being in tune with what's *right*. There is only one reason he would give up his most cherished possession. It's the same reason God gave up His most cherished possession."

She swallowed. "Love."

"Not just any love. It's called *agape*. He did it because he thought it was best for you. You needed to take your job in Seattle. Yes, it gave him the vote on the zoning board to help preserve the neighboring property as open space, but he would have paid you rent for the rest of his life. He wanted you to have the freedom to choose where you lived, what you wanted to do, whether or not it included him. If it included him, nothing would tie him down back here."

"He was going to follow me."

"He was going to *visit*. He never would have moved until you invited him. Nicole was toxic to him. Somewhere along the way in that relationship he took his eyes off God. He calls it his time in the desert. He went from being friendly and outgoing to majoring on being so caught up with her demands, he couldn't see straight. He worked triple time to please her with money. He lost all common sense when she left because she never told him why. He took off after her because he needed an explanation."

She stared at him, uncertainty still written in her creased forehead.

"Brady never stalked Nicole. After he got to California, it took him a while to track down where she was living. She traveled for her job; she didn't have an office. He never called her. He went to her apartment *one* time and simply asked her why. She said she didn't love him anymore. He told me that it was in that moment that he saw how blind he had been. Unfortunately, before it sank in, the boyfriend came to the door. Brady realized that they'd been living together for a while and..." Cal shrugged. "He slugged the guy. Your classic knight-in-shining-armor reaction. He got on a plane that night and came home."

"But he was arrested."

Cal hesitated. It was a black memory. He had to think it through, get to the end of it, to the fact that it had been the catalyst prompting Cal himself to put his faith in Christ. "I took the call from the Los Angeles police, then I went out to the house and arrested him." He briefly closed his eyes.

"How awful!"

"You're telling me. Anyway, we were just taking his prints when Nicole's pitiful excuse for a conscience kicked in. She called and they worked it out. She dropped the charges, kept the ten-thou..." He stopped.

"Ten thousand? Ten thousand dollars?"

"Ugly ring. Bottom line, Gina, he loves you. I've never seen him so happy or clearheaded. He's a better person with you. He wants what's best for you and, if that means moving halfway across the country, so be it."

She exhaled. "Cal, I do love him. That hasn't changed. I just need to process the whole thing. Maybe we moved too quickly." She eyed the diamond on her left hand.

Cal noticed it wasn't quite as big as he remembered Nicole's, but then Gina the practical vet and natural beauty would not have wanted or needed it so. "Okay. I'm sorry for intruding—"

"You're no intrusion. You're a part of Brady's life. An integral part." She stood on her toes and kissed his cheek. "Part of the equation to life with Brady here. If I left..." Tears ran down her cheeks. She wiped at them and sniffled. "So," her voice rose, forcing a perky note, "assuming this hurdle gets jumped, we should have dinner with you and Tammy."

"Yeah. Well, take care. And call me if you want to know about any other stupid things he's done, like how he blew the game against Orion."

She smiled. "Okay. Thanks, Cal."

Outside in the crisp football-season air, he felt sad. Tammy refused to have dinner with Brady and Gina. Brady had supposedly snubbed her at one time. Now that he thought about it, it wasn't right that he wasn't allowed to be with his best friend and his best friend's fiancée. Talk about losing all common sense because of a woman! It wasn't right that he felt guilty accepting a pie from Lia. Especially banana cream.

Something was going to have to give here.

Twenty-Three

From her front window, Isabel watched Tony stride up to her house, hurrying through the breezy afternoon turned too cold for early October.

Her throat caught. He wore that soft crew neck blue sweater beneath a black sport jacket. It would hurt to look at his eyes because they would glisten brilliantly like a hot summer Mexican sky...and she would remember again.

Blue jeans made him appear younger than his 32 years. You'd think after 32 years he would have grown kinder.

Isabel considered not opening the door. It was late Saturday afternoon, time for the movie date they had planned earlier in the week. Since talking with Cal Thursday night, she had been praying for this confrontation. No, she hadn't prayed Thursday night. She had been too angry then. Friday she told Celeste—the most trustworthy woman on the face of the earth—all the details Tony knew about Brady. And then she started praying.

Celeste had called her five times since, advising her not to lambast him. "We need you to persuade him," she said. "Coerce him, but *gently*. Ask him to please exclude from his story the part about Brady's incident in California." She argued that Tony needed their prayers and forgiveness.

As far as Isabel was concerned, Gina and Brady could forgive him if they wanted to. She figured her role was to set him straight. It wasn't *her* life he was into destroying.

No...he'd already done that.

The doorbell rang.

203

Her face felt warm. This wasn't a good sign.

She leaned her forehead against the door. *Father, I'm losing it. I know I'm despicable, but he's off the charts. He doesn't deserve—*

There was a loud knock.

Isabel yanked open the door and hollered, "Tony Ward, how *could* you?"

At least he didn't smile. Holding open the exterior aluminum door, he lowered the hand raised to knock again. "May I come in? It's freezing out here."

She stepped aside.

"Thanks." He eyed her warily, opened his mouth as if to say something, and then closed it.

"How could you?" she asked again, quietly this time.

"I take it this has something to do with Brady's skeleton?"

"For starters."

He lifted his arms and then dropped them at his sides in a helpless gesture. He walked over to the couch and plopped onto it. "Izzy. It's my job."

"Don't give me that line! You don't drive a wedge between two people just to feel a sick satisfaction that you've somehow avenged your sister's death. That is *not* your job! That's twisted and mean and underhanded."

"My job is twisted and mean and underhanded, and it gave me no satisfaction whatsoever to hurt two of the kindest, most refreshing, most delightful people I've ever met."

The tirade she'd phrased and rephrased for almost 48 hours crumpled like a pinpricked balloon. "Why did you do it, then?"

"Come, sit down."

She shook her head.

"Brady Olafsson is too good to be true. Readers wouldn't believe a word I wrote about him."

"That's your excuse? So you won't look foolish?"

"No. I wanted to make him human. I mean, I asked, but you couldn't even tell me something like he's got an enormous ego or hoards his money or kicks his dog. That's not *real*, Iz. Brady's more believable, more approachable, if some dent in the armor shows up."

"You just sacrificed two people, not to mention all their friends you'll hurt—"

"By being authentic? Come off it, Izzy. Brady knows he's a public figure, open to scrutiny. He doesn't really care what people think of him—"

"Except for Gina!"

"Except for Gina. If they can't weather this storm, they weren't meant to be. He'll thank me for forcing the issue."

"Talk about ego."

He leaned forward and propped his elbows on his knees. With a start she noticed he needed a shave. Tony never needed a shave.

Lacing his fingers together, he stared down at the carpet. "You're right, Iz." His voice was barely above a whisper. "The real reason is that I want revenge. I want to punish every Christian who ever influenced someone through music, books, or art. I want them to suffer for their proselytizing."

"And you don't proselytize in your own way, you reporters? The whole point in your writing is to change readers' beliefs about something. You plant doubt about someone's integrity. You slant a story so people will be afraid to buy a certain product. Or that they'll support or not support a certain company. You make or break movies, books, plays, and political candidates all the time."

Head still bent, he didn't respond.

She realized this wasn't the point. "Oh, Tony. Your sister gave up drugs! Nobody made her go to Colombia. I don't know. Maybe she did have a crush on a band member, but from what you've told me, I know she fell in love with Jesus. And she wanted to love her enemies, like He said. It's a radical teaching. She thought going would make a difference."

Still no response.

Isabel knelt and touched his arm. "I am so sorry that she died. There's no human explanation why."

When he looked up at her, she saw unshed tears in his narrowed eyes. "Oh, there's an explanation. It's because she fell for a bunch of nonsense."

"You're right. That is the human explanation. But from a supernatural standpoint, there's something else going on here that we can't understand. Tony, life doesn't end when this body dies. And while our hearts are breaking, Joanna's alive and well, in the presence of Jesus Christ, and she understands why it happened."

Tony closed his eyes and pinched the bridge of his nose. "You sound like Brady's book."

"Really?"

"Haven't you read them?"

"*I* have. Have *you*?"

"Started the first one this week."

"And?"

He shrugged a shoulder and gave her a small smile. "Now there's a guy too good to be true."

"But He's God!"

"But...it's fiction and unbelievable and yet supposedly true. I was hoping we could talk about it over dinner."

Still on her knees, Isabel wrapped him in her arms. As if struck by lightning, she propelled herself backwards and landed on the floor with a loud thump. "Ouch!" She crinkled her nose. "Sorry. I forgot we're not hugging."

He didn't laugh, only gazed at her as if in amazement. "How do you do that? Hug me as if I'm not the pariah you know I am?"

She started to nonchalantly lift a shoulder when it flashed through her mind that she did not hug him of her own accord. It was Jesus in her hugging him...forgiving him. "It's called forgiveness."

"I think I could use some more of it." He stood and held out his hand to her. "And I promise it's got nothing to do with kissing."

"Well, if you promise." She let him pull her to her feet and take her into his arms. As she slipped her arms around him and heard his heart beat in the ear she pressed against him, she began to pray in earnest for his soul.

A mental fog settled in early Sunday morning. Isabel awoke startled, a subconscious thought bursting into the conscious: She was in love with Tony Ward.

No, she loved Tony.

More precisely, she had never stopped loving him.

Which was why she hated him.

That was when the fog crept in.

Last evening with him felt like a distant memory. Instead of a movie and pizza, they had driven into Rockville and eaten at a homey Mexican restaurant where they sat for almost three hours before the conversation flagged.

Tony pondered minute details of Brady's book. The fictional account of someone meeting Jesus—in this case a sister of Peter's and a blind man—was the catalyst for debate. It was exhilarating and exhausting, satisfying and disconcerting. Tony argued and he belittled. Isabel defended and challenged and finally ended with a question, "Yes, but what if it's all true?"

Not replying, he stared at her, those deep-set blue eyes intensely somber, threatening to unravel her.

Thankfully, the conversation didn't turn personal as it had earlier in her house. Yet they lingered, as if not wanting to part, at last concluding that they could still catch a late showing of the movie. The remainder of the evening was casual. As lifelong friends might do, they laughed, shoulders brushing, heads bent together, fingers touching in the popcorn bag. She dabbed butter from his chin. He grasped her hand, pulling her at a run through the cold night air to his car. At her front door they shared a brief hug.

"Tony, do you have to use it?" The unsettling question of his story and Brady had remained just below the surface all evening.

"I don't know." He hugged her again, her neck in the crook of his arm as he kissed the top of her head. "I'm writing tomorrow, all day, just me and my laptop in my little Valley Oaks furnished apartment. Then I'm heading home. Mind if I stop by your girls' meeting on my way out of town?"

"More research?"

"Mmm..."

"Truth."

"Probably, but I really want to say goodbye."

"Gina will be there."

His breath frosted the air. "Well...good. That's good. If she'll listen, I can tell her goodbye, too. And she can tell me good riddance."

Isabel giggled into his shoulder. "You can stop by for a *minute*. The girls will enjoy ogling the city slicker."

"You're sure?"

Isabel kicked off the covers now. No, she wasn't sure, but when his arms were around her she would agree to just about anything.

Still? After all these years?

She made a strangled noise of frustration and padded down the hall. Her usual Sunday routine was out of the question. First off, she'd better give Gina a heads-up call. Then she would go into East Rockville, sit in a pew between her *mamá* and *papá* at the church she had grown up in, hear the word of God in her native language, and try to put some order to the disarray that had become her life.

Twenty-Four

While shaving Sunday morning, Cal considered the advantages of a goatee. Tammy had nixed the idea of growing one. He hadn't even bothered to mention that as fall turned to winter, his goatee sprouted into a full-fledged beard. It was his annual custom, now past due to begin.

He arrived at church with 30 seconds to spare and hurried up a side aisle as the organist played the opening bars of a song. He slipped midway into a pew, grabbing a hymnal from its bracket. Beside him, a black-haired woman turned and smiled. It was Lia...with short hair!

She grinned, pointed at her head, and nodded.

He blinked. "What'd you do?"

She only sang, holding up her hymnal to show him the page number.

Turning his attention to the music, he gave her sidelong glances. By some standards her hair wouldn't be considered short, but compared to yesterday's ponytail swishing to her waist, this was short. Parted on the left, it hung thick and straight to just beneath her chin, a shiny swoop of jet black that set off her dark eyes and accented her creamy skin. Except for subtle eyeliner and glossy lipstick, she wore no makeup. Not that the smooth porcelain needed it. Not that Tammy's pretty face needed it either, but that didn't stop her from caking it on.

The music came to an end. As they sat, Lia palmed the bottom edge of her hair, patting it, and whispered, "So what do you think?"

Cal wasn't good at faking compliments. Her long hair had been the most appealing thing about her. One of the most, anyway. Involuntarily, he winced.

She laughed quietly and leaned toward him, stretching to whisper in his ear, "It's good to have an honest friend."

Cal was like the gum he chewed. Lia couldn't unstick the thought of him. This had been going on for a while, not just since Friday night when they nearly kissed, but especially so since Friday night. Whatever that had been!

Turning toward him now, she squinted against the sunlight as they walked toward her car. "I've moved the back room key from the desk drawer and hidden it in the laundry detergent. I usually use the one I keep on this ring with all my other keys."

"And where do you keep that ring?"

"With me. When the store's open, it's in a drawer behind the counter. If I'm home, it's usually in my handbag, upstairs."

"Will you tell Chloe where you hid the key?"

"Cal, she lives there with me. In an emergency, she may need to use it."

"Kids talk."

"She won't if I tell her not to."

"You give her an awful lot of responsibility for a— How old is she?"

"Nine. Nine year olds are capable of extraordinary responsibility. She's better than I am on the cash register."

He grunted a monosyllabic reply. "Did she tell you if Chelsea had friends over Thursday night while she was baby-sitting?"

"I asked. She said no one came. They did art projects all evening." She didn't mention that Chloe had already been in bed a while when she arrived home from the book club. In her opinion, casting shadows of doubt over Chelsea wasn't necessary. Lia opened her trunk, removed a large manila envelope, and handed it to him. "Here are the copies of invoices and everything." Closing the lid, she scanned the parking lot, watching for Chloe.

"Thanks. Try not to worry."

"Are you kidding? I feel like I need an armed guard just to walk upstairs to the apartment!"

He squeezed her elbow. "Hey, I'll figure it out." It was his larger-than-life cop tone. "And remember Philippians 4:6 and 7. Be anxious for nothing, Miss Impressively Independent."

It worked. A small smile tugged at the corner of her mouth. "Thanks."

"You're welcome. Have you talked with Chloe's dad again?"

"Unfortunately, yes." She pressed her lips together and then exhaled loudly. "Scratch the unfortunately. Why, yes," she attempted a cheery lilt, "I have talked with him and the conversation went rather well. I'm letting her visit him next weekend."

He gave her a thumbs-up sign. "Way to go."

"I sure hope so. Will you stop staring at my hair?"

"Oh, uh, sorry. It just takes some getting used to."

"Well, get used to it when I can't see you. You're giving me a complex."

He crossed his arms and made an exaggerated show of studying her from every angle. "Why did you do it?"

"Why not?"

"It looked great the way it was."

She rolled her eyes. "Now you tell me."

"Never thought about it."

"Typical male. Don't know what you want until it's long gone."

"Typical female, always changing to keep up with the latest fashion." Something flickered in his eyes.

Unintentionally, the bantering had turned flirtatious. The scales they had kept so delicately balanced tipped, and the momentum pushed her comeback off the tip of her tongue. "Accuse me of paying attention to fashion, will you? No way now am I telling you why I did it, Deputy Huntington."

"Have it your way. We're not supposed to be friends anyway, right?" The early spring green of his eyes reflected the noon sunshine, his cheeks folding like an accordion behind his big grin.

She looked away, speechless at the surprising jab of hurt. *Well, you asked for it,* she chided herself, *playing with fire. And yes, you did tell him you shouldn't be friends...for Tammy's sake.*

He cleared his throat. "Here comes Chloe. Well, thanks for the papers. I'll study them and hopefully come up with a simple explanation for the missing drugs."

She nodded and gave him a tight smile. "Bye."

"See you." He threw her one last puzzled look and left.

Lia watched him stride away, his broad teddy bear shoulders draped in a white shirt with thin, subtle green stripes, its long sleeves rolled up his forearms. His thick, bristly, light brown hair was cut neatly across the back of his square neck.

Strike two. Their easygoing relationship had just turned serious.

Strike one had been his tendency to avoid Chloe. Fear of little kids. Lia had seen it often enough.

Not that she was pitching to him in the first place, but she should pray for a strike three. She was enjoying his company way too much and even missing him. Actually wondering what that kiss would have felt like. Ridiculous! After all these years of guarding her time and her heart, of protecting her space with Chloe, she wasn't going to throw it away and lose herself to a man as her sister had done...just because a pair of green eyes danced in the noon sunlight, warming her like the first hints of spring.

Come to think of it, there already was a strike three. Tammy. He was crazy about—if not wholeheartedly devoted to—a beautiful woman.

Good. No reason for Lia to complicate her own life by encouraging his friendship...or whatever the correct term was. *May he buy his toothpaste elsewhere!*

~

Cal made one last sweeping glance over the thinning crowd outside the church. No Brady. No Gina. No Isabel. No Tony, who had become a regular in recent weeks.

He made a beeline for Celeste. Unlike the pastor himself, Peter's wife would get straight to the heart of the matter. And she wouldn't invite him yet again to the men's weekly Bible study/prayer breakfast.

"Celeste. Morning."

"Hi, Cal." She smiled and waved goodbye to the last departing parishioner.

"Any idea where Brady and Gina are?"

"Afraid not. They talked with us briefly on Friday. Peter suggested they get away to some quiet place and be alone, but you know it's harvest season. Brady's in the fields."

Cal knew. Brady would have shown up in boots, jeans, jacket, and cap, harried from taking precious minutes away from his combine. They were probably working 12-hour days. There would be no time for a getaway soon. Brady loved farming and he loved the farm. He was part owner. It was his responsibility. Even the writing would be put on hold until a rainy day. But could he put Gina on hold and survive?

"Don't look so worried, Cal. Pray for them."

"How were they?"

"Cautious. Gina held his hand the whole time. He looked more distraught than she did. I'm certain they're determined to get over this bump in the road."

"Celeste, the eternal optimist."

"Never." She laughed, her freckled nose all scrunched up. "They just need some healing time."

"Okay. Thanks."

"I saw you with Lia."

He clenched his jaw. *Valley Oaks women and their preoccupation with observing every single conversation. They really should be deputized—*

"What did you think of her haircut?"

"It's, um, different."

"Cal, that's not the point! She donated her hair to be made into wigs for cancer patients. Isn't that wonderful?"

"Hmm. I didn't know you could do that."

"Yes. Did you sign the petition yet?"

"What petition?"

"Cal, you really should get out more. Some HMO is going to cut out independent pharmacies like hers. Without their support, she'll go out of business. We can't lose her!"

Lia needed money? What was it she had said? *Oh, please don't shut me down. I don't know how I'm going to make ends meet as it is!*

An ominous scenario began to form in his mind. He fought the urge to suppress it. After all, such thoughts were part of his job.

Twenty-Five

Isabel attended her parents' church with them but begged off dinner at home. It wasn't an afternoon for the happy chaos of sharing a meal with at least half of her six siblings and their families. She headed instead to the river.

It was a beautiful fall day, full of cool air and warm sunshine. Glorious reds, yellows, and oranges painted the hilly landscape of trees. The river, about half a mile wide, sparkled a silvery gray. She left her car in a lot and found a vacant bench near the riverbank, away from the walkway jammed with a steady stream of joggers, bicyclists, and strollers.

Church had filled her with a delicious sense of peace, and she intended to savor it, wringing every last drop into her frantic heart.

Her *abuela*, her mother's mother, dominated Isabel's thoughts. Listening to the church service in Spanish always brought her to mind. She had been the happiest, most contented, most devout woman in the world.

Isabel brushed away silent tears. Her *abuela* had been gone just over two months now. Oh, how she missed her! How she needed to talk with her! What insight would she wisely reveal?

She thought back to college days, to that spring vacation she spent in Mexico with Tony.

It had been a whirlwind trip. Of course, Puerto Vallarta had been their destination, not the hot dusty remote area of Leon. But Isabel had declared she would not set foot in Mexico without visiting her *abuela*. Tony promised he'd go with her. After three sun-and-tequila-soaked beach days, they rented a car and drove seven or eight hours inland.

The middle child of seven, Isabel had discovered at an early age the solution to her attention cravings: It was in Mexico on her *abuela*'s lap. Her grandmother never traveled to the States. By the time Isabel was 12, she was traveling alone or with some relative to visit her, choosing outdoor plumbing and hauling water over the conveniences of home for months at a time. Every penny she earned or was given went towards a ticket of some kind, be it plane, bus, or train.

It wasn't that her *abuela* was a pushover. Her thick dark hair grew silver-streaked, and she always wore it in a long braid down her back. She was short and strong as an ox. Widowed at an early age, she raised eight children on her own. Though kind and generous to a fault, she reprimanded Isabel two minutes after meeting Tony.

Shorter even than Isabel, she reached up and gently took hold of her chin, gazing into her eyes, boring into the depths of her soul. She spoke in Spanish because she did not know English. "Are you married?"

"No."

"Then you are sinning." There was steel in her *abuela*'s voice.

"*Mamá!*" She tried the most respectful address.

The woman shook her head vigorously. "You think I can't see? Does your mother know you're sleeping with him?"

Tony understood enough Spanish. He slipped back outside.

Isabel knew declaring innocence was pointless. Instead, she challenged, "How do you know?"

Her *abuela*'s eyes filled as she caressed Isabel's cheek. "It shows, Isabel. Your mother hasn't noticed?"

"No. I don't know. She hasn't spoken of it. Stop trying to make me feel guilty!"

"The Holy Spirit does that. You know the Word of God. I taught it to you."

"But in the States, it's different. Everyone—"

"Shush. You know better. Do you love him?"

She nodded.

"Will he marry you?"

The subject hadn't come up. She shrugged.

"Foolish girl..."

Still, her *abuela* welcomed them into her home. She fed them, laughed with them, teased Tony, planted Scripture in their minds, and assumed rightly that they would go with her to church. Isabel spent two nights snuggled beside her grandmother while Tony slept in an abandoned camper at the neighbor's.

How did she do it? Unconditional love poured from the woman, but Isabel knew she had broken her *abuela*'s heart.

A few months later, when classes ended, Isabel returned to Mexico alone. Tony was long gone, and her life had fallen apart.

Foolish, foolish girl.

Isabel sat long at the river, remembering her grandmother. Since childhood, Isabel had known where to run for the unconditional love that carried her safely along life's journey. There was a void now. And then Tony had come, reminding her of the guilt, reminding her that there was no longer anywhere to run.

Her grandmother's words came to her. "It's not me, Isabel."

How had she explained it?

"It's God who forgives, God who loves. Just be still and let Him do that."

Be still? Isabel hadn't been still for years. Life was full...of good things...work, friends, choir, family. Always Christian music playing at home and in her car. Most weeks she was only home long enough to read a chapter from the Bible and sleep. There was no *stilling* time.

"I'm sorry, Father."

A dull rushing noise filled her head. A deep sorrow took hold, as if she were physically seized by giant pincers. Her body literally ached. Instant tears burned her eyes, a voiceless cry scraped her throat raw.

She knew that she was—at last—being still, and that He was listening.

Twenty-Six

Isabel walked through the dimly lit church foyer in Valley Oaks. It was Sunday evening, and she had arrived early for her Bible study with the high school girls. The place was empty except for a few other groups scattered about the building. Adult groups were meeting in homes.

She felt as if she floated. At the river that afternoon, the ache had eventually melted away, leaving in its wake an indescribable quiet. She was forgiven. She was loved. Nothing else mattered.

"Isabel!"

She turned and saw Gina approaching. "Gina! Didn't you get my message about Tony being here?"

"Yes."

"And you still came?" They hugged each other tightly.

"Isabel, Tony was only the messenger." She smiled that dazzling smile of hers. Casually dressed in blue jeans and a white cotton sweater with her brown hair pulled back in a ponytail, she was incredibly attractive. The girls were going to love personally meeting Brady Olafsson's fiancée.

Fiancée? Isabel grasped her left hand and looked at it. The diamond caught the dim light. She breathed a loud sigh of relief. "Are you okay?"

"Well, I know he's not a stalker, but I keep waiting for him to get possessive with me. I mean, I don't expect him to, because he never has. Yet..." She shrugged. "It's a trust issue. I need some time to process things."

Isabel gave her another hug. "In the meantime, I imagine you've got him wrapped around your little finger."

Gina laughed. "If I truly wanted the moon, I think he'd get it for me!"

Tony followed Isabel's directions and went down the steps to the church basement. The musical sound of feminine giggles led him from there.

He went to a set of open double doors at the end of a hallway. Inside a large room lit by lamps, about a dozen teenage girls sprawled on couches, chairs, and the carpet, Izzy and Gina among them. Bookshelves and posters lined the walls. The scent of chocolate drifted into the hall.

Izzy waved and came over to him, her petite figure making her appear as youthful as the girls. "Hi."

"Hi. Looks like a fun group."

"Come on in."

He caught Gina's eye as she made her way over to them. "Mind if I talk to Gina first out here?"

She winked at him and went back into the room.

"Gina."

"Hi, Tony."

"I'm sorry." He decided against using his line that he was just doing his job. It wasn't exactly the truth in this case. "I don't know what else to say."

She studied his face for a moment. "That about covers it. On Tuesday, it would not have covered it, but tonight…I forgive you."

"Thank you. Are you—" He stopped from asking if they were going to make it. That was brazenly personal; his trademark, yes, but not for tonight. "I hope everything works out for you."

"Thank you." She paused. "Um...if I were you, I'd be very careful. You know Brady is into breaking noses."

"I'm on my way back to Chicago this very moment."

"Maybe you'd better stay there a while." Her face lit up then in what Brady called her "Miss America" smile.

He shook her proffered hand. *One classy lady.*

"Coming in?" she asked as Izzy joined them.

"I don't know—"

Izzy grabbed his arm. "Yes, you're coming in. But the conversations do not leave this room." She closed in on him, her nose nearly touching his. "Got that, Mr. Big Shot Reporter?"

"Got it."

He found an armchair outside the loop of girls, near the door. As usual, his natural curiosity quelled any discomfort. Well, that plus Izzy and Gina and their... Their what? Acceptance? He might as well admit it. Their words and behavior encompassed much more than acceptance. Such a vague, generic term. It was forgiveness, nothing less.

He listened attentively. The girls, still munching brownies, quieted down. Someone said a short prayer. Izzy introduced him as Mr. Big Shot Reporter "who is not taking notes!"

He held out his empty hands.

"Ladies, pretend he's not here."

Gina spoke next. She was there as a guest to talk about her career as a veterinarian.

Tony marveled at the dynamics. There was nothing like a roomful of females. The topic digressed, as he knew it would. It went from Gina's love of animals and early start as a wildlife park employee to what it was like living in California to how she met Brady Olafsson.

"Oh, he was such a pain in the neck. He thought I was a California snob. And I was." She laughed with the girls.

"And I thought he was an arrogant, goofy—he kept telling me these ridiculous jokes—guy from a town I couldn't find on most maps. Now here I am, living in that town, *engaged* to him."

The discussion flowed freely, the girls eager for more details about the elusive author. Tony missed how the group segued into premarital relations, but there it was. Captivated, he wished he could meld into the upholstery and remain unnoticed. But nobody glanced back at him. Izzy didn't look over. It seemed they'd forgotten he was there. Or didn't care. He stayed put.

Izzy interrupted when Gina turned pink. "Girls, this is getting a little personal for a stranger to the group."

Gina replied, "I don't mind. Really. I want to say this for your benefit. Brady and I are waiting. I know that sounds wild in this day and age, but we believe it's for our best that God wants us to. It's not something we're going to regret. I'm not saying it's easy. I've suggested on more than one occasion that we run over to the courthouse, get that marriage license, and grab Pastor Peter. Other times—" She fanned herself and laughed. "Whew. Maybe this is getting a bit too personal."

The girls laughed.

"No." Gina held up a hand. "It's good that you hear this. We'll be holding hands or kissing—yes, we do kiss—and literally jump apart. One of us says, 'I can't handle this right now.' We go to opposite ends of the room. We play Scrabble. We go for a walk. We hang out a lot with other people."

Tony wouldn't have believed it coming from someone else. But he had seen these two people up close. They were strong enough and Brady was zany enough to behave in such an unnatural manner.

Izzy had the floor now. "Girls, I want to talk about the other side of the coin. What happens when you don't wait?"

It was what they had talked about the night she cried so hard, full of guilt for their past relationship. Curious how calm she was now, her voice low and even, her eye contact taking in every face turned her way. Except for his.

"As we always remind each other, our times here are private. They are not a source for gossip. If, however, you need to share my story with someone, maybe a boyfriend, you have my permission. Okay?"

There were nods around the room.

"I was in college, mixed up, and yet so in love with life. I knew I could do it my own way. I thought I had met my future husband. We didn't wait...and I got pregnant."

The group drew in a collective breath. Tony mouthed a silent, "Whoa." This was news to him. He wondered when it happened. Before they met or later?

"It ended in a miscarriage when I was about three months along. The whole scene disrupted my life. I never went back to school. That guy is not my husband today." She paused, again making eye contact with the girls one by one. "I lost a baby, I never got a college degree, and I cheated any man I might marry." Her tone grew passionate. "Ladies, I cheated on Jesus, too. I disobeyed Him. There's this chunk of guilt that still weighs on me because nothing can take away the fact of what I did. I know He has forgiven me, but in all these years I haven't yet been able to let it go completely. I am *still* learning what that means. It doesn't go away overnight. When I was your age, this was not the journey I planned on taking."

For a few moments, there was complete silence. Then one of the girls raised her hand. "Can I talk about what I did?" she whispered.

Tony slipped through the door. Now it was getting too personal. He didn't want to be there when they remembered he was listening.

He hurried down the hall.

Well, that explained why Izzy was hiding out in Valley Oaks. It probably also explained why such a good-looking chick had no suitors. Poor kid, never graduating. And dragging around all that guilt about boyfriends and getting pregnant wasn't healthy. He wondered again: What good is faith?

⁓

As the girls filtered out the door, Isabel struggled with a barrage of emotions. She had just publicly, diligently pointed out in minute detail her ugly past, the things she hadn't shared with her closest friends in Valley Oaks.

She felt exhilarated and drained. She felt exposed and yet wrapped in the mantle of God's love like never before. And now she felt doubtful. Had it been a wise choice?

Although her times with the girls were pretty free-floating, their discussions revolved around a Bible study booklet. The personal experiences Isabel shared usually concerned life in the present. She had never plunged to such depths of her past. She had never planned to do so. These girls were so impressionable. Would it be further gossip for the Valley Oak's gristmill? Would it be condoning harmful youthful behavior because in the end God made it all right? In spite of her honesty, they could have no clue as to the price she paid. Teens were incapable of comprehending future consequences.

Tonight had not been on the agenda. How they went from Gina's experience as a veterinarian to Isabel's college years, she had no idea.

A few of the girls displayed no reaction...a few gave her extra-tight hugs...a few avoided eye contact...and Tony disappeared at some point along the way. What had *he* thought?

While sharing her story, she had forgotten he was there. It was as if time and space faded from view as she focused on those precious young faces. She was aware only of her passionate longing for them to understand her stumbling, so that they might not do the same.

Gina turned to her now as the last girl left, her face beaming. "Oh, Isabel! I had no idea!"

"That I was pregnant? I hadn't told—"

"No! No! I had no idea that women could *connect* like that. That we could talk so freely about real life and mistakes and forgiveness. That we could—Oh, I don't know! It was as if we walked alongside those girls on their journey and said, 'I've been here; learn from my experience.' Isabel, we really could have made a big difference in one of their lives! But it wasn't us. Jesus was so palpable I could have *touched* Him. I think I heard Him *breathing* beside me!"

Isabel stared at her. She had forgotten how young Gina's faith was. Tonight had been a wild ride even for Isabel, and for her such sweet times of sharing were a commonplace occurrence. No wonder a new believer like Gina was ecstatic. A nonbeliever would have been skeptical and—Walked out the door. Like Tony. Why did she even imagine he would have waited around?

Gina gave Isabel a fierce hug, laughter and words still bubbling forth. "I can't wait to tell Brady! He'll be asleep already, but I've got to wake him up. This won't keep. Do you need help here?"

"No, you go ahead, Gina. Thank you so much for coming. You sparked it all."

"I did?"

"Are you kidding? You and Brady are like this ultimate romantic couple." She grinned. "The girls didn't want to hear from a single, 'hasn't had a good date in ages' girl like me!"

Gina hugged her again. "Thank you! Okay, bye!" She hurried through the doorway.

Isabel glanced around the room. Just a couple of napkins to throw away. A cup. An empty brownie pan to take home.

"Isabel!" Gina's voice carried into the room a beat before she appeared, breathless and red-faced. "Do you know what I just realized?"

"What?"

"You didn't go around telling the world your story until it was time when someone could benefit from it, like these girls tonight. That fact doesn't make you any less trustworthy of a person. Does that make sense?"

Isabel tilted her head, unsure.

"It's like Brady. He couldn't or didn't want to tell his story until now. For whatever reason. And that's all right. And it should be all right with me even though I thought he should have told me. Yes?"

Brady had his reasons, Isabel had her reasons, God had His reasons. Her throat tightened. Lips pressed together, she smiled and gave her friend a thumbs-up sign.

Gina gave one back, grinned, and rushed off.

Isabel sank onto a couch and wept.

Twenty-Seven

The teapot slipped from Lia's hands and clattered into the sink.

Her mother put an arm around her shoulder. "Dear, let me fix the tea. Go sit down."

"Thanks, Mom." Lia unclenched her fists and joined her dad at the table.

It was Thursday afternoon. Chloe was due home from school shortly. Her parents had taken time off from their jobs to drive from Chicago and pick up their granddaughter.

Susie Neuman was the daughter of immigrant parents with a trace of a Chinese accent coloring her words. She was a student when she met Jack at Northwestern, her tall, handsome economics professor. They were the greatest parents anyone could ask for, which was one of the reasons Lia had moved away from them. They had raised her to be independent, to dream big dreams. Independent dreamers didn't live next door to the folks, even if they did borrow money from them.

Lia's dad patted her hand. "Don't worry, honey. It'll work out."

"Which part?"

He smiled and removed his horn-rimmed glasses, diminishing the professorial image. He was tall and gangly with still-thick, longish silver hair. "Chloe, Nelson, your business, the mysterious theft, the subtle prejudice here. All of it."

She had to smile at his certainty. "One way or the other, you mean."

"Of course. You wouldn't want it any way other than God's way. Success or failure."

"Did I make a major mistake by coming here? You have money wrapped up in this, too."

Her mom kissed the top of her head, placed two cups of tea on the table, and settled her petite frame into a chair. Her short black hair emphasized the roundness of her face, her dark eyes brimmed over with love for her now only child. "You gave up your dream to be a doctor. But the part about living in a small town not too far from the city was still alive. A place where you could get to know people and serve them." She smiled. "Valley Oaks and the pharmacy are just that. We all agreed it appeared to be a good environment for Chloe. Give it time. Maybe you'll even meet your pediatrician here and give me more grandchildren!"

Lia couldn't help but smile back at her. *All this melodrama and Mom brings that up!*

"Lia," her dad added, putting down his coffee mug, "we also all agreed the business details fell into place. Our money is your money. We trust in you and what you're all about."

Their support was as reliable as the daily sunrise. "But it seems I've bitten off more than I can chew."

He grinned. "That's never stopped you before."

Her mother placed a graceful hand on her arm, smoothing the lab coat's long sleeve. "With God's help it has never stopped you before."

Lia nodded. "All right. It's what I needed to hear. Of course. Now, about Nelson."

An almost undetectable glance passed between her parents. Lia knew they were here only because they agreed with her decision to allow Chloe to visit with her biological father. But the hurt was never far from the surface. The man had killed their other daughter.

"You're sure, Mom? Dad?"

Her mother nodded, reaching for her dad's hand as she said, "Nelson told you just as he told us: He has changed. He's rebuilding his marriage, his family wants to meet Chloe, he's attending church. For Chloe's sake, we should give him the benefit of the doubt. She needs to know him."

Lia listened to the phrases that echoed those of Celeste and Isabel. She worried, though, because Nelson knew the buzz words that would resonate with them: church, change, family. He could use those words to manipulate them, to get what he wanted. But why would he even want to bother with his illegitimate daughter at this stage? Unless he truly had changed. Unless God truly had answered the prayers of her parents and their church.

Her mother wasn't finished. "I think we're called to give him the opportunity to change. Your dad agrees."

He nodded.

Lia sighed, still struggling with the decision. "And you promise you won't let him talk you into letting her spend the nights with his family? That's asking too much of Chloe." *And me.*

Her dad crossed his arms, her mother lowered her eyelids. No, of course they wouldn't. They loved Chloe as much as she did, and the schedule was set. Nelson would take her for Friday evening dinner and then a visit to the zoo on Saturday. No more.

"Maybe you'll visit the zoo this weekend? You haven't been there for a while, have you?"

Her dad narrowed his eyes slightly. Lia knew he was trying to hide the twinkle. He'd probably considered the very same thing.

She stood, teacup in hand. "All right. I'd better get back downstairs." She had left Dot in charge of the pharmacy counter, knowing she would call if things got too busy. The remainder of the store was in Anne's capable hands.

Her mother smiled. "We'll wait here for Chloe."

Her dad put on his glasses and held the newspaper up in front of his face.

"Your dad doesn't want to get in Dot's way."

Lia grinned all the way down the staircase.

⌒

A short time later, quick goodbyes were said on the sidewalk in front of the shop, squeezed between the filling of prescriptions. Lia kept telling herself it was better this way. If they lingered, she could very well lose control and change her mind. Extra-tight hugs were shared all around.

Anne and her daughter Mandy stood with her, waving until the Neuman car could no longer be seen across the town square. Mandy went to Anne's car parked nearby on the street.

"Be right there, punkin," Anne called. "Lia," she said in her matter-of-fact tone, "you're coming to dinner tonight."

"Celeste already invited me."

"Are you going?"

"No. I'd rather curl up with a good book. You know, I never have enough time to read..." Her voice trailed off.

"And cry yourself to sleep."

She met Anne's penetrating gaze. "So?"

"So, nothing." Anne hugged her. "Call me or just come over if you change your mind and want company. We'll be home all evening."

Lia waved as her friend drove off, blinking back the tears, fighting down the nausea, wishing she hadn't let Chloe out of her sight.

~

The night was long. Lia curled up all right, but it was in the dark without a book and nearer a fetal position than a cozy one. Things only got worse when little Soot leaped onto her bed and nudged herself under her hand. She must have been lonely in Chloe's room.

Lia cried her eyes out and finally began to name her concerns out loud to Jesus, wanting desperately to feel His arms around her.

"Please, don't let him drink. He promised not to. Please, don't let his children be mean to her. Please, let the zoo outing be fun tomorrow. Please, if his wife is there—Oh, Lord, how can she forgive him? Does she know You? Or is she just so out of touch..."

It struck her then. That's what she should be praying for: his entire family. What a dysfunctional mess they must be! And she'd sent Chloe right smack into the middle it!

She moaned through the scenarios which that thought created, until at last even she tired of her complaints. Sitting up, she began to focus on praying for the Greene family.

After a time she felt calmed and reassured. God was with Chloe, and He loved her better than she could.

Before snuggling down under the covers, Lia went to the kitchen for a glass of water. Even with the blinds closed, the street lights lit her way, shining brightly through the windows that faced Walnut. At the sink she peeked through the lace curtain. A squad car was parked just across the alley, in the small lot behind the grocery store, facing her back door. A shadowy figure sat behind the wheel. A rather large shadowy figure.

Well, it wasn't the arms of Jesus around her...but it came pretty close.

Twenty-Eight

"Cal!" Tammy pouted.

He kept his poker face. No two ways about it, the woman knew how to whine, drawing his name out into two syllables. "Tam, it's business. I'll be right back. Don't pay the check." She had a thing about picking up the check, making a show of treating him. It had begun to feel belittling.

Tammy's blonde hair swung as she turned her head toward the window.

Cal slid from the booth and moved across the noisy, crowded main room of the Pizza Parlor. The building was turn of the century, an unlikely spot for pizza, but the Parlor had been serving the best homemade food in a 30-mile radius since he was a sixth grader. He grabbed a vacant chair and carried it to the booth where Isabel and Lia sat.

"Hey, ladies." He swung the chair around and straddled it. "Mind if I interrupt a minute?"

Lia glanced over. "Hi, Cal."

"Cal." Isabel shook her head. "You are such a romantic. In uniform, at the Parlor, on a Saturday night date. You can't top that."

"Mind your own business, Mendoza."

She rolled her eyes. "It's his cop tone."

He leaned toward Lia. "We're still looking over your papers. So far everything is in order, numbers and dates add up. I don't know what to say."

She pushed a fork through her salad. "Go back to your cop tone. Tell me you've got it all under control."

He heard the worry in her voice. "More phone calls?"

She looked up. "Occasional hang-ups."

"Nelson Greene?"

"I don't think so. We've talked a couple of times, and Chloe is with him now. I don't think he has a reason any longer to intimidate me."

"Maybe not."

"Nice goatee."

He stroked his chin, proud of his five-day effort. "Thanks."

Isabel added, "Fall must be here. So what do you think of Lia's hair?"

He exchanged a glance with Lia. They both chuckled self-consciously. He switched subjects. "How's business?"

"It's great, for the moment. I've got until the end of the month before the insurance company pulls out. In the meantime, Alec Sutton is working on things at Agstar. We hear he has some influence."

Isabel laughed. "Anne calls him a *semi*bigwig."

"And, of course," Lia continued, "I'm not the only one who needs their support. All the independent pharmacies in the other outlying towns need it, too. A lot of people are working on it. We'll see."

He asked, "Otherwise?"

"Otherwise, Cal," she said, her voice softly going up a notch, "I quit and spend the rest of my life paying off a business loan." Her forehead wrinkled.

Isabel poked his arm. "Hey, Huntington, we're having a night off here. Don't you ever take a night off?"

No, he didn't really. Tonight's standing dinner date was pizza wedged in before he left to take over Hawk's shift because Hawk was taking off early. When that shift ended, Cal's would just be starting. The dinner date also happened to include subtly interrogating a business owner who had the motive and the means to steal her own supply of morphine.

He stood. "Have a nice night, ladies."

Lia cut into her steaming manicotti. "It's a weird feeling. I don't know if I've been robbed or not. The evidence is there, but not the means."

Concern lined Isabel's face. "Do you want to stay with me? I have an extra bed."

"Thanks, but no. I refuse to let it disrupt my life. I've got to get over this Chloe-Nelson hurdle first. And you're helping with that by offering to hang out with me tonight. After Thursday and Friday nights, I've had my fill of self-pity."

"My pleasure. It's not like I had anything else going on."

"Tony's gone?"

"Indefinitely. Back to Chicago."

"I can't read you, *Izzy*. Are you happy or sad about that?"

"Hmm... content. Lia, um, I've never told my Valley Oaks friends about part of my past with Tony. We lived together for a few months before he graduated. Thank you for not looking disgusted or shocked."

Lia laughed. "We all do things we wish we hadn't."

"Did you?"

"Of course."

"Live with someone?"

"No, but I had my sister for a role model of what not to do, and I had my hands full caring for Chloe. Now what guy is interested in that? Anyway, Isabel, my life isn't over yet. We don't need to compare wrong choices."

"Sins."

"Right, sins."

"Okay. Tony graduated and left without even saying see ya, it's been fun, goodbye, keep in touch. *Nada*." She paused, glancing around the restaurant. "I...I spent that summer with my grandmother. The guilt became unbearable, but I didn't take her advice to just confess it and ask forgiveness until years later. All I wanted was Tony. I thought he loved me and would come for me. But he didn't. You know what I finally had to face? I've been holding that against him." She held out her arms, palms up. "After all these years, I just forgave him last week. Isn't that wild? And besides that, I admitted feeling that there was no way God could really forgive me for my relationship with Tony. Well, that's just denying everything about my faith in Jesus. So I had a long talk with Him and...and I finally let it sink into my heart."

Lia smiled. "It's a lifelong process, huh?"

"Amen." The worry left Isabel's eyes. "I even hated the name Izzy because it was his special name for me. It seems so childish now. Anyway, this all came together Sunday afternoon. That night he came by my girls' group at church. I wanted him to stay so we could talk afterwards. I hadn't planned on discussing premarital sex with the girls, but it came up, and I felt it was time to share my story."

"Kids need to hear real stories like that."

"I hope so. I didn't use his name and say outright that the guy sitting by the door was the one I lived with. He left before I noticed, so we didn't talk. I...I don't know how he reacted. Another non-goodbye. He probably thinks I'm a real fruitcake. Maybe I won't hear from him again, but that's fine." She sounded as if she meant it, but chewed her bottom lip.

"And yet...you care about him."

"Oh, Lia, once I got over fussing about him being in town, it was like we picked up where we left off seven years ago.

Like a hand in a glove." She waved her fork, dismissing the thought. "History. Now, what's this between you and Cal?"

The water halfway down Lia's throat changed direction. She choked. No words came out. She clamped a napkin to her mouth and coughed.

Isabel burst into hysterical laughter and collapsed against the back of the booth, sliding down the seat.

Lia wiped her eyes. "Noth—"

"No way! You can't deny it now, girl!"

People in the booth across from theirs turned to watch them.

Isabel waved.

"Isabel!" Lia hissed.

"They can't hear us above the music and that group of kids behind you."

She frowned.

"Hey," Isabel leaned across the table. "He and Tammy are gone, and I told you, they're not engaged or all that devoted to each other. He's fair game."

"Does it show?"

She went into hysterics again.

Lia stared at the side wall.

"Lia, he can't take his eyes off you. I saw him when we sat down. He kept glancing this way, right at you. Then when he finally came over, you wouldn't look straight at him. My guess is it's mutual. What does he think about your hair?"

"He liked it long."

Isabel hooted, drawing more stares in their direction.

Lia thought of how he had touched her hair that night they stood between the shelves. He seemed fascinated with its length. The next afternoon she had it cut. "Isabel, I don't want to care for him that way. He's involved with Tammy. He doesn't like kids. I might have to leave town."

"Surmountable, in Christ. All of it."

She folded her arms. Why not say it out loud and stop denying what was happening? "We click. We're comfortable being quiet together. He appreciates my cooking. He's tender and so thoughtful. He sees a problem and fixes it. He likes his work. He doesn't talk too much, and he never complains. And…his…" She winced. "Biceps."

That sent Isabel into another giggling fit.

Maybe confession wasn't such a good idea.

Twenty-Nine

Standing behind Lia in the alley at the pharmacy's back door, Isabel shivered in her lightweight fleece jacket. "I dread the thought of winter. The only good thing about it is Christmas can't be far behind. Hey, Lia, let's unpack your Christmas order!"

Lia glanced over her shoulder as she turned the key. "On a Saturday night?"

"Sure. It's only nine o'clock. Besides, I can't wait to see your selection. With your taste in gifts, I figure I can do half my holiday shopping right here. If you get into toys, I could do all of it." She followed Lia inside. The desk lamp cast a dim glow about the small room.

"All those boxes came yesterday." She flipped on the overhead light and pointed toward a cluttered corner beside the basement door. "If we can at least organize some of it, then stocking the shelves won't take as long."

"We'll have to do that soon. You know how women like to Christmas shop early."

"That's good, since I need to sell it all as quickly as possible." She shrugged out of her coat.

"Lia, did you know the petition has over 300 names on it?"

"Really? I guess somebody in Valley Oaks does like me."

"It'll work out— What's wrong?"

Lia clutched her arm and stared beyond her shoulder with terror-stricken eyes.

Isabel turned around. "What?"

"That door's open!" she hissed.

A few feet behind her, the door leading into the shop was all but shut. A hairline of the night-light shone around its frame. Lia always kept that door locked! Isabel pushed her friend back toward the alley door.

Lia was rooted to the floor.

She shoved harder. "Go! Someone might be in there! Or upstairs!"

That got a reaction. Five seconds later they were banging shut Isabel's car doors and she had the engine running. She slammed the car into gear, and they flew out to Walnut where she braked a short distance across the street.

They craned their necks to look out the back window toward the alley, their breath coming in short bursts. "Lia, we should call Cal. The cops. We need a phone."

"My keys are back there in my coat pocket! The door's not locked. Maybe I didn't even shut it."

"Hon, I don't think that matters at this point. You're sure you locked the inside door tonight?"

"I never *not* lock it. Yes, I'm sure."

"Then we better get help." She pondered where to go. Except for two restaurants and the gas station, the town had folded up for the night. "You know, the whole world has cell phones except you and me. And I'm not using the pay phone in the grocery story parking lot. Let's go to my house."

Lia grabbed her arm. "What's that noise?"

She listened.

"It's the alarm! I didn't turn it off when we ran outside!"

"So the cops should be on their way?"

"Soon. Security calls me. If I don't answer, they call 911."

"All right. We'll wait." She cracked her window open. Cold air seeped in with the blare of the alarm. Nearby two renovated houses faced the street; one was an insurance office, the other a real estate company. Both closed, of course. "That's obnoxious. If you had neighbors, *they* would call the police."

"The video store is open! It's always so loud, though, they probably can't hear it. I doubt they'd even bother to call if they did. The kids who work in there are strange. Isabel, this is ridiculous sitting here. If somebody were inside, the alarm would have sent them running by now."

"But we haven't seen anyone."

"They could have run out the front or been long gone before we got here. I'm tired of being afraid in my own home. Between those stupid phone calls and Nelson disrupting my life, not to mention that insurance company mess, I've about had it." She opened her door.

"Lia! Wait! I'll drive back into the alley." Isabel's hand slipped off the gear shift. Adrenaline pumping, it took her long moments to maneuver the car in reverse. "I don't think you should go inside. Cal would say do *not* go inside."

"For goodness' sake, this is Valley Oaks. Someone is just trying to scare me, not hurt me. If they were going to hurt me, they would have done it before now." She climbed out.

Isabel followed more slowly. The alarm was deafening here. She hesitated. They really shouldn't go inside.

But Lia already had her hand on the doorknob.

When he heard the report, Cal was out on Coal Creek Road 20 miles southwest of Valley Oaks. Technically, the call wasn't his jurisdiction until his shift started at 11:00. Technically, Benny Richards could handle it. Technically, he should butt out. Technically, he should cruise west.

But it was Lia.

He switched on his lights and roared north.

Since a week ago Friday night, when he had come within a gnat's length of kissing her, Lia came to mind every time he picked up his tube of toothpaste, every time he drove near the town square, every time he walked out of the Community Center, every time he prayed—and he was getting into the habit of praying throughout the day. Often.

Technically, Eliana Neuman was invading his space.

Richards' cruiser blocked the alley. Cal parked on the side street, cut the engine with one foot out the door already, and then halted before bounding down the alley.

Was this getting personal?

Richards would look at the simple facts. A brick had been thrown through Lia's alley window. Morphine was missing from its place on the shelf. There had been no sign of forced entry. She could be responsible for those things and made up the story about the phone calls.

But he knew her, and intuition said she wasn't responsible.

Intuition or something else? The impenetrable dark eyes, the smooth skin, the sense of humor, the mouth that reminded him of a bow tie? The beautiful black hair she cut off the day after he touched it?

He slammed the car door shut and strode to the alley door. After a quick jab to the doorbell, he turned the knob. It wasn't locked. He went inside and spotted them through the open door leading into the store. Benny Richards stood against the wall, notepad in hand. Lia and Isabel sat in the wicker chairs, confusion on their faces and in their slouching shoulders. A quick scan of the pharmacy revealed nothing out of place.

Richards threw him a puzzled look. "Huntington, what are you doing here?" With graying hair and medium build, Benny still cut a daunting figure in his uniform as he loomed over the women.

Resisting the urge to pull Richards down with him, Cal sat. He also used his size to intimidate. This wasn't the time. "Just following up. Lia, how are you doing?"

A shadow of relief crossed her face but was quickly replaced by a baffled frown. "The Oxy-Contin is gone."

It was listed with the Schedule II narcotics, those the Drug Enforcement Administration tracked. A powerful pain reliever, on the street it was known as oxys. It was a step up from the morphine and codeine that anyone could recognize. "Somebody knows what they're doing. What happened?"

Richards answered, "We've been through this, Cal."

"Humor me. I was here when she discovered the other missing drugs."

The cop rolled his eyes.

Lia glanced anxiously between the two of them until Cal leaned sideways, blocking her view of Benny. "Isabel and I..." She spoke quietly, not in her normal big-city friendly tone. "We came in about nine. That door was open a crack, and I know it had been locked." She stopped.

"What did you do next?"

Isabel groaned. "We got out of here, but then the alarm went off, and Lia marched right back inside."

He touched Lia's shoulder. "Lia Neuman, don't ever, *ever* do anything like that again. Do you understand?"

In the norm, she would have argued with him, pointing out that the alarm would have scared off anyone inside, that she was going to get to the bottom of this nonsense. She only blinked unfocused eyes, as if her mind were miles away.

He lightly squeezed her shoulder and dropped his arm. "What did you find inside?"

Isabel answered, "Everything looked normal until Lia checked the narcotic drug shelf."

"Lia, how certain are you that you locked the door?"

The black eyes seemed to recognize him again. "I never *don't* lock it. Today I locked it about two o'clock when I went up to the apartment."

"Any visitors after that?"

"No. I only used the alley door. I went out and did errands in Rockville, came home, and then Isabel picked me up at seven."

Richards shifted his stance. "And Isabel didn't come inside at that time?"

"No, I told you I met her outside in the alley."

"So she didn't see that this door was shut or locked?"

Lia shook her head.

Cal knew what Richards insinuated. No one to vouch for Lia's story. He didn't want to go there. "What about the key you moved from the desk? Is it still hidden?"

"I don't know. I didn't look."

He stood. "Let's go."

She seemed uncertain, and then she slowly made her way into the back room. He followed, concerned about her hesitant movements. There had been no smiles, no jokes, no outburst of frustration, no sign of determination to fight this. Fear was closing in, obscuring her typical spunky demeanor.

Alongside the washer and dryer, a shelf held laundry items. She lifted off a box of powdered detergent. It wobbled in her hands.

Cal reached over, took it from her, and set it on the dryer.

She dug inside of it, spilling granules of soap powder every which way.

"Here, let me." He pulled her shaky hand from the box and plunged in his own. "Maybe there's a print on it. How far down did you bury it?"

"Not far. What's he getting at? Deputy Richards." Fear was evident in her strained whisper.

He ignored the question. "Maybe we should dump this—"

"I know what he's getting at."

"Don't worry about it, Lia. It's just procedure." His fingers landed on the key. "Here. Obviously no one found it." He lifted it carefully by its edges, pulled a tiny plastic bag from his pocket and slipped in the key. "Sorry about the mess." He held the box at the edge of the dryer and brushed the spilled granules into it.

"So." Richards had entered the back room. "How'd they get in so smoothly without a key?"

"I figure the first time they found the key in the desk drawer right next to the door. Obvious place to keep it. They borrowed that for a while and had a copy made. Actually, this looks like a copy. Lia, where's the original?"

"On my key ring. No, that's not right. There was only one original. The one in the desk."

"The one that should have been in the detergent box here?"

She nodded, her forehead scrunched in a frown.

Proved his point. "Benny, did you check upstairs yet?" He scanned the small back room and spotted the basement door. The basement. Why hadn't he thought of that before? There must be an outside window to it. "Or the basement?"

"Not yet. Terry's on his way to check for prints."

"Okay. We'll go upstairs, see if anything was disturbed there."

"Let's get a search warrant first."

"Richards, she's not hiding anything." Behind him, he sensed Lia stiffen.

Benny's eyes narrowed. He paused before answering. "Let's just make sure we do this one by the book."

In the end they allowed Lia to gather a few personal belongings. She was going home with Isabel.

Cal hovered near the bathroom door while Lia rummaged through the medicine cabinet. She stuffed things into a clear plastic baggie she had grabbed from the kitchen. Cal hoped that his presence would prevent Richards from digging through her overnight bag. The other deputy waited downstairs with Isabel while Terry dusted for prints.

"Here, Cal." She held the baggie up now in front of his face. Inside was a toothbrush holder, toothpaste, a hairbrush, a bottle of facial lotion. "Satisfied?" She brushed past him. "Come on, let's go search my dresser drawers!"

At least her hints of anger were an improvement over despair. He stood a discreet distance from her open bedroom door as she reached into the closet.

"You'd better search this, too!" She pulled out a black duffel bag and flung it toward him.

He caught it. "Lia, I'm sorry. It's for your own protection."

She slid out a drawer. It crashed to the floor, silky contents spilling over the edges.

Cal entered the room and pulled her into his arms. "It's okay."

She cried softly against him.

"Shh." He touched her head, holding her tightly. "Lia, don't worry."

"Do you think I took the drugs?" Her upturned face was damp with tears.

The night vanished. For one eternal moment there was no time, no investigation, no past, no future, no one waiting downstairs. There was only Lia. He kissed the crease between her brows, he kissed the corners of her eyes, he kissed her dewy cheeks. And then he kissed her lips, and he wondered why he had waited so long. He only stopped because the cop niche in his mind signaled there was an urgent matter at hand.

They stared at one another.

She swallowed. "Calming the distressed victim, I take it?"

"Mmm, something like that." He smoothed her hair back from her face. "Please don't cut any more off?"

She pushed herself from him, gave him a half smile, and knelt beside the drawer.

"Need some help?"

She pulled out something yellow and flannel. "Will you grab Soot there? She'd better come with me."

He noticed the kitten slinking down the hallway and retrieved it.

"Cal, I want to be here when you search things."

"No, you don't. It would feel like a violation."

She crossed her arms and shuddered.

"Lia, I promise, I'll take care of your belongings."

"It's not just that. There's...something else."

There was a twisting in his stomach. "Something else?"

"They might plant evidence. They want me out of town."

Relief surged through him. She wasn't hiding anything. "Who does, Lia?"

"People like Benny Richards."

"No, no. Benny's a good guy. Hey, where's my Miss Impressively Independent?"

The tears spilled again. "Oh, Cal. Did you like her?"

"I liked her a lot."

"But you never kissed her."

He grinned. "Next time I see her I will."

Thirty

Unintentionally, Tony tuned out the young woman sitting across the table from him as she gave the waiter her dinner order. The downtown Chicago restaurant they sat in was the latest rage among those who were in the know. Tony deduced this not because he was in the know, but because the clientele was the under-30 glitz, the prices outrageous, the waitstaff informal and gauche, the atmosphere cacophonous. The only journalists in the place were himself and Brandy.

He reminded himself that yes, indeed, her name was Brandy. He should accept that as fact, given the dual byline coming out in the Sunday *Tribune*. They had just put to bed a collective piece about a complex murder investigation. Late tonight it would be in print: Anthony Ward and Brandy Kettelson. Why not Elderberry Kettelson? Or Cognac Kettelson? Or Scotch—

"Yo! Mister." The waiter waved a hand in front of Tony's face. "How about your order?"

"I'll have the same."

"Got it." The kid left.

Brandy giggled. "Something else we have in common. A passion for meat loaf and garlic mashed potatoes."

Yeech! That's what he ordered?

His mind wandered again as she chattered. She was cute, with long, natural blonde hair. Long legs, short skirt. Mediocre writing ability, but she interviewed like a banshee, which could be a plus under certain circumstances. She was

248

new and appreciated his tutoring her through this assignment. Dinner was her idea, her treat.

He stifled a yawn. The place made him feel old. No, not old, rather...bored.

What was Izzy doing now? Ten o'clock on a Saturday night? Reading alone...laughing with good friends...jotting down new ideas for interviews...joining her girls for a campout... She wouldn't be chattering at him, nudging his shin with the toe of her shoe, making silly innuendoes.

If Brandy only knew... He didn't get involved, not in one-night stands or short-term or long-term relationships. He had neither the time nor the mind-set. The last time he felt any interest had been three years ago. Or was it four? The wacky actress... What was her name?

A chunk of iceberg lettuce appeared before him.

Cold and tasteless. Kind of like his life. Kind of like the life of everyone he knew.

Except for Izzy. She was everything he wasn't. Warm, full of love, interesting and interested, giving, strong and secure in her faith, no masks, not claiming perfection. To her it seemed that every day was a new adventure, even at her little radio station in Valley Oaks. Maybe she was in hiding, but then, who wasn't?

Here he was, hiding from himself. His ugly, cold, tasteless self.

He wanted to see Izzy. Immediately. As in *yesterday*.

"Brandy." He carefully folded his napkin and laid it on the table. "Look, I'm really sorry, but I...I can't stay."

"What?"

He stood, pulled a fifty from his pocket and set it beside his napkin. "I—" There was no explanation that would make sense, not even to himself. "I just can't stay. Something has come up."

"Since when!"

"Here, you'll need cab fare, too." He dug for a twenty, laid it atop the fifty, knowing the total wouldn't cover two meat loaf dinners in that place, but it was all the cash he had.

"Tony! What kind of weirdo are you?" A familiar sullen expression crept across Brandy's features.

How was it that all of the under-30 females these days had lips that so easily, so often *pouted*?

Correction. Izzy was under 30 and hers didn't.

He hurried toward the exit.

The red dial in Isabel's spare bedroom clock radio glared in Lia's face. How could it only be 3:16?

What was Cal doing now? Removing the cushions from her couch? Emptying her refrigerator? Rummaging through the linens?

She rolled over onto her other side.

As long as it was Cal and not that macho cop Benny Richards... She trusted Cal. She had trusted Cal even before he kissed her.

The tickles swished again, the sensation of floating gossamer brushing her from head to toe.

Oh, Lord! What happened to the three strikes?

Evidently the feeling she had tried to ignore was mutual. But they *had* to ignore it. There was Chloe and the failing pharmacy and Tammy. And now Deputy Sheriff Richards insinuating that she had stolen the narcotics.

She flopped onto her back.

Cal's kisses had soothed her, calmed her, cleared her head so she could pack. Did he know they would? Or did he just want to kiss her? Well, obviously he wanted to kiss her, but surely he didn't go around kissing every damsel in distress.

No, it was just like Cal to accomplish two goals in one efficient motion.

She kicked off the covers. This "damsel in distress" role made her skin crawl.

When she and Cal had gone downstairs and she saw the other man dusting black powder on the latch of the half door between the counters, the room began to spin.

Isabel stood and took Soot from her. "Can we go now?"

Deputy Richards never took his eyes off Lia. "Miss Neuman, maybe you should take something to help you sleep. You've had a tough night here."

She shook her head and murmured that the OTC stuff made her sick.

He gestured toward the counter, toward her supply of prescription drugs. "I'm sure you know what would be helpful."

A surge of anger pumped adrenaline through her. He just assumed—!

Behind the policeman, Cal caught her eye and cocked his brow. She wasn't going to convince Richards tonight that she was innocent. There was no reason to try. They all knew that she wasn't allowed by law to prescribe for herself. She knew, and Cal knew intuitively, that she didn't. She had turned on her heel and walked out the door.

She looked at the clock again. Just 3:22.

Tomorrow would be a nightmare. Could she make it to church? Could she drive to pick up Chloe? Could she clean up the pharmacy in time to open on Monday? Would they even allow her to open?

She had to stop this train of thought. She flopped onto her side.

Better to think instead about Cal. Not of the three strikes against him, but rather of his strong arms around her.

Cal draped the yellow crime tape across Lia's back door. Dawn was still an hour away. Stars sprinkled the dark sky, and his breath steamed the cold air. He zipped his jacket more snugly and joined Benny beside his squad car parked in the alley.

"Cal, I agree the town won't want her shut down long, but I can't come in today. I promised the wife and kids we'd drive out to the pumpkin patch."

They still needed to search the store and the basement. The apartment search was finished and naturally had produced nothing incriminating. Cal had already made a mental checklist of the favors he'd call in to rush the lab work on the prints, but finding someone to help scour the pharmacy on a Sunday afternoon might be next to impossible. The staff had been short-handed lately. Benny had just put in a double shift.

"Don't worry, Benny. You need to be with your family. I'm off until Monday night. I'll put in some extra time, see if we can't hurry things along. Besides the fact that we didn't find anything upstairs, my hunch is Lia Neuman does not deal drugs except as a pharmacist."

"Yeah, I agree, but still, you never know. No forced entry. What are we supposed to think?" He punched Cal's arm and laughed. "Hey, if I didn't know you were dating Tammy Cassidy of all gals, I'd say you were a little sweet on this foreigner. You were up there alone with her for an awful long time. And I saw how you tried to keep things in order while tearing her place apart. Well, I'm out of here. See you."

"Yeah, see you."

Cal walked along the back of the store, around the corner, and down the long side of the building that bordered Walnut. Retracing his steps, he shone his flashlight at the base of the walls. Interesting. There was no basement window until he reached the video store's back door. He knelt on the rough alley surface and studied it closely. It appeared caked with dirt inside and out, as if it hadn't been touched in years.

He climbed into his own car and headed for the Gas Mart. During the two-minute drive, he stopped thinking. Inside the brightly lit gas station, he didn't think. He poured a cup of coffee, grabbed a fresh donut, and made small talk with the clerk and a semi driver. He was on cruise control.

Then he returned to his car and sat, sipping the hot, inky liquid the Gas Mart owners called coffee. Finally, he let the thoughts come.

The last few hours had been spent with Benny, sifting through every inch of Lia's apartment. They examined closets, clothes, dressers, her niece's room, kitchen cupboards and drawers, refrigerator, trash, and a box of mementos, the contents of which concerned her sister. Cal knew he had done a thorough, professional job. No one could accuse him of anything less. No one could accuse him of letting personal feelings get in the way. Only now did his stomach twist at the thought that they had somehow desecrated what should have been private.

He learned details that threatened to clog his brain. She kept coffee beans and flour in the freezer, ibuprofen in a cupboard above the fridge. She hid a fifty-dollar bill under the kitchen radio. He knew the brand of Lia's soap, shampoo, hand cream, and lipstick. Her one perfume bottle looked expensive, called Dolce Vita. Either it was brand new or she used it sparingly. He guessed the latter to be true. The sheets on her full-size bed were yellow flannel with a tiny flower print. Her nightstand held Christian books, nonfiction, of the type Brady passed on to him and Pastor Peter quoted from in his sermons. On the dresser was a framed photo of her family. She was young, probably a teenager. Her older sister resembled her, though she was thinner, her hair shades lighter than jet black, her mouth not a soft bow tie. Their mother was distinctively Chinese, pretty, with an expression of happiness that practically jumped out of the photo. Their dad towered over the women and appeared the standard gaunt image of an intellectual with his light hair that may have been pulled back into a ponytail.

Cal sipped the coffee.

If he were sweet on—He cringed, remembering the way Benny said "the foreigner." If he were sweet on Lia Neuman, then he had to excuse himself from this case.

But he wasn't sweet on her because he was more or less going with—whatever that meant this many years out of high school—Tammy. Everybody knew that.

Then why had he kissed Lia?

And why was he already looking forward to the next time he could kiss Lia?

This was crazy.

That was the word. He wasn't sweet on Lia. He was crazy about her, and he might as well admit it, but just not too loudly yet. He wanted to get to the bottom of the thefts, of the harassing phone calls. It had to be someone in Valley Oaks because the situation with Chloe's dad seemed to be sorting itself out, eliminating him as a suspect—

Chloe.

He'd forgotten about Chloe.

Thirty-One

Isabel prepared a whole pot of coffee. She expected Cal to drop in at any moment. His shift would be ending about now, and she doubted he'd go home without first checking in on Lia. She didn't think it was her imagination that something had connected between her friends. Connected nothing. Sizzled was a better description. Sparks fairly flew as Cal escorted her and Lia out of the pharmacy last night, carrying Lia's bag, the two of them lingering beside the car while Isabel got in and started it.

Lia still slept. No doubt she had lain awake for hours. Although she was strong in her faith and confident about herself and smart about business, last night harshly undercut all of that. The thought of some intruder sneaking into the store, which was also Lia's home, and taking prescription drugs chilled Isabel. On top of that, Benny Richards insinuated that Lia was responsible! To have Cal calmly explain that searching the apartment was necessary procedure didn't help one iota.

As if on cue she heard Cal's tapping on her porch door. She unlocked the kitchen door, walked through the adjoining screened room and unlocked the exterior door. As she suspected, he was still in uniform, the short brown leather jacket bulging with cop gear. Along the sides of his goatee, his face needed a shave.

He stepped through the door, worry etched into his wrinkled brow. "How's Lia?"

"Asleep. Want some coffee?" She led him into the kitchen. "Notice I had that outside door locked, just like you always harangue me to do?"

"Uh, now that you mention it, yeah. Good."

She poured a large mugful and handed it to him. "Last night scared me enough."

He sat at the table and stared at nothing in particular.

"Want some eggs? Cereal?"

Cal shook his head. "No, thanks." Now he eyed the mug in his hand as if unsure how it got there.

"So what happened last night?"

"We turned Lia's home upside down."

"And?"

"And nothing." His steely cop look closed in. "It's my job."

Isabel shivered in spite of the sweats she wore.

"Hi." Lia stood in the doorway, Isabel's white robe covering yellow pajamas. Her eyes were almost swollen shut, her hair disheveled.

Cal stood, took a step toward her, then hesitated. "Lia."

Isabel wished herself far away. "Hey, you two, pretend I'm not here. As a matter of fact, I'm not here."

Too late. Lia's form was buried in brown leather before Isabel could duck out.

Cal rested his chin on Lia's head. "Mendoza, forget you saw this, okay?"

They held each other tightly for a few moments and then sat side by side at the kitchen table, fingers intertwined on it. Their hostess had disappeared into another part of the small house.

Lia smiled. It was true. She hadn't imagined his feelings for her. "Isabel guessed already."

He squeezed her hand. "Lia, we can't have anyone else guessing. Do you understand? I should quit this case, but I want to get to the bottom of it. I'm afraid the investigation would just drag on and affect your business. I mean, it's not a problem as long as you're not a suspect."

"What exactly is not a problem?"

A grin slowly spread across his face, crinkling eyes that were incredibly green in the early morning light. "That I can't stop thinking about you."

"Oh."

"That kind of thing could cloud my ability to reason."

"I see." They stared quietly at each other. Lia cherished the moment, but knew they had to deal with other problems. "Am I a suspect?"

"Well, technically you're not cleared yet. We have to search the store, and even then, until we get proof you're not illegally selling drugs, somebody like Richards won't let it go." He grinned again. "I'd rather it be me than him watching you closely."

She did too. "So now what?"

"I need to file the report and then sleep. I'll take you home this afternoon and help you clean up. I'm sorry. I did the best I could to keep things in order."

She stretched up and kissed his rough cheek. "Can I open tomorrow?"

"No."

She blew out a breath. "Okay. I didn't think so. I was supposed to pick up Chloe today at my parents' home in Chicago, but she can stay an extra day. There's no school tomorrow. I'll go then."

"Leaving town is not a good idea."

"What?"

"Don't leave town."

"Cal, why don't you just arrest me?"

"Because my China Doll is not going to jail."

It cut through the frustration and exhaustion. She laughed.

"I'll take you to Chicago, hon."

"I can't ask you—"

"You didn't. I offered."

She didn't know what to say.

He shrugged a shoulder, a small smile lifting one side of his mouth.

The doorbell rang. From where they sat, the front door was visible across the living room.

Isabel called out, "I'll get it."

"Lia." Cal squeezed her hands again, his forehead creased. "We'll figure this out, and then there will be time to figure out...us. That is, if you think there's something to figure out?"

"About us? Oh, most definitely, Deputy."

As Isabel approached the front door, Cal let go of her hands and pushed himself to a standing position, kissing her temple on the way up.

Isabel opened the door. "What are *you* doing here?"

Tony stepped inside, wearing a grin, navy blazer, sweater, and slacks. "Picking you up for church. Hey, what's going on? You're in sweats. Cal's in uniform. And Lia's in pj's?! How come you three Christians aren't ready to go?"

Tony wanted to straighten his tie, but he wasn't wearing one. Instead he smoothed his navy blue blazer, threw back his shoulders, and surveyed the unoccupied room.

Reverend Peter Eaton's office overwhelmed him. Most of the four walls were covered in floor-to-ceiling shelves chock-full of books. The sanctuary's muted greens and oak accents carried over into here. Two overstuffed chairs and a coffee table filled one corner. Two padded, straight back chairs faced an enormous desk, upon which were the requisite family photos, pen holder, paper weight, and computer. His feet sank into plush carpet. The view through two narrow windows revealed shrubbery and a sliver of the Valley Café's back door across the street.

He was familiar with such bookshelves and desks and carpet. No, it wasn't that which overwhelmed him. It was something else, something intangible. The air was thick with it.

Tony had gone alone to church, his three new friends too discombobulated to join him. No wonder, after the night they'd been through. Izzy made him promise to tell the pastor's wife what had happened at the pharmacy.

Which was why he was standing here at this moment. When he found Celeste Eaton in the lobby after the service and explained the situation, her sparkling eyes and freckled, elfin face had gone lifeless. She had grasped his elbow, steered him down the hall, and ushered him into the office ten minutes ago, assuring him she would return soon with her husband. She wanted him to hear this.

He studied the book spines now, searching in vain for a familiar title. At the sound of knuckles rapping, he turned. The door opened and Reverend Eaton entered his office.

"Tony Ward. Nice to meet you again." The pastor shook his hand and pointed to an armchair. "Have a seat. Celeste has gotten waylaid." He settled into the other armchair.

Peter Eaton did not resemble Tony's image of a pastor. He wasn't sweet-faced, nor was he over 60. He wasn't even over

50. His unruly red hair, barrel chest, and craggy face suggested Ireland.

Tony met the pale blue eyes and said, "South-side Chicago. Your dad was a cop."

The man burst into deep, rich tones of laughter that must have carried throughout the building. He wiped at his eyes. "Bingo!" He leaned forward. "But 'twas me grandfather, on me wee mother's side, who was the cop."

Tony grinned.

"And you're a reporter," the brogue was gone, "for the *Tribune*."

"You had help, Reverend."

"Ah, I could have figured it out without my wife clueing me in. And we're Celeste and Peter, by the way. Sorry to keep you waiting. Please, tell me what happened."

Tony relayed the events of the night before as he knew them. There were drugs missing and the pharmacy wouldn't open Monday morning. It was a mystery how anyone had entered the store without being detected, which seemed to place Lia in a dubious position.

Elbow propped on the chair arm, Peter held his chin, his wide face creasing. His eyes focused some place Tony couldn't see. After long, silent moments, he put his arm down. "Thanks, Tony. We'll get started right away."

"Started?"

"On praying. We have a telephone prayer chain. Quite a few people will know by this afternoon. You didn't tell me anything classified, did you?"

"N-no."

"You look doubtful."

"Prayer? I mean, what's God got to do with this?"

"Lia needs His strength and comfort. Cal needs His wisdom. The perpetrators need His justice and forgiveness.

The town needs the pharmacy. And the drug addicts need healing."

That sense of being overwhelmed settled on him again, and he heard himself speaking unintentional words. "My sister was a drug addict. Becoming a Christian got her killed."

"Oh, Tony, I'm so sorry. What a dreadful heartbreak for you and your family." He paused and again his eyes momentarily focused elsewhere. "Please, tell me what happened."

"She followed a Christian rock band down to Colombia—"

"What was her name?"

"Joanna Ward."

"Joanna Ward was your sister?" His jaw dropped. "Martyred about two years ago with five other young people? Weckel, Ruud, Piccurelli, Miller, Helms...and Ward."

"You *know* about it?"

"Tony!" His brows shot up. "Everyone interested in Latin American missions knows about it! Men from the guerilla group responsible for their deaths have actually stopped working for the coca growers. They've relocated their families and are struggling, but they're Christians. They meet as a church. God answered your sister's prayers."

Tony felt as if a noose dropped down around his neck and twisted. "And that's why she died? So a bunch of illiterate natives can get together and sing on Sundays?"

Peter gazed at him.

"Look, I'm sorry if I'm being rude here, but that's hogwash." His breath came in short puffs.

"Tony, there's no way you can begin to comprehend unless you know Jesus."

"Well, what I know of Jesus—" Izzy burst onto his mental screen. Izzy's softness, vulnerability, laughter, forgiving attitude, arms wrapped around him... "What I know is insane."

"Or supernaturally real."

"I've taken up too much of your time." Tony stood. He really was suffocating now. His legs felt the lack of oxygen. It was as if thick tree trunks replaced them. He plodded to the door. "Excuse me. Please."

Thirty-Two

"Great chili, Izzy." Tony stacked the four bowls on Lia's kitchen table and carried them to the sink.

"Thanks." *So why did you hardly eat any?* She didn't budge from her chair at the table, wondering for the umpteenth time today where she stood with Tony, where she wanted to stand with him. Not sure how to get answers, she only discerned that it was not yet the time to voice her questions. Trouble was, it hadn't been the appropriate time all day and it was getting late. He was leaving tomorrow and couldn't easily return. His apartment lease expired in a few days.

Cal and Lia were in the living room behind her. After Tony returned from solo church attendance, the four of them had spent much of the afternoon and evening at Lia's apartment. She and Tony helped replace the things Cal and Benny's search had left in disarray. Although Cal had warned them, she hadn't been prepared for the mess they encountered. When they arrived and saw the contents of cupboards spread about the kitchen, Lia had gone strangely quiet while Isabel went ballistic. Cal unobtrusively touched the back of Lia's head and whispered in her ear.

Tony's demeanor didn't change at that point. He had been subdued when he came to her house after church, and for the most part he had remained subdued all day. But she wasn't about to ask him why. She knew why.

She figured he wanted to discuss her confession from last week's youth group meeting. But he would choose a private

263

time, not in the company of Lia and Cal. He probably didn't know what to make of her story. *Still, you'd think he could communicate something. A simple, "Can we talk later?" A wink and, "That was quite a revelation." A quick, "Sorry I haven't had a chance all week to call."*

She watched Tony rinse the dishes. She felt physically stretched to the limit, unable to offer any more assistance on any level. Lack of sleep, dinner preparations, cleaning Lia's apartment and then the store downstairs after Cal searched that area had all but drained her. On top of that, she didn't know what she wanted or expected from Tony. Her emotions jumped from ecstatic to apprehensive to angry. She sat quietly, reserving just enough energy to convince Lia that she was coming home with her.

"Izzy." Tony threw a dishtowel at her and winked. "How about some help? Leave the lovebirds alone."

She joined him at the sink. "What makes you think they're lovebirds?"

He stared at her from the corner of his eye. "Pretend you're Tammy and take a gander."

Isabel peeked over her shoulder as she dried a handful of spoons. The television was on now, newscasters' voices coming from it. Cal's arm was across the back of the couch. Lia's legs were tucked beneath her, and she leaned against him, her head resting on his chest. "She's a crime victim."

"Mm-hmm." He turned toward her, touching his forehead to hers, and whispered, "Tell me, if you were a crime victim, would he sit like that with you?"

Isabel winced.

He handed her a wet bowl. "I didn't think so. But I would." He plunged his hands back into the sudsy water.

"Oh, really?" She lowered her voice, "And would that make *us* lovebirds?"

"Good question. What do you think?"

"Hey, you're the one who started this!"

"Okay. Well, I think we'd be pretty close to it."

She rolled her eyes. "You mean, if I got robbed, you'd be my boyfriend?"

He grinned and playfully shoved his shoulder against hers. "That's nonsense. I think you're as exhausted as I feel. Can we go now? You can come back in the morning and finish these up."

"Tony, it's only four plates and that grilling pan." He had made his famous toasted-cheese-and-tomato sandwiches. "We'll take my chili pot home, though. I'll let it soak overnight."

"Hey, you two," Lia called out. "Stop doing the dishes. Go home."

Isabel shook her head. "Not without you, sister."

The lovebirds left their perch on the couch and walked across the room. Cal said, "I'm going to stay with her."

Isabel felt her eyebrows go up and her eyes widen. *Stay out of it, girl.*

Cal continued, "I want to get down to the basement and finish this search so Lia can open on Tuesday. But I don't want anyone to know I'm here." He threw Isabel a stern look.

She held her palms up in surrender. No way was she going to question his motives tonight.

Tony nodded. "You're going to bait the bad guys."

"I hope so. Tony, would you do me a favor and drive my truck home, go in the house, and turn on a light? Make it look like I'm there?"

"No problem, but size-wise, I can't pass for you."

"It's dark. If my suspicions are correct, they're not watching that closely. As long as my truck and Isabel's car are gone, that'll be enough for them to assume Lia's either alone or not here."

Isabel said, "But I thought they took all the drugs."

"No. I think you ladies interrupted them last night. If they knew about the Oxy-Contin, there are others in the same category they didn't grab. They'll be back soon."

"But why does Lia have to stay?"

"Nosy Mendozy."

"Cal!"

Tony nudged Isabel. "Someone is framing Lia. If she leaves with us and returns to find the drugs gone again, we're witnesses to her innocence. Wouldn't work."

Isabel was horrified. "Why would someone want to frame her?"

Lia answered, "They hate me because I'm different."

Cal shook his head. "No, if that were true, it would just be kids vandalizing the store or your car. It runs deeper. Someone wants you *discredited*."

Isabel sat in her dark kitchen, waiting for Tony to come to the back door with Cal's keys. After dropping them off with her, he was going to walk down the block to his apartment.

All this cloak-and-dagger stuff had frayed her nerves almost beyond endurance. She was the first to leave Lia's. Cal promised he'd watch her walk across the dark alley and get into her car, but the thought of other eyes noting her movements unsettled her. He had said that someone must have followed them last night to the Pizza Parlor and then signaled the thief when Lia and Isabel left the restaurant.

Driving quickly across town, she parked on her street and raced into her house, immediately shutting the door and locking it. She had never felt frightened before in Valley Oaks!

Tony was to have made his exit a few minutes after she did, wearing Cal's coat to add some bulk to his slender body. He needed to reattach the yellow crime tape across Lia's door, then drive the truck home. That left the parking lot and alley empty except for Lia's car.

Isabel berated herself. Lia should not have stayed there, even with Cal! It didn't matter what their silly theories were. She should be here, safe inside Isabel's home.

There was a knock on her porch door. Isabel went to let Tony inside. Silently they walked through the porch and into the kitchen. Only a dim light shone from the living room.

Tony set the keys on the counter beside the sink, brushing her shoulder. "Izzy, you're shaking. Are you okay?"

"I...I..." She gave up the attempt to say she was fine. She wasn't fine. "No."

He hugged her tightly for a long while.

It wasn't the comfort she wanted. His nearness only intensified the battle. She loved him, but not just in the way she had been trying to convince herself, as a friend. He was the music and the radiant sunlight she had stopped missing. Until now.

"Izzy." He spoke into her hair. "I have to go home tomorrow."

And when he left, the void would come, silent and grey.

"I don't know when I'll be back." He kissed her then, almost desperately, almost as if he too craved the fading music and light.

After a time he whispered, "My, my, Izzy Mendoza. I had no idea Christians kissed that way."

She pushed herself back, keeping him at arm's length, her breathing ragged. "Wrong thing to say, mister!"

"Hey, I'm only teasing."

"Well, stop with the Christian put-downs!" Her voice rose. "We're not some subhuman species to be mocked whenever you feel like it!"

"Oh, you're a different species, all right." His chuckle was derisive. He dropped his arms and stepped away from her. "Human, but definitely not of this world."

"You're right. You and I are from two different worlds, and we will never ever see eye to eye. We don't even have the first thing in common! I don't even know why you're here again!"

"How else am I supposed to process this information?"

"Like you always do! With your own sharp mind, with absolutely no hint of the hand of God working through it all."

"You knew? All along?"

"Of course I knew! Who else could be the father? There was never any other possibility."

"What? What are you talking about?"

"The baby! What else would I be talking about?"

"My sister!"

"What about your sister?"

"Eaton told me the people who killed her are Christians now, and instead of toting machine guns, they go to church. And that's supposed to make me happy!"

She let the surprising words register and then lowered her voice. "Oh, Tony. I didn't know."

Only the sound of their breathing broke the stillness. His eyes were hidden in the shadows, but she sensed their confusion.

"Izzy, what do you mean by who else could be the father?"

He hadn't caught on. All day long she had been misreading him. "Wh-what I told the girls last Sunday night. I thought you would figure out I was talking about you. I was pregnant when you graduated. I wasn't sure until—"

"I was going to be a *father* and you never told me? Well, that really takes the cake. And I thought you were the one honest friend I had."

As the door slammed behind him, Isabel flinched.

Thirty-Three

Cal leaned against the refrigerator, arms folded, watching her clean up. He avoided the kitchen window. "Lia, pretend I'm not here."

Fat chance of that, she thought, putting the last plate away in the cupboard. "Why don't you go on down to the basement and get started?"

"Because you're about two stages beyond exhaustion, but you think you have to stay up with me. I want to make sure you go to sleep."

Tears filled her eyes. His attention made her accept the truth of what he said. She needed sleep, but she was fighting it. "I'll just be a few minutes."

He bowed, holding a hand to his chest. "Thank you, Miss Impressively Independent."

Lia changed into jeans and a sweatshirt and washed her face. Too much had happened in four days. Chloe had survived the separation and time with Nelson. Lia hadn't heard details yet, but her niece's voice over the telephone was normal. Lia herself had survived the separation. She had survived another theft. She hoped to survive the role of sitting duck. What she feared she could not survive was Cal. He whittled diligently away at the independent defenses she had spent years putting into place. All he had to do was look at her now and she forgot someone was stealing narcotics from her. If asked, she wasn't sure she would know her name.

Maybe it was exhaustion. She gathered a sheet, pillow, and blankets and carried them to the living room where she found Cal dozing in the recliner.

His eyes opened when she walked past him. "Lia, I don't need that stuff. I'm working tonight."

"They're for me. I can't sleep in my own room."

"Why not?"

She turned her back and spread the bedding on the couch. "It seems too far away."

"Suit yourself." He climbed from the chair. "I'm going to turn off the lights like you normally do." He switched off the lamp next to the chair, went to the kitchen and flicked off the light, then headed down the hallway toward her bedroom.

Evidently he knew her routine. How many nights had he sat outside her windows? She yawned and crawled onto the couch, snuggling under the blankets, ridiculously complacent given the daunting events of recent days, from theft to Nelson to—*May as well admit it!* To feelings for Cal. *Feelings?* That was putting it mildly.

He returned, his path lit only by the street lights shining through the closed curtains, and knelt beside the couch. The scent of peppermint filled the small space between them. "Are you afraid?"

Only of falling for you... She reached for one of his hands and took it between hers.

"Lia, just say the word, and I'll stay right here until you go to sleep."

"It's not that. It's—" In the cozy shadows and the hush of their soft tones, in the comfort of the already familiar rough texture of his strong hand, she found her voice. "I've started dreaming again about...about wanting to share all the details of my day-to-day life with someone. I haven't allowed myself to dream that way for *years*. I never thought it would be possible to meet— Oh, for goodness' sake, I'm sorry. That was way too much information! I've probably scared you right out the door."

He hesitated and then cleared his throat. "Well, ten days ago, you'd probably be looking at my backside right about now. I wouldn't have had a clue as to what you're talking about because... Lia, I've never imagined such things. But now...now I know exactly what you're talking about."

A comfortable silence hung between them for a few moments, and then Cal stood. "Okay. So you're all right if I go downstairs?"

"As long as you don't leave, I'm fine. Are you all right?"

"Got my cell, flashlight, and cup of coffee. What else is there?"

"My prayers."

"I'm counting on those. I'll be here when you wake up. 'Night, China Doll."

"'Night, Teddy Bear." She gave his hand one last squeeze and let go.

He walked through the dim light into the kitchen area, stopping at the table to collect his things. He picked them up, then set them down, and strode back to the couch.

"There is one thing more." Again he knelt beside her.

Lia smiled. "I thought you said no more until we figure things out."

"I did. Dumb idea."

It was the best goodnight kiss she'd ever had.

Halfway down the steps to the back room, Cal halted and reminded himself that whistling and the pounding of feet were not the best of surveillance techniques. But he felt he would burst if he did not whistle and pound his feet. He wanted to dance the "If I Were a Rich Man" jig while singing at the top of his lungs.

Well, he'd just have to stuff it for now and not think about what happened to his heartbeat whenever Lia looked at him.

Cal breathed a prayer for God's guidance and then quietly descended, using only his flashlight to illuminate the way. He crossed the back room to the door tucked beneath the staircase. It led to the basement flight of steps. Again he noted that there was no lock on the door. He opened it and continued his descent.

Before dinner that evening he had made a quick run-through of the basement. Lia said she seldom went down there. The ceiling was low. Boxes stood about, abandoned by previous owners, filled with newspapers and junk that might be interesting to a Valley Oaks history buff. She planned to examine them some year when she had the time.

If she had ever taken note of the small door across from the steps, half hidden behind the furnace, she probably thought it led to an old root cellar. Cal suspected it led into another basement, the one beneath the video store.

His light landed on a small white box sitting atop a stack of large cardboard boxes. He read the label. *Oxy-Contin.* That hadn't been there earlier. How inane were these guys? Like Lia would stash something in plain sight!

He made his way across the square room. The building had been built in 1908 and now housed the pharmacy, video store, and florist. It had hosted a variety of businesses over the years and not necessarily three at a time. Walls had been added and torn down. It was more than likely that the basement had been a common area in the early days.

Shining his flashlight on the door now, he studied it closely. It was set in the concrete block wall just across from the bottom of the stairs, placing it under the back room.

Made of grey metal, it was narrower and shorter than an average door and nearly blended in with the wall. Its hinges were not visible from his side. He would have to push it open. Surrounding dirt and cobwebs appeared disturbed, but not enough to indicate that the door had been opened recently.

But of course it had been.

Hoping to preserve fingerprints, he covered the doorknob with a handkerchief and lightly touched it. It was locked. From another pocket he pulled a tool and went to work on the lock. Within moments he turned the knob and gently pushed the door open.

The other room was dark. Cal briefly considered calling Benny, before deciding to just take a quick look around. Maybe they were only leaving "evidence" in Lia's basement.

Ducking, he stepped through the doorway, sweeping the flashlight beam on the dark floor. There had been traffic—

A movement on his left registered—too late. A blinding pain split through his head, stunning him so that he scarcely felt the cold steel blade cutting into his side.

Lia awoke with a start. What was it?

She didn't move, listening intently and hearing only the apartment's night hums. She peered into the shadows until her eyes hurt. Nothing moved. The microwave oven's digital clock displayed 11:42. She hadn't been asleep long.

And then she caught the scent...a faint, acrid whiff.

In one motion, she threw off the covers and slipped her feet into loafers. She raced through the apartment and down the stairs. At the bottom she hit the light switch, illuminating the back room.

"Cal!"

She flew to him. He lay sprawled face down, across the threshold of the basement door. Smoke rolled out above him.

"Cal!"

Taking hold of the legs of his jeans, she pulled with all her strength. Below his feet the basement glowed as if the noonday sun shone in it.

"Oh!" She yanked his legs clear of the door and slammed it shut.

Phone! She needed a phone! Where was his cell? She had seen him stick it in his back pocket. It wasn't there!

Her eyes burned and she choked. They had to breathe! She jumped up and ran to fling open the alley door. The alarm screamed.

Was he breathing?

She grabbed towels from the dryer top, threw them in the sink and turned the faucet on full blast. "Cal! Cal! Talk to me!"

She pulled the wet towels from the sink, wrang them out, and held one to her face as she ran back across the room to his side. Smoke curled beneath the basement door.

What if the floor caved in?

Lia pulled him over to his side. "Oh, dear God!"

He was covered in blood...but at least she could see he was breathing.

She laid a damp towel across his nose and mouth, then pushed aside his sweatshirt, looking for a wound.

Blood ran from his left side. She pressed her towel against it, straining to hear sirens above the alarm, crying, wondering how she could drag him eight feet to the open door.

Would the firemen half a block away hear the alarm? Was anyone there? They were volunteers! Were they all sleeping at home?

She dashed to the desk, grabbed the phone, and dialed 911. "This is Lia at the Valley Oaks Pharmacy. There's a fire here!"

Not waiting for a reply, she dropped the receiver and plunged back to Cal's side. The linoleum beneath her shins felt hot. She heard crackling now, coming from the other side of the basement door.

There wasn't time!

A strength not her own propelled her arms to push him, then pull, rolling him onto his stomach...then onto his side...then onto his back...then onto his other side. He was losing more blood, but—

The basement door burst into flames.

Thirty-Four

In the ambulance, Lia clung to Cal's hand, washing it with her tears while the paramedic cared for him. She had no sense of time passing. When the sirens and the motion stopped, they pulled him out and whisked him away. She collapsed against someone, the sobs growing stronger.

They put her in an examination room, though she protested. "Just a quick check over," a nurse said. "Your voice is raspy, and you're covered in soot and blood."

Soot!

No, Soot was still at Isabel's. He was okay.

And Chloe was fine. She was with Mom and Dad...in Chicago.

And Cal. Cal was fine. He was breathing. He was fine. He was fine. Wasn't he? It was Cal's blood on her hands, on her sweatshirt, on her jeans...

Isabel and Anne appeared at her side, and in time they absorbed her trauma with their hugs, tears, and prayers. The blurring sensation eased. She spoke coherently to the doctor. No, she did not care for any relaxant. Her friends helped her into the clothes they had brought and helped her clean up.

They moved out to a waiting area, a brightly lit open space where people milled about. The horror was closing in again, pulling blinds on her peripheral vision, numbing all sensation to the here and now.

Anne nudged her onto a stiff chair, tucked a thin flannel blanket around her, then gently took hold of her chin. "Lia, you need a pill."

She shook her head and curled her legs up underneath herself. She had to stay alert for Cal.

Someone sat beside her. "Lia." It was Brady, his voice husky. He hugged her fiercely. "Thank you for saving his life."

When he let her go, Gina appeared and silently embraced her.

Pastor Peter came next. He knelt in front of her and grasped her hands, his warm face an instant comfort. "How's our heroine?"

Lia had no idea one person could shed so many tears in such a short amount of time.

Ted Rickman, manager of the grocery store, stood behind Peter. "Lia, I'm so sorry, but everything is going to be fine. I just talked with one of the firemen. It's not as bad as it could have been. There's smoke damage throughout, but the fire was contained in the basement and back room. Your inventory might not be in too bad of shape. The video store is intact. Your car is fine."

She could not comprehend if that was good news or bad news. She only wanted to know one thing, but no one would tell her. Maybe Peter would. She sought his face again. "How's Cal?"

"We don't know yet. He's still in surgery."

"But he was breathing!"

"Excuse me." It was Benny Richards.

Brady groaned. "Aww, Benny, can't this wait?"

"Sorry. I need to ask a couple questions."

Isabel moved from Lia's other side and Benny sat down. "Ms. Neuman, what happened?"

"There was a fire—"

"Start at the beginning. What was Cal doing at your place?"

Yes, Cal had been at her apartment. But what *was* he doing there? He was just...just *with* her. She was falling in love with him. And he cared for her. He truly did. He kissed her. He offered to take her to pick up Chloe tomorrow, but first he had to— "He wanted to finish the search."

"In the middle of the night?"

"He wanted to be there, in case they tried something again. He thought they might try something again. He went down to the basement; I fell asleep on the couch. I woke up and smelled smoke. I found him..." Fresh tears again.

"Where did you find him?"

"Lying in the back room. In the doorway, his legs kind of hanging down the basement stairs. He was bleeding. I..." She what? She remembered only screaming.

"You got him to the alley?"

"The firemen didn't come. There was smoke. There was no time..."

"He weighs over 200 pounds!"

Peter touched her arm. "Benny, Jesus and adrenaline work wonders."

In the dark alley she had cradled his head in her lap while pressing her hand against his side. "Why was he bleeding?"

Benny said, "You don't know?"

She shook her head.

Brady squeezed her arm. "Benny—"

"He was stabbed, Ms. Neuman."

Someone's arms came around her, muffling new sobs.

The nightmare dragged on for Lia. Anne massaged her shoulders. Isabel brought tea. The group grew larger. Celeste and Britte arrived with sandwiches for everyone. Conversations floated around her, as if part of a dream.

And Tammy came with Dot. They sat on the other side of a magazine-strewn table, across from Lia.

Tammy's eyes were red rimmed and mascara streaked, though her blouse and blue jeans were neatly pressed, her lipstick in place, her blonde hair cascading in fresh curls. "Lee, what was Cal doing there?"

Isabel leaned forward, intervening. "Working."

"In the middle of the night?"

"It's his job and it's dangerous."

"I know that!"

Dot patted her hand. "It'll be all right, dear. Lia, you probably can't open the store right away, but I don't see how I'm going to make it without working. My husband's laid off."

Isabel said, "There's cleanup duty. Maybe moving inventory."

Dot sniggered. "I'm a pharmacist's technician. I don't do cleanup. There's a special service that does that. They come in after a fire and take care of everything. Your insurance will probably pay for some of that."

Lia tuned them out.

Cal hadn't had time to tell Tammy, of course. Did he even have something to tell her? He indicated so, hadn't he? He wanted a relationship with Lia, didn't he? That's what he had said. Not in so many words, but that's what he meant. *Didn't he?*

Isabel was speaking. "Lia saved Cal's life."

Dot turned to talk to someone else. Tammy dabbed her eyes with a tissue. "Cal means the world to me."

Isabel squeezed Lia's hand.

Lia set down the styrofoam cup. Tea was spilling over the edges.

A nurse in aqua-colored scrubs appeared in the middle of the hovering group. "Who belongs to Mr. Huntington's family?"

Isabel replied, "He doesn't have any relatives locally. We're all his friends, from Valley Oaks, just like family. How is he?"

"He's out of surgery."

Isabel hugged Lia. "Thank You, Jesus."

"The doctor wants to talk to the family or, I guess in this case, those closest to Mr. Huntington. This is too many people."

Isabel stood, pulling Lia up with her. "The three of us are close friends. She pulled him from the fire, and I live next door to him."

Tammy stood. "I'm engaged to him. Practically."

"I'm his pastor."

Brady spoke over Peter's shoulder, "I've been his best friend since sixth grade."

The nurse shook her head. "All right. You." She pointed. "One, two, three, four, five. No more. We'll go to a conference room."

She led them down a hall and into a small room with four padded chairs. Brady and Peter remained standing as the nurse shut the door.

The doctor entered a few moments later. He introduced himself to everyone, shook hands all around. "Young lady, that was quite a feat you managed. He wouldn't be with us right now if you hadn't found him when you did. The knife wound itself wasn't seriously deep, probably due to the muscle it encountered on its way in. However, the smoke inhalation and blood loss did a lot of damage. And he's experiencing some swelling in the brain. There's a goose egg of a bump on the back of his head."

Nausea swept over Lia.

The doctor continued. "He's in critical condition in intensive care."

"Can we see him?" Brady asked.

"No, not just yet. He's not conscious. I can't give you a timetable, but he's in excellent, *excellent* shape. The next 24 hours are crucial, but I'm certain as I can be that he has a good chance of pulling through."

A collective murmur of relief and thanksgiving went round the room.

"He needs to rest now." He glanced at the wall clock. "Perhaps later this morning his fiancée can see him."

"Thank you, Doctor," Tammy gushed. "I can't tell you how happy this makes me! He doesn't know it yet, but I'm carrying his child."

Thirty-Five

Sitting on her living room floor, Isabel played with Nutmeg and Soot while inconspicuously keeping an eye on Lia.

Her friend sat primly on the rocker, her hair pulled back in its usual, albeit shorter, ponytail. She wore a long denim skirt that belonged to Anne and a forest green sweater of Gina's. In a little over 72 hours Isabel had witnessed Lia emerge from a zombie-like condition and slip once more into her familiar big-city-style persona.

Before daybreak Monday at the hospital, Lia finally succumbed to shock. It happened almost simultaneously with Tammy's announcement. The surgeon who had apprised them of Cal's situation noticed Lia's unresponsiveness and shallow breathing and quickly took charge. She didn't protest when they put her in a room and offered sedation.

Isabel brought her home Monday night. Because of the damage to the stairwell, Lia wasn't allowed up into her apartment. A fireman brought her handbag over so she had her wallet at least. Friends generously shared clothes and personal items.

By Wednesday afternoon Lia had arranged for a cleanup company to begin working Thursday. Area pharmacists had dug into their inventories, organizing enough supplies to get her started. Aaron Thompson had offered an unused space attached to his medical office. She would open up temporary shop on Saturday.

Isabel wanted to give credit to Lia's strong faith, but she suspected the source of her courage to move on had more to do with Tammy's news than faith. It hardened something in Lia, pushing her a step beyond confident assertiveness. Isabel surmised this because Lia refused to visit Cal. The last she had seen them together they were snuggling. Since then Cal had put his life on the line to protect Lia and Lia had saved his life, endangering her own in the process. The natural progression here was not to ignore the man.

Not that Cal would have noticed. He still remained unconscious.

Benny Richards was sitting on the couch. He wasn't nearly as large as Cal, but he still occupied a lot of space in his brown uniform with his gun, radio, handcuffs, and other thingamajigs hanging about. Their paths had never crossed until the other night at the pharmacy. That afternoon he was decidedly kinder in tone. She was glad he was finally addressing them by their first names rather than "Ms." He told them to call him Benny. He had even thanked Lia three times for saving Cal.

"Lia," he said, "I have to say I toyed with the idea that you knifed Cal. If you were strong enough to pull him out, you were strong enough to stab him."

"But why would I do that?"

"Cover up the fire you set. Then you got cold feet about committing murder, so you dragged him out. You needed the insurance money. Everyone knows you're hurting with the Agstar program pulling out."

Lia stared at him for a moment, expressionless. "So what changed your mind?"

"The general consensus in Valley Oaks is you're the greatest thing to come along since peanut butter and jelly."

She only blinked in reply. "About the officer sitting outside Isabel's house here all night... I appreciate it, but I really don't think anyone is out to hurt me any more than they already have."

Isabel shuddered. "I, on the other hand, invited the guy to spend the night inside."

"Well, he's staying put," Benny pronounced without reservation. "Somebody tried to kill Cal, and since you all made it look as if you were home alone, Lia, they obviously didn't have any compunction about taking you out with him."

Isabel asked, "The guard will stay put at the hospital, too, won't he?"

"Yeah." He raked his fingers through graying hair. "We may have found what Cal was after. The fire inspector let me climb down into the basement this morning. What do you know about that door down there?"

"Door?" Lia frowned. "Oh, I've seen it. I never bothered to open it. I hate spiders and it was covered in webs. I figure it leads to a closet or a—What are they called? Where people store potatoes."

"Root cellar. No. It was locked from the other side. I suspect it leads into the video store basement."

Isabel gasped. "Then—"

"That's how someone got inside!" Lia completed the thought.

"Right. How's your relationship been with Mitch Conway?"

"Fine. I mean, he doesn't shop in the pharmacy, but he's polite enough when Chloe and I rent videos. Oh." She frowned. "There was a thing with his son, Damon. He brought in a prescription for codeine cough medication. A week later he wanted a refill. I said I had to call the doctor, and if he approved it, Damon could pick it up later. The doctor didn't okay it, and the boy never came back. But—but he's just a kid. Maybe 12?"

"Thirteen. And his friends are 19. He's bad news, though I didn't think he was this bad." Benny's pager beeped. "Isabel, may I use your phone?"

"Sure. There's one in the kitchen." She stood, moving out of his way. "Lia, remember when Cal said someone wanted to discredit you? What would that have to do with kids stealing drugs?"

Lia shrugged. "It doesn't make any sense. I can't figure it out. I'm just trying to remember why it was I wanted to move to a small town and open my own business."

"You will get through this, Lia. And then you'll remember."

Benny returned. "Ladies, that was the hospital. Cal just woke up."

Cal fought back the grogginess with every ounce of strength he could muster. He was convinced that lead weights sat on his eyelids.

Tammy's tears weren't helping. "Oh, Calhoun Huntington, what am I going to do with you?" She clung to his shoulder, the only spot on his body that didn't seem to be hooked up to something.

Monitors beeped. Wires and tubes hung all over the place. Every breath he took felt like a knife piercing into his ribs.

There had been a knife. That much he remembered. And smoke. And crawling up the steps.

Benny Richards walked in. "Hey, welcome back."

"Thanks."

"Tammy, we need to talk business before he goes nighty-night again. Mind stepping out?"

She pouted and then she bent over and kissed his cheek. "Ooh. When are you going to shave that thing off? I'll be right outside the door. With that nice policeman. *He* doesn't have a beard."

Benny shut the door behind her. "Feel like talking? I'm only supposed to stay for three minutes."

"Is Lia all right?"

"Sure."

"Did she get hurt in the fire?"

"Not a scratch—Man, didn't you hear?"

"Hear what? I just woke up, and Tammy's been bawling the whole time. She did tell me today is Thursday."

"She didn't give you the scoop, huh?" He shook his head slightly. "Cal, Lia saved your life."

"What?"

"Yep. She woke up and smelled the smoke. Found you, rolled you right out into the alley before the firemen got there. Good thing, too. That back room was in flames when they arrived."

Cal closed his eyes. *Lia saved my life? Pulled me outside?*

"Don't go to sleep! I've got two minutes left. Tell me what happened before you got hit on the head. We found the door in the basement. I take it that's what you were checking out. Does it lead into the video store basement?"

"Yeah. I went through it."

"Huntington! What a bonehead thing to do! You almost got yourself killed."

He didn't have the energy to defend himself. "I stepped just inside. Didn't hear a thing. Noticed a movement when something hit me on the back of the head. I vaguely remember a knife being shoved into my side. I do remember waking up and smelling smoke. I could see the steps. Last I remember was hauling myself up them..." *Praying for Lia.*

"That's attempted murder. Who do you figure?"

"It's Conway's property. He's always hated me but I didn't think enough to kill me."

"I don't know. If he knew he was looking at a stiff sentence for stealing drugs, he might choose getting rid of you over prison."

"But I still didn't have proof he was in on the drug thing."

"He wouldn't necessarily know that. Could be his kid and friends. Some of them aren't from Valley Oaks. Maybe it's them and not Mitch. You look like you're fading. I suppose you left some of your blood beyond that door. I think it's time for a search warrant."

Cal gave him a weak thumbs-up. "Go get 'em, pal."

Lia hugged Chloe until the little girl protested.

"Aunt Lia! Where's Soot?"

"Sleeping with Nutmeg in the kitchen. Go." She smiled and then fell into her mother's embrace. It was the most comfortable place she'd been since falling asleep on her couch as Cal whistled his way downstairs.

Lia almost gave way to tears again. She was so grateful to be alive...so grateful for her parents' love...so grateful for Chloe. But she held back, afraid that if she started crying once again, she would never stop this time.

"My daughter, the heroine."

"Oh, Mom."

"Why don't you go see him? Chloe and I will unpack and fix dinner." They were moving into Isabel's house. Her father hadn't been able to come, but her mother was staying until Monday.

"There's just too much to do with the store. And he's still in intensive care. Visitors are restricted." *Only* fiancées *are allowed to visit.*

"But he'll want to thank you."

"That can wait. I need to get back over to the new store. It's really a makeshift affair, but I think it can work for a short while. Mom, you won't believe how people are helping."

"Lia, they like you here. Don't give up too soon."

She had told her mother over the phone that she had decided to sell the business. "We'll see. Are you sure you'll be fine?"

"Isabel said to make myself at home, so I plan to do just that. We've brought food. Chloe and I have shopped. You both have new clothes. We'll get organized."

Lia smiled. "Thank you, Mom. Chloe's going to use the spare bedroom. It's small, with a single bed. You and I are out here on the hide-a-bed."

"Suits me just fine. Your friend Isabel is a gem to welcome us this way."

"She is that. God is good." Lia said the words because she accepted them as fact, but it felt as if her rock-solid faith had liquified. Why had God opened her heart only to break it?

Isabel perused the mail at the radio station, waiting to identify the station and give a weather update at 5:00. That week had been a topsy-turvy chain of events.

Exhaustion had set in after she brought Lia home from the hospital. Between Saturday's short night and Sunday night's vigil for Cal, she had been running on empty. Not to mention Tony's abrupt, angry departure sandwiched in between...

She ached for him, berated herself for letting him down. She prayed nonstop, almost mantra-style, "Lord, heal Cal. Lord, heal Tony's soul." *Lord, heal Cal. Lord, heal Tony's soul.*

She exchanged her early morning shift with another announcer and slept away much of Tuesday, as did Lia. She was an easy house guest. They both recognized their nerves were worn raw. They were content to snack instead of cook real food and to sleep rather than chitchat. The air was heavy with Tammy's announcement.

It was Thursday already. Susie Neuman had arrived with Chloe that afternoon. Isabel already knew Chloe and Lia were delightful. After meeting Susie, she concluded delightful was a family trait. Isabel had a distinct impression that they would be fed well, the house would be cleaned, the laundry would be folded and put away.

And...Cal had woken up. *Thank You, Lord. Heal him completely. And heal Tony's soul.* Too many emotions swirled through her.

A letter caught Isabel's eye. It was some sort of a general announcement about a new Spanish-speaking station soon going on the air in the Chicago area. They needed announcers.

Isabel dropped the paper as if it burned her fingers...as if it were a burning bush.

It happened that instantaneously. She knew her life would never be the same again.

Thirty-Six

Cal stared out the window and thought about how grateful he was. He was alive. He didn't feel as bad as he did yesterday. He was out of ICU and sitting up in a bed near a window. Benny had found traces of his blood in the basement of the video store. Mitch was under arrest. His fingerprints had been found on both handles of the basement door as well as the latch of the half door in the pharmacy.

He thanked God for all these things, and then he faced what he could no longer ignore. He had to break things off with Tammy. Poor girl was here all the time.

And Lia wasn't.

He tried not to dwell on that fact, but it bothered him. He couldn't help wondering why she didn't come. Of course she would be busy recovering herself, not to mention regrouping business-wise. Tammy said that Dot was working today, Saturday. They were opening next door to Aaron Thompson's office.

Then, too, Lia was independent...impressively independent. Nothing like Tammy...

Also, visitors had been restricted in ICU. Even Brady, who should have been nearer a family member than Tammy, was only allowed five minutes, just long enough to let him know he talked often with Cal's mother. Her health wasn't the best, and it was difficult for her to leave home in Florida. Cal had talked with her himself yesterday, assuring her that she needn't come.

Tammy had been granted special privileges because for some reason they believed she was his fiancée. One of the nurses had referred to her that way when they moved him this morning. Now that he thought about it, she did act more possessive than ever, as if they *were* engaged.

Well, he'd had enough. Why should he be chasing a passing fancy rather than the woman he wanted to spend the rest of his life with? That lesson had hit home about the time he passed out on Lia's basement steps.

~

A knock woke Cal from one of his perpetual naps. "Come in."

It was Brady. "Hey, bud. I hardly recognize you without all the tubes. And sitting up even." He walked over to the bed and grasped his hand. "Man, I'm glad to see you're coming back. You sure put us all through one rough week."

Cal grinned. "You think you've had it rough?"

Brady laughed.

"Combining over?"

"It's raining."

He glanced out the window. The sky had grown dark and a steady rain beat against the window. "Hmm. Guess I missed that development this afternoon. I sure hope this sleepiness goes away soon. Is it still Saturday?"

"Last I checked it was."

"So what are you doing here? If you're not in the fields, you should be with Gina. Win back that woman's trust."

Brady's grin widened. "Already did."

Cal held up his palm for Brady to slap. "What's your secret? More flowers?"

"No way. Flowers wouldn't touch this one. God had to intervene. She went to Isabel's youth group. I don't know what happened there, but she said it helped her understand more about trusting God instead of people. And then after this incident with you." He shook his head. "I don't know. It really scared all of us, but she said it also woke her up. She took time off from work for a week just to ride around in the combine with me."

Cal let out a mellow whoop.

"We're going out for a special dinner tonight. I'm going to propose to her all over again, this time in private, on my knees."

"Congratulations, Brade."

"Thanks. You're still planning on being my best man?"

"It'd be an honor. Just give me a few days to get back on my feet."

Brady smiled. "Just a few days, huh? So where's your sidekick? Tammy has been here every time I've come by."

"Well." Cal took a deep breath. "Got a little catching up to do with you. This morning I broke off whatever it was she thought we had going between us."

"What?"

"You know I wasn't in love with her. We had some good times together. But after I met Lia, I knew the difference between a good time and sharing a life. I haven't stopped thinking about Lia for weeks now— What's wrong?"

"Cal! You're not this callused, I know. I mean, I don't hold it against you. We all make mistakes, but you made a commitment to Tammy."

"I did not. The nurses seem to think we're engaged, but that's hogwash."

"You can't turn your back on her now!"

"Brady, what is it I'm missing here?"

He groaned. "Oh, man, she didn't tell you."

"Tell me what?"

"Cal, Tammy's pregnant."

Thirty-Seven

Lia sat beside Chloe on the bed in Isabel's spare room, snuggling. It was Tuesday night, just over a week since they had been alone, but it felt like months.

Her mother and Isabel were gone: her mother back home after nourishing them for five days with her marvelous cooking and infectious laugh; Isabel to Chicago for a job interview. The healing had begun.

She opened the pharmacy on Saturday. It was a drugstore in the strictest sense. There were only drugs available. Smoke and water from the sprinklers had ruined everything. The Christmas inventory stacked in the back room had been destroyed by the fire.

Insurance money would carry her for a while, hopefully long enough to sell the business and at least break even. After closing Saturday afternoon, she let Dot go. She couldn't afford her financially. That morning she realized that neither could she afford her emotionally. The woman informed her that Tammy had suffered a miscarriage, but Cal was sure to stay loyal.

Lia hugged Chloe tightly, shutting out those details. "So tell me. How was the visit with your dad?"

"He was nice."

Well, that wasn't much information. "Did you meet his family?"

"No. Just the two of us went to dinner and the zoo. He said his other kids were busy, but maybe next time they could meet me."

Next time? Lia groaned to herself.

"Aunt Lia. I've been thinking. Do you think I can call Mommy Mom? Mandy doesn't say mommy anymore."

"That's a good idea. Your mom would like that."

"Aunt Lia?" She raised her face, those big blue eyes boring into Lia

"Hmm?"

"Sometimes I call you my mom when I talk to the other kids. Is that okay?"

"Sure, honey. I'm your adopted mom, even though I'll always be your aunt." She hugged her silently for a few moments. "Did your dad say he would call you?"

"Yeah. Can I see him again?"

"Do you want to?"

"Yeah. I mean, yes."

"We'll see. You better get to sleep now."

"Okay. I love you."

"Love you, too, sweetpea."

Lia carried bed pillows to the front room. In an effort to keep Isabel's home neat, her mother had folded up the hide-a-bed every day and stacked the pillows in Chloe's room. Lia wasn't sure how long she could keep up the chore. Hopefully they could move back into the apartment in a few weeks. The workers had allowed her upstairs that day. The smoke stench gagged her. Could it ever be washed out?

A knock on the front door startled her. She knew Mitch Conway was locked up and that the deputy guard no longer needed to park on the street overnight. Like the smoke odor, though, she wondered if the fear would ever subside.

She turned on the outside light and looked through the door's peephole. It was Cal. Another kind of fear rooted her feet to the floor. He knocked again.

She knew she would have to face him sooner or later. *Dear Lord, give me grace!*

She slowly opened the door. "Hi. Isabel's not home."

"I wanted to see you. Mind if I come in?"

She stood aside and let him pass, and then she shut the door. Perspiration beaded on his forehead. "Cal, it's 40 degrees and you're sweating!"

He sank onto the nearest chair, his face pale behind the full beard that had grown during his hospital stay. More than ever he resembled a teddy bear with his bristly face matching his light brown hair. He panted.

"Are you all right?"

He waved a hand. "I'll be fine. Walking across the yards felt like a major hike. The back doors are closer, but I didn't want to frighten you by banging on the porch window."

"You just got home today!" Naturally she had heard the news. "You shouldn't be out at all!"

"No choice. My thanks are long past due. Lia, thank you for saving my life."

She sat on the couch. "You're welcome. You're not taking very good care of it right now."

"I'll be fine. I'm a tough cop." He paused, his breathing more even. "Except when it comes to you."

She allowed herself to meet his eyes. What would be his excuse? It didn't matter. There was no place for him in her life now.

"Lia, I about went nuts when you didn't come visit. Then on Saturday Brady told me what Tammy said. No wonder you hadn't shown up! But I've been going crazy since then, not being able to come and explain."

"Cal, save the effort. At this point, it doesn't matter. We had a good friendship. You helped me out a lot, and I got you away from the fire. I guess you could say we're even. There's nothing else between us."

"Lia! Tammy's not pregnant!"

"I know that. Dot told me she lost the baby."

"There never *was* a baby!"

She blinked, trying to process this information.

Cal heaved himself from the chair and lumbered over to the couch. He sank onto his knees before her. "Lia, I have to explain something. Growing up, playing football, Brady was always my quarterback. After I became a Christian, he kind of became that again, only in real life ways. He's always telling me what plays to run. Which ones not to run because they won't work."

He stopped to catch his breath. "The point is, as far as I know, there's only one natural way to make a baby, and it just didn't happen. Tammy thought she could trick us into being engaged, get the whole town assuming we were together. She figured no one would tell me since I supposedly didn't know. If I did hear, she could chalk it up to gossip. In the meantime she conveniently had a 'miscarriage.' What she didn't figure on was me breaking things off. She didn't really love me. I guess she thought I was a good catch or something."

Lia's throat tightened. She touched his beard and whispered, "You are, Cal. You're a very good catch. But I'm not fishing."

Cal stumbled back across the darkened lawns to his house, his head swimming. He knew Lia watched, concerned that he had pushed himself beyond the limit of endurance.

He had, but it wasn't physical. He felt a fierce loathing toward Tammy, which scared him. He desperately wanted to turn back time, to spin the earth backwards until he sat again in Lia's apartment, kissing her goodnight, deciding against searching, deciding to sit and simply watch her sleep.

He climbed his front steps and leaned against a porch post, panting and sweating.

It didn't feel as though he'd been stabbed. Instead it felt as if that knife had filleted him open, exposing his heart to damage he never would have imagined possible.

Oh, God!

He went inside and made his way to the kitchen and the bottle of pain pills, which he told the doc he didn't need. He swallowed two.

He had talked with Lia for over an hour. She explained that circumstances made her realize that Valley Oaks wasn't working out for her. She was selling the business as soon as possible and leaving no later than the end of December. There wasn't enough space in her life for a relationship. As she had said when they first met, she wasn't looking for one.

"But I love you, Lia."

"It's only infatuation, Cal. There hasn't been time for love to develop."

She wasn't the soft woman he remembered.

Now he realized she was running scared. She had been thrown off course, choosing Chloe over her own dreams, working hard to carve out a new life for them. She was impressively independent and not about to give that up to some guy she wasn't sure she could trust. Where should he start? Would flowers help?

Try prayer, bud.

He didn't know if it was his own consciousness or Brady or the voice of Jesus Himself, but he recognized it as the place to begin.

Thirty-Eight

Isabel stood on Michigan Avenue across from the *Chicago Tribune* Tower, the sky a brilliant blue against the nearly white stone that soared heavenward.

She closed her jaw. At the radio station where she interviewed, they teased her about behaving like a tourist. She wondered now if Lia could help her develop a big-city air about herself. Teach her how to dress and walk, how not to gawk with her mouth hanging open.

But this was procrastinating. She wanted to see Tony, to apologize, to...well, to just *see* him.

Swallowing the intimidation that kept welling up, she made her way across the busy boulevard, dodging people in the crosswalk. Where in the world did all these people come from? Where did they all live? And park their cars? And buy groceries?

She went inside the building and eventually found herself standing before a security guard.

"Anthony Ward," the woman said, reaching for a telephone. "That smart-alecky reporter. You sure you want to talk to him, honey? You look way too sweet for the likes of him." She pressed the phone pad buttons. "Used to be I could send you right on up. Too many threats these days. I seem to remember one or two against him in particular. What's your name?"

"Isa— Izzy. Tell him Izzy is here."

"Mr. Ward, this is Sheila downstairs. There's an Izzy here to see you. Oh! He hung up. Rude, rude, rude! You'd think he'd at least—"

Isabel somehow made her way back out to the sidewalk, blinking rapidly to keep the tears from falling. Now that certainly manifested a big-city attitude. She dug in her bag for sunglasses and a tissue. Well, she had tried. If he didn't want to see her... Sunglasses in place, she glanced to the right and left in what she thought was a nonchalant manner. Where was her car again? The people at the radio station had given her directions to the *Tribune* building, just a short distance across town. There was no reason to stay and so much to do at home. And she had promised to work early tomorrow—

"Izzy!"

She turned to see Tony running toward her.

"Izzy! What are you doing here?" He didn't smile, but he wrapped her in a brief hug.

"Um, looking for you."

He cocked an eyebrow. "Do you want to walk a bit? We can find a bench."

"You have time?" She tried to sniffle unobtrusively.

"Sure." He grasped her elbow and steered her toward the river, across a type of courtyard and away from the avenue.

They walked without speaking for a few minutes. After descending a stairway, they reached a sunny bench in a quiet area overlooking the river. Across the way, skyscrapers rose, the early afternoon sun glinting off their black windows.

"Izzy, you're the last person I would expect to show up here."

"Guess what? I'm taking your challenge."

He shook his head and leaned forward, propping his elbows on his knees. "And which one would that be?"

"The one about not hiding away in Valley Oaks."

"Iz, you know I'm full of hot air. You shouldn't take me literally. It's bad for your health."

"Tony, I'm sorry for not telling you about being pregnant. I should have told you years ago. I certainly should have told you before now."

"I'm sorry for jumping down your throat. I had no right to get nasty with you. If I were you, *I* wouldn't have tried to tell me. Once a jerk, always a jerk. I pushed you so far out of my consciousness that after one feeble attempt to call you that summer, I forgot about you. I mean, I totally forgot about you. Now I know I did that consciously, because I was falling in love with you. And that, above all, gave me the heebie-jeebies."

You loved me? She fought down the emotions his confession ignited. "I've blamed you all these years for not coming after me and making an honest woman out of me."

He looked back at her. "I should have. I'm sorry."

"You didn't know."

"I'm sorry you had to go through it alone. I'm sorry you never finished college."

"I survived. I can always go back if I want."

"I'd pay for it."

"Hey, it wasn't entirely your fault." She smiled. "You can pay for half."

He turned again toward the river. "I feel like I've lost a sister and a child."

She rubbed his hunched shoulders.

He sat quietly for a while. She wondered if he blinked away his own tears. "Iz, I can't write the article. Every time I try to work on it, I have this image of you walking away. And you're walking with my sister. My mind goes blank." He straightened, put an arm across the bench behind her, and smiled in that crooked, self-deprecating way with his head tilted. "Heavy, huh?"

"What does it mean to you?"

"God's leaving old Tony Ward out in the cold."

"Why don't you come in?"

"Hmm. Like that song you sang to me at breakfast. Just come in and leave all that guilt outside."

"That's all there is to it."

He drew her closer and hid his face in her hair. "You are so beautiful, Isabel Mendoza." He let her go and crossed his arms. "Now tell me why you really came to Chicago."

"To see you." She smiled. "I came for a job interview, but I think I came for that because you were here. I needed to apologize before any more time passed."

"Job interview? In Chicago?"

"Mm-hmm. Radio announcer for a Christian Spanish-speaking station. Enough of a challenge to meet your standards?"

"I'd say so. Did they like you? Silly question. Of course they loved you."

She shrugged. "They have to think about it. I have to think about it."

"You'd leave Valley Oaks?"

"It may be time. I'm also considering missions work in Mexico. My heart is still there."

"If you moved here, I'd be like your only friend in a hundred-mile radius." He winked. "So how are things in Valley Oaks? Cal solve the pharmacy thefts yet?"

"Oh, you haven't heard!" She filled him in on details of the attack and fire. "He got out of the hospital yesterday."

"Poor guy. I'll give him a call. How are the lovebirds?"

"Well, not so good. Tammy has sort of moved in and claimed her territory." She decided not to fill him in on all the sordid details. "I should go. Don't you have a deadline or something?"

"Actually, all of my writing seems to be a bit off these days, but yes, I do have work to do."

"Tony."

"Uh-oh. It's her serious tone."

"There's a Spanish-speaking church here." She pulled a pamphlet from her bag. "I went last night with the family who let me stay with them. There's a pastor visiting here all week from…Colombia."

He went still.

"He knows about your sister and her friends. Some of the people he ministers to met her." Isabel folded the pamphlet in half. Pushing aside his crossed arms, she opened his sport coat and stuffed it into his inside pocket. "Go. Listen to him; they have interpreters. Stay after and meet him." She met his deep-set blue gaze. "My challenge to you."

Tony watched her walk away and bit the inside of his cheek. She wore black boots, a long gray straight skirt, and a black jacket. The red highlights in her hair glinted in the sun.

She looked too small under the huge buildings, too pure and innocent for the likes of Chi-town. Not fragile, though. No, she wasn't fragile. She could move to the big city and fashion a life, making borders out of ideals and integrity. But…she would choose Mexico. Her talents lay in the city, but she would choose the extreme route. Just as his sister had done. And she would walk away from him and not turn back, just as in the image he could not erase. Just as his sister had done.

He may have been falling in adolescent love with her seven years ago, but this was different. He could not remember what life was like before he entered that vet's office in Valley Oaks two months ago. Only two months? A lifetime.

Just now, he had asked her to keep him posted on her job decision. She smiled in that enigmatic way of hers, kissed him on the cheek, and left.

He knew that kiss had meant goodbye.

Tony sat in the back pew of the tiny church, totally absorbed in the service. He had even stopped listening to the translator, hearing the preacher's Spanish and somehow—after all these years—understanding it. The short, mustached, European-looking man stood before the pulpit, no notes, words flowing effortlessly, hands gesturing elegantly.

Tony's vision blurred, creating the sensation of swimming underwater. He stretched one hand to the back of the wooden pew in front of him and clung to it. It was as if the water parted, giving him a clear, tunnel-like view of only the preacher. *What am I doing here?*

After Izzy stuck the pamphlet in his pocket the other day, it crinkled whenever he moved. It sat on his kitchen table for twenty-four hours before he decided. He would take her challenge because he didn't seem to have any other option. Through no choice of his own, his life was on hold and he didn't know for what. He would go to the service and meet God and tell Him what he thought. He would set straight once and for all those hapless folks who thought he should celebrate his sister's sacrifice.

The tears started as the little man neared the conclusion of his passionate talk. The preacher spoke of obscene poverty and of unfathomable joy. He told of how people braved threats of guerillas, how Bibles were treasured, how many miles people trudged in order to join with other believers. He spoke of young Americans who loved their enemies...and of how their deaths had softened some of the hardest of hearts.

After the service, the man reached Tony before he was able to uproot himself from the pew. Their eyes met, and he sensed that somehow the preacher knew.

The man grasped his shoulder. "My friend, I am sorry for your loss."

"How can I forgive the men who killed my sister?"

"You can't. Only Jesus can. Jesus living in you can forgive them. Do you want to forgive them?"

"I can't carry around this...this..." *Name it, Tony. Say it!* "This *hatred* around anymore."

"Then ask Jesus to live in your heart. He'll set you free from the darkness you walk in now." He laid a hand lightly on Tony's head, murmured a prayer, and moved away.

The underwater sensation returned. His face was wet. His palm ached from its grip on the pew. His chest felt as if a sumo wrestler sat on it.

I'm sorry, God! I'm sorry!

What had the preacher said? What had Izzy said? What had JoJo said? "Ask Jesus to live in your heart."

I don't understand any of it!

He could barely breathe.

Just ask.

All right!

"Jesus," he whispered, "live in my heart? Please?"

The sumo wrestler vanished, leaving a gaping hole in his wake, ripping the breath from Tony's lungs. The ache was unbearable.

And then a warmth began to seep in around the edges, a fluid heat absorbing the pain, consuming the hatred, engulfing the doubts. An implosion of love.

His tears continued long into the night. He had met God all right, but it was most decidedly not on Tony Ward's terms.

Thirty-Nine

"Cal," Isabel called from his kitchen, "I'm going to do a little housekeeping out here."

"Go for it." He sat in his recliner in the living room, hand on the remote, eyes glued to a televised soccer match.

"Chloe," Isabel called out again, "you okay for a bit?"

Cal glanced at the girl sitting across the end table from him. She sat on the edge of the other, smaller recliner that had been his grandmother's. He couldn't read her expression. She had come over with Isabel that morning, the two of them carrying enough casseroles and loaded grocery bags to keep him going for a week.

"Yes, Isabel," she called back.

She was a polite little thing, with big blue eyes that always unnerved him because it appeared there was a lot of activity going on behind them, but he couldn't imagine about what. What in the world could nine-year-olds have to think about? He remembered that night he ate dinner at Lia's. Chloe had giggled and even hugged him goodbye. Since then, he hadn't really noticed her much.

Except to realize that she was an awkward obstacle in Lia's life.

No, that wasn't it. Lia was devoted to her well-being and enjoyed her immensely. Her stepmother role came naturally. Even when she talked of not being married because the guy would have to accept Chloe as a daughter, there had been no trace of complaining or self-pity.

He was the one who found Chloe an awkward obstacle.

What an idiot!

Chloe was nearer to Lia's heart than anything. The way to Lia's heart was nothing less than through her niece.

But she was a kid! She was everything Cal was determined to avoid. He had never been around kids, had no desire to be around them. He remembered being one: he remembered the best times were when he was with his dad. And then his dad died.

What was it Lia had said? *They're just short people, Cal.*

He cleared his throat. "Do you like soccer?"

"I like gymnastics."

"We can probably find some of that." He picked up the remote and began flipping. "I've got a gazillion sports channels."

"Isabel doesn't have cable. Do you like cartoons?"

"Can't remember the last time I saw one."

"Aunt Lia only lets me watch two on Saturdays."

"Have you watched your two today?"

"Yeah. I mean, yes."

"Well, you're in my house now. I think I want to watch a cartoon."

Chloe giggled, slipped off her shoes, pulled up the recliner's foot rest, and settled back.

Lia parked in front of Isabel's house and muttered aloud to herself, "This isn't working."

Cal lived way too close for comfort.

And he had started an ongoing Chinese checkers tournament with Chloe. He wasn't leaving his house much yet, which meant Chloe went over there, which meant Lia had gone to collect her three times in six days. Not to mention the night before when he baby-sat while she and Isabel went to Club NEDD.

As long as she didn't have to see him, she was fine. Well, as fine as one could be living with a friend, sleeping in her living room, dispensing drugs from an oversized storeroom, and wondering how much money she was going to lose when all was said and done.

But when she had to see him and look into those green eyes and sense his teddy bear presence, still strong and yet weak from the recent ordeal, then she felt overwhelmed and inundated with conflicting emotions. Anger, sadness, joy, confusion. Floating gossamer tickling...

Well, not tonight. It was Friday. A father-daughter/mother-son date night for fifth graders was being held at the school. And she had to deal with Nelson's visit. Chloe had called and invited him. He was due to arrive in ten minutes.

Lia hurried inside the house and stopped short just inside the door. Across the living room she spotted Cal sitting at the kitchen table, arranging marbles on a playing board.

He looked up and grinned. "Hey, Aunt Lia." It was his recently acquired mode of addressing her.

"You left your house!" She dropped her coat and bags where she stood. The mail she had picked up at the post office fluttered to the floor.

"Yeah. I even walked to the Center today. Of course I was too exhausted to work out, but I got there. Isabel was called to the station for some emergency, so I came over about five to keep Chloe company while she gets ready for her big date."

"Cal, she's nine years old. She can stay by herself for an hour."

He shrugged.

Chloe emerged from the hallway and twirled around the front room, grinning. "What do you think?" The red party dress and black patent-leather shoes her grandmother had bought sparkled in the lamplight.

Lia clapped. "You're beautiful!" She smiled to herself, noticing the slightly askew barrettes in Chloe's black hair. "Absolutely perfect."

"Chloe, you'll be the prettiest one there." Cal stood in the kitchen doorway.

"Do you think so?"

"Definitely."

"Is my dad here yet?"

Lia hugged her. "Not yet, sweetpea. It's still early."

Cal said, "Hey, how about some checkers while we wait? You're still beating me. I gotta catch up."

The two of them laughed and headed into the kitchen. They paid no attention to Lia's sigh.

Forty-five minutes passed. Chloe grew quieter. Lia dropped a pan, an onion, a fork, and cut a finger. She didn't know what would be worse. Dealing with Nelson or dealing with his no-show. She gave up cooking dinner and sat down at the table.

Cal stood and patted Chloe's shoulder. "Well, I better go. I'll beat you tomorrow, though, Chloe. You have a good time tonight. See you, Aunt Lia." He sauntered through the kitchen and out the back porch.

"Chloe, he probably got hung up in Chicago traffic. You know how that happens."

She nodded, her eyes on the marbles, her little forehead pinched.

"Do you want a snack?"

She vehemently shook her head and then flew from the table and down the hall.

Lia listened to her sobs until the bedroom door slammed shut. Then she stood and marched to retrieve her handbag from the floor by the front door. She dug out Nelson's cell phone number. If necessary, she would beg him to get here as soon as possible or make it up in some extravagant way. He wasn't going to get away with this. He would not break Chloe's heart and get away with it.

She returned to the kitchen, yanked the phone from the wall, and punched in the numbers. No answer. Not even a voice mail. Oh! She would kill him!

Her thoughts echoed in her head. *Kill him?*

What was wrong with her? She sank onto a chair. The world had grown ugly and she with it. *I don't even like myself anymore!*

Lord, I'm sorry.

How long since she had prayed? Sincerely prayed and listened for His leading? She was too wrapped up in her troubles. Too determined to take care of business and not feel anything. She knew how to do that. She was an expert at that. It was how she had turned her back on a normal life, adopted Chloe at the age of 21, and bought her own business. Except this time she had even turned her back on Chloe and her heavenly Father.

She laid her head on the table and prayed. Knowing she invited a dreaded crying fit, she told God everything and asked Him for everything. The tears came, but they cleansed this time. She sensed the beginning of a healing.

A noise outside on the darkened porch startled her. She looked up. Isabel had told her to keep that door locked! Her heart pounded in her throat as the kitchen door opened.

It was Cal. Relief flooded her. "What…" Her jaw locked open halfway through the one-syllable word. Deputy Sheriff Cal Huntington was wearing a black suit.

He shut the door. "Sorry, I knocked. Guess you didn't hear." His shirt was white and his tie red, the same bright red of Chloe's dress. His light brown hair and beard appeared shinier and even combed. He must have showered.

Lia managed to close her mouth. She had never seen him dressed up before. The man was…gorgeous.

He smiled sheepishly. "I figure every little girl needs a dad, even a temporary one." He pointed toward the living room. "Did he show up?"

"Who?"

"Chloe's dad."

"N-no. She's in her room."

"Okay." He strode past Lia, a scent of Polo trailing behind him.

Holy smokes!

And he's here to mend Chloe's broken heart.

"Whew!" It was a loud expulsion of what little breath she had left.

Chloe burst through the front door, a tiny red teddy bear clutched in her hand. "Aunt Lia! We went to the Pizza Parlor for ice cream and everybody was there!"

Lia set aside her book on the couch and stood. "I wondered where you were!" She hugged her niece. "It was getting so late!"

Cal shut the front door. "Sorry. We should have called."

"Oh, goodness. I wasn't worried. She was with you."

Chloe rattled on about the evening. "Cal had pizza too because when we got to the school most of the tacos were gone so he didn't get to eat much. But we got to play games, and we won this teddy bear. Cal said I can keep it. And—" A yawn interrupted.

Lia hugged her again. "I want to hear all about it, but we'd better let Cal go home."

Chloe giggled and ran over to him.

He knelt and caught her in a bear hug. "Thanks for letting me go with you, Chloe."

"Thank you!" She reached into his chest pocket and pulled out a piece of gum. "That's where he keeps it, Aunt Lia. Bye, Cal." Again she giggled and raced toward the hallway.

"Isabel's sleeping!" Lia turned back to Cal. "How can I thank you?"

"My pleasure." He sounded sincere. "She wore me out, but it was worth it to see her laughing again."

"And I thought kids scared you."

"They did." He smiled, those beautiful green eyes of his crinkling. "Goodnight, Lia. See you tomorrow."

The guy sounded pretty sure of that.

Except for attending the morning church service, Isabel spent much of the weekend with Lia unpacking inventory and stocking shelves at the freshly painted pharmacy. Countless others had also offered their assistance. Most of the Chamber of Commerce members had helped move things. Cal hauled stuff in his truck. All the Club NEDD ladies pitched in at the store, preparing it for the next day's grand reopening.

Now, late Sunday night back at the house, Isabel and Lia were beyond tired and feeling slaphappy. After Chloe had gone to bed, they polished off a plate of cookies someone had left at the store. The house was in total disarray. Isabel refused to do anything that resembled putting something away. She plopped on the couch, content to digest all that butter and sugar from a prone position.

Lia got down on her hands and knees. "Isabel, I can't let this mess go any longer. You've done so much for me. The least I can do is pick up a few things."

"Lia, stop!"

"Oh, good grief. There's mail under the couch. I must have dropped it here Friday night."

"There's no mail delivery on Sundays. Leave it until tomorrow!"

"Look at this. You've got something from a missions board, and I have something from that insurance group." She sat cross-legged on the floor, her eyes wide.

"Lia, we won't sleep tonight if we open those."

"Don't be silly." She ripped open her envelope and her jaw dropped. "They've rescinded their decision to cancel me and the other independent pharmacies. They will continue to pay for Agstar employees' prescriptions. They're even making it retroactive, to cover from November 1 last week."

Isabel sat up and cheered. "Yea! How's that for answered prayer and petitions and Alec and Anne Sutton pushing their weight around?"

"I...I don't know."

"You don't know? Doesn't this mean you can stay put and not sell?"

"I don't know anymore if that's what I want to do." She shrugged. "I guess this will make it easier to sell the business."

"Lia, what's going on?"

"I've already talked with a broker. He has a couple of interested parties."

"But what about your life here?"

Again she shrugged. "You're leaving. The back room still gives me the willies. And I do not want to live in that upstairs apartment. Chloe wants to live closer to her grandparents, which of course I knew in July, but you know what they say about 20-20 hindsight."

"You have other friends. You can live in this house as long as you want; the landlords are the best. And Chloe's only nine. You can have a life of your own, Lia. Keep going after your dream."

"That went up in smoke, figuratively and literally. The shop can be fixed, but not my trust."

"You didn't really think Cal had been a perfect saint his entire life, did you? When I first met him he was a nice guy, but our paths didn't exactly cross."

"It's not that. The whole incident reminded me that getting involved is simply not worth it. I think it's best that I focus on raising Chloe and just work for someone else. I can find a niche in Chicago and send her to a small, private school."

Isabel didn't respond. She disagreed, but sensed that Lia wasn't about to reconsider at that moment.

"Open yours, Izzy."

At this point whatever it contained couldn't make the evening more somber than it was. She opened her envelope. Then again, maybe it could. "They can take me on immediately." She blew out a breath. "I can be in Mexico before Christmas."

"That's wonderful! It's exactly what you wanted. Right?"

"Right." It felt as if something shifted, as if some subtle piece of herself broke away. "I guess so."

Bundled in her winter jacket, Isabel drove along the two-lane county highway, passing vast, open farmland toward the radio station. Though the corn had been harvested, brown soybean plants remained in some fields. Here and there patches of trees filled a hillside. For the most part, they raised stark limbs toward a gray sky. Oak trees clutched crispy brown leaves. Some deep yellow leaves still brightened the landscape. The midwest remained true to form. It was November.

She was not going to miss the cold winter.

She glanced down at the passenger seat again, making sure the letter was there, reminding herself that it was the right thing to do.

Writing the letter of resignation ranked right up there with telling her mother about her plans to move. Anguish met her in every direction.

She knew the station needed at least two weeks notice to replace her. By quitting now she could give that to them and still have time to move out of the house and store her things...and tell her family goodbye.

Lia would take over renting the house. After figuring in the cost of redoing much of the apartment and replacing many things, plus heating it during the winter, the price of the small house seemed affordable. There was enough insurance money left over to help.

And, she thought, *it gives Lia time to reconsider. Cal is so in love with her.* Not that he had told Isabel, but it showed. It especially showed in his kindness toward Chloe. Cal was not one for spending time with kids.

Last but not least, the timing gave the Chicago station four more weeks to decide. She had called them back once. They hadn't resolved some issues yet.

Now it was all in God's hands.

Forty

"Cal," Lia pressed the phone to her mouth and stretched the cord to its limit as she walked between the drug shelves. There were customers in the store. "I thought you weren't supposed to work yet."

"The doc said no patrolling. Tonight I'm filling in at the desk. That's why I won't make it to the checkers game with Chloe."

"I know you've been spending a lot of time with her, but you just can't promise a little girl you will do something and then not do it."

"I'm sorry, Lia. It can't be helped. She'll understand. You keep telling me how responsible she is for a nine-year-old."

But this is different! "All right. Thanks for calling." *At least.*

"Tell her I'll try—"

"Cal, don't. Just don't. You'll only set us all up for disappointment. I have customers. Goodbye."

"All right. See you."

Lia scanned the store. No one needed her just yet. Anne had the front covered.

It was Friday, two weeks since the father-daughter date night. Cal had become a fixture at Isabel's house. Lia grew weary of the effort to ignore him. He didn't try to romance her. He hadn't even brought the subject up again. And that wore down her defenses, allowing his friendship wiggle room.

316

Isabel would be leaving for Mexico in about two weeks. Her absence would create empty hours. Lia would automatically turn to their neighbor and that wiggle room would expand. And then one day, like today, he wouldn't show up. Why complicate their lives?

She pulled a business card from her pocket and dialed the broker's number. It was time to pursue the sale of the pharmacy.

Tony sat at his *Tribune* desk and phoned Izzy's radio station.

"Good morning," a chipper female voice answered. "This is WLMD. How may I help you?"

"Hello. I'm a friend of Izz—Isabel Mendoza. I'd like to send her a fax. May I have your number?"

"Sure. Let's see where is that? Oh, here we go." She gave it to him. "Isabel is here now. Would you like to talk to her?"

"No, thanks."

"You almost missed her. Tomorrow is her last day working here."

"Really?" His chest constricted. Should he ask? "Where's she going?"

"Actually, I don't know. I'm filling in for the secretary. Isabel said something about not being cold this winter. Sorry. Are you sure you don't want to talk to her?"

"Yeah, I'm sure. Thanks. Goodbye."

"Goodbye."

He sat at his desk, transfixed, imagining Izzy stringing Christmas lights around a crude dwelling under a hot Mexican sky.

It was out of his hands. Is this where God came in? *God, please let it make sense to her.* He typed in the fax number on his computer and sent the article on its way.

～

After leaving the station Friday afternoon, Isabel stopped in the library, plunked down some change on the counter, and went to the copy machine. A few minutes later she was back in her car, making a mental checklist, choking back tears.

Which was why she hadn't called Tony. Blubbering wouldn't communicate anything, and it seemed that was all she could do since reading the article he had faxed to her. Well, blubber and thank God.

She would start with Brady and Gina. Brady had been the catalyst for Tony's visit to Valley Oaks. He would get the first copy. If they weren't at his house, she would leave the papers stuck in between the doors. Next she would drop a copy off at Celeste and Peter's, and then at Cal's.

After that she would go home and blubber some more. She would reread the beautiful, haunting words of the article he had entitled "Just Come In." It was an intriguing look at Brady's stories, of their influence on readers. It was a human look at Saint Brady without the innuendoes or details of exposé. It was an honest representation of Christianity. His sister's story was woven throughout.

And it was all written from a broken heart where Jesus surely must be living now.

Forty-One

The wind almost whipped the pharmacy door from Lia's grasp as she shut it behind her last customer. She turned the lock. It was one o'clock on Saturday, the end of a long week. Another long week. It was time to take stock again.

She sat on the stool behind the front counter. Chloe was content in the back room. It didn't seem to upset her the way it did Lia, who had even started parking her car on Fourth Avenue and using the front door exclusively.

She knew Chloe lounged on a new rug with Soot, watching the little television Nelson had sent to make up for missing the father-daughter outing. His excuse had been work, which seemed to satisfy Chloe along with the TV.

The store wasn't what it had been. Merchandise was sparse on the shelves. The gift section was a quarter of what it had been, but she couldn't afford to replace the Christmas items lost in the fire.

She missed Dot. No, she didn't miss Dot. She missed Dot's help with prescriptions. Lia needed to hire and train someone new. Just today one of her regular customers highly recommended a friend who would soon be looking for a job. No, if she were staying, she would hire someone new. For now, she could manage.

Next week a potential buyer planned to visit again. She was comfortable with that, with moving forward on the sale.

They would live in Isabel's house. She would shut down December 31, whether or not the business sold. Between Chloe's school semesters in early January, they would leave

Valley Oaks and move in with her parents. Temporarily. She was comfortable with all that.

This day had been like most of her days in the store. The minutes stretched like a gold chain. Each customer, with a personal story of laughter or tears, was like a pearl or a precious stone attached to that chain. She felt as if she had to return the necklace to the jeweler. She *wasn't* comfortable with that.

Cal had strung a more precious kind of necklace through her world. But...but he would only break it again and again if she stayed. She wasn't comfortable with that.

The phone rang. She scurried to the back of the store, wishing she could afford an extension up front.

"Hello?"

"Lia, is Nelson there?" It was Cal.

"Not yet. We're meeting him at Isabel's at two." Chloe's dad was coming to take her to Rockville for a movie and dinner. Lia wasn't looking forward to that, but—

"Listen carefully. I want you and Chloe to stay at the store. Lock the doors. Turn on the alarm and don't let anyone in."

"What's wrong?"

"Lia." His exasperation came through loud and clear. "Just trust me and don't go meet him. I'm on my way from the courthouse."

"Cal! I will not disappoint her again—"

"Mitch Conway just confessed that Nelson Greene paid him to discredit you and put you out of business. He wanted evidence that you were an incompetent guardian for Chloe. He's got no business taking her— The point is, there's a warrant out for his arrest. If he shows up at Isabel's, we'll pick him up there. Highway Patrol may find him first."

Lia's knees buckled. "Cal!"

"Honey, don't panic on me now. I'm 20 minutes away. Just wait for me there. Please!"

"We will."

"All right." He hung up.

Lia clung to the counter. Why had Mitch started the fire? Did Nelson want her dead? Chloe had been in Chicago that weekend. How convenient. But why the attack on Cal?

"Aunt Lia, what's the matter?"

"Oh, Chloe." How was she supposed to explain this to a child?

Isabel jumped at the crack of thunder. Out here at the studio in the middle of acres and acres of farm fields, storms were always wild. It could be frightening, but she loved the intense display of God's power.

The lights flickered. No problem. The generator would kick in if the power went out. She knew her way around the workings of the station. The only problem was her own energy. She had been there since five that morning. If she wanted to drive she was free to go, leaving everything automatically programmed. But she wanted to stay. Even without the storm as an excuse, she probably would have stayed. It would be a good last day on the job, long hours of howling wind and talking into her microphone to familiar listeners. And she felt like talking since she couldn't dance on the wind.

The impact of Tony's article still burst like the thunder and lightning. It was another type of an intense display of God's power. She hadn't been able to call Tony yet. She truly did not know what to say to him. She hoped he would call.

But maybe he didn't know what to say either. Perhaps it was all said in the unsaid.

~

Lia had moved the stool to the front window. She sat as if glued to it and watched the storm. The bare trees in the town square across the street were almost bent double. The rain battered against the sidewalk, bouncing crazily. Streams ran along the curbs. An hour had passed since Cal called. He said he was 20 minutes away. She shivered. It was past two o'clock, the time they were to have met Nelson.

Chloe had reacted badly. She yelled that Cal was making it all up; her daddy wouldn't be mean. Lia had not told her details, just that Nelson was in trouble and wouldn't be coming today. Cal had told them to wait at the store. She ran upstairs then, and Lia had heard her footsteps pounding into her bedroom.

She wrinkled her nose now, thinking of Chloe burying her face in bedclothes that still smelled of smoke. Lia reconsidered going up to console her. Maybe she had calmed, but...she needed time alone to deal with it as best a nine-year-old could. Lia would step in later for damage control. Quite honestly, at the moment she didn't think she was up to it. How could she have ever trusted Nelson? She knew better. She knew all along. She had known ever since Kathy became involved with him. He had promised he would always take care of Kathy, that he was leaving his wife. And then, while Kathy was being sick in the bathroom, nauseous in her pregnancy, he put the moves on her little eighteen-year-old sister out in the living room. Revulsion swept through her at the memory. There had been other occasions, Lia crushing his ego every time. The man probably truly hated her.

To top it, he understood how to play the Neumans as the fools. "Fools for You, Lord. Where are You in this?"

"Lia!"

She cried out and leapt from the stool.

Cal was striding up the center aisle, rain dripping from the rim of his deputy's hat and short jacket. "I told you to lock the doors and set the alarm!"

"I did!"

"Well, I just walked right in. Where's Chloe?"

"Upstairs." Their eyes met.

Cal beat her to the staircase and flew up them two at a time. "Chloe! Chloe!"

They frantically raced through the small apartment. Chloe and Soot were gone. Only her favorite stuffed animal—the red teddy bear she and Cal had won—remained, lying on her bedroom floor.

"Oh, Cal! He took—"

He grabbed her and held her tightly, the rain from his jacket soaking her lab coat. "No, no. We picked Greene up at Isabel's. He's in the back of a squad car on his way to Twin Prairie. He can't harm her now. Was she very upset?"

She nodded against him.

"She knew how to turn off the alarm. She's just run off, mad at the world. She can't be far. Maybe she's back at Isabel's. Or my house. She knows where I hide the key. Let's go."

In less than five minutes they had roared in his cruiser halfway across town while he radioed in the situation and a description of Chloe. "Is she wearing her red jacket?"

"And blue jeans. Black boots."

Together they dashed into Isabel's house. Lia's voice grew hoarse from shouting Chloe's name.

Cal grabbed a raincoat from a closet and draped it over her. "Come on. Let's try my place." He held her arm as they ran, sloshing through puddles that dotted the back yards

His two-story house took longer. There were more closets, more nooks and crannies. At last they huddled together in the kitchen and asked each other, "Where would she run to?"

Lia said, "Mandy's? I'll call the Suttons and other—"

"The phone lines are down." He grasped her by the shoulders and leaned over to make eye contact. "Honey, the phone lines were down when I called you."

"Huh?"

"God let me get through. He's here. He's in this. He protected you from going to Isabel's. Are you with me?"

She nodded.

"We'll find Chloe. All the fire volunteers heard the report. They're out looking."

"In this storm?"

"Yes. Listen, I want you to wait back at Isabel's."

"Where are you going?"

"To Chloe's favorite place."

Lia couldn't think straight. "Where's that?"

"It's behind the Suttons."

"I don't know—"

"She told me once, over checkers. I'm sure that's where she would go."

"I'm going too."

"No. She may show up back home."

"She's my responsibility!"

"She's ours, Lia. I should have nailed this guy a long time ago and not let him hurt her or you. I'm sorry. You'll only be in the way. I will find her. I promise. Your responsibility now is to pray."

Forty-Two

Forty-five minutes outside of Rockville, Tony's car radio picked up Izzy's voice.

That voice. The lilting tones were more musical than music itself.

"The national weather service has issued a severe thunderstorm warning. That means it's here, folks. It also means stay put. If you're out driving, well, you shouldn't be. Go home. If you're not near home, find other shelter. The temperature is dropping. This rain may turn into sleet by evening. It looks like you're stuck with me for the duration because I'm not driving in this. It's 3:00. There's a glorious display of God's power right outside my window. Lightning is dancing across the sky. Unfortunately, all that power knocked out the phone lines. That means you can't call in and complain—or keep me company. Enough chitchat. Let's listen to some more music."

That answered the question of why he couldn't get through with his cell to the station or her house. At least he knew where she was.

The car hydroplaned. He eased his foot on the accelerator, both hands white-knuckled on the steering wheel. This trip was going to take a lot longer than the 45 minutes to Rockville. Valley Oaks was another 30 minutes, the station ten minutes beyond that on a good day. If this storm kept up, he was looking at over two hours.

"The first song we're going to hear is from Margaret Becker. I'd like to dedicate it to a special friend who recently decided to 'Just Come In.' Welcome home, Tony."

A sensation flowed through him, an overwhelming, indefinable sensation that took his breath away. Did one ever get used to these surprises? Things like this had been happening right and left for over three weeks now. Things like selling the article in spite of its change of focus... The timing of picking up her broadcast... The words she spoke... That song... His world collided with the cosmic on a daily basis.

Thank You, God.

On top of everything, Izzy understood his article. But was it enough to keep her from moving to Mexico?

He didn't know. That's why he kept driving through this horrendous thunderstorm, hoping sleet wouldn't force him off the road. No, not hoping. Praying.

Cal parked at the barn behind the Suttons' old farmhouse on the edge of town. Neither of their cars were in the drive, but he spared two minutes to bang on their back door. It was locked and nobody answered. Typical Sutton family Saturday. They wouldn't be home.

He jogged around the barn and hit the grassy waterway that ran through the field. The rain still pelted him. The wind howled across the barren plain. Bits and pieces of cornstalks left behind by the combine swirled in the air. Thick clouds hung low in the sky, darkening the area as if it were evening.

His lungs burned. His legs ached. His side throbbed. He was seriously out of shape.

What hurt worse, though, was this love for a woman and her child. It was indescribably all-consuming. He never would have thought such feeling possible. He had searched for lost children before, but that was a mental process. This tore at his insides. If Chloe were hurt... If Lia was dealt that blow... If Lia left...

He couldn't think this way. Now he understood why you didn't get personally involved with a case. Your brain shut down.

But he knew where he was going because he knew how Chloe reasoned. He had been watching her up close now for three weeks.

Her favorite place was also one of his favorites as a kid. This pathway veered down a hill, giving way to a meadow that was never planted. In the middle of the meadow stood a magnificent lone oak. At some point through the years, boys had nailed boards to its trunk, making a crude ladder up to the lowest limb. Cal remembered falling out of it one spring and breaking his arm. Fortunately, it hadn't interfered with his sixth-grade football season.

The reason the meadow was never planted was because it flooded. When the creek overflowed during heavy downpours, it gushed over its banks, and the meadow became a rushing stream, at times almost a river.

He catapulted himself down the hillside now, the wind whipping away his shouts of "Chloe!"

Squinting as he ran, he took in the scene at a glance. Like some giant cardinal, a red jacket caught his attention through the oak's brown leaves. Bless Chloe and her favorite color. All runaways should wear red jackets. She wasn't on the lowest limb. What was she doing? Dark water raced at the base of the tree, surrounding it 20 feet out. At least she was up in the tree.

At least the lightning portion of the storm had moved from the area.

Thank You, God.

He calculated as he raced to the stream's edge. How low had the creek been? Average. It had been a wet autumn. The meadow was probably saturated when the rain started. When had it started? A few hours ago. Last he heard two inches had fallen. The worst wouldn't catch up to this area for a while. How had the ground shifted in the years since he'd been here? Ruts? Gullies? He didn't know.

But he knew he would wade into it.

The ice cold water took his breath away as it rushed up over his boots.

"Chloe!"

"Cal!"

"Stay put! Wait for me!"

His right foot sank into a hole. The water whooshed at his thighs. He pressed on, and then he was out of it.

He reached the tree, grasped a board, and climbed. Reaching the lowest limb, he heaved himself onto it and sat in the crook, his legs dangling. He looked up, panting.

Chloe stood above him, two branches up, hugging the tree. The red hood of her parka was tied tight under her chin. "Cal, Soot won't come down. Can you get her? She's up there. See her? *You* can reach her. You're tall enough."

Cal waited to catch his breath before replying. The words "hug" and "strangle" came to mind. Here she was, risking her life and tearing out his heart and Lia's, worried only about a stupid cat! "Chloe! Soot can take care of herself. We've got to get out of here right now, before the water gets any deeper!"

"But she's scared! Look at her!"

Cal craned his neck. He could easily reach the kitten...if he climbed to where Chloe stood.

Lord, is this what being a dad is all about?

Forty-Three

Isabel was in her element, no doubt about it. The storm raged outside. The satellite was down. National news was on hold. Her future—as in where she'd be living and working next month—was undecided.

But she sang at the top of her voice, twirling through unoccupied rooms, looking out windows in every direction. She had her unseen, silent audience scattered about surrounding counties, a studio full of music, and the means to share it.

And she had the letter from Chicago, addressed to her at the station's post office box rather than the house. It waited in a pile of mail for the secretary to deal with on Monday. Nosy Mendozy had been snooping.

And covering it all, like her silky pink security blanket of childhood, she had the knowledge that Jesus would work it out. Hadn't He always?

Headlights flickered now past a window, turning off of the highway. Who was out driving through this? The storm had tapered, but only within the last 15 minutes.

A long set of songs had just begun playing; nothing required her attention. She hurried to the front door and saw through the glass someone approaching.

Tony?

Isabel unlocked the door. "Tony! What are you doing out in this?"

He grinned. "You didn't answer your phone."

"It's out of order. Did you drive from Chicago? Here, give me your coat." She took it and hung it on the coat tree in a corner.

"The trip only took twice as long as normal. Didn't seem that long, though. I've been listening to you. Great radio personality, Izzy."

She smiled back at him. "Thanks."

They stared at one another. Evidently he didn't know where to begin either. "I heard the song."

Tears sprang to her eyes, and she went to him.

He wrapped his arms around her. "I hope those are happy tears?"

She nodded.

He held her tightly and whispered in her ear, "Thank you for not giving up on me."

"It wasn't me."

"I think I'm beginning to understand your convoluted reasoning."

"Isn't it wonderful?"

"Yeah, it is." He brushed the tears from her cheeks.

"Tony Ward, I've been missing you for years. Oh! I did not mean to say that out loud."

"And why not?" He locked his hands behind her waist.

She leaned back to take in those deep-set eyes, the narrow nose, and that crooked grin. "It might give you ideas."

He blinked. "Izzy, you're not teasing me, are you?"

"Do you want some soup?"

"Izzy!"

She bit her lip. *Oh, Lord!* "No, I am not teasing."

"Okay. I do happen to have some ideas."

"How about some coffee?"

He kissed her cheek. "I love you, Isabel Mendoza. I think I probably did before, but now... Can we start over? After all these years? I want to share everything with you. All my thoughts, my time, my work." He paused. "Will you please reconsider moving to Mexico?"

"Oh, Tony. I don't think I've ever stopped loving you." She took a deep breath. "I'm taking the job in Chicago. There's no way I'm running away from you again."

His laughter filled the studio. He whooped, and then, meeting her eyes, he grew serious. "I won't run away from you again either."

"I'll hold you to that."

"Izzy, does this mean I didn't have to risk my neck driving for hours through this crazy storm? We could have just talked on the phone later?"

"Well, I don't think that would have worked quite the same." She slid her arms more snugly around his neck.

When they kissed, Isabel felt a flickering of something new ignite between them. They were on the threshold of a different kind of love that didn't resemble the past.

She smiled as their kisses slowed. "And besides, I hadn't decided which job I was going to take. Not until the moment I saw you standing outside the door."

Lia stuffed another sweater into a plastic grocery bag and tied the handles together. There. Plastic worked just as well as Samsonite. No reason to replace the smoke-scented luggage. She wasn't taking a trip—probably would never ever be able to afford to take one again—she was just moving. Most of her and Chloe's belongings were already stacked by the front door. They'd toss their grocery bags into the car trunk and be out of there right after dinner.

If Chloe came home.

Lord! Help him find her.

How long had he been gone? Night had fallen already, the black clouds hurrying it.

Lord, keep her safe.

It was like sliding to the edge of a panicky abyss, peering over its edge, and then jumping back to cling to the hands she knew held them all. Then it would start all over again, the sliding and the jumping. Nervous energy drove her to this manic fit of packing. She would be finished when Chloe got home. *If—*

The front door banged open. "We're home, Aunt Lia!" two voices rang out, followed by laughter.

Lia raced to the living room. "Oh, Chloe!" She caught the little girl in her arms and squeezed her. "Thank You, Lord."

"I'm sorry, Aunt Lia."

"You'd better be! Thank you, Cal!"

He was wiping little Soot's paws on the mat just inside the door. "You're welcome."

"Oh, Chloe! You're soaking wet and freezing. Let's get you out of that coat. Look at your boots!"

"It's raining cats and dogs!" She giggled, yanking off the muddy boots. "It was almost raining Soot, huh, Cal?"

He roared with laughter. "Almost, Little China Doll."

Lia paused a moment, holding Chloe's arm in midair, and then she finished pulling off the girl's jacket. "You need a hot bath. Go!"

"Aunt Lia!"

"Now! You'll get sick."

"We have things to discuss!"

"You mean like how I'm going to ground you? Like how you're going to lose every single privilege you've ever known in your short life? It can wait!"

"Yeah, well, every little girl needs a daddy."

"What?"

Chloe looked somewhere beyond Lia.

Lia turned. Cal was pointing his thumb in the direction of the hall. She spun back to Chloe.

The girl opened her mouth as if to say something but then turned and skipped away. Soot bounded noiselessly behind her.

What was going on?

"Cal." She faced him again. He looked as if he'd been swimming. His wide-brimmed hat and leather jacket dripped. Raindrops clung to his beard and mud to his boots. His brown pants were a shade darker, soaked through. "Oh my goodness. Where did you find her? Never mind. You need a hot bath, too. Thank you for finding her." She would have opened the door for him, but he was blocking it.

"You going somewhere?" He nodded toward the piles of grocery bags. Clothes, shoes, and daily miscellany were clearly visible through the plastic.

"I'm leaving. This was the last straw. Chloe and I don't belong in Valley Oaks."

"Is that so? If you ask me, this is not the time to make a major decision." His voice was even, the cop tone distinct.

"I'm not asking for your opinion."

"You're just reacting to a terrifying situation."

"I've been considering it for some time."

"Since when? Since Tammy lied to you?"

She blinked. "That's got nothing to do with it."

"Hogwash." His tone remained on even keel, though his words stung. "You know, you think you're so independent, but you're just afraid of letting people care for you, specifically a man, more specifically m—"

"That's not true!"

"It is. I know Miss Impressively Independent, and she would not run away."

"It's exactly what she would do!"

"I suggest you hold off on deciding about leaving. For goodness' sake, Lia, you're shaking like a leaf. I can see it from here."

"I don't have to answer to—"

The door behind Cal opened, and he moved aside. Isabel and Tony came through it, both grinning.

Isabel said, "Cal! You look like a drowned rat! What's going on?"

He answered, "Long story, but Lia will have to tell it. Excuse me. Hey, Tony. You're back again."

Tony reopened the door for him. "Yeah. Got a favor to ask. Mind if I sleep at your place tonight? Isabel won't let me stay here."

"No problem. Coming now?"

"One minute." He turned to Isabel, cupped her face in his hands, and kissed her. It took longer than a minute. "Okay. Let's go, Cal."

Lia stared at a rosy-cheeked Isabel.

She grinned back at her. "Long story."

Forty-Four

While Chloe soaked in a hot bubble bath, Lia dug through the grocery bags piled near the front door, searching for the girl's pajamas. Isabel suspected a diversion was in order and announced they were having an indoor picnic. She stacked peanut butter and jelly sandwiches and a plate of veggie slices on a tray, and then poured hot chocolate for herself and Chloe. For Lia she fixed a cup of a calming herbal tea. The woman was a mess—rightly so—though she hadn't shed a tear yet. Her dark eyes were wide and she trembled. Once Chloe emerged from the bathroom she could scarcely stop hugging her, and her conversation was almost incoherent.

Chloe helped Isabel carry the meal into the front room where they had pulled out the hide-a-bed. Isabel set drinks on the end tables and spread a tablecloth over the bed. They all sat cross-legged around it and said grace as the wind still howled outside.

Isabel grabbed a sandwich. It was late. The last she had eaten was long before Tony... She smiled inwardly. Tony... She tucked that thought away, but it left her feeling somewhat lightheaded. "Okay, Chloe, you go first. Tell us all about your adventure."

"Aunt Lia will kill me."

"I won't, sweetpea."

"You yelled at me when Cal brought me home."

"That was just because I was so scared."

Isabel patted Chloe's hand. "It's what parents do when they're upset."

335

"Cal didn't."

Lia replied, "Cal's not a parent."

"Well, he's almost like my dad. He's *better* than my dad. He said my dad's pretty sick and will have to stay in the hospital for a long time."

That's one way to put it, Isabel thought. She had heard about Mitch's confession and Nelson being picked up right outside her door.

Chloe was still talking. "Cal said we have a standing date for Sunday school. He's picking me up tomorrow. What's a standing date?"

Isabel jumped in before Lia could sputter whatever was on the tip of her tongue. "It means it happens regularly. I'm glad I wasn't here when you ran off. Otherwise your aunt and I both would have been yelling at you when you got home. Where did you run off to anyway?"

"The tree behind Mandy's house." She told them about her favorite place, a climbing tree down in a meadow. "I wanted to come home. It was so cold! But Soot was being naughty. She kept climbing higher. Cal came and he climbed higher than she was, so he got her. Then we got down, except the water was so deep Cal had to carry me. I rode on his shoulders all the way to the hill."

Lia blanched. "Water? What water?"

"Cal said it was from the creek, but it sure didn't look like the creek. He said it always floods around the tree when it rains real hard, like today."

"How...deep was it?"

She shrugged. "Cal said his gun didn't get wet and that was a good thing. So it wasn't *that* deep."

Not that deep only meant it didn't come up to his waist. Isabel thought her own eyes must be as wide as Lia's.

"He had some blankets in his police car, and he wrapped me up in one. I got to sit next to him on the way home."

Isabel asked, "And he never yelled at you?"

"Nope. But he said if I ever did anything like that again, he was going to wring my neck." She giggled. "But he wouldn't really do that."

Lia clutched her cup of tea. "I know you had a good reason to be mad. It's okay to get mad, but please, please don't run off the next time."

"Aunt Lia, did Cal hug you?"

"What? When?"

"I said you were really going to be mad, and he said oh, he would just hug you and then you'd be all right. Did he?"

"He was wet and cold. He needed to go home so he wouldn't get sick."

"He can hug you tomorrow then."

Isabel glanced at the stack of plastic grocery bags. Lia wasn't going anywhere tonight, but she seemed determined to run off exactly the way Chloe had. She wouldn't be sticking around for any hug.

Lia tucked Chloe into her little bed in the spare room. She had hoped her niece would sleep with her on the hide-a-bed. Lia was having a difficult time letting her out of her sight, but evidently Chloe was not affected in the same way. Talk about impressively independent.

She and Isabel tidied the kitchen.

"Lia, was Nelson really arrested in my front yard?"

"I think so. I wasn't listening too closely when Cal was telling me. We were driving over from the pharmacy. I believe he and Benny waited inside your house. When they saw Nelson walk up to the front door, they got him." She shivered.

"Too much excitement for one day."

"That's for sure. I don't think I can go to sleep."

"But you need to. You're exhausted."

"I am. However," she smiled, "I'm awake enough to hear your long story, the one that led up to that kiss!"

Isabel grinned. "Tony showed up at the station. He drove for hours through the storm so he could talk to me face-to-face and convince me not to move to Mexico."

"And why is that?"

"Because he loves me!" She laughed out loud. "Oh, Lia, it's as if life is all brand new with him, with us. It would be totally unbelievable if I didn't know God specializes in the totally unbelievable. And guess what else? The Chicago station sent me a letter. It was at the station. They offered me the job! They need to know by Tuesday."

"Let me guess. Mexico? Or Tony and Chicago? Rather obvious choice, I'd say."

"Well, I didn't think so. I mean, I read the letter, but still, why go to be near him and not be a part of his life? I didn't know he cared for me. From his article, I assumed he's turning his life over to Christ, but I didn't know he felt anything beyond a friendship based on some long-ago past. Oh, Lia. I never thought we could love each other again and in a grown-up way."

A knot of envy twisted in Lia. *I'm sorry, Lord.* "That's wonderful, Isabel."

"Now, back to you. It sounds like things are pretty serious." She winked. "Between Chloe and Cal. What do you think?"

"I think he's turned into a great surrogate father, but we are leaving here. I'm glad you'll be in Chicago. We won't be that far from you."

"Lia, Cal loves you."

"I don't know about that, but I do know that I don't love him."

"You did until the Tammy thing."

Lia shrugged. "I'm destined to be a single mother living near Chicago."

"Why?"

"I don't know why. That's God's area of expertise. I just know I can't stay here."

"What makes you think that?"

"Human nature. My experience says Cal will let me down. Tammy was just the wake-up call."

Lia felt something sandpapery trace lightly along her cheekbone. Fingertips? They must belong to Cal. His were rough like that. You didn't nab bad guys and climb trees and keep your hands soft.

She kept her eyes shut and snuggled more deeply into the pillow. "It's too early to get up."

"It's time for church." It was Cal.

"Mmm. But I was still awake when the sun came up."

"You fret too much, China Doll. Go back to sleep. I'm taking Chloe to Sunday school. We'll see you later. Come over for lunch. Okay?"

"'Kay."

Peppermint-scented lips grazed her temple.

When Lia awoke she saw Isabel's front room curtains. Although they were shut, she could tell that the sun was high in the sky. It must be late. She wore her watch to bed because there wasn't a clock in the living room, but she didn't pull her wrist out from the covers. She wasn't ready yet to let go of the sensation.

It was a peculiar sensation, a cross between a warm bubble bath and eating chocolate. It felt like Christmas morning. It felt a little like being five again and holding her dad's hand as he walked her to school. It was a little like that dream a few months after Kathy died. In the dream she glimpsed her sister in a crowded room, laughing, calling, "Lia, I'm fine!" It was anticipation…fulfillment…security…and joy. All rolled into one sensation.

What had she been dreaming?

Cal. She dreamt Cal came while she slept, and he said he was taking Chloe to Sunday school.

Cal.

The sensation remained.

Cal. Calhoun Huntington.

"Lord, I've made up my mind!"

Imagine having Cal beside her every time she woke up. Lia sat up. "Lord, don't make me change my mind!"

Something across the bed caught her eye. On the end table was a single red rose in a crystal bud vase.

She groaned, threw back the covers, and climbed out. Where was Isabel? Lia glanced at her watch. They were very late for church. "Chloe! Isabel!" She hurried down the hallway. The bedrooms were empty. "Chloe! Isabel!" She ran back out into the living room and pulled aside the curtains. Isabel's car sat there. Cal's truck was gone. Tony had driven over last night, but his car was gone.

The sensation returned full force, this time with a tickle like floating gossamer brushing her from head to toe. Maybe it hadn't been a dream.

～

God changed her mind. Sunlight crystallized the new day, chasing away the fears of recent weeks as it did yesterday's storm. Chloe was safe today because Cal loved the little girl. He had nurtured their friendship and become privy to secrets such as a favorite place she would run to when upset. And why had he spent all that time with Chloe? Because he had a special passion for children? Hardly. It was because he loved Lia. Pure and simple. To run from that was a slap in the face of her heavenly Father. Pure and simple.

Shaky from the revelation, she tried on three different outfits, unsure what to wear to Cal's for lunch. Jeans? Slacks? Skirt? She chose black slacks and a red turtleneck sweater.

When she noticed his truck was parked again on the street, she decided to wait a bit for Isabel and Chloe to show up. Anxiety gnawed at that absorbing sensation of bubble baths and chocolate threatening to squish it. Maybe it had been a dream. The rose was for Isabel from Tony. Maybe Cal *was* just interested in Chloe's welfare. Maybe he wasn't interested in pursuing a serious relationship with her. Maybe...

Thirty minutes went by. Chloe and Isabel didn't show up.

Lia grabbed a jacket, strode out the back door, across the yards, and up to his kitchen door. The crisp air, so clean and calm, bit at her, stealing her breath away. She knocked.

He opened the door. "Come on in. I didn't know if you'd remember my invitation. You were pretty sleepy. Lunch is almost ready."

She followed him into his kitchen that smelled of tomato sauce. A soft flannel shirt hung from his broad shoulders and was tucked into blue jeans. She asked, "Where's Chloe?"

He stood at the stove, stirring. "Tony and Isabel took her out to lunch."

"I just came for my hug."

He turned, his clear green eyes questioning.

"Chloe said you had a hug for me last night. I didn't collect it."

"I didn't think you needed it. Do you need it?"

"I'm going to need at least one every day for the rest of my life. Do you have that many?"

He turned back again to the stove. "Hmm. It sounds as if Miss Impressively Independent is back, making decisions."

"It's about time, don't you think?"

"Well, let's get one thing straight. I'm in charge of making proposals around here."

"Fine! I just came for a hug."

He tapped the spoon on the edge of the pot, set it down, and turned. "You sure?"

She nodded.

He smiled and held his big arms wide open.

She stepped into them and took her first normal breath since... Since? Since the fire, weeks ago. He embraced her in a bear hug. "Oh, Cal. I wanted to run so far away from this."

"But you didn't. Hey, I seem to remember making a promise to you about when Miss Impressively Independent showed up again."

She smiled up at him. "Hey, I seem to remember that promise."

"I'd better keep it. I hear you can't make a promise to a big girl and then not keep it."

"It would break her heart."

He lowered his face and whispered, "I promise I will not break your heart."

When he kissed her, all the built-up tensions of the past weeks scrambled into oblivion. "Mmm, I think I'm going to need at least one of those every day, too."

"You got it, China Doll." He kissed her again. "What is it?"

She hesitated. "Cal, I'm scared."

"Of what?"

"Trusting you."

"Listen." He lifted her chin and lowered his face until those lovely eyes were all she could see. "I am not Nelson Greene. I do not resemble any of the weak ninnies you dated who didn't know the first thing about commitment. I love you, Lia, and I will never leave you or Chloe."

Like that rainy night in the alley when he first strode into her life, she sensed his big teddy bear shoulders coming alongside, lifting the burden she carried. He had been doing that ever since. And she had subtly been leaning more and more on his trustworthiness, falling in love.

"I love you, Cal."

He grinned his big grin, the one that pressed his cheeks into an accordion now hidden behind a beard. "Yeah?"

"Yeah. But I did want to marry a pediatrician."

"Really?"

"Mm-hmm. I had everything planned out. Then Chloe came along, and now *you've* come along. I don't know about giving up—"

He rumbled like thunder and kissed her again, this time with an urgency. "Marry me? Soon?"

When she could catch her breath, she asked, "Is that one or two questions?"

His beard scratched her cheek as he murmured, "Mmm, two. Will you marry me?"

"Yes."

"Soon? Before a pediatrician comes along and sweeps you off your feet?"

She chuckled. "I think you already did that."

Forty-Five

Lia stood in the wide, arched opening between Cal's dining and living rooms. It was Thanksgiving Day, much to her surprise. The usual weeklong fanfare of preparations had been eclipsed by life in the sleepy little town of Valley Oaks.

Nelson Greene was history—for many years to come at any rate. Documented phone calls between him and Mitch Conway, withdrawals of large sums of cash, and Mitch's confession guaranteed that he would serve a sentence behind bars. Chloe might want to meet him again some day when she grew up, but his record would prevent any judge from granting him custodial rights as her biological father.

Mitch, on the other hand, was guilty of attempted murder but would soon be eligible for parole. The knife was found in a trash can in the alley with no fingerprints on it. Cal patiently explained the whys and wherefores of plea bargaining while Lia ranted and raved at the unfairness of it. Mitch paid teenagers from Rockville to harass her with phone calls, the letter, the doorbell ringing, and the broken window. He stole the drugs himself, going through their connecting basements, and started a new side business in dealing. Nelson figured if Lia were discredited, he could more easily gain Chloe, supposedly because he loved her. Now that was a twisted form of parental love if she ever heard one.

When things weren't happening fast enough, Nelson upped the ante and suggested a fire the weekend Chloe was gone. Cal surprised Mitch at the wrong time. Or as Cal said, the right time. Fire damage was minimal and they were alive.

Thanksgiving Day sprang on them almost unawares. Her parents hadn't come. They celebrated the day as usual, in Chicago with relatives. Lia chose to remain at *home*. She smiled to herself. Less than a week ago she had packed her belongings in plastic bags, frantic to run away from home.

Earlier she, Cal, and Chloe had enjoyed a quiet dinner at his house, making plans that took her breath away. Afterwards, they watched football together, during which they determined that two people could fit at the same time in Cal's large recliner. Chloe sat in what had already been dubbed her own recliner, the one that once belonged to the woman recently renamed *Great*-Grandma Huntington.

Now it was early evening as Lia stood in the archway. A deep sense of belonging flowed through her as she silently observed the scene before her. The living room overflowed with a gathering of her new friends, all of them talking or laughing. They occupied every couch and chair and most of the floor space. The lamps were lit and the square coffee table held Chloe's Chinese checkers board, full of marbles at the moment. It was the center of a round-robin tournament...an incredibly clamorous round-robin tournament.

Isabel and Tony had arrived after having dinner in Rockville with her family. It had been Tony's first meeting with them. He had pronounced himself a success, even with her four brothers. Isabel seemed unable to stop grinning.

Tony was spending the week at Cal's, helping Isabel prepare to leave the following Monday. Lia would remain in the house and use her furnishings while her own were being refurbished. Meanwhile, Isabel would stay with a family in Chicago while she hunted for an apartment.

Anne and Alec Sutton had descended, bearing three children and enough turkey and rolls to feed everyone sandwiches later. Lia appreciated the open welcome Anne had always displayed toward them. Her little Mandy and Chloe were the best of friends.

Gina and Brady arrived after their dinner at the Olafsson farm. Cal's best friend had given Lia an extra hug. "Thank you, Lia. Cal has never been so content." They brought along Gina's parents from California, Maggie and Reece.

Celeste and Peter Eaton came with their three children and the pastor's bulky Day-Timer.

He raised his voice now above the clamor, calling out, "Who wanted to schedule something?"

Brady announced, "I did!"

Reece stood, hands on hips. "Just like an Olafsson, barging in. *I'm* the one who asked him to bring his calendar."

"Well, that may be, but everyone knows Gina and I are planning our wedding." Not one to back away from a challenge, even from Gina's dad, Brady stepped over sprawled bodies to reach him.

Nose to nose with his much taller future son-in-law, Reece continued, "I asked Maggie to marry me long before you asked Gina."

"Before Labor Day weekend?"

"Oh, you're counting that showy public proposal? I heard you had to ask her all over again."

Brady scowled.

"That one doesn't count. Before your *second* attempt, I proposed. We were on a gondola in Venice and the sun was setting."

"You're counting *that* one? That was your second honeymoon. How can you propose on your honeymoon? Especially a *second* honeymoon?"

"I can because I did."

"Mother!" Gina cried. "Do something with him!"

Maggie laughed. "I can't, honey. He's a new man these days. Besides, I accepted, and our schedule is very tight."

"But you're already married!"

"Not to this man."

Gina rolled her eyes and groaned.

Reece looked over at Peter. "We want the Saturday between Christmas and New Year's. And we want it in that little chapel outside of town, not in your big church."

Brady's jaw dropped. "Excuse me! That's *our* date! And we need the big church."

The teasing debate continued amid much laughter and raised voices.

Still standing in the doorway, Lia leaned back and threw an anxious glance up over her shoulder. "Cal?"

He secured his arms around her and whispered, "Don't worry, China Doll. I already talked to Peter. He penciled us in."

Harvest House Publishers
For the Best in Inspirational Fiction

Linda Chaikin
Desert Rose
Desert Star

Mindy Starns Clark
THE MILLION DOLLAR
MYSTERIES SERIES
A Penny for Your Thoughts
Don't Take Any Wooden Nickels
Dime a Dozen
A Quarter for a Kiss
The Buck Stops Here

Roxanne Henke
COMING HOME TO
BREWSTER SERIES
After Anne
Finding Ruth
Becoming Olivia

Sally John
THE OTHER WAY HOME SERIES
A Journey by Chance
After All These Years
Just to See You Smile
The Winding Road Home

IN A HEARTBEAT SERIES
In a Heartbeat
Flashpoint

Craig Parshall
CHAMBERS OF JUSTICE SERIES
The Resurrection File
Custody of the State
The Accused
Missing Witness

Debra White Smith
A Shelter in the Storm
This Time Around
Let's Begin Again

THE AUSTEN SERIES
First Impressions
Reason and Romance

Lori Wick
THE YELLOW ROSE TRILOGY
Every Little Thing About You
A Texas Sky
City Girl

CONTEMPORARY FICTION
SERIES
Bamboo & Lace
Beyond the Picket Fence
Every Storm
Pretense
The Princess
Sophie's Heart

THE ENGLISH GARDEN SERIES
The Proposal
The Rescue
The Visitor
The Pursuit

The author invites you to contact her at:
sallyjohnbook@aol.com